ROMAN'S KISS

Isra looked ahead, down the valley, and saw a thick cluster of horses reemerging onto the road leading from Kerak's sandstone motte, a red and white banner flickering like a tiny scrap in the sunset.

She looked up at Roman, but his face was turned to the sky now, as if he was contemplating something only he could see.

Then he turned his head toward her, held out his hand.

Isra placed her fingers into his palm and let him pull her to her feet. Once she was standing he drew her against his chest slowly, deliberately, wrapping his uninjured arm around her shoulders, and Isra held her breath as she looked up and he lowered his head.

"I can wait no more," he whispered against her mouth, and then he kissed her . . .

Books by Heather Grothaus

THE WARRIOR

THE CHAMPION

THE HIGHLANDER

TAMING THE BEAST

NEVER KISS A STRANGER

NEVER SEDUCE A SCOUNDREL

NEVER LOVE A LORD

VALENTINE

ADRIAN

ROMAN

HIGHLAND BEAST
(with Hannah Howell and Victoria Dahl)

Published by Kensington Publishing Corporation

ROMAN

The Brotherhood of Fallen Angels

Heather Grothaus

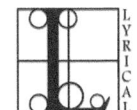

LYRICAL PRESS
Kensington Publishing Corp.
www.kensingtonbooks.com

LYRICAL PRESS BOOKS are published by

Kensington Publishing Corp.
119 West 40th Street
New York, NY 10018

All Kensington titles, imprints, and distributed lines are available at special quantity discounts for bulk purchases for sales promotion, premiums, fund-raising, educational, or institutional use.

Special book excerpts or customized printings can also be created to fit specific needs. For details, write or phone the office of the Kensington Sales Manager: Kensington Publishing Corp., 119 West 40th Street, New York, NY 10018. Attn. Sales Department. Phone: 1-800-221-2647.

Lyrical Press and Lyrical Press logo Reg. U.S. Pat. & TM Off.

First Electronic Edition: July 2016
eISBN-13: 978-1-60183-400-3
eISBN-10: 1-60183-400-4

First Print Edition: July 2016
ISBN-13: 978-1-60183-401-0
ISBN-10: 1-60183-401-2

Printed in the United States of America

Always.

Prologue

August 1179
Syria

The wall came down no more than fifty feet behind Roman, the already hot air contracting around him like a shroud, then exploding with a roar of flames. The blast lifted him from his feet and sent him flying over the bodies of the slain workers who had, only a moment ago, been being prepared for burial. He slammed into the hard-packed dirt and then skidded and tumbled for several yards, his rough brown tunic seeming to melt into his skin.

He realized the instant he came to a stop that it wasn't a friction wound he felt; the back of his tunic was afire.

He slapped at the flames and flung himself onto his back as a pair of screaming pillars of fire ran past him, but Roman could barely hear them above the loud squeal the explosion had stuffed into his pounding, spinning head. They weren't flaming pillars; they were men. Men on fire.

Roman pushed himself up on his elbows and looked at the southeast corner of Chastellet's bailey. Where carefully crafted rectangular stones—many of which Roman Berg himself had set—once comprised the fortress's key defense, the wall sagged, framing an inverted wedge of white-hot Syrian sky beyond. Roman's eyes burned and his nose ran as the air was filled with the stink of naphtha and burning sand, burning flesh.

His head jerked as a hand gripped his right biceps. He hadn't heard his apprentice approach, hadn't been able to *hear the slim man's shouts over the twisting whine still swelling in his ears. But Osbert's mouth was moving wildly, his teeth flashing behind cracked lips as he pulled futilely at Roman with one hand while gesturing with the pick in his other to the barracks left standing against the eastern wall. Roman glanced in that direction, but the shelter held little interest for him as his eyes gaze fell upon a hunting falcon tethered to a post just outside one of the doorways. The bird of prey's hood swiveled and twitched, as if listening to the commotion Roman could not hear. Roman found himself fascinated by the creature's movements . . .*

A hand struck Roman's cheek, and he reluctantly turned his attention back to Osbert.

Come on! his apprentice mouthed, spittle flying, his eyes bulging.

Roman frowned, hesitated. He was confused. What was happening? Why had the wall fallen? Why were there little shadows crawling like insects across Osbert's face, across the dirt of the bailey . . . ?

The arrow shaft appeared in Osbert's neck so suddenly, it was as if by magic. Blood spurted out of the hole in the side opposite the fletching. Although Osbert's mouth opened once again in preparation for what Roman surmised was to have been a scream of agony, he doubted any sound emerged. The apprentice pitched forward onto Roman, the man's pick arcing smoothly down into the dirt, and he felt Osbert's hot blood soak through his tunic and run down his chest as arrows suddenly fell like rain on the bailey.

Roman pushed the apprentice's body from him as he skittered backward. A zinging pain shot up his left arm from his smallest finger and he jerked his hand from the yard, looking at the arrow that had shot a wedge of flesh from his hand before burying itself deep in the dirt. Another landed precisely between his bent knees. Roman's head swam, throbbed; his tongue seemed to swell in his mouth.

Stay still? Move? What sort of nightmare was this?

Roman looked up and saw Chastellet's remaining workers, Templars, servants—all that were left on this sixth day of siege— crisscrossing the bailey frantically, many of them pausing in midstride to demonstrate the bow-backed pose of defeat before crumpling to the ground, their bodies stubbled with arrows. Roman staggered to his feet at last, shook his head violently despite the pain it caused.

His hearing came back with a slow whoosh, letting in the roar of screams, the pounding of feet, the clanging of metal. Reality crashed upon him as surely as the wall that had crushed the men standing just behind him: Chastellet had been breached. The wall had been the first wave of attack.

The arrows falling around him with whistles and pings: the second wave. Which meant . . .

Roman again raised his eyes to the collapsed section of wall just as the undulating crowd of Saracens crested the rise and charged toward the opening. Some were on horseback, some afoot. All with weapons raised and yelling their terrible, unintelligible screams.

The third wave.

Roman reached down and retrieved Osbert's pick from the dirt, all the while keeping his eyes on the force advancing toward him. The warrior monks were already engaging the invaders, their long, double-edged swords swinging without hesitation. But even Roman Berg—never a warrior until six days before—knew the sheer numbers of Saracens pouring into Chastellet's walls meant defeat was expected.

He thought briefly of Lord Adrian Hailsworth, Chastellet's architect and Roman's principal at the site, and wondered if the brilliant man would live to see the total destruction of the fortress both men had labored over in their own ways.

He thought of Lord Constantine Gerard, a layman general of noble rank who was to have left Chastellet a week earlier. An earl, Roman thought. Was he already dead?

They were both good men, noble men, casually treating Roman as their equal. Even Hailsworth—arrogant as he was—had taken to the practice of deferring to Roman's skill and experience when appropriate. Now whatever differences between Roman and the titled men's backgrounds and pedigrees were truly washed away, as Roman would battle as they battled, fight as they would fight, to defend the place Roman considered to be the pinnacle of his life's work.

The fortress that would likely become his tomb.

He began to stride toward the line of Templars who were miraculously holding back the onslaught against them. Without pause, he reached down and pulled a broadsword from the limp grasp of a fallen soldier. But he kept the pick in his right hand; it was familiar there, and he knew just how to utilize it.

As if his earlier thoughts had conjured the man, Roman saw Constantine Gerard leaping and sidling through the fight toward him. His helm was missing, but he held forth his long shield as he dispatched a rogue attacker. Somehow, Roman must have caught Gerard's eye, for the general paused and banged his sword against his shield before raising it in Roman's direction.

"God be with you, brother," he shouted at Roman.

Roman lifted his weapons and crossed them with a clang over his head. "For Chastellet!" Roman returned against the cracking of his voice.

And then General Constantine Gerard was gone, the last of him Roman saw was his tawny mane flowing behind him as he threw himself into the thick of the battle. Roman turned once more toward the breach, walking deliberately, his weapons flanking him like the squires he had no right to claim.

Yes, he knew he could fall this day. But for as long as he was able to swing his tools, he would swing.

He stopped then and braced his feet as a Saracen soldier broke away from his comrades and galloped toward him on horseback. The man's robes rose and fell in rhythm to his mount's charge, and he held a long scimitar in his right hand, a small hatchet in his left, guiding his finely built horse with nothing more than his knees.

Roman crouched lower, holding forth the broadsword and drawing the pick behind his head. He opened his mouth to let out a cry of attack . . .

He came awake with a gasp, inadvertently sucking in some of the silty dirt from the floor of the cave. Roman fell into a coughing fit as he sat up fully, noticing that he clutched at his shoulder out of habit.

He released his arm and reached for the now nearly empty skin of wine the Spaniard had left behind for him.

"To pass the time, yes?" Valentine Alesander had said with a wry grin as he'd tossed it down from atop his horse. Then he'd disappeared down the trail in the spreading dusk.

A short, creaking chirp echoed in the cave, interrupting the memory.

Roman gained his feet and walked to the opening of the cave where the hunting falcon was tethered. He stroked Lou's back with one finger as he looked down on the walled city of Damascus, which would soon lay in shadow for the third time with Roman as witness. Three days. Valentine Alesander had left Roman in the cave three days ago.

"They will be praying soon," Valentine had said. "It is my best opportunity."

Roman scrubbed a hand over his bristly face as if he would wipe the thick air and his troubled thoughts away. Then he sighed and placed his hands on his hips. It was of no use; the cave seemed to be full of ghosts now: days past living on in his dreams, voices in his head.

Something had gone wrong. Either the Spaniard had been caught or he had not even attempted to gain entry into Saladin's prison to free Adrian Hailsworth and Constantine Gerard. Perhaps he had instead maneuvered his horse around the wall and gone on past the city, taking the sack of Chastellet coin with him. He'd already proven he could disappear into the native population; Roman had nearly killed Alesander himself upon their first meeting at the ruined fortress, thinking him Saracen.

Roman stalked to the back of the cave, squatted down, and checked his bag again; it was still cinched tightly, the other sack of gold secure inside. Then Roman rose and paced the width of the crude shelter.

Whether Alesander had absconded with the coin or been captured himself, there was clearly no one to rescue Roman's friends. And if the Spaniard *was* caught, his blood was on Roman's hands. Roman's shoulder ached where the man had reseated the joint for him, dislocated for weeks, and he kneaded the biceps which seemed so much smaller than it had been only weeks ago.

Valentine Alesander had rescued him from the midden heap of Chastellet—its cisterns stuffed with corpses and its walls adorned with carrion birds; rescued him from the cesspool of his own mind, which echoed with the screams of the dying; the sounds of arrows finding deep flesh; the shame of being the one left behind, the one left alive. The Spaniard had made Roman's body whole again, despite the healing gashes and still-dark contusions beneath his tunic and chausses. And he had led Roman to Damascus, where the only two men on earth Roman could claim as friends were being held by the conquerors of Chastellet.

If they weren't already dead.

Roman, like Chastellet, had fallen. Had he not been struck so many times to the temple, perhaps he would have realized the true folly of dragging himself into the exposed bailey once more to save the life of the hunting bird left abandoned and tethered to its perch— the same one that now stood guard at the cave's entrance. But in Roman's swollen, fevered reasoning, there had been naught else for it. His weakness and injuries had rendered him incapable of saving Chastellet, but there had been a creature before him—one totally innocent of man's folly and politics—that he *could* save. He had decided to let the attempt be on his soul, then, and damn him if it would.

Lou chirped again—a questioning sound—and Roman went once more to the falcon, who had come to mean so much to him since that bloody day.

"Naught else for it again, is there, Lou?" he said quietly, stroking the bird's feathers. The falcon tolerated Roman's touch, but Roman knew he was impatient. Lou needed to fly. And so did Roman.

He looked back to the opening of the cave. If he did nothing to save the three men hidden somewhere in the city below, he might as well return to the ruin that was Chastellet and drop from a rope hung from its highest crumbled wall. It would be better than rotting here in this cave, waiting for a Spaniard who was clearly never coming back.

Roman returned to his satchel again, picking it up and looping the strap over his back before donning the leather hood that fit tightly over his skull and draped onto his shoulders like a short cape. He had no robe, no cloak, nothing else to disguise his large body and English coloring. The hood would have to do. The guards would likely kill him as soon as he passed through the gates any matter, if he made it that far.

He had no gauntlet for Lou, but the falcon had been content to ride upon Roman's shoulder from Chastellet. He picked loose the leather tie keeping the bird prisoner, and then leaned down, easing the falcon onto the edge of the hood.

"Going on an adventure, Lou."

The bird didn't respond, but sidled a bit higher on Roman's shoulder, closer to his ear. Roman found the weight of the creature, the grip of its talons, comforting, as if he truly had a comrade in the falcon.

"I'll not keep hold of your tether, though," he said, turning and walking out of the cave without hesitation and setting his boots upon the narrow, twisting animal path that led down the hillside. "I'm likely walking to my own death, and I'd not have yours on my conscience as well. I'll remove your hood before I enter the city. You'll be free."

Roman considered as he tromped down the mountain in the lengthening shadows that, if he were being truly magnanimous, he would remove the bird's blind now. But he could not yet bear it—the thought of being totally alone at what could again be the last hour of his life. That void had been with him since he was a boy, had it not—the solitude? He thought with some shame that he should be used to it by now.

He walked quickly among the dunes dotted with scrubby brush at the base of the mountain, seeking the shortest path to gain the packed road leading into the city. Roman guessed that a lone man afoot with nothing more than a single bag was unlikely to draw immediate scrutiny from the guards atop the wall. The sun was swiftly sliding down the sky behind him, throwing a long, deep shadow on the road before him, and Roman hunched into it, made it his companion along with the falcon on his shoulder.

When he was within a stone's throw of the wall, Roman stopped abruptly and, before he could think himself out of it, reached up and gently slipped the leather string from Lou's leg and then the hood from the falcon's head. The bird blinked and tilted its head wildly, seeming to drink in the sight of the wide-open sky.

Roman gave a shrug of his shoulder. "Go on, then." The falcon flapped its wings for balance and then settled back against Roman's ear. "Go on." He shrugged again.

This time Lou crouched low and leaped from his shoulder, the quiet whoosh of its wings sending a crisp flip of air across Roman's face. He watched the falcon fly low over the ground for several yards before flapping in earnest and pulling himself up, up, up into the darkening east over the walls of Damascus. The falcon cried out once, and it caused Roman's heart to flinch.

But then he tucked the falcon's hood and tether beneath the flap of his bag and headed into the night himself, his head down, his eyes only on the road. Roman had lost any traces of hesitation he'd felt in the cave. He had set his aim now, freed his obligation, and there was no fear in him of what might happen once he reached the gates, the streets of the city, the prison. His feet fell like hammers beneath his gaze, working to chip away at any obstacles he imagined he might soon face.

So intent was he upon his purpose that it was quite a surprise to realize he had passed through the walls and was in the city. The spicy, fecund smells pressing around him and the sounds of his footfalls muffling gave him a physical start, as did the blaring of a horn that shot the thick, still air, and then another, and the warbling sound of a song in the familiar yet still foreign tongue. Roman glanced sideways and behind him to see the guards closing the gates to the city, not twenty feet beyond his heels, shutting out the last rays of the sun disappearing over the rolling land.

The horns continued to sound, and Roman realized he was caught up in a current of citizens all heading in the same direction. His heart pounded despite himself, and he hunched his shoulders further, crouched lower on bent knees as the slimness of the general population became glaringly apparent. The narrow black space of an alley between sandstone buildings came upon his left side suddenly, and Roman stepped into it as swiftly as a gust of air, slinking back into the deep shadow and straightening his aching back against the wall of the building.

He watched from the shadows as the stragglers, mostly boys and young men, ran down the center of the street, hands clapped down on their caps as they hurried to answer the call to prayer. Another moment and the ruddy street would be deserted.

Then what? He had no idea in which direction to go. Wandering aimlessly through the maze of pathways connecting the straight and orderly streets might only be enough to render him completely lost, and then, when the faithful flooded the city again on their way to their homes . . .

He dared lean toward the opening to glance in either direction. There were no clues whatsoever as to where the city housed its prisoners. He pressed his back against the building once more with a sigh. And then his heart stopped as he caught sight of the woman standing against the wall directly opposite him, so close that he could have touched her without fully extending his arm. The last slash of sunlight slunk away from her face, hidden in veils, as the alley was dipped in indigo. He didn't know how she had come upon him so suddenly, so silently.

"Pardon me, mistress," Roman said brusquely and looked away, turning toward the street once more. There was nothing for it now but to go. He could not inhabit such a close space with a woman of this culture; it would certainly mean his death, and likely hers, if he were caught.

Not that he thought to be spared if found alone either.

But before he could step from between the buildings, he felt a hand upon his arm, staying him. Roman paused, but dared not turn to look at her.

"What is it you require of me? I do not speak your language."

"Not to worry—I speak yours," she replied. "I will not raise an alarm to betray you, you must believe me." She tugged on his arm so that he turned to face her once more. "We have not much time before it is discovered I am gone."

"I fear I am unable to give you whatever it is you seek," he said, feeling her touch conspicuously upon his arm. He could smell the soft, heady, feminine scent of her in the close alley and it made his skin flush beneath his coarse tunic.

"It is I who shall give to you," she said, and then slid her palm down his forearm to grasp his fingers, stepping backward as she did so, pulling Roman's arm away as if she would lead him.

He understood, then.

Roman pulled free from her grip. "I cannot tarry with you, woman. I am looking for someone in the city."

She dropped her arm to her side and stared at him for a moment. "I know why you have come. I will take you to your friends, but you must come with me now."

Roman hesitated. If she was a prostitute, the only place she would likely take him was to her keeper, where Roman would certainly be robbed and probably killed. She couldn't possibly know who he was looking for. But she'd mentioned friends, plural, when Roman had only mentioned he was looking for some*one*. . . .

"Where is this friend of mine?" he challenged.

"They are still imprisoned, if that is what you are asking."

A chill shook his spine. This smelled of a trick to Roman. Likely the guards atop the wall had caught sight of him entering the city but lost him in the crush, and had sent this woman to seek him out during the prayer. He couldn't risk it.

"You're wrong," he said, and began backing away from her, toward the edge of the buildings where ambient light in the sky from over the mountains urged him to quit wasting time and *search now.*

"They die at dawn," she called after him. "The two soldiers. A Spaniard as well, if you know of him. One may not live to see morning, he has been tortured so."

Roman paused. "Who?"

"I have heard him called Hails-worth."

Lord Adrian Hailsworth, Chastellet's architect.

The woman continued, as if she sensed his hesitation. "I can convince you not standing here. You must trust me, and you must follow me now. If you do not, I shall have no choice but to leave you. You will soon be discovered on your own, and they will have no mercy on you."

"How can I know you will not betray me?"

She shook her head, a rounded shadow in the already dark alley. "We must go now." She held out her hand.

Roman understood he had two choices: deny the woman and strike out on his own or follow her. If he followed her, she could lead him directly to his own death. If he denied her and she was in league with the guards, she would raise the alarm immediately.

But perhaps the worst outcome of all was if he denied her and she was telling the truth . . .

He stepped toward her suddenly and took her hand. "If you lie, or if we are caught, you will regret it, mistress."

"That I well know." She didn't waste time with mincing steps, and soon they were running between the close-set buildings that leaned together like crowded molars in the dark, humid mouth of a beast. She led him around sudden corners, pulled him across wide, deserted thoroughfares until they came to an enormous, long building on the north side of the city, its pitched roofs black and sharp looking in the gloom.

Over the growing sounds of night, Roman could hear the droning prayers emanating from inside the building. The entire male population of Damascus was contained within its walls.

"Are you mad?" he demanded, pulling free from her in the street.

"Do not slow—no! Hurry!" She grasped his hand again and yanked, but she could not move him.

"You lead me here of all places? It can only mean my death!"

"*You* will be the cause of your own death *and* your friends' if you do not come out of the street!" she hissed angrily and then stepped toward him to look up into his eyes. In the next moment, she ripped the veil from her face, and Roman could see the cuts and deep bruises on her delicate cheeks, the swollenness of one eye. "They beat me, tortured me, too! They have killed those whom I love and yet I have no choice but to stay!" She was nearly gasping in her anger.

"Who did this?" Roman queried, shocked at the woman's delicate beauty crushed beneath the heavy weight of the violence visited upon her.

"The prison is below," she said, ignoring his question and pulling on his arm again as she refastened her veil with her other hand. Roman fell into a trot once more; he had no other option at the moment.

"Follow the corridor at the bottom of the stairs," she continued as the very building they ran past seemed to watch their flight. "Turn right at your first opportunity. The cell you seek is at the very end—the only one. There should be but a lone guard at this moment. You must dispatch him quickly, though, and do not exit to this courtyard; it is the way the others shall return."

"Then how are we to escape?"

She pulled him behind a short wall that seemed to enclose a small garden beyond, and also served as the lintel for a black rectangle of doorway that led down into further darkness. The woman was gasping, and Roman could feel her trembling in his grasp. For all her demands and vows of revenge, she was terrified.

"You must pass this entrance and continue on through the entirety of the prison. There is another exit."

"Only one corridor?"

She shook her head. "No."

"Which one do I take?"

"I know not. I have never been below."

Roman dropped her hand with a breath of agitation and turned in a short circle until he was once more facing the black doorway. The chanting from the domed building had stopped.

"I thank you for your help, mistress," he said gruffly. "If, indeed, you are helping me. I will be in your debt." He stepped toward the descending stairs.

"Wait," she called, once more laying a hand on his arm. "I have a message for the general."

Roman felt his eyebrows raise. This woman had a message for Constantine Gerard?

"He must not return to his home. England is against him now, as they are the other one—Hails-worth. The general has been marked a traitor and is wanted by his own crown. His family is being watched."

Roman nodded. "Very well. Again, I shall be in your debt."

She let her hand slide from his skin slowly. "Do not forget me, then."

A screeching cry split the night, and then a dark shadow shot from the sky and lighted upon the wall above the doorway. It sidled awkwardly along the rough surface, bobbing and ducking until it was near enough that Roman could determine its character.

"Lou?" he asked softly.

The falcon flapped-hopped the short distance separating it from Roman, settling on the leather of his hood once more, fidgeting, adjusting, its weight obviously increased.

The woman stepped close to Roman and hesitantly reached up toward Lou with one hand, her wide sleeve sliding up to reveal a slender arm adorned with golden bracelets that tinkled in the thick air. The falcon ducked away at first and then shot its beak forward, nibbling curiously at her fingers.

"Lou," she whispered. Then she stroked his wing with one finger while speaking a stream of foreign words to the falcon, who seemed to listen intently, swiveling his head to look at her and then the sky with alternating eyes.

The woman abruptly stepped away and began walking backward, looking at Roman as she went, as if she was loath to lose sight of him. "Go now. You have only moments."

Indeed, Roman heard the distant sounds of a crowd, and although he could see nothing over the wall when he turned his head, he knew the time of prayers was over.

He looked back for one final glance at the beautiful, mysterious woman who had brought him thus far, but the street behind him was empty. She had already disappeared into the city.

Roman ducked through the doorway, pushing all thoughts of her away as he descended the stairs as quickly as he could. A moment later, he had found the right-hand turn, and now he ran through the corridor, his wide shoulders nearly brushing the walls, his hood only inches away from the undulating ceiling. A haze of torchlight shone around the corner ahead, but Roman did not slow.

And so he took the guards by surprise—two instead of one. They rose from their crouched positions before a wrought door, one still rolling the woven mat he had knelt upon. Roman came to an abrupt halt and was unable to stop himself from glancing through the bars to his left.

There, chained by his neck to the back wall, was General Gerard, his tawny mane now long and stringy around his face as he lifted his head to investigate the crashing footfalls. A shadow against the far-left wall of the cell grew taller, and then Valentine Alesander stepped into view, his Saracen robes swinging.

Near the Spaniard's feet lay a long, crumpled pile of rags.

Adrian Hailsworth.

One of the guards shouted at Roman, his foreign words challenging yet hesitant, as if he was unsure what to make of the giant man who had appeared in his prison with a falcon upon his shoulder.

Roman glanced down at the man's waist and saw the ring of keys dangling there. Then he looked both guards in the eye in turn.

"I've come for my friends."

Chapter 1

October 1181
Melk, Austria

Roman Berg rather enjoyed being a criminal.

He paused on the steep hillside, one knee cocked to brace his sandaled foot against the slope, his palm pressing the jagged gray bark of an ocher-tinged cedar. He tilted his face up at the faded sky peeking through the tallest branches already stripped by the autumn storms and listened. The cry sounded behind him and Roman turned, scanning the islands of blue within the dark sea of the canopy. A quad-pointed shadow swooped diagonally overhead, soaring toward the river. Roman pushed away from the cedar and sidestepped down the hill to follow the falcon.

The dried leaves scraped and poked his instep, twigs trying to wriggle between his toes. He held out his arms for balance as he leaped over a small outcropping of gray rock, his monk's robe snapping taut with the motion. He was smiling, but that was not unusual. Weren't all criminals as happy with their lot? Roman thought they should be.

He paused against another tree, directing his labored breaths through his nose in order to listen more closely. There! The tinkling of the bells tied to Lou's leg sifted like ghostly music through the breeze. The hunting falcon had landed. Roman turned and set off to the east through the trees, more quietly this time. He directed his gaze to the treetops as he stepped slowly, carefully; he loved to watch Lou at the hunt.

But the rustling of leaves sounded suddenly out of time with his own footsteps, and Roman stopped. There it was again: something rolling in the underbrush. It sounded as though it were being made by a creature too large for even the noble Lou to pursue. A person, then? Few from the village would wander up from the riverbank to scale the steep slope below Melk, and he couldn't think of any of the brethren besides himself who would have reason or desire to take such a laborious stroll.

Perhaps Stan at one time would have, but the general was different since his wife and son had been killed; he had no interest in much of anything anymore. Adrian was continually occupied with his studies and duties, faithfully observing the hours of prayer while Maisie tended a stall in the village. Valentine spent most of his hours gazing rapturously at Mary or little Valentina, nearly four months old now.

The rustling erupted again, loud and frantic and fast this time, and accompanied by what sounded to Roman like gasps for air. Had he heard a word in those breathy gulps? He felt his brow crease and he cocked his head, listening, watching, in much the same manner as Lou. He flinched at the short, shrill scream that filled the humid space between the trees.

It sounded like a woman.

Lou chose that moment to cry out, from the same direction in which the scream had come, and so Roman began walking once more, although not so quietly this time; he didn't want to be accused of being a voyeur should he happen upon two young people from the village seeking the wood for a romantic interlude. He saw a flash of white through the tree trunks ahead, and Roman leaned and weaved, trying to discern its origin. The sliver of brightness stuttered rhythmically and was now accompanied by smacking and thumping sounds.

If Roman hadn't known better, he would have thought perhaps someone was doing a very good job of taking a sound beating.

Lou cried again, and Roman's eyes instinctively went up. He saw the hunting falcon perched on the spindly pinnacle of a dead oak tree, bobbing in the air, the faint sounds of his bells now recognizable behind the rustling below. Lou stretched out his wings as if he was preparing to swoop down on the unseen quarry, but then flapped himself back into place, clutching the tree in an agitated manner before crying out again.

Roman's frown deepened and he headed toward the sounds. "Hello there," he called out, adopting his Brother Roman persona—which really wasn't much different from his true personality. "Peace be upon you."

He weaved through the trees, and the white form ahead grew more clear. It was a person, bent over in the underbrush, but Roman couldn't yet tell if it was a man or a woman.

"Have you lost someth—" The friendly query broke as Roman's feet stopped and the figure ahead raised fully.

It was a dark-skinned man—Saracen dark—wearing the flowing costume of his homeland, white except for the bright red splatters adorning its front. His head was wrapped in a close, dark turban and the slender face below it held wild eyes, a mouth pulled wide in either pleasure or fury. The man's hands—slick with blood—went to the sash tied around his robe, where a woven scabbard dangled. In a blink, the man had drawn a curved scimitar and pointed its angled tip in Roman's direction.

"This is none of your concern," he said with a thick accent. "Go back the way you came, lest you wish this day to end very badly for you."

Roman got a cold feeling in his chest and took a step closer to the man, peering into the brush at his feet. "No need to threaten me so— what have you there?" His eyes caught sight of a swath of lavender-colored silk; at least, it had at one time been lavender. Now it was mottled with dirt and leaves and wide, wet patches of black.

The Saracen stepped between Roman and whatever lay in the scrub, holding his scimitar in both hands now. "I told you, come no farther. I will kill you."

Roman held out a supplicating hand. "Listen here, now; I mean you no harm. As you can see, I am but a simple monk, and you seem to have found your way onto abbey land. I have no intention of robbing you, so if there is aught I can do to direct you in the way you mean to go, I—"

"Help," a choked voice called from behind the Saracen, and Roman was certain it was a woman. "Help me."

Roman frowned and glanced at the cloth-wrapped bundle again before returning his eyes to the dark man. "What exactly are you doing here?"

Before the Saracen could answer, the voice from the bundle called out again. This time, the plea made his blood freeze in his veins.

"*Roman.*" His name bubbled and cracked in her throat as she gasped.

The robed man cocked his arms so that his weapon was raised

near his right ear. "I warned you twice, false priest. Now I shall send you to your judgment and lay up my own reward."

Roman raised his palm higher. "I wouldn't do that if I were you. Put down your blade and step away from the woman."

The Saracen rushed forward, drawing back the scimitar even farther.

Roman's vision seemed to tremble, his peripheral sight blacking out until only two tiny pinpricks of light were available to him, both showing the robed man who now seemed to be impossibly small, impossibly far away, and moving so slowly he might be a statue.

The sound of his own breath was a roar in his ears; his arms and legs felt as though they had shimmered away into nothing, leaving only the growl in his head and the tiny vision of the man before him, who meant to end his life. Who had meant to end the life of the woman still lying in the brush, somewhere beyond the terrible thunder that deafened him.

He might just as well be in the Damascene dungeon again.

Roman.

There should be no Saracens at Melk. Melk was safe. His friends were safe. If they were discovered, Roman's happy existence was over.

He couldn't let that happen.

His vision and hearing came back with a whoosh and the Saracen was upon him now. But it didn't matter, as his hands had already reached out, his arms moving, lifting, twisting, as if of their own accord. The sizzle of cold along his biceps was barely noticed, the crunching sound of bone nothing more than a flinch and a whisper.

And then the Saracen fell to the brush at his feet with a crash of leaves and moved no more. Roman looked down at the man over the heaving cowl covering his chest and then nudged him over with a sandaled foot. Dark eyes stared, unseeing, at the tree canopy.

Ahead, Lou screamed, and Roman looked up to find his falcon still observing the scene below. His attention was drawn by a wet sensation on his hand, and when Roman lifted his right arm, he saw the streams of blood threading from his fingertips. His eyes traveled up to his right biceps, where the brown wool of his habit was slashed open, revealing the gash that split his pale skin from shoulder to elbow.

"This is bad," he mused aloud. He ripped off the remainder of his sleeve and tied it as best he could around his arm, using his teeth to pull tight the knot. The blood coursing down his forearm barely slowed.

Roman stepped to the bundle of lavender silk, which had not moved or spoken again. He knelt, feeling the slight wobble in his knees, and pulled away a bloodied swath of fabric. His heart seemed to stop beating in his chest.

It was indeed a woman, her face a puffy sea of swollen bruises and trickling blood. Her nose was likely broken, her lips split and crusted, her eyelids fat and prickled with starburst patterns Roman knew would rapidly spread in a deep indigo over her skin like oil on water. Her arm was bent awkwardly behind her body, her bare feet torn and scarred, poking out from beneath the ragged hem of her robes. Roman touched her cheek and she whimpered.

This was not just any woman.

If Roman had thought her injuries dire the first and only time they'd met on that fateful eve in Damascus, her condition now was so much worse. The Saracen had nearly beaten her to death, likely would have achieved that very goal had Roman been a moment or two later in happening upon them.

Had Lou not cried out and led Roman to her.

For all Roman knew, she might yet die, even should he take her to the abbey for care. She was dangerous to the Brotherhood. If she had found them, it meant others could be right behind her—others, like the man who had seemed intent on killing her. Were they from Saladin's camp?

Or Glayer Felsteppe's?

How had she gotten there, and what did she want?

"This is very bad," he corrected his earlier assessment of the situation as Lou screamed again from his perch.

The woman on the ground had obviously been hunted, chased, tortured. The very woman who had saved his three friends' lives and, in essence, joined the Brotherhood together, for good or ill. Would he now repay her by leaving her to die?

The ground seemed to spin beneath him, and Roman dared a glance at his arm; his brown wool sleeve was now black, glistening. The leaves beneath his sandals were splashed with his own blood. If he didn't do something now, they might both die here in the wood.

He gathered the nearly weightless woman in his arms and stumbled up the hill toward the abbey, one name throbbing in his mind, keeping time with the sloshing, sluggish heartbeat in his ears.

Stan. Stan. He must reach Constantine.

It seemed to take an age to gain the top of the steep slope, and then another still to walk along the lengthy and windowless curtain wall. Roman stumbled around the corner, his sandals no longer able to clear even the meanest pebbles as he dragged his feet along, and at last he saw the tall winged statues guarding the gates. They seemed to meet, trade places, and then multiply before his eyes as the world began to slowly tilt. The woman's arm had fallen from across her stomach and now dangled and flopped as he staggered toward the opening, too weak now to shout, too desperate to stop. His knees were bowing in response to the crazy tilt of the ground.

Constantine . . .

He made it as far as the gates before he was at last spotted. In a slow, slowing heartbeat, a flood of robed monks rushed toward him from garden beds and dooryards. Roman crashed to his knees as— thanks be to God—Constantine pushed his way to the crest of the wave and was the first to join Roman in the cold dirt of the bailey.

So stupid. He was so stupid. Now everyone would see. Everyone would know. Victor would worry.

"Roman," Stan said, giving him a shake. "What happened?"

Roman tried to focus on his friend's face. No one could find out about the Saracen. No one could find out about *them*.

"Body," Roman whispered, his nose nearly touching Stan's. "In the wood."

His world went dark then, and the ground rushed toward him over the woman's limp form. Even in the darkness, he could feel strong hands take him up, could hear Lou crying as he circled overhead.

Isra came into consciousness with a sob. She hurt so badly—her face, her head, her arm; her lungs felt as though they were being shredded with each shallow breath. She tried to writhe onto her side, but a pair of hands on her shoulders stayed her, pushed her back onto the mattress.

"You canna turn over. Lie still now."

Isra wanted to open her eyes, see the woman who owned the strange accent and who smelled of flowers, but her lids were so swollen that trying her hardest only rewarded her with a sliver of indistinguishable light. Her head screamed in protest and so she closed her eyes again and managed a thin whimper.

"I'm certain you're in a great deal of pain. Perhaps he'll bring you a draught."

Who? Isra wanted to say. *Who are you? Where am I?*

The gurgle of water being wrung into a basin filtered through the terrible agony in her head, and a moment later a heavy, icy cloth was pressed to her swollen, throbbing eyes. Isra tried to turn away, but her strength was as that of a newborn babe's against the steely fingertips that held her temples. She thought her mind must be playing tricks on her, for she was certain she heard a beastly roar from beyond the walls of her prison; a chattering; birdsong.

"Shh. Stop that now. I'm trying to help you."

Isra tried to lie very still while the frigid sodden cloth seemed to push her eyeballs to the back of her skull. The throbbing steadied, but her stomach roiled. She tried to swallow down the pressure in her throat, but her muscles would not obey, and she knew she would choke to death should she vomit.

She'd seen it before, after all.

And just like that, it all came back. Huda's small, broken body, her dusky skin covered in blood-smeared bruise points that would never fade. The bile on the side of her face, drying in her hair, the smell of sweaty men and spicy incense and fear.

They'd left her on the floor like rubbish.

Isra began to weep silently, the slight heaving of her chest enough to set off the bright starbursts of pain once more, but they paled in comparison to the misery she felt in her heart.

Perhaps a door opened; somewhere behind her there was a sound like wood against stone and, for a brief moment, a cacophony of squawking and growls. Isra didn't care enough to call out, to try to pull the now lukewarm cloth from her eyes to see who had come into the room. It didn't matter. Huda was still dead, and she had failed. Perhaps her mind had only been playing tricks on her on the hillside; she hadn't found Roman Berg and she never would. They would find her and kill her, if they hadn't done so already.

The woman must have lifted the cloth herself and was now wiping at her eyes. Isra could feel the crust taking many of her lashes as it was scraped free, slicing into the tender flesh of the corners. Isra tried to turn away.

Let me be, she tried to say. *Just let me die.* But all that came out was a pathetic whine.

"Stop that, I said," the woman snipped. "I'm nae accustomed to playing nursemaid, so if you wish any care at all, you'll be still." The steely fingertips came back to the crown of her head as the rag was applied to her face more briskly.

And then, as if the woman was indeed speaking to someone who had entered the room, "She's only been awake for a few moments. I doona think she can speak verra well."

"English or at all?" a man asked in a low, emotionless voice.

"It was nae language I've heard before." The hands left Isra and she heard a splash, as if the rag had been tossed into the basin. "I've done all I'm willing for now. How is Roman?"

Isra's head swiveled at the mention of that name, and she strained to open her eyes, fought to raise the arm that wasn't pinned to her side.

"*Oh-man*," she called out as the light again pierced the slivers allowed by her swollen lids. The attempt at his name was strangled and nasally, her nose was completely blocked, the syllables zinging in her bones.

"That enlivened her," the man said. Isra heard the scrape of chair legs and fought to focus her eyes through the blinding light. "Can you hear me well enough?" he asked near her ear. She felt him take her hand in his, and the touch of his skin made her stomach roil again. "Squeeze my hand if you can understand me."

Isra squeezed.

"Very well. Now try to tell me your name."

"Roh-man."

"No. I need to know who *you* are. What is your name?" The man repeated the question in Arabic.

She turned her head away from him in answer.

The man sighed and seemed to speak over Isra's body. "Could I trouble you for a cup of water?"

"Great gods. I may as well take off me shoes and don a cap while I'm about it."

A moment later, Isra's head was raised and a cup pressed to her lips. The water just wet her tongue when it was withdrawn. She tried to open her mouth and follow the cup, but it was taken away. The man's voice was very close to her face now.

"What. Is. Your. Name?" he demanded.

Isra tried to lick her cracked lips. "Roman."

He leaned so close now, Isra could feel his breath on her ear. If his proximity was not enough to set her insides to trembling, the dark sincerity of his next words nearly caused her to retreat once more into unconsciousness.

"Hear me now, woman: We have perhaps saved your life. But if you do not tell me now who you are and why you have come to this place with that name on your lips, come nightfall, I will carry your body to the river myself." He paused, and the scant space between them was filled with only his breath in his nostrils. His whisper chilled her. "I will stand on the shore and watch you drown."

Isra's heart trilled in her chest. She could tell by the lack of emotion in the man's voice that he was confident in what he said, and that he would not hesitate to follow through with his threat. That they knew of Roman Berg was clear; perhaps he was at this place even now.

But she could not determine if they knew him as trusted allies or as foes. Anything she told this stranger could put Roman in even greater danger.

If she said nothing, they were going to kill her.

Isra fought to open her eyes again, straining to focus until she could make out the shadowy image of a man's face. He had leaned slightly back from her and was now studying her—not with pity for her condition, but with a wariness that made Isra's skin crawl. She had no doubt that he would leave her to die; hadn't she seen that very look of apathy, that hard-heartedness dulling the eyes of so many men before?

She swallowed several times to work open her airway enough to speak. The man leaned forward, turning his ear toward her mouth as if he understood she was preparing to form words. It was clear he was used to having his commands obeyed. Isra tried to raise her head to bring her lips even closer to his ear. She wanted to make sure he heard her.

"As you wish."

He exploded from his seated position, and Isra could see his shadowed arm as it raised. She closed her eyes.

But no blow fell, only the sounds of wood against stone again and a confused shuffle of footsteps and movement.

"Stan? What are you doing?"

"You shouldn't be up. And why didn't *you* tell me he had woken?"

"I was coming to tell you now, yes? As you can plainly see, he would no do as I asked. Who is she?"

Footsteps came close to her, and Isra tried to force her eyes open once more, hoping against hope as the conversation carried on in the room without her.

"I don't know," her interrogator said. "But I've a feeling we're about to find out."

Isra felt her hand being taken up once more, in a grasp that was rougher, larger than the palm of the man who had threatened her, and yet this touch was gentle, protective. At last she could make out bright blue eyes and the impossibly blond hair that now curled around chiseled cheekbones. She felt the painful welling of tears in her eyes.

"How are you feeling?" Roman Berg asked.

Her throat convulsed and she had to swallow down the overwhelming emotion as best she could. "Your hair is long." Her words were garbled, broken whispers, and yet she saw that he had understood her by his look of surprise and then the half grin that came over his lips.

"It's been a while since last we met," he conceded.

"Roman." His name was spoken in warning by the man behind him who had threatened her.

His expression sobered. "I need to know your name. If I—we," he corrected, "are to keep you safe, you must tell us how you found me, and why you are here."

Isra tried to roll her eyes around the room and look at the two men and the red-haired woman who had come to stand behind Roman. It was not hard to determine that the man with the long auburn hair had been her inquisitor; his eyes were haunted, his face haggard even from several paces away. The dark-haired man could have been from her own country, and yet Isra surmised he was the infamous Spaniard of the group by the sound of his accent when he had spoken moments ago. All three men, including Roman, were wearing monk's robes.

"Your friends?" she rasped.

Roman hesitated a moment before nodding his head.

"From Damascus?"

He only stared at her, his lips in a line.

Isra understood. "My name," she whispered, trying to command her swollen lips and tongue to enunciate clearly, "is Isra Tak'Ahn." She paused to swallow. "I've come because you must return to Syria."

Chapter 2

Roman sat at his spot at the large table in Melk's secret library, the silence so palpable it seemed to press against his throbbing arm. Someone—Valentine? he hadn't thought to ask—had stitched his wound, and now the muscles beneath it screamed and burned. He judged that he had lost quite a lot of blood by the way his head swam and his stomach roiled. But he had refused Stan's order to return to his cell and his bed.

Constantine sat in his usual chair, in his usual posture: forearms braced on the table, his hands linked, head down. He'd said nothing since he and Roman and Valentine had left Maisie Lindsey with Isra. Valentine sat to the right of Roman, attending his cuticles with a short blade while the three of them waited for Victor and Adrian to join them.

They entered through the door that led to the gatehouse, the skinny old abbot preceding Adrian, who carefully pushed the heavy door shut.

"My apologies for the delay, gentlemen," Victor said, coming to take his seat on Roman's left side. "The brethren have been set astir by the goings-on this afternoon."

Adrian came around the far side of the library to deliberately pass behind Roman. He stopped near his chair and squeezed Roman's left shoulder. "Doing well enough?"

Roman gave him a sideways nod but didn't meet his eyes.

Adrian clapped his shoulder a pair of times before continuing around the table to his own seat, something Roman was still not used to, after so many long evenings of Adrian sitting removed from the group near the window, preferring his own misery for company. The red-haired woman caring for Isra had changed Adrian Hailsworth deeply.

"I was certain Brother Hilbert was going to follow us all the way into the gatehouse," Adrian commented, adjusting his seat as he settled in.

"As was I," Victor muttered. "Hilbert is a capable servant, but at times too exacting." Victor looked around the table at each man in turn before settling on Roman. "Where is she?"

Roman opened his mouth, but it was Valentine who answered. "Below. In one of Wynn's empty cells."

Victor nodded. "And the . . . other?"

"Also below," Valentine answered, holding forth his hand to examine his fingernails. "In one of the no empty cells."

"There will be bones," Adrian said. "The larger ones, any matter."

The abbot inclined his head in acknowledgment. "They will be interred in the crypt for the indigent, God have mercy on his soul." Victor crossed himself.

And then Roman knew what they were talking about. It seemed as though everything had been taken care of; he had been taken care of. Perhaps it was because he still felt so weak, but the idea of these men taking such pains for him this afternoon caused a lump in his throat.

He cleared it as quietly as possible before asking, "Has anyone seen Lou?"

Valentine was putting away his blade. "He had flown back to the mews and was crying to get in. I saw him as I was coming up from the river, so I pause a moment for him. You're welcome."

All eyes turned to the Spaniard, but it was Constantine who spoke.

"You stopped to let a falcon in a cage while dragging a dead body?"

"He'd had a trying morning as well, yes? He was tired. And I was no so much dragging the body. It is no as heavy if you tie up the hands and feet just so and then wrap it—"

"*Did anyone see you?*" Victor interrupted, holding forth one palm with a pained expression across his kind face.

Valentine looked offended. "Of course no."

"What's going on?" Adrian interjected.

All eyes in the room turned to Constantine. But when the general looked up again, it was to pin Roman with his gaze.

"Well? You are the only one she'd talk to."

Roman shifted in his chair, adjusted his throbbing arm. His forehead prickled with sweat. "She is the woman who found me in Damascus. The one who led me to the prison." He paused a moment. "Isra Tak'Ahn."

"Egyptian surname." Adrian's brow was creased in a frown. "Why is she here now looking for you? And how did she find you?"

"The how of it I don't yet know," Roman said. "She is too weak to speak at any length. But she told me that we must return to the Holy Land. That King Baldwin's life is in danger. There is a plot to assassinate him."

"Apparently the Christian king's life is no the only one in danger," Valentine said, "if the package I dragged through the wood is any measure. Perhaps Saladin's men?"

"Perhaps," Victor conceded. "But there has been a well-respected truce between Saladin and Baldwin for at least two years. I've had no word to indicate it's imperiled."

Valentine sniffed. "A time of truce would seem to me to be the best time to attempt an assassination."

"That is not Saladin's way," Constantine argued.

"No," Adrian said, a hint of his old bitterness creeping into his words. "He would rather torture his enemies slowly."

The silence grew thick again for a moment.

Victor cleared his throat. "Why did she seek you, Roman?"

"I don't know." Roman shook his head. "Perhaps she feels I owe her a debt and she has no one else she can trust. That night in Damascus, it almost seemed as though she was taking revenge against someone by helping me. Perhaps one of the higher-up generals?"

Adrian pulled a face but said nothing. Constantine regarded the table once more.

Valentine leaned forward, one arm along the edge of the table. "She wishes you to travel all the way back to Syria, you, who would be the most conspicuous of us all, in order to warn Baldwin that—in a time of war, mind you—someone at some time might try to kill him?"

Roman opened his mouth but then closed it again. His thoughts were tied up in knots. At last he said, "I don't know what she wants, Val."

"It sounds like a trick to me," Valentine said, relaxing back in his seat. "Though why should we care if it is true? Baldwin is a leper. His days are already numbered. Adrian is too well-known, as are you, Stan. I certainly will no leave my women to save the life of a rotting man who has done nothing for those who sought to preserve his fortress. In fact, he would likely try to kill any one of you himself at first sight. Let him die, I say, by whatever means befall him."

Roman caught movement out of the corner of his eye, and when he turned to the left, he was shocked to see Constantine nodding.

"I agree, Valentine."

Adrian's brows raised. *"What?"*

"Baldwin would never believe any of us." Constantine kept his eyes on the tabletop as he explained his reasoning. "He thinks us traitors, when in his heart, he should know the three of us would be the last men on earth to ever betray him."

"To betray Chastellet," Adrian added with a wistful tone in his voice that made Roman's heart flinch. He'd loved that fortress as much as Roman.

"Kind of you to exclude me." Valentine sniffed and waved a hand toward Roman. "I have only been made a criminal by this business, when I had no part in it save to help a man out of the goodness of my heart."

That at least made Adrian grin. "You were a criminal long before you met us."

"And I had to give you a sack of gold in order for you to help me," Roman added.

But Constantine was having no part of the attempt to lighten the mood. "I was to have already left Chastellet," he said pensively. "The day of the siege, I should have been on the Mediterranean, en route to Benningsgate. But Baldwin beseeched me stay, look over Chastellet in his absence. Only a short journey. He said he trusted Glayer Felsteppe not, and would rather have him under his thumb." He paused. "Had I died in the final battle, perhaps he would have thought otherwise. But instead, I am here, and my family are dead. My home lost."

It was as if the room had been surrounded by a thick, dank cloud of despair, humid with sorrow and regret. No one spoke, for none of the men could refute what the general had said.

Then Constantine stood up from his chair and all the men looked at him: his rumpled clothing, his wild hair, his red-rimmed eyes.

"Let him die," Stan repeated. "The woman, too. We cannot let her leave now that she has discovered our identities and our location."

Constantine stepped away from the table and began walking toward the door, and Roman's head was spinning too much to form enough of a thought to stop him.

But Victor intervened, taking hold of Constantine's forearm as he passed and rising. "I cannot allow a murder in God's house, Constantine," Victor warned. "In my house. Has the woman not suffered enough? What is her crime that she should be put to death?"

"What was Christian's crime?" Constantine said, shaking the abbot off. "What did my little boy do that warranted his burning to death in his home, along with his mother?"

Then Constantine leaned into Victor's face, his mouth pulled into a grimace, his posture threatening. Victor did not shrink away.

"If you let this woman go free, she will run to the first coin she can find to trade what she knows. The village and all the countryside around Melk will then be filled with criminals the like you've never even *imagined*. Think you they would bother determining identity once they discover we have been posing as monks? They will kill everyone here, including you.

"If we were to depart Melk after she betrayed us," Constantine continued, leaning away from Victor and looking at all the men, "there would truly be no protection for the brethren. And where else in the world would we go? Wyldonna, to be devoured by beasts or drowned by creatures of the sea? I would not trade the life of even the basest beggar of yonder village for that woman's, let alone the lives of the men who reside within these walls."

Now Constantine looked at Roman. "Get rid of her by morning or I will."

He strode to the secret door that led to the larger library and was gone a moment later.

Valentine drummed his fingertips on the table. "It is nice that he is talking again, yes?"

"I don't understand," Adrian said. "Constantine's attitude toward Baldwin is perhaps justified, but why should he hold such hateful feelings toward the woman who effectively saved our lives in Damascus?"

"Because," Roman said in a low voice, the realization resting on him as heavy and real as a block of granite, "if he could return to that time in the past, knowing what would become of his family, his home, he would not wish to have his life saved. The three of you were only hours away from death in the prison, Constantine only hours away from avoiding a long life without his little son."

Roman had felt the very same after Saladin's army had lain ruin to Chastellet and left him alone with nothing but corpses and carrion birds for companions.

"I do no doubt that you are right, my astute friend," Valentine allowed with a tinge of admiration in his voice. "However, there is much to be said for Stan's reasoning. The woman has seen us and knows where we have hidden away. I have a wife and child now; Adrian his own woman. We can no risk discovery."

Victor rejoined the discussion, sitting once more in his chair. "Roman, do you feel the woman would betray us?"

"I don't know," Roman said. "She refused to tell Constantine anything before I entered the room. Not her name, not why she was asking after me. I can only surmise that is part of the reason the Saracen bothered to beat her so badly rather than just kill her outright once he'd caught up with her. Perhaps she has more to tell us, if only we give her the opportunity to heal—and to live," he added.

"I agree," Victor said.

Adrian nodded. "As do I."

The men looked to Valentine, who was wobbling his head from side to side, contemplating the ceiling. Finally, he sighed. "Agree. For the time being."

All four men stood, and Roman tried to be as inconspicuous as possible as he braced himself on the edge of the table. His head swam still, and the gentle candlelight in the library seemed to throb for a moment.

"Constantine will not like being overruled," Victor said. "I don't know how he will take the news that she still lives on the morn. He is a man of his word."

"I will sit with her," Roman said. "I will not let him harm her, not only for her safety but for Stan's own good. Perhaps there might come a day when he would bitterly regret such an action."

"Thank you." Adrian nodded toward Roman, and he was again made aware of the change in the formerly snide and bitter man as the four of them made their way to the gatehouse passage.

Valentine struck Roman on his uninjured arm. "Yes, that is a good idea, my friend. He will have a most difficult time climbing over your large body when you faint. But you? You will no even feel it. Brilliant."

Roman gave his friend a shove that nearly sent Valentine from his feet. "Then you'd best bring me something to eat, you sneaking Spaniard."

"I'm certain Brother Wynn has sufficient provisions to sustain you. Plenty of hay and leaves; perhaps some delicious grubs, yes?"

"Won't you precede me down the stairs?"

Valentine grinned over his shoulder while he stepped into the black corridor. "So you can push me down them?"

"Don't worry; you won't even feel it."

Isra could feel the redhead's eyes on her as if they were tethers holding her to the pallet. She couldn't have moved even if she'd wanted to, her body was so sore, but even had she been well, she doubted she was brave enough to test the woman's unspoken threat.

She was a prisoner here.

No matter, that. She'd been a prisoner the whole of her life, really. A prisoner dressed in the finest silks and jewels, provided the best food and drink, her health and grooming looked after in the most meticulous ways. But she had never been free.

Isra shifted her gaze and confirmed that the woman was indeed watching her closely, a frown of concentration across her pale face. Her eyes sparkled like emeralds, and Isra thought she would rather enjoy looking at the woman had she not felt so threatened by her.

"Are you going to kill me?" she rasped.

The woman's eyes widened a bit. "I didna know you were awake. 'Tis difficult to tell with your eyes as swollen as they are." She crossed her arms over her slight chest and leaned back in her chair. "*I'm* nae going to kill you, nay. What their plans are, I doona yet know. You're a danger to them; surely you ken that?"

Isra swallowed, and yet the words still broke in her raw throat. "I know."

"You've much death around you already."

The statement brought to Isra's mind her mother, and Huda, and the man she'd killed on her last night in Damascus. Her eyes strained with the desire to produce tears, but none would come. She said nothing.

The redhead sat up and scooted to the edge of the seat, reaching out her hand. Isra tensed and heard her own gasp.

"I'm nae going to hurt you," the woman said. "I just want to—"

"Maisie." The word caused the woman to withdraw her hand and look crossly at whomever had entered. It was a man's voice, but not one Isra recognized from earlier.

"What?" the woman demanded. "I only thought I'd see—"

"The less you know of her, the better for you," the man replied, coming at last into Isra's line of sight. He had brown hair laying over his shoulders, a slender, pale face. When he reached out his own hand toward the woman and she took it, Isra saw swirling black designs on his forearm. "Come. You're being relieved."

"By who? *Him?* Doona be ridiculous," Maisie scoffed. "He's in nae condition to sit up with her all the night."

"He's not keeping her company," the long-haired man said, and then pulled the woman away, giving Isra a curious look before both he and the woman were gone. She heard him speak in a low voice again. "You will fetch me at any time if you have need of me? I must have your word or I shan't leave at all."

"I will. Val will be here soon to look in on me."

Isra's heart skipped in her chest. He'd come back.

She heard the door scrape closed and then heavy footsteps growing louder as he approached. He took the seat Maisie had recently vacated, but beneath his huge frame it seemed a child's chair. He pulled his right arm toward him and held the elbow in his palm.

"Are you awake?" he asked.

"Yes," she whispered. She tried to ask what had happened to his arm, but her words were like gravel in her mouth.

Roman leaned forward and retrieved a cup that was out of Isra's line of sight. "You must either hold up your head or try to grasp the cup. I fear I have only one capable arm at the moment."

Isra lifted her right hand from the pallet and saw that it trembled. She wrapped her fingers around the cup and discovered the tips beneath her nails were quite numb. She grasped it as firmly as she could. While she concentrated on lifting the cup, Roman slid his wide palm beneath her head and lifted.

Her lips stung as she fitted the rim to her mouth, the sweet taste of the water made salty by her own blood. But each swallow came easier, as if the water was holy elixir in this strange prison. She drank it all.

Roman eased her head back down onto the hard pallet and then took the cup from her before sitting in the chair again.

"You are injured," she said, her words smoother but still heavy with rasp.

"A gift from the man I found you with," he said. He paused, as if waiting to see if she would ask the question she was too frightened to give voice to. "He is dead."

Isra closed her eyes for a brief moment. *Thank God.*

"Are there more following you?"

She emerged from the darkness once more at his question, to look at this man who seemed to be the embodiment of light with his pale skin, his curling, almost-white hair, and his glittering blue eyes. She was still so afraid. Afraid of the people who effectively held her captive, afraid of this strange land, afraid of Roman Berg's question, afraid of what a truthful answer might mean for her.

But she would not lie to him.

"I do not know. Probably."

He said nothing, only nodded while he dropped his gaze to the floor for a moment. Then his face raised again and Isra was enchanted by the way his eyes seemed to hold all the colors of the sky.

"Why are they hunting you?"

Isra swallowed. No lies.

"I killed the man who was to lead the party meant to kill Baldwin. Certainly when they found him dead and me missing . . ."

Roman continued to watch her, his eyes flitting over her face as if trying to discern the truth beneath her swollen features.

She continued. "They likely think me to have gone to Baldwin or to one of his vassals. But at least one tracked me here. There could be more."

"Why have you come? Why have you sought me out?" he asked. "We are strangers, and you owe the king of Jerusalem nothing."

"That night in Damascus," she said, her voice already beginning to weaken again, "I was seeking revenge against a man named Abdal. He killed my mother. I knew that your friends' capture and death meant great honor for him, and I wished him destroyed."

"Abdal is dead."

"I know," she said. "But there were many evil men ready to take his place. The man who came after him is even worse and has stolen the last thing in my life that I held dear. It is he who has made the pact to kill Baldwin in a time of truce, and I must see that he fails."

"You came all this way, risked your life, thinking to convince me to return to Syria to exact revenge for you?"

Isra tried to shake her head, but it was little more than a weak wobble. "I am not so selfish, my lord. The man who took Abdal's place is called Hamid. He has been promised a great deal of gold to assassinate the Christian king for an Englishman named Glayer Felsteppe. I believe you know of him."

Roman only stared at her, and she could not tell what he was thinking.

"Spies have been placed in the different kingdoms of the Holy Land. There will be minor attacks in the coming months meant to draw both sides out, and when Baldwin nears the north country before the spring, he will be killed."

"Why?" Roman asked.

"Because," Isra paused to swallow again, "there have been rumors that the men charged with the betrayal of Chastellet have been wrongly accused. And this Glayer Felsteppe is to receive a very wealthy English estate. In the spring."

"Baldwin could see him ruined before he gains his title."

Isra only blinked.

"Who is Hamid's English connection in the Holy Land?" Roman pressed.

"I do not know his name. A titled lord. Trusted by Baldwin, but frustrated with his lack of power. Would you be able to find him?"

Roman shook his head with a grimace. "That could be anyone in the whole of Jerusalem. Even Baldwin's own family." Isra could not tell if he was in pain or chagrined by the holes in her information. "It is not my area of expertise. My duties at Chastellet did not involve mingling with the nobility."

"You were a soldier, my lord?" Isra said, shocked at this information. "How then did you escape the siege?"

He met her eyes. "No. I was a craftsman. A stonemason. I built Chastellet."

The admiration she already felt for him grew in her chest. This was no pampered lord; no soldier charged with saving his comrades and superiors. Before her was simply a man who had been intent on rescuing his friends. And his reward had been that his freedom and his livelihood were taken away.

But the admission seemed to have made him uncomfortable, and so Isra did not press him. Indeed, his face now bore deep lines of pain and fatigue, and Isra knew she was the cause of both this day.

"Thank you, my lord," she said. "For saving me. For listening to me."

"Go to sleep," he said. "We will talk more on the morrow."

"Will you stay with me all the night?" she couldn't help but whisper, and even she heard the fear in her voice.

"Yes," he said. "I, too, might sleep. If the man comes who first questioned you, you must wake me. He—" Roman closed his mouth in a grim line. "Wake me if he comes."

"As you wish, my lord," she said.

"I'm no lord."

"As you wish." Isra closed her eyes and took as deep a breath as her searing lungs would allow. By the time she exhaled, she was asleep.

She had never felt so safe in all her life.

Chapter 3

Maisie Lindsey relieved Roman the next morning, although Adrian must not have been completely comfortable with his wife being in the cell with Isra by the conversation Roman heard just beyond the door. But eventually, Maisie did enter the chamber, bearing a tray of food and drink as well as a fresh pile of cloths and a basin of water, along with a small pot of dried plant matter.

"How is she this morn?" Maisie asked as Roman rose from his chair.

"Still sleeping," he said, sidestepping around the perimeter of the chamber to give Adrian's wife room to put the tray down. "She had a bad night."

Roman did not elaborate upon Isra's weeping and moaning episode in the deepest dark, or how he had been unable to withstand the sound of her misery and had escaped the cell to stand on the far side of the fountain for many long moments, keeping close watch on the doorway. When he'd returned, she was asleep once more.

"I'm nae surprised by that," Maisie said, coming to lean over Isra. "She's taken quite a thrashing. Much more and she wouldna have survived."

Roman had no response to that. His own arm was searing, throbbing heat at the moment, his back ached, his head pounded, and he needed to make water.

"I'll return in but a moment," he said to Maisie as he made his way toward the low door.

"Rest a while in your chamber," Maisie instructed, pouring from a pitcher into a cup. "Victor shall come before the noon meal."

Roman paused. "Is that wise?"

Maisie glanced up at him as her hands readied her supplies on the tray. "Of course it's wise. Of all the people at this abbey, think of those with whom Constantine would nae readily come to blows for disobeying him. I count three, myself."

Roman had to grin as he considered there could be no other woman on the planet more suited to bringing Adrian Hailsworth to heel. He inclined his head toward her in acknowledgment and turned to leave, intending on seeing to Lou right away.

"Oh," Maisie called after him into the gallery. In a moment she was standing in the doorway, cloths in her hands. "Valentine asked me to tell you that he has taken to the mews this morning."

Roman nodded and made his way toward the stairs to behold the pale Brother Wynn descending, his personal stench preceding him like a rolling fog. The man gave Roman a distracted smile and bow, which Roman returned, and then held out a short, waxy-looking stick. After Roman took it, Brother Wynn first pointed to his own biceps and then Roman's before giving a wave and disappearing into the blackness below with an eye-watering breeze.

As Roman climbed the stairs, he wondered how he had come to have such people around him, such friends as these.

Was Isra Tak'Ahn's presence a threat to all of them?

The ointment disappeared into Roman's sleeves, along with his hands. As much as he wished to indeed seek his bed and put to good use the medicine gifted by Wynn, he needed to talk to Constantine first.

Roman found the general once more in the abbey's manicured bailey, where the majority of the brethren were readying the plantings and beds for the coming winter. Stan was working with his back to Roman, using a wide, stiff rake to smooth a section of needle mulch. The bailey was peaceful, quiet, only the sounds of tool and branch and leaf stirring on the crisp breeze. Roman stepped into Constantine's peripheral vision and gave a bow.

Stan glanced up, pretended a return bow over his rake, and then turned his attention back to the curved red slivers beneath his sandals.

Roman waited for Constantine to stop, but it soon became apparent that the man had no intention of giving him any attention at all. So Roman did the only thing that came to his mind. He strode to the nearest arch and retrieved a rake and then joined Constantine in the garden bed.

The motion of pulling the rake was so terrible that Roman was soon forced to use only his left hand, tossing the head of the tool out onto the mulch and then grasping the middle of the handle and lifting, dragging it back. The activity caused sweat to break out on his forehead instantly in the sunny bailey, and his increased heartbeat caused his arm to throb like a rotten tooth.

After several moments of Constantine glancing back at Roman with ever darkening glares, the general stalked to the archway and tossed his rake against a wall before disappearing inside the doorway that led to the gatehouse. Roman followed with a silent prayer of thanksgiving as the cool darkness flashed over his fevered brow. After a quick glance around, he stepped up behind the statue of Michael and ducked into the twisting corridor.

Stan had left the silent stone door standing ajar, and Roman pushed it to carefully, noting that the general had taken up a place before the secret library's only window, a stone-edged arrow slit where Adrian Hailsworth had spent countless days lost in his own misery.

When his vision cleared from the pounding of blood behind his eyes, Roman at once repeated the information Isra Tak'Ahn had relayed to him the night before. He embellished nothing, belittled nothing, reciting everything as closely as he could as to how he had been told.

Once Roman had finished, he waited in the silence for several moments for a response from Constantine.

"Why do you believe her?" he said at last.

"I don't know why she would lie."

Stan turned his head to look over his shoulder at Roman. "Perhaps the four large bounties offered for our capture?"

"She risked her life to come here. She nearly died as it was. And she saved you and Adrian and Valentine in Damascus. She saved me as well. I never would have been able to find you on my own, and if I had been caught . . ." Roman let the thought trail away. Constantine wasn't stupid, after all. He knew perhaps better than anyone what would have happened to Roman had he been captured inside the city walls. "She never demanded payment for leading me to you that night."

"She is demanding her payment now."

Roman took a step into the room. "By giving us an opportunity to stop Glayer Felsteppe from orchestrating the murder of a man who was at one time one of your closest friends and possibly clear our names? Is that a payment or another debt we could never come close to repaying?"

Constantine spun around. "*You* tell *me*, Roman. She purports not to know who the English contact in Jerusalem *is*. Have you any idea how many states you would have to search? How impossible it would be for you to access the caste of nobility where you might ferret out the traitor? Or were you planning to simply march into Baldwin's salon and announce as fact rumors relayed to you by a common *whore* wanted for *murder*?"

Roman felt his head draw back as if Constantine had struck him. He had to wait several moments for his heartbeat to slow before speaking. "It is true that I know little about Isra Tak'Ahn beyond what she has told me. And I have no idea how we would locate Baldwin in time to give him the information he needs. But that's why I have come to you, Constantine."

Stan turned back toward the window and muttered, "I'm not the general any longer."

"You were never my general," Roman said. "I've come to you as my friend. As my brother." He stepped to the table now and sat down in his chair. "If we are to act, it must be in one accord. Aren't we accused together?"

"I don't trust her," Constantine said. "She cannot be allowed to leave the abbey."

"I will go with her. I have no wife, no child." He regretted the words as soon as he'd said them.

A long, cold silence filled the library. "She has already killed at least one man. You may underestimate her cunning."

"If you trust me not either, then come and be my keeper. Face Baldwin yourself." Sweat broke on Roman's brow and he rose again, suddenly filled with an agitation that made him unable to sit and caused nausea to cover him in gooseflesh. "It is the last chance I can see to clear our names, and what better way to do it than by saving the king's life?"

"You're wrong, Roman," Constantine said. "I do trust you. I simply don't care if Baldwin dies."

"You'd better bloody well care," Roman growled as the vision of

Stan blurred and doubled for just an instant. "It is his word that damns or clears us. If he dies before we are vindicated, we will never have our lives back."

"I don't have a life to return to," Constantine spat.

"I'm certain Adrian would like to see his brother and his father before he dies," Roman said. "Think you Valentine and Mary wish to raise their child in a cloister of monks?"

Constantine spun around, but the dark glare on his face changed in an instant. "You don't look well, Roman."

Roman opened his mouth to reply that he didn't *feel* well either, but the vision of his friend went foggy, blurring at the edges, and gave him such a start that his lips felt gummed together. He reached out his good arm to brace himself against the table, but his hand seemed to swipe through nothing.

The fog grew brighter and brighter until Roman felt it swallow him up completely.

The first thing he saw when he opened his eyes was Constantine's face, his friend's brow creased in concern.

"Did I break the table?" Roman muttered.

Stan's frown deepened. "What?"

"When I fell. Did I break the table?" He raised up his head to see if he had reduced the Brotherhood's meeting place to a pile of splinters.

But when he looked around, instead of shelves of manuscripts ringing the room there was nothing but gray chiseled stone. A figure moved over Stan's shoulder and Isra Tak'Ahn came into view. The bruises on her face seemed to be healing quickly.

"We brought you to the woman's cell."

He found Stan's eyes again. "How long have I been out?"

"Two days."

Isra moved around Stan, and Roman could see that she carried a cup in her hands. She ignored the general's dark look as she leaned close to the pallet, sliding her fingers behind Roman's head and lifting.

He had never seen a smile so serene. "I can be of use to you now."

Roman swallowed the wine in the cup, trying to look anywhere but at those deep brown eyes that regarded him with a kindness he did not understand. But he could not look away for long, the almond shape fringed with thick black lashes so appealing to him.

He swallowed and leaned back. "Thank you."

"As you wish." Isra backed away from the pallet and moved to stand beyond the scowling Constantine again. Roman wished she would come sit at his side.

"How do you feel?" Constantine demanded.

"I feel fine," Roman said, wincing a bit at the pain his words caused in his head. He tried lifting his arm, hissed when the bending of his elbow caused a burning pain below his shoulder. "My arm hurts."

"We had to lance your wound. It had festered. But Brother Wynn has doctored you well."

"What did you tell Wynn that he would not grow suspect of such traffic in his demesne?"

"He told me nothing," a voice said from closer to the door, and in a moment, the albino monk reached Roman's side, a tray in his hands. The cell was instantly filled with his odor. "And I have no wish to know." He set down the tray and then placed his fists on his hips, looking Roman over from head to toe while he continued to speak. "You should have gone immediately to your cell with the balm I gave you. We would have had none of this."

The albino sighed. "You're looking fit enough, though. So up with you now. Up, up!" He grasped Roman's left arm in two places, squatted, and pulled in such a manner that Roman felt his body being lifted.

No single man had been able to move Roman before, especially not one whose head came only to the middle of his chest. He found himself quite disconcerted with the situation: Constantine and Isra in a cell together, Brother Wynn playing physician, himself being unconscious for the better part of two days.

The pale monk poked and prodded, squeezed and wiped, muttering and humming to himself all the while. Isra stood in the shadows along the wall, and Roman could not make out her features. At last Wynn straightened and looked to Constantine.

"The fever has gone from his arm. He will be well soon."

Constantine nodded. "My thanks, Wynn."

"If there's nothing else, I'm off to bed." He turned to Roman and patted him on his left shoulder. "Rest well, big fellow." The albino shuffled from the cell without another glance over his shoulder.

Once the door had closed, Roman looked to Constantine. "Stan? What are you doing here?"

The general kept his eyes trained on the floor somewhere in the area of his feet. Constantine hardly ever looked up anymore. It was as if his burden of sorrow had become so great that it had physically impaired him.

"I owe you an apology, Roman." He glanced up, meeting Roman's eyes for only an instant and then dropping his gaze again, nodding almost imperceptibly, as if he were hearing a conversation in his own head. At last he muttered, "I suppose it could be Raynald of Chatillon."

Roman winced. "Who could what?"

Isra stepped just inside the glow of the torch. "The traitor who has schemed with the Englishman to see Baldwin dead?"

Constantine shook his head. "No. Raynald wouldn't have schemed directly with Felsteppe. That would be too easily turned on him. I think Felsteppe has used his connections in Saladin's camp to encourage a pact with the traitor. Perhaps a senior adviser in Raynald's company. Felsteppe knows the leaders of the states well: their means, their frustrations. No doubt he has been kept well-informed as Baldwin's hero." Stan all but spat the last word.

Roman was still hesitant to draw any conclusions. "You wish to return to Syria and warn Baldwin?"

Again, Constantine's tangle of hair shook. He looked up. "I'll stand with you, whatever you and the others wish to see done. But I will not go. You need to understand the danger you will be in."

"We can't simply let him die, Stan," Roman said. "He was once your friend. And his word could be the very thing that clears us all."

Constantine only looked at Roman with deep sadness in his eyes, and Roman knew in that moment that Stan didn't really care if his name was ever cleared.

Roman nodded and held out his left arm.

Constantine took it, and the two men sat connected for a moment before Stan rose from his seat. He once more averted his gaze. "You have been excused from your regular duties. Wynn has requested your assistance with the lairs."

Roman nodded. "I'll come to you when I have made my decision."

"Good night." Stan turned and left the cell without a glance for the woman still skirting the pool of torchlight.

"At least he did not speak of killing me," she mused, and then she turned her gentle smile upon Roman. "Perhaps he is beginning to like me."

Chapter 4

Roman left her cell soon after, promising Isra that he would return after the brethren of Melk had broken the fast together the next morn, and he was true to his word. The screeching of the wooden door across the stony floor startled her from her pacing, and she held her breath as she turned to see who had entered.

The blond man had changed into a cowled robe, and his hair was dark gold, the damp ends curling around his temple and square jaw. His right sleeve hung limp, the obvious misshapenness across Roman's midsection indicating that he was wearing his arm in a sling close to his body. Isra's stomach clenched as it flashed through her mind that his injuries were entirely her fault. He could have been killed.

Lou perched on Roman's shoulder, but Isra could not see the falcon's sharp black eyes for the hood that it wore. Roman turned and pushed the door of Isra's cell closed before reaching up and removing Lou's hood.

"It's best to keep him blind down here. No telling what he might get after otherwise. But I thought you'd like to say hello."

"Good morn, my lord." She approached both man and bird and reached up a crooked finger to stroke the falcon's wing. "Good morn, Lou." The bird swiveled its head to investigate who was touching him. "I am happy to see you again."

Lou considered her, and Isra smiled at the majestic-looking creature while addressing his owner. "This is a strange place for a religious house."

"Wynn is a strange man," Roman hedged.

"He is a wise man," Isra argued, reaching up once more to stroke the bird. She hesitated when he shied away, but then turned his head as if granting her permission. "His knowledge of healing is great.

Why would such a man be kept hidden away in the bowels of the abbey?"

"Oh, he isn't kept hidden away," Roman said, and then cooed and clucked to Lou as he replaced the small leather hood. Isra was disappointed; she loved to look at the bird. "This catacomb is paradise for our pale brother. Would you like to see? I have been caged long enough. Perhaps you feel the same."

Isra thought Roman would be shocked at how close his words were to the truth for her. But she felt she must ask, if only for the safety of him and his friends at Melk. "Is it not dangerous to risk me being seen?"

His grin was boyish. "I assure you, no one comes down here of their own accord unless they must, and Wynn is already very aware of your presence. Ready?"

Isra nodded, wondering what horrific things she would see. The sounds in the night were unnerving enough. But she followed Roman from the cell, trusting he would not lead her into danger.

The gallery beyond was as empty as it had been the handful of times she'd spied it through the doorway of the little barred window. Because of its location beneath the massive abbey, there were no windows, making it nearly impossible to determine whether it was day or night save for the meager light that filtered down the wide stairs from above. But all the torches between the doors were lit and cast a soothing glow over the smooth stone floor and bubbling cistern.

Isra followed Roman to the edge of the fountain.

"Can you guess what is here?" he asked, looking down at her from his considerable height. He seemed a mountain inside this stone cavern, and yet Isra was comforted by his presence, rather than intimidated. "Surely the sounds have given you clues."

She looked around at the nearly identical doors. "A prison of some sort, I can only assume." Her eyes found his again. "Or a hospital? A place to care for those who have gone insane? Brother Wynn would be a capable caretaker."

"Close," Roman said. "But it's not ill monks Wynn cares for. He fashions himself a modern Noah, Melk his own personal ark."

Isra's eyebrows rose. "The prophet?"

"Yes. Wynn has made it his holy mission on earth to—" His explanation was interrupted by a door banging against the stones, and the sound of the albino monk shouting as he backed through the far-thest doorway to the left of the steps, a long staff in one hand and a short whip in the other.

Isra only now noticed that a pair of wrought-iron gates had been swung shut at the bottom of the stairs, sealing off the only exit from the dungeon.

"Well," Roman said, "I'll let you see for yourself."

Isra turned her head to watch the monk back from the cell and into the empty floor of the far gallery. He held the staff and whip away from his body, moving them up and down.

"Hie! Come now. Come now," Wynn called in a steady voice. "Hie!"

Her eyes widened as half of the wide head appeared in the door-way, the orange and black and white stripes recognizable. She gasped as the tiger took two slow steps into the gallery and then yawned, the torchlight causing its long, pearly fangs to glow.

"Hie, now!" Wynn commanded, cracking the whip and causing the tiger to advance in the direction away from the weapon. It began padding toward the fountain, its shoulders rolling. It stopped as its glowing eyes caught sight of the people standing on the opposite side of the pool, but began walking forward almost at once, an air of cu-riosity quickening its lazy strides.

"Roman?" Isra asked, unable to keep her hand from inching up to pinch a fold of his robes at his left elbow.

Lou squawked.

"Perhaps I could have chosen a better time," Roman allowed. "I thought that was the striped horses' cell."

"Stay where you are," Wynn called out, striding behind the tiger and heading around the fountain toward them. "Don't think to run. Brother Roman, you will wish to remove Lou's hood."

Isra began to tremble as Roman did as he was bade without com-ment, and she couldn't help her start as the tiger reached the far edge of the pool and stepped up on the smooth stone edge. It crouched there and drank, its wide, flat tongue scooping up the water, but its eyes stayed locked on the people across from it.

Isra felt they were locked on *her*. Her fingers took more of Roman's habit into her fist, until she could feel the warmth of his arm beneath the cloth on her skin.

"She's had her fill," Wynn explained, "so she'll likely have little interest in eating you. But she will be curious. Only be still, and do not turn your backs to her."

To Isra's dread and fascination, the tiger raised its head and began walking in its rolling gait atop the pool's edge toward her.

"Have no fear," Wynn insisted, although Lou did disembark from Roman's shoulder just then with a warning cry, and the albino monk shoved his way between Isra and Roman, breaking her link with him and holding out his staff across Isra's chest. "She's only curious."

The tiger slunk around the perimeter of the pool closer to Isra, and the water splashing from the fountain seemed to grow as loud as the roar of a waterfall. On such an elevated walk, the animal was as tall as Isra, and its head appeared so wide that she could not have encircled it with both arms. It snuffed and blew, lowering its still dripping muzzle as it slowed to a stop before her, taking up her scent. Isra, too, could smell the tiger's unique odor, warm and musky, deep like amber inside her head. She forced herself to swallow.

"Easy, easy," Wynn said in a low voice, and Isra could not be certain whether the monk was speaking to her or to the creature.

The tiger pushed its head forward beneath Wynn's staff, snorting at Isra's borrowed gown and then swinging up to brush its nose against her shoulder. Isra felt the damp imprint left by that firm bump and then squeezed her eyes shut as the wide head was suddenly before her face, misting her skin with its humid breath, its whiskers stiff as they dragged across her skin. She gasped through her nose as the tiger pushed its face into hers and then rubbed, running its wide head down the side of Isra's cheek and then onto her chest.

She dared open her eyes and her hands wanted to lift, to instinctively bury her fingers into the deep fur around the tiger's face in much the same manner in which she had been unable to resist touching Roman's falcon, but Wynn's solid staff cracked down on her wrists.

"No, lady," Wynn said in a low voice, and Isra understood that the staff had not been for her protection from the tiger.

Then the tiger moved on, stopping before Roman to sniff at the lumpiness of his robe and then finishing the circuit of the pool's ledge to take up a spot on the far side. The tiger lay down, one paw hanging over the stone edge to dangle in the water, the tip of its tail swishing.

Isra blew out her breath at last, realizing she had been holding it for most of the encounter.

"My apologies, Wynn," Roman said from the other side of the albino. "I wasn't aware you would be exercising her this morning."

"Think nothing of it, my brother," the monk replied, tucking the handle of the whip beneath his rough cincture. "Indeed, this is not our routine, but she has only just finished the last of—" The albino glanced at Isra so quickly that she could almost convince herself that she had imagined it. "Her meal. She's not been about for several days."

Terrible screeching and banging noises erupted behind the trio, causing all three heads to swivel toward the opposite end of the gallery. Isra saw little brown hands reaching through the barred window of one of the doors, a dreadful cacophony behind it.

"Well, blast," Wynn said. "Better release them before they render us all deaf. They'll have nothing else but to be let out if Princess is about. Do you stay or go?" Wynn demanded.

Roman looked at Isra and raised his eyebrows.

"As you wish," Isra said, lowering her eyes, but inside she trembled with anticipation.

"We'll stay, if we won't be a hindrance," Roman told the pale monk. Wynn moved away and she dared a look at Roman. He was watching her. "Are you not frightened of what wild beasts Wynn might next introduce?"

She shook her head. "There are worse things to be frightened of than animals."

Her answer seemed to be punctuated an instant later by the skittering, dashing, screeching brown balls that flew across the stones around their feet, causing Isra's skirts to sway. The creatures swarmed over the ledge of the fountain, their long tails held erect behind them, and overtook the tiger so suddenly that Princess squealed and went over the side of the fountain into the pool, her big paws swiping in the air, slinging up wide arcs of water.

The monkeys dashed away, chittering and screaming in what sounded like delight.

"They torment her so when they know she is too fat to be nimble," Wynn chortled as he came once more to stand between Isra and Roman. "She behaves as though she would kill each one of them and eat them as raisins, but I can't help but think she has grown attached to them. They are the only creatures who will come near her. She is getting old. She needs a mate." His face turned toward Isra. "I don't suppose you know of anyone with a male tiger, do you?"

Isra pressed her mouth together into a grim line. "I am sorry. No." The monk turned back to watch the monkeys frolicking in the water. "Ah, well. God's will be done."

"Is she tame, then?" Isra asked, finding herself unable to keep from asking after the majestic tiger who had pulled herself out of the pool, shook, and was lying along the stone edge once more, licking one massive paw. "Princess."

The albino looked at Isra as if she'd just turned into a monkey herself. "*Tame*? Lady, this is no domestic creature who lurks inside a gentle stable seeking rodents. She is *tigris*. More specifically, she is a man-eater."

Isra's eyes went over the monk's head to Roman's face, as if he would give her some reassurance. But he seemed as enthralled by the albino's speech as Isra.

"Oh, yes," Wynn continued, looking across the pool at the stunning animal who had turned her attention to grooming her chest. "Tigers can come to have a taste for human flesh. Princess killed and consumed more than a score in her village before she was captured. Why do you think they brought the—"

"Wynn," Roman warned in a low voice.

The monk quirked his mouth and then continued, hardly skipping a beat in his story. "She was on her way to be used for sport in the south of France, I believe, when I purchased her."

Isra didn't know whether she was horrified or amazed. "You do not fear her? Down here, all alone?"

Brother Wynn rocked back on his sandals, as if considering her question. "The day I am afraid of her is the day she shall kill me. So, no, lady, I am not afraid. That is the way with tigers. You must always face them. Always command them. The moment you allow yourself to believe the tiger cares for you, the tiger is your friend, you have *tamed* the tiger, that is when the tiger loses all respect for you. They kill animals they feel are lesser than them, weaker than them. Sometimes, too, they eat those animals." The monk sniffed.

"How do you come to know so much about the creatures?" Isra asked, slightly unnerved at the man's outlining of the bloodthirstiness of the animal lounging not thirty feet from them.

Wynn glanced at her, a frown creasing his forehead over invisible eyebrows. "God has given me this knowledge. It is my holy mission. Why else would I be here?"

"Thank you for allowing me to see her," Isra said, dropping her eyes to the stones for a moment. When she raised her face it was to find Roman's eyes again. "I would prefer to return to my cell now, if it will not disturb Brother Wynn's charges."

"Not at all," Wynn said, already sliding his whip from his cincture. "She needs to exercise her limbs, any matter. She lies about enough." The monk moved away from them and around the fountain toward the tiger, who watched the albino over one shoulder and flashed her teeth. Wynn cracked his whip and raised both arms in response. "Hie now, you great sloth. Come! Up with you!"

"I think it best we go now, before Wynn becomes more enthusiastic about exercise, don't you?"

She smiled her agreement and let him lead her back to the safety of her own cage. Unlike the tiger, Isra felt afraid of the open, of the unknown. Princess was fierce, fearless, a man-eater.

Then the thought of the man she had killed in Damascus came charging through her memories; the worst of all the things she had seen and done and been forced to do in the past three years swirled in her mind, causing her face to flush with blood and her heart to pound.

And she wondered if, even though it was Roman Berg who pulled her into the cell, it was she who was leading him to damnation.

Roman shut the door behind Isra. There was no bolt on the inside, but he was confident enough in Wynn's rule over his subjects that there was nothing to fear from the creatures milling about the gallery beyond the wooden barrier. He went to the table near the cot and unrolled the map he'd brought earlier. The table's surface was not wide enough for the chart, so he spread it on the clean, rough stone floor, tucking one curling side under the legs of the table. He placed the toe of his right sandal on the other end of the map. Isra came to sit above him on the pallet, her feet tucked to the side and one slender arm holding her while she leaned over the diagram.

"We are here," Roman said, pressing the index finger of his left hand in approximately the middle of the continent. Then he reached up to the tabletop, breaking off a long, curling piece of cooled yellow wax from the base of the metal candleholder. He snapped it in half and placed one piece on the area he'd indicated.

"Here is where we must go." He dropped the other piece of wax east of the Mediterranean, west of Damascus. Then he looked up at Isra, who was frowning at the map. "What way did you come?"

She only continued staring at the map, her eyes becoming a little wider, her face a little pale under her olive complexion. "Where is Constantinople?" she asked, her voice carrying a heavier hint of rasp than it had since she'd first awakened.

Roman pointed to the little spit of land between the Mediterranean and the Black Sea.

Isra's lips parted and she was as still as one of the statues in the abbey's bailey for a moment. Then she turned wide, frightened eyes to Roman. "Where am I?" she asked in wonder.

"You don't know?"

Isra shook her head.

Now it was Roman's turn to frown. "You're at Melk Abbey. In Austria."

"Austria," Isra echoed in a whisper, dropping her eyes back to the map on the floor. He saw her throat move as she swallowed.

"Isra, how did you get here?" Roman asked.

She raised her face to look at him and her eyes welled. "I walked," she said, her voice cracking.

His heart flinched in his chest. "Alone? From Damascus?"

Isra nodded and then swiped her fingertips under her eyes before the tears could spill over. "What month is it?"

"October." He tried to keep his voice even. "When did you begin?"

Her voice was thin and reedy when she answered. "July." She swallowed again. "That would explain why it is so cold."

Roman felt his jaw grow tense, and he had to look away for a moment. Was it even possible that this woman had walked to Austria alone—a journey that had taken her four months—while being hunted the entire way? That she hadn't known what month it was, or where she'd ended up? It didn't seem conceivable.

He looked back to her. "You must tell me how you knew where I was. How you found me." He heard the threat inherent in his tone, but he could no longer be gentle with her. What she was suggesting was so unlikely that Roman feared Constantine's wariness of the woman could be warranted.

She shook her head, and for a moment, Roman wondered if she

would refuse to tell him. But then she met his eyes. "You will not believe me."

He had no choice. "If you do not tell me, Isra, I will be forced to report to my friends that you cannot be trusted. I doubt I need remind you what their initial plans for you were."

She winced, as if he had physically struck her. Her shoulders rounded, her head ducked. She hadn't shown this weakness to Constantine; was it an act for his benefit? Did she think him naïve?

Was he naïve when it came to her?

"I snuck through the city gate at night, behind the men who led the patrols," she said in a steady voice, although she wouldn't meet his eyes now. "I followed in their wake to the base of the hills, and when they returned to the city, I fled north into Mumed-Adin. I hid in the brush when the sun rose."

All Roman could see of her face was the black fringe of lashes above the tip of her nose. "That night, I carried on toward Antioch."

Roman frowned. "You came directly here from Damascus. You instinctively knew the route to take and where to find me."

"No," she whispered. "There were many nights I went in the wrong direction. At first I did not know."

"You didn't know what?" Roman demanded. He felt his heart growing cold in his chest and he didn't care for the feeling at all. The feeling of being made a fool of. The feeling of knowing this woman was sealing her fate with every word she spoke.

"My lord, as I have told you, my mother is dead. But she came to me in my dreams while I hid in the daylight. She led me on the correct paths."

Roman stared at the top of her head. He didn't know what to say. But he had no need to say anything, for Isra continued. "It was many weeks before I realized that when my sister came to me while I slept, I was in danger."

"Your sister—she is dead, too, I suppose?" Roman was shocked to hear the condescension in his voice. It sounded unlike him even to his own ears.

Isra gave a tight nod.

"You're right," Roman said. He took a moment to collect himself, while the coldness in his heart turned fully to ice. "I don't believe you." And then he slid his sandal from the map and pulled the other edge from beneath the table legs. He rose and then awkwardly rolled up the parchment against his torso with one hand, the little pieces of wax flying across the floor.

"Her name was Huda," Isra whispered. "She was ten years old."

Roman kept rolling the map.

"Hamid and some of his men killed her. They . . . they raped her." Her voice grew hoarse.

Roman walked to the door, prepared to take his chances with the tiger outside the cell. Surely the animal could not be more blood-thirsty than this woman.

"Wait!" she cried, and although Roman did stop, he didn't turn. He could hear her scramble from the pallet and stumble across the floor toward him.

"Please," she said, and he felt a tugging on the back of his robe. "My lord, I beg you: Look at me."

He dared a glance over his shoulder and was startled to see that Isra was on her knees behind him, a fold of his habit clenched in both her fists. She stared up at him with wide, pleading eyes, the wet tracks on her cheeks glistening over the indigo and green bruises.

"Hamid will kill your comrade, Baldwin," she said in a whispered rush. "If he succeeds, you and your friends will never be free. There is no one else to stop him—Saladin is in Egypt." She paused, swallowed, inched closer to him on her knees. "I must see that Hamid fails. For Huda. For my mother. I do not believe you are so cold-hearted that you could not care."

"You don't know anything about me," Roman said.

"I know that you are loyal, and brave. Kind." Her voice broke on the word, and despite himself, Roman felt a crack appear in his resolve. "I knew it the moment I saw you that night in Damascus, when you came to free your friends. *That* is why I have come to you. Why I have come all this long way to find you."

"Although I am not of any noble class, I find it difficult to accept that your family, your village, would not rise up against such atrocities as a woman and her young daughter so brutally killed."

Her mouth turned down even farther and she looked sad enough to dissolve away into the stones. "We had no family. No one in the city would ever come to our aid."

"Impossible," Roman said. "That night in Damascus, you were dressed in the clothes of a wealthy woman, with jewelry on your arms, silk about your head." He dropped the rolled parchment in his hand before reaching down to jerk his robe from her grasp. "Someone would have helped you."

Her support gone, she fell to her palms on the stones and let her head hang there while it seemed a sob tried to fight its way from her throat. She gave a long sniff.

"No one," she wept. "There was no one I could turn to save you. You must believe me."

Without knowing exactly what he was doing, Roman dropped to one knee before Isra, seizing her arm with his left hand and yanking her upright to her knees.

"Why?" he gritted between his teeth. "Tell me the truth!"

Her mouth was pulled wide in either fear or agony—Roman could not tell which—and he wondered if she thought he was going to strike her. The idea of it had never entered his mind, and even he found himself quite shocked at this action of taking physical hold of her.

"Because I am unclean!" she wailed and then covered her face with both hands as she sobbed.

Besides Isra's jagged weeping, it was very quiet in the cell while the meaning of what she'd said sank in on Roman. Stan had been right after all, at least about one thing. Hadn't Roman himself guessed as much when first she had come upon him in the Damascene alley?

"Your profession . . ." he began and then stopped. He couldn't bring himself to say it out loud. "Your mother, as well?"

Isra nodded into her hands.

"But the sister you spoke of—surely not she?"

"No," she sniffed. She turned on one knee and faced away from him as she gained her feet, pulling out of his now weak hold. She walked to the pallet and withdrew what appeared to be a wadded kerchief from beneath the edge of the thin ticking. After blowing her nose and wiping her face, she took a deep breath. But when she spoke again, she did not face him, instead seeming to prefer to address the blank wall before her.

"So now you understand why no one cared to help us."

It did explain many things to Roman: the abuse of her person he'd witnessed that night in Damascus, how she was able to receive such sensitive information from one of Saladin's generals, her manner of dress and freedom in the city at night, why no one would raise objections to the murder of her mother or the young girl who was her sister.

Roman didn't know what to say to her, didn't know what to feel as he stood and watched her thin back, the sharpness of her shoulder blades tenting the thin material of the borrowed gown she wore. The roll of her black hair was just visible beneath the hem of white linen over her head.

She had sold her body to any man who could pay for it. How could he trust that she would not sell him at her first opportunity?

"If you still cannot believe me," she began in a husky voice, "tell me now, before you leave me. I will be no further trouble to you or your friends. You shall have no worries that I might lead your enemies to you."

"Constantine will never let you leave here alone," Roman said.

Isra nodded, and her eyes still seemed to be trained on the kerchief wadded in her hands. "He will have no fear of me after tonight." She looked over her shoulder at him, and Roman realized that each time he had seen Isra Tak'Ahn, her face had borne the evidence of abuse. Although he knew her bruises would fade, the damage in her eyes was so deep that Roman wondered if anything could heal her.

Roman frowned and walked across the cell floor toward Isra. When he was two paces from her side, he held out his left hand, palm up.

"Let me have it."

"No," she whispered. Then she raised her head and looked into Roman's eyes. "It is the only guarantee of freedom I have. I have no family. No friends. I will not be forced into bondage ever again."

"Isra," he said, "let me have it."

She shook her head.

"You said only moments ago that I was the only person you could turn to; the only person you could trust. Is that true?"

She nodded only slightly.

"Show me how much you trust me," he said and lifted his palm toward her.

A gold-handled dagger crawled from the wadded folds of the kerchief like a gilded caterpillar from its cocoon, a smooth, polished ruby for an eye. Isra placed the weapon in his palm, the blade pointing back at her, and her fingertips trailed down the beveled metal edge, as if at any moment she would seize the dagger back again.

Roman closed his hand over the gold hilt and drew it behind his back, out of her sight. He turned and walked back to the cell door, stopping to pick up the discarded map with the same hand that held Isra's confiscated weapon.

"Wynn!" he called through the small barred portal. Then he looked back at Isra, who stood just as he had left her: her hands hanging limp at her sides, her shoulders sloped, the corners of her mouth drooping. "A few days," he said to her. "I'll send someone to prepare you."

The door pushed open and Brother Wynn poked his head through the space, an odiferous cloud preceding his white hair. "Ready, then?"

"Prepare me for what, my lord?" she asked, and the anxiety in her voice was so heavy that Roman felt a pinch of guilt for leaving her this way. "Will you come again?"

But he didn't trust himself to speak and so he only nodded to Wynn and then followed the albino as he backed from the doorway. Roman didn't look back into the cell as Brother Wynn pulled the door closed.

"Lock it, if you would," Roman said. "And keep watch over her if you can. She is . . . distraught."

The albino's eyes met Roman's, and for the first time, Roman recognized the shrewdness, the deep compassion in Brother Wynn's oddly colored gaze. "As anyone would be, I'd wager. She's an exquisite specimen. Holding up remarkably well in spite of her mistreatment."

"That she is," Roman muttered and then headed toward the wide steps that led to the abbey above. To a world of quiet orderliness; of prayerful meditation and clear answers to questions of right and wrong; of confession and penance and redemption. None of which would help him or Isra Tak'Ahn now.

What Roman needed were lessons on deception. Tutorials on disguise and perhaps thievery. Insight into dealing with a fragile woman of questionable background.

Fortunately for Roman, Fallen Angels Abbey was home to the one man in all the world who could educate him thusly.

Chapter 5

At least one week passed. Isra was not quite certain the exact length of time; days and nights seemed to melt together in the dismal dungeon of the abbey, and she herself felt much like one of the albino's charges while her body continued to heal but her mind grew more frenzied.

In those long, lonely hours, broken only by her forays into the gallery chaperoned by Brother Wynn and the visits by the brusque, red-haired Maisie Lindsey, Isra wondered whether she would ever see Roman Berg again. He might believe her, but she doubted he trusted her. Perhaps one of the other three men would put an end to her. Or the redhead would slip a poison into the rich red wine she brought every night that seemed to make it easier for Isra to sleep. Maybe it was already poisoned, and one day she would simply not wake up.

But then why let her linger?

On what she thought might be the seventh morning since Roman last left her, it was not Maisie Lindsey who came through Isra's cell door bearing the morning tray but a chestnut-haired woman with a delicate brow and a kind face.

"Good day," the woman said with an inquiring smile as she balanced the tray on her shoulder with one hand and pushed the door closed with the other. A well-worn satchel, round with its hidden contents, hung from her crooked elbow. "I do apologize for not calling on you sooner. It was not my wish to delay our acquaintance."

Isra backed into the darkest corner of the cell as the woman slid the tray onto the small table and then swung the satchel onto the rumpled pallet. Despite telling herself that she had accepted whatever fate was hers, Isra suddenly had more than a little fear at what the next hour held for her.

"Hello?" the woman called, cocking her head and leaning to the side, as if she was attempting to peek behind the shadow that hid Isra like a curtain. "I'm Lady Mary Beckham. I've brought you something to eat, if you'd care to . . ." She gestured to the table and then stepped back, folding her hands before her waist and waiting.

"Why have you come instead of the other woman?"

Mary's eyebrows rose. "Oh, I—" She held out her open palms. "Didn't Roman tell you that he would send someone to help prepare you? Maisie is quite the wonderful guardian, but I have a bit more"— she wobbled her hands up and down, as if they were scales, gave a shrug of her shoulder—"*understanding* of what you will soon be enduring. Roman and my husband thought it would be best if I readied you. I've brought some suitable clothes and—"

"Readied me for what?" Isra interrupted, her heart pounding. The woman seemed very sure of herself. As if there were nothing at all wrong with the situation in which she now found herself. But then again, she was an actual English *lady*. Isra had never seen a female member of the English nobility before, let alone been locked in a chamber with one.

Especially one who might be preparing her for execution. Isra had heard that titled people enjoyed very strange diversions.

Mary Beckham dropped her hands to her sides and looked nonplussed for a moment. "And I thought no one told *me* anything. Your journey. You and Roman are leaving the abbey today. I thought he inform—"

But Isra didn't give the woman time to finish her sentence as she came from the corner and threw her arms around Mary Beckham's slight shoulders. She quickly remembered herself, though, and drew away, her hands clenched before her chest, her eyes on the floor, but she couldn't suppress the smile on her lips.

"Forgive me, my lady," Isra said, bowing. "I should not have touched you so. My joy has made me reckless."

To Isra's surprise, Mary Beckham laughed and then reached out to take Isra's hands in her own. "Good heavens, dear; there is naught to forgive. I would be overjoyed myself were I about to depart this smelly prison. And I have been reckless myself a time or two."

She led Isra to the pallet and guided her to a seat. "In fact, I must admit that I am rather envious of you."

Isra took the cup Mary Beckham pressed into her hands while her eyes were trained on the woman's pale, serene face. "Envious of *me*?"

Mary sighed and seemed to stare into nothingness, a slight smile curving her lips. "What grand adventure must await you!" She came back to the present with another longing sigh and bent to the tray, stuffing a knife's blade of fig paste into a hunk of bread. "Completely dangerous of course. It shall be a miracle if neither of you are killed. Arrested, at the very least." The woman turned and pressed the sweetbread into Isra's other hand and then straightened, her hands on her hips. "Do you suffer seasickness, by chance?"

This Englishwoman was clearly of the eccentric sort.

Isra shook her head.

"Very good." Mary sat down on the edge of the pallet next to Isra and dragged the satchel onto her lap. "They've not given us much time, so while you break your fast, I will ready your costume."

"Costume?"

Mary paused and looked to Isra, her mouth open as if about to say something. But then she closed her mouth and smiled while she reached out and patted Isra's knee.

"Welcome to Fallen Angels Abbey, Isra Tak'Ahn," she said, her brown eyes dancing, "where your old life disappears and you can become whoever you wish." Mary squinted sideways before looking at her again. "Eventually. But first . . ."

The Englishwoman stood and pulled a long length of what appeared to be soiled, yellowing bed linen from the satchel, unfurling it with a sharp snap. It looked to Isra to be a corpse shroud, stained terrible browns and blacks and ochers.

When Isra looked up at Mary Beckham, the seemingly unflappable Englishwoman's face was beaming and there was a somewhat devilish sparkle in her eyes.

"*Vamanos*, dear."

Roman walked around the short, two-wheeled cart a final time in the dark bailey, crouching to check the axle, shaking the long poles and harness attached to the sleeping gray donkey. His breath billowed out of him in great clouds of steam as his sandals crunched over the frosted gravel. Out of one of the black archways came Constantine and Valentine, their arms laden with parcels. Adrian and Father Victor came next, followed by Maisie Lindsey, who bounced and shushed a mewling baby Valentina in her arms.

Stan waited at the rear of the cart while Valentine slid a hidden latch beneath the bed. A moment later, the Spaniard lifted the boards of the platform as one unit and Stan stepped forward, sliding the parcels he carried into their hiding spot. Valentine lowered the cart bed and then tossed a rough sack into a corner near the driver's seat before turning and taking his infant from Maisie. He turned Valentina facedown and tucked her under his arm with his palm spread beneath her narrow chest like one would carry a piglet, and the child quieted.

Adrian followed Father Victor to the front of the cart, where the abbot hung a censer to a staff affixed to the driver's seat. The two men walked around the sleeping donkey and then Victor turned and carefully took a wrapped object from Adrian. The thing was soon hung in a similar fashion as the censer but tethered to the seat by a cord. Victor whisked the covering away and the metal dome glinted in the dim light of the single torch. Adrian returned to the censer while Victor faced Roman.

"Keep it lashed until you are well south of the village. Let it ring freely after that, even should the sun not yet have risen and the road appear deserted."

Valentine came to stand at his side. "Thieves often wait in the wood along the road for a mark to pass before making themselves seen. If they hear the bell well in advance, they will no bother giving chase. And if they do give chase . . ." Valentine reached into his deep cowl and withdrew a long, leather-sheathed dagger, which he handed to Roman.

Roman took the blade and reached inside his robe to attach it to the leather belt around the tunic he wore beneath. The smell of incense wafted on the thin, cold air, and Adrian joined the group a moment later, pausing to take Roman's still weakened right hand in his own and pressing a small but weighty bag into his palm.

"That should be enough to last you until Venice."

Victor came forward again as Adrian stepped away to join his wife. The abbot held forth a sealed document. "In case you have any trouble. A declaration in my own hand, avowing to your permission to transport our afflicted brother to his final rest in the holy city of Rome."

"Burn it once you reach Venice," Constantine said. "And then follow the plan as we have created it. Any problems—"

"I know," Roman interjected. He placed the bag of resinous incense on the driver's seat with a sigh. He sounded curt and sought to soften his tone. "My thanks, Stan."

When Roman turned back around, everyone in the group was facing the back of the cart. Mary Beckham approached, leading what appeared to be a phantasm from beyond. The group parted and in a moment, Roman and Isra faced each other.

"Good morrow," he said to her. "Are you prepared?"

"Lady Mary has tutored me well," Isra said with a slight bow, although her eyes darted to the sides at the people staring at her. "I shall bring no shame upon you. Lou?"

"It is safer for him here," Roman said, uncomfortable with the woman's obeisance, while at the same time reminded of his guilt for leaving the falcon behind.

He was saved in that moment by Adrian, who nudged Victor with his elbow. "Shall we get on with it?"

Victor nodded, pulling a small booklet from his robe while Adrian removed the censer from its staff.

"What are they doing?" Roman asked Valentine quietly, and when the Spaniard just frowned and shook his head, looking straight ahead at the old abbot, Roman asked more loudly, "What are you doing?" His head swiveled as Adrian began to circle the group, sending waves of incense floating through the air.

Victor began to recite the prayers, and Roman listened carefully to the Latin, his eyes slowly going wide.

"Are you giving us last rites?" he demanded.

"Shh," Valentine said. "You do no wish to go to heaven?"

Victor took the censer from Adrian and stepped up to Roman, swinging the receptacle toward him and then walking around Roman in a circle. He then went to Isra, who seemed hesitant to come fully into the group of people gathered in the frigid bailey. The abbot whispered something to the woman, who shook her bowed head. She looked up into Victor's face and replied in such a low voice that Roman could not hear.

Then she sank to her knees in her macabre costume, and Victor laid a hand on her head while he prayed a prayer Roman was unfamiliar with before clouding her kneeling form in the fragrant incense. He helped her to her feet and led her to the back of the cart while Isra wiped at her eyes with a ragged hem of linen. Victor left the woman there while he handed the censer back to Adrian, and the two of them walked about the cart again.

Val handed the baby to his wife and turned to Roman then, distracting him from the forlorn sight of the woman. "I can no bear to watch you go," he said candidly, even though the same rakish smile was across his face. "So I will be the first to bid you farewell." He reached out his right hand and grasped Roman's, placing his left hand on the top of his shoulder at the crook of his neck and squeezing. "Farewell, my friend."

Roman felt a catch in his chest. This was happening far more quickly—and with more intensity—than he had imagined. The thought of never seeing Valentine—of never seeing any of his friends again—shook him so suddenly he felt the tremor of it to the soles of his feet.

He pulled Valentine into a gruff embrace. "Thank you."

Valentine clapped Roman's back twice and then pulled away. "Remember what I have taught you, Roman Berg. Adios." Then the Spaniard took Valentina from his wife and strode toward the darkened arch of the abbey. He did not look back.

Lady Mary stepped to him with a sweet smile. "Do you remember what you told Valentine the morning he and I left Melk?"

Roman didn't trust himself to speak so he just shook his head as Mary took both his hands into hers. It was like holding a kitten's paws.

"You said, 'Come back to us, Val.'" Mary's smile faltered, and so she swallowed and then renewed the attempt. "I know my husband could not bear to speak it aloud for doing so would allude to the idea that anything else was possible. And so I shall say it for him: Come back to us, Roman."

He nodded. "I will do my best, my lady."

Mary wrapped her arms around Roman's middle and spoke into his chest. "I know you will. You always do."

After a final squeeze, she slid her arms from him and turned to Isra, who dropped her eyes and gave a shallow bow.

"I am in your debt," Isra said.

But Mary pulled the woman aright and embraced her as well, waiting until Isra had hesitantly laid her hands along her back in return before speaking.

"Have a wonderful adventure, Isra Tak'Ahn. Godspeed. You are in the very best of hands." She pulled away and looked into the woman's eyes.

"This I know, my lady," Isra said solemnly, and then glanced over Mary's shoulder at Roman.

The look was a bolster to his shaky emotions. He was leaving his friends, leaving the haven he had found at Melk, but it was for a purpose he would not shirk. He was protecting this woman, protecting his friends, Baldwin, all of the brethren still asleep in yonder darkened cells. It was a heavy burden.

But Roman had always been strong.

Then Mary was gone, having disappeared the way her husband had escaped. And before him stood Victor.

"God's blessing upon you, Roman." Victor made the sign of the cross before him.

"Thank you, Father," Roman said. "I—"

"I'll go open the gates," Victor interrupted, stepping around Roman and crunching away into the darkness. Roman turned to watch him go.

Constantine's gruff voice called his attention back to the cart. "Let's see the cargo settled."

Maisie helped Isra into the bed of the conveyance while Constantine and Adrian shook out a large canvas and lashed one edge behind the driver's seat. Isra lay down on her back and Adrian's wife leaned over the side of the bed and squeezed the vague shape of her arm before withdrawing and turning to Roman. Behind her, Constantine and Adrian drew the canvas over the bed, closing the woman from Damascus in darkness.

"I shallna embrace you," Maisie said with a lift of her chin. She met his eyes, and Roman understood.

Maighread Lindsey had a strange and special gift, and it was clear she had no desire to risk catching a glimpse of whether or not he would return. He was glad she did not.

Roman gave the woman who was once a queen a short bow. "Until we meet again, then."

A ghost of a smile played across Maisie's face. "Until we meet again."

The clang and scrape of the gate echoed in the bailey when Adrian finished the knot at his corner of the canvas and, brushing his hands together so that the sleeves of his robe rose and displayed the fantastic black markings on his forearms, he strode to Roman.

"The weather will be more fair once you have reached Venice," he said. "Be sure to hang the sick flags and build a sizable fire at night." Adrian met Roman's eyes. "Take care, my friend."

The two men embraced and then Adrian took Maisie's hand and was gone, leaving only Roman and Constantine in the bailey, along with the silent woman hidden away in the cart.

Stan was walking about the cart a final time, making a show of checking the canvas lashings. Roman waited until he had played out the act to his satisfaction. At last, the general turned to him.

He withdrew a sealed square of parchment similar to the one Victor had given him and hesitated for only a heartbeat before handing it to Roman.

"Not that I am certain you will have chance to deliver this," he said with a cynical lift of his eyebrow.

Roman took the message. "Who is it for?"

"Baldwin. No one's eyes save his. If you cannot place it in his hands, burn it." Stan looked up. "God be with you, brother."

Roman's composure suffered a blow at hearing the same words from Constantine's mouth that he had spoken on the day of the fall at Jacob's Ford.

Roman held out his hand. "For Chastellet," he said, calling down with all his might the power of the phrase with which he had answered Constantine before he had plunged into battle, helmless, hopelessly outnumbered, gravely betrayed. They had lived that day.

But Constantine shook his head as he looked at Roman's outstretched hand. "No. We can no longer save Chastellet." He looked up. "All we have is one another." And then he grasped Roman's hand.

"For one another, then," Roman echoed and took Constantine's forearm with his other hand, gritting his teeth at the sight of the once formidable general's bloodshot and glistening eyes.

They broke apart and turned away from each other, Roman striding toward the front of the cart and Constantine dissolving into the fortress that was Melk. Roman climbed up on the seat and picked up the reins, adjusting his position and flicking the donkey awake.

"Ha!" he called, and the cart lurched forward.

Roman couldn't see Victor in the darkness as he rolled through the gates and past the enormous winged statuary to either side of the path, but he could hear the abbot's quiet Latin. The smell of the incense smoldering at his side stung his nose and made his eyes water, his throat itch. Roman swallowed hard and set his jaw.

It was time to return to Damascus, to once more save his friends.

Chapter 6

Isra fell asleep not long after the cart began moving. She had not rested well in her subterranean cell, but now that she was swaddled and hidden away in the back of a rough cart driven by Roman Berg, she felt as if nothing could harm her. There were no strangers, no soldiers, no walking through the night in a land populated by people who stared and frowned suspiciously at her shadowed self. She was alone with him now and he had a plan. The relief of it caused her to drop into a defensive slumber almost instantly.

She had no idea how far or for how long they had traveled when she woke, only that the sun outside made bright lines above her head where the canvas met the seat and over her feet at the rear of the cart. Her throat was dry and a bit sore and the bones in her spine felt bruised now where they pressed into the hard bed through the gauzy linen.

She waited what seemed like an hour to see if Roman Berg would make any attempt at conversation. He did not. Perhaps he had guessed that she'd fallen asleep. Should she call out to him? What was the risk of her speaking if they were traveling through a village or passing other pilgrims on the road? Would they hear her and grow suspicious? Was she expected to remain still and silent the entire day, only to emerge at night?

Perhaps she should have been more inquisitive with the English lady. Isra could withstand whatever hardships this part of the journey necessitated; Mary had said they should be in Venice within a week, depending on the rains, and then the cart would be sold for passage on one of the trading ships bound for Alexandria. It was only so close to Melk they must be cautious, and Isra had faced much worse conditions than being borne along a road in a cart, after all, especially since the redheaded Maisie Lindsey had slipped a blade under Isra's hip as she'd made a show of squeezing her wrist. Roman had yet to return her mother's dagger, but thanks to Maisie Lindsey, she was once again armed, and with no mere eating utensil.

She felt the cart begin to slow then, the bumps and ruts raising the bed in a slow, exaggerated fashion as it rolled to a halt. Isra closed her eyes and blew a long breath between her lips. She raised up on her elbows and turned her face toward the bright line of sunlight above. She drew in a breath and opened her mouth, readying to call out to Roman.

"Ha—"

Her words were cut off as Roman Berg's voice sounded over them in the same instant she had started to speak.

"Good day, gentlemen," he said. He hadn't stopped for a rest; he was *being* stopped. "God's blessing upon the three of you."

By three men.

Isra lay back down as slowly and quietly as she could, her breath frozen in her chest, as if the strangers beyond the canvas could detect the slightest motion of her inhalations. She raised her hand to pull up over her face the linen cowled around her neck and then lifted her right hip to slide the dagger from its sheath. She pushed the case farther beneath her buttocks and lowered her hip over the blade, her fingers gripping the handle beneath the long, draping sleeve of gauze covering her hand. In no more time than it took her to blink, she was still again, her body rigid as she concentrated on the voices beyond the canvas.

"Good day, friar," a man said. "What brings you to our humble burg?"

"Only passing through," Roman replied.

"Passing through to where?" another voice demanded, and Isra could hear the clop of a horse's hooves growing louder, as if whomever spoke was drawing their mount nearer the cart bed.

"Rome." Isra noted that Roman volunteered no information.

"Taking the church's spoils to your leader, eh?"

A third man's voice joined the conversation, meeker, younger than the other two. "I don't think that's what he carries."

"Did you not hear the bell?" Roman asked, and then Isra nearly jumped out of her skin as the thing clanged.

"Aye, we heard it," the first man said. "But you don't look like any priest I've ever seen."

"I'm not a priest," Roman said. "I am in penance for the crimes of my previous life. It is why my superior thought me the best to transport our ill brother to his eternal rest in our holy city."

"Ill brother, eh?" the snide man commented, and the sound of his horse drew even nearer. "What's in the sack?"

"Resin," Roman said. "For the censer."

"What's he ill of?" the young man asked.

"He's a leper," Roman said. "At least he was this morn. He could be dead by now. I was hoping to draw nearer the city before that happened. Bodies tend to stink even in this cool weather." Isra heard a rustling. "Here is a letter from my abbot, giving me permission to be away from the abbey."

"Melk, eh?" the first man mused after a moment. Isra heard more rustling and the cart rocked. "What are you doing?"

When Roman answered, he was alongside the cart, even with Isra's head. "I'm taking up the canvas so you can see the grisly mess yourselves. You won't be swayed by my word or the vow of my abbot, so . . ." He broke off, and Isra heard the dusty scrape of sandals on the road.

"Yes, open it up," the snide man encouraged. "I'll be pleased to cleave your skull when I see with my own eyes a cart full of golden chalices and silken robes."

"You'd better put down that ax before you hurt yourself," Roman said good-naturedly.

Isra began to panic. They were going to remove the canvas. Her face and body were covered, true, but did her wrapped figure closely enough resemble the corpse of a monk? What would happen if they suspected her? What if the man chose to test her by striking her with the ax? Or striking Roman?

What if they were caught and traced back to Melk?

What would happen to Roman's friends?

What would they do to Isra, if they didn't kill her?

What if they decided to keep her?

She gripped the handle of the dagger and shimmied it higher on her palm in the instant before a corner of the canvas above her feet flapped and then was thrown back in a bright triangle.

"Only a moment while I get the other side," Roman said amicably.

Isra saw a shadow flit across the open section of the bed. "Ezzer, I think he speaks true. Look."

More footsteps drew near as it seemed Roman was taking his time with the other corner of the canvas.

"Oh, hell—look at that!" a man cried out in disgust. "Cover it back up, man! Cover it up! Is it your wish to taint the entire village?"

"Not at all, brother," Roman replied and—in a much quicker fashion than that in which he'd undone it—the corner of the canvas was once more secure. "I could use a bite, though. Perhaps I might take my rest at yonder tavern and inquire as to whether they have a room to let."

"The bloody hell you will," the snide man said. "You'll get your great arse back in your cart and take your damned rot with you and not come back."

"You'll show no charity to a brother of God on a mission of mercy?" Roman needled.

"Here," the younger voice called out, and Isra heard a slight clink. "For your trouble, friar. Godspeed to you."

"The Lord's blessing upon your merciful heart, lad," Roman said, and Isra could hear the sincerity in his voice.

"Go on, then!" the first man demanded. "Go! Be swift! Go!"

The cart rocked and then lurched forward with a skull-jarring jerk, and the road passed beneath her with a fury that brought only peace.

Isra released the handle of the blade and brought her hands up to cover her face, her heart racing and her breath heaving in and out of her at last. They had almost been caught already, only hours after leaving.

"Isra?" she heard Roman call from beyond the canvas.

She swallowed. "Yes?"

"Are you all right?"

"Yes, my lord."

"I'm not your lord."

"I am very well."

"I'll stop the cart when we are in the wood once more. It shan't be long."

Would they ever be far enough away to be safe?

"No, do not stop," she said. "Do not stop until dark."

* * *

Roman drove the cart and the donkey until he could no longer reliably make out the road before them. At a wide bend where the tall grasses spread into spent fields to either side, he eased the cart off the road and toward a lone tree, its long, low branches spread like gaunt arms.

The donkey was tired, he was tired, his backside was numb; he could only imagine the state Isra Tak'Ahn was in, having been trapped in the blackness of the cart bed since before dawn. He'd stopped twice after their close call in the village to relieve himself and allow the animal a rest while he rationed the foodstuffs in the sack behind his seat. Isra had at first refused to emerge from the cart. Indeed, she had declined the carafe of wine and only partaken of a handful of leathery apple sections.

He circled the cart around the tree so that it was once more facing the road before climbing down from the seat with a groan. He looked around at the darkness and saw no village, no cottage, not even a humble hay shed.

They were alone. Probably.

"Are you awake?" he called.

"Yes, my lord."

"We've stopped for the night. I'm going to set up the flags and tether the donkey. Can you persevere a few more moments?"

"Yes, my lord."

Roman stood there looking at the blackness of the canvas. He didn't know of another woman—not the patient Mary Beckham and certainly not Maisie Lindsey—who could withstand being in that cart bed for another instant without raising issue.

"You're certain?"

She hesitated, and Roman thought her next words would be a plea for freedom.

"You think perhaps I should not come out at all?"

He frowned. "No, that's not what I mean. I just need to—" He broke off. "I'll return in a moment, all right?"

"As you wish."

He opened his mouth, then closed it and went to retrieve the block from under his seat to prop up the cart tongue before freeing the little gray donkey. Very shortly thereafter, the cart and animal were encircled by a long strand of pennants held aloft by short stakes. Roman stepped over the low boundary and walked ten paces before planting a single flag. Ten more paces toward the road he sank another deep into the soft ground. Then he turned and headed back toward the cart.

"The sky is clear," he said, throwing back the canvas as if turning down bedcovers. A warm, musty smell wafted up from the cart bed, and he wondered how she had withstood such a close space for so many hours. He went to the end of the cart and let the gate down as her ghostly shrouded figure sat up. "It should be pleasant for sleeping."

He held out his hand toward her, but she ignored it, gripping her satchel to her chest and scooting to the edge of the cart farthest from him before sliding to the ground. She clutched at the side of the cart as she stumbled around the end of it but seemed to regain her balance quickly as she started off toward the wide gnarled tree.

"I'll lay a fire," he called out after her.

She did not acknowledge him, only passed the tree and stepped over the sick flags to disappear into the fringe of tall weeds at the edge of the field.

Roman grabbed the small bag behind the driver's seat and tossed it to the ground as he walked toward the tree himself, scanning the ground beneath it and collecting limbs and twigs until his left arm was full. Then he chose a spot between the tree and the cart to scrape the dead grass away with his sandal until he found damp dirt. He dumped his wood and then squatted, building a conical structure of twigs and leaves before reaching for the bag and removing the flint and fluffy tinder.

He was laying sticks on the fledgling fire when Isra stepped back into the circle of flags. She went to the cart and spread her shroud on the side of it, then returned to stand across the fire from Roman, her satchel still in her hand. She was looking at him for the first time since early that morning when he raised his face to her.

"There is more wood on the edge of the field. Shall I retrieve it?"

Her eyes seemed puffy in the shuddering yellow glow of the flames, and he wondered if she had been crying.

"Thank you," he said.

She set her satchel down and disappeared again.

While she was gone, Roman went to the secret compartment of the cart and withdrew the sack containing their foodstuffs. By the time Isra returned with a sizable amount of sticks and branches, Roman had visited the babbling creek across the road from their camp to fill their small bucket with water and then laid their meal upon a cloth: a large round of bread, hard cheese, pickled eggs, and a carafe of wine.

She seemed to take great pains to lay each stick neatly just beyond the fire before coming back to kneel at the edge of the cloth. Her head was bowed and she seemed to be waiting.

Roman thought it was perhaps her way to say a blessing before a meal and so he cleared his throat and recited one of the prayers the fat Brother Hilbert imposed upon the brethren at Melk before they dined. He skipped a great part of the middle, true, but even after he had crossed himself and looked up, Isra made no move to touch the food.

"Do you not care for cheese?" he asked and reached for the bag he'd set aside. "I believe there are some nuts—"

"I am only waiting for you to first be satisfied," she replied. "I will eat after you."

Roman froze, the bag hanging suspended from his hand. "Why?"

She looked up at him then. "Why?"

"Why won't you dine with me?"

"It is—" She paused, and the firelight emphasized the peaks and valleys of her frown, the hollows of her eyes and temples. "It is improper for me to eat before you. We are not equal."

Roman set the bag straight down while still in his fist. "How exactly are we not equal?"

"My lord—" she began, a pained expression coming over her oval face.

"No," he interrupted. "Isra, I mean in no way to be harsh with you, but I have told you before that I am no lord. And certainly not yours. There isn't a drop of titled blood in my veins. It's improper for you to refer to me as such."

Her frown intensified. "Shall I then call you master?"

"No!" Roman said, horrified.

She dropped her eyes back to the untouched meal. "I do not understand. Forgive me."

"I'm sorry, I didn't mean to shout," he said. "You've done nothing wrong."

"What is it your wish I should call you? Please, have mercy and tell me, for I do not wish to incur your scorn again."

Roman stared at her. "Scorn? I'm not—" He paused and took a

deep breath. "Roman. Just call me Roman. And we shall eat at the same time."

Her eyes flicked up. "As you wish. I shall call you Roman." She reached out and picked up the bread. She tore it in half, although one side was considerably larger than the other, and then handed the larger piece to Roman.

"Thank you," he said. He gestured to her with the hunk of bread and then took a large bite. He was still chewing when he saw the little smile come over her face as she at last brought her own morsel to her mouth, nibbling on it.

He'd eaten first, just as she'd wanted.

"I see what you did," he said after swallowing the hard, lumpy dough.

"I should never think to hide anything from you," Isra replied. She returned her bread to the cloth and picked up the carafe. "May I pour you some wine?"

He reached out and took the carafe from her. "You're not my servant, Isra."

The woman placed her palms on her thighs. "I owe you a debt I can never repay in this lifetime. You must allow me to serve you."

"I do believe our debts to each other negate any repayment," he said and poured two cups of wine. "I've never had a servant in my life, and I'm not about to allow it now from the woman who saved my friends from execution."

"That which I did was also for my own benefit," she admitted.

"Perhaps that is true," Roman allowed. "But it doesn't change the fact that what you did saved the lives of the three men who I consider my only family." He took a drink, if only so Isra would. She had to be thirsty.

The dark-haired woman lowered her cup. "What of your true family? Were you an orphan?"

Roman picked up one of the eggs and took a bite, taking a moment to think upon a subject his mind hadn't come near in years.

"No, I wasn't an orphan," he said at last. "I had a mum and a father. Brothers and sisters, too, although I can't recall how many or their names. More than I could count on one hand. The earliest memory I have is of our small home." He paused. "I haven't seen any of them since I was six."

Isra selected the smallest piece of cheese. "What happened to that boy who was yet so small?"

Roman laughed despite the vague feelings of sadness this discussion was rousing in him. "I wasn't small, even then. It's actually the reason I was sent away. My father said I ate too much, so he found an apprenticeship for me in the city. A stonemason who needed another slave. My departure brought much-needed coin into their house." He glanced up and saw that Isra was looking at him levelly, and there was no pity or regret in her eyes.

"You clearly performed your duties well."

Roman nodded, feeling the sadness fade away. "That I did. I had my own crew by the time I was twenty. Five years after, I was my own master." He popped the last of the egg into his mouth.

He thought he saw something like admiration shining in her eyes, and Roman had to admit that it gave him a feeling of pleasure.

"You are not beholden to any lord? To no king?" she asked, a tinge of amazement in her voice as she tore a small piece of bread from the portion she still claimed.

Roman shook his head. "Only to the man or principality that hires me."

"You enjoy more freedom than the wealthiest lord, then."

He chuckled as he raised his cup to his lips. "I used to," he said before taking a drink.

Isra dropped her eyes again, and so he thought to soothe her worry. "At Melk I do not toil for months in desert heat. It is a good life."

She glanced up for only an instant, and it gave Roman relief to see that she no longer wore the chastised look he'd seen a moment before. He wanted to inquire as to her own past—the mother, the sister she'd lost—how such a beautiful and well-spoken woman had come to be enslaved in the basest of occupations in Damascus, but he did not want to see a reemergence of the fear and anxiety that had only now faded the slightest bit. And so he finished his meal much as Isra finished hers, in peaceful silence.

They gathered up the remnants of the food, returning the supplies and Isra's satchel to the compartment hidden beneath the cart bed.

"The sky is clear," Roman pointed out again as he fastened the latch. "It will likely become quite cold tonight; I'll sleep beneath the cart."

She was gathering her shroud from the side of the wagon as he spoke, and she looked up at his words. "No," she said, and then seemed to temper her tone. "Would that you allow me the freedom of lying on the ground. I grew used to sleeping out of doors on my journey, and I fear the cart bed has made injury to my back." She didn't look at him as she gave her reasons, only draped and folded the lengths of cloth between her fingers.

Roman frowned. "I do not care for the idea of you being exposed in the night. If someone should by chance come upon our camp, I would not be able to reach you easily."

She did look up then. "If I am only under the cart, I can more quickly escape."

He understood. He opened his mouth, but a faint rumbling from beyond the glow of their fire caused both their heads to turn. While Roman stood still, his eyes straining to pick out any movement along the dark horizon where the road lay, Isra dropped the clothing in her hands and stepped quickly to the fire. She kicked the bucket of water across the base of the coals and then grabbed a cracked, crooked branch, dragging the broken end in a zigzagging pattern through the ash. Besides the faint hissing of doused wood, no evidence of the fire remained, and although Roman lamented the loss of their warmth for whatever time they would be about before sleeping, he was impressed with the woman's forethought.

The desperate are often resourceful by necessity, he acknowledged, and he wondered how many times she'd had to perform the same action with her own lonely fires on the many nights of her journey to Melk. The idea gave him a feeling of unease in his stomach.

Then she came to the back side of the cart and squatted behind it. Roman joined her, bracing one hand on the splintery wood to duck his head and peer beneath the cart. He reached into a fold of his robes and withdrew the small golden dagger he'd confiscated from Isra days ago and held it out to her. She wasn't looking at him, though, so he whispered her name.

Isra looked down at the blade he held toward her, handle first. She reached out to take it, but when she did so, her hand was not empty. She had to maneuver a much larger knife in her palm in order to take possession of the small dagger, and Roman was quite surprised she had managed not only to acquire such a deadly weapon but that she'd apparently had it readily at hand the entire time of their supper.

As if she could hear his thoughts, Isra whispered, "Maisie Lindsey." Roman smiled to himself in the dark, but the distraction was quickly forgotten when Isra again whispered, "There."

He looked toward the road again and could now make out the soft, swinging glow of lanterns hung on the hooks of moving conveyances. By the heavy, muffled sounds of many hooves and the orchestra of creaks, Roman could only surmise that whoever passed was of a large party. The first of the wagons drew even with their camp and then passed, but the sounds of approaching travelers only grew louder. Soon, the faint whisper of a melody being plucked on a lute, the rhythm of a tinny drum, reached his ears, and then the murmurings of voices, the high-pitched shout of a woman's laughter, the arguing drone of men's voices, the barking of numerous dogs.

It was an enormous traveling party. Roman hadn't seen one so large since his time in the Holy Land, when the families of nomads would move themselves and everything they owned across the desert.

A horse from the procession whinnied and their little gray donkey behind them responded. Roman felt his shoulders tense, but the line of wagons did not pause.

"It's a caravan," Isra whispered at his side as still the party passed by.

"A caravan of what?" He looked to her, trying to make out her features in the darkness, but her eyes were fixed on the road, and all he could see was her gently rounded profile.

She shook her head.

The last of the wagons finally passed, although the rattling cacophony of conveyances swelled in the air. Roman could not imagine any town who would grant them entrance at this time of the night. He thought of the wide place he and Isra had stopped to make camp and gave a moment's wordless thanks that it wasn't any larger.

He rose to his feet, as did Isra, and both of them stared for several moments in the direction in which the caravan had gone.

"Will you not reconsider sleeping in the cart?" he asked.

"No," she said. She looked up at him. "I do not wish to disobey you."

He watched her for a moment. He knew if he commanded her, Isra would obey. But he could see the fear in her eyes, and he did not want to be a cause of it. Perhaps she was in slightly more danger sleeping on the ground, but perhaps not. After all, if a person of ill intent sneaked up on their camp in the night and wasn't detected before reaching whoever it was on the ground, both of them would be in dire straits.

"Very well," he said, and then went to ready his meager bedclothes: an extra robe and his satchel for a pillow. "Perhaps you would take the canvas to lie on so as to avoid the damp."

"Thank you," she said and took it from him. In a moment, she had disappeared under the cart.

Roman climbed into the now open bed and adjusted himself, trying as best he could to keep the cart from rocking. His feet hung off the end, the wood digging into his calves until he bent his knees and pulled his legs up.

He turned over onto his side and pushed the satchel into the board behind the driver's seat, trying to give the stiff pillow as much volume as possible. Then he sighed, resigning himself to the idea of his skull pressing against wood all night.

The darkness at last grew still as the rattling echoes of the caravan faded away.

"Good night, Isra," he said.

The silence was complete for a long moment.

"Good night, my lord."

"I'm not your lord."

"Good night, Roman."

Chapter 7

Isra closed her eyes, but her mind would not quiet. Her ears were attuned to the slightest whisper of wind against the land, the creak of the branches of the trees. In only moments, she could make out the steady rhythm of Roman Berg's breathing above her. And although his close proximity did make her feel much safer than she'd ever felt while sleeping on the road, her brow still creased with unease. Every so often, the breeze carried to her a hint of a shout or a clang or a single note of music, so faint that perhaps no one but Isra could have heard it.

It was the caravan. And it had stopped not so far down the road.

Slavers, performers, Romani . . . the group could be comprised of any sort of individuals. But they were traveling into the darkness, which meant they were used to being turned away. So whatever their kind, their repute was of the ill sort, and well they knew it. Isra didn't think they had noticed their tiny camp in the darkness set so far back from the road, but she wasn't sure enough to relax.

Should she wake Roman? And tell him what? That there were people camped down the road from them? That was a situation they would encounter many times during the course of their journey, and Isra knew she couldn't fall to pieces each time they were passed by travelers or someone noticed her at all.

But there was something about the group that had passed—something—she couldn't sort it out in her head. It wasn't exactly fear, it wasn't attraction; perhaps an anxious curiosity to know the nature of the danger or nay that was so close to them, sleeping in the darkness.

She told herself she was only foolish, squeezed her eyes shut, and finally forced herself into a tense, fitful slumber.

The creaking of the cart bed above her woke her—not long after dawn, by the gray haze that curtained the landscape beyond her meager shelter. She looked down past her bent knees, curled beneath her blanket, and saw Roman's sandaled feet touch down onto the ground. As they moved around the side of the cart before her, Isra gathered her legs and rolled out the opposite side and stood. They faced each other over the open bed.

"Good morn," he said, and Isra thought he looked like a disgruntled little boy, his white blond hair flipped up at his crown where it had bent into place while he slept. She thought it looked silky and soft, like angora, and she wondered if it would feel as such should she pull a lock of it through her fingers.

"Good morn," she replied and then dropped her eyes, bending at once to gather her bedclothes while the large man moved away from the cart.

It was only a moment later that she heard his muffled curse.

She looked, still turning the roll of blanket in her arms, to find him just coming to a stop near the tree, the thick fog blanketing the landscape around their camp like an enchantment. He was turning in tight circles, and from his hand hung a short portion of rope. Her eyes went to the tree.

The donkey was gone.

Roman turned to her and their eyes met, and in that moment Isra felt a weight of guilt descend upon her. She should have woken him last night; she had known something was wrong, but she had ignored it; she should have stayed awake all the night and listened instead of sleeping. She could have prevented the theft of the animal, but now the donkey was gone.

And it was Isra's fault.

A sick, cold, trembly feeling took over her middle and she felt heat come into her face, but before she could apologize, Roman's eyes went over her shoulder and he began marching toward her.

She frowned, but she was not afraid. No matter that she was prepared to take the blame for the loss of the donkey, she had no fear at all that Roman Berg intended to strike her. Indeed, he strode through the area where the line of sick flags should have been and past her to the front of the cart. Isra turned and then she, too, stared at what had caught Roman's interest.

The censer was gone. Likewise the bell.

Isra looked over her shoulder to where the blackened remains of their fire lay damp and glistening with dew. The thieves had even taken the neat pile of branches and twigs Isra had gathered the night before.

She looked back to Roman, her mind in a panic at what this would mean for their journey, and opened her mouth to beg his forgiveness.

"Isra, I'm sorry," he said before she could speak, one hand on his hip, the other swiping at his forehead. "Our first night on the road and I've not proved myself a capable protector."

"No," she stammered. "I . . . I heard them making camp not far from us after we retired. I should have alerted you that they were nearby, but I was afraid you would think me overanxious. The loss of your belongings is the fault of my pride."

He stared at her for a moment, and then a slight grin came over his face. It was so unexpected that it caused Isra to frown.

"Why are you smiling?" she asked. "We have lost our animal, our implements of disguise, even the wood for our fire."

"I suppose it's the irony of it all," Roman said. He held his arms out from his sides, turned his face up to the misty gray sky, and gave a loud bark of laughter. After he let his arms fall back down he turned to her. "Before we left Melk, my friends tutored me on surviving the journey." He walked toward her and then past her, and when he continued talking, Isra felt she had no choice but to follow him if she wanted to hear what he was saying.

And she most certainly did want to hear.

"Adrian schooled me on the geography of the terrain and weather patterns of the season; Valentine advised me on the roles we would play and how best to stay true to them; Constantine warned me of the dangers inherent in each of the territories we would pass through and which leaders were corrupt." He bent as he walked, gathering the leftover bits of fallen wood that would have to suffice for their fire.

"And each of them impressed upon me—over and over," he continued in an affected accent, "*do not deviate from the plan, Roman. Stay with the plan. No matter what, Roman, you must follow the plan exactly.*" He laughed again and then glanced at Isra as he once more passed her on the way to the small circle where they'd made their fire the night before. "Do you know why they did that?"

Isra blinked. She hadn't been certain he was speaking *to* her rather than simply voicing his irritation aloud.

"No. Why?"

Roman dropped the pile of wood onto the damp coals and looked up at her, his hands going to his hips once more and his grin taking over his mouth. "Because I am terrible at playing along."

Isra felt her eyebrows knit. "'Playing along'?"

"Pretending to be something I'm not."

"You seem to have done well at pretending to be a monk," she offered.

"I haven't really pretended anything," Roman said as he went to the bag that was—thankfully—still in the bed of the cart. "The camaraderie there is not unlike what I have found in a work camp, although there is much less swearing and it is considerably cleaner. I do many of the same things I would do in my life did I not live at Melk—I work, I pray, I cook." He squatted by the wood and began to remove the flint and tinder from the bag.

"I do not understand," she said, "why they would be so concerned with you not following a plan when there is so much at stake for both you and your friends."

"That's just it," he said and paused for a moment while the sparks flew from the stone onto the fluffy wad of tinder. Roman leaned spindly twigs against the tiny licks of orange and then turned his cheek against the ground to blow up the fire. He sat up and reached for another handful of damp wood. "It's precisely when there is so much at stake that I tend to . . . deviate from the generally accepted course."

"You do not seem deviant to me," she defended.

He arranged the little finger-width branches in a cone and then dropped his palms to his thighs. "Think back to when first we met."

Isra did not have to rattle her brains to retrieve the memory of it from her mind. Indeed, for many, many months, her memories of Roman Berg were what had kept her alive.

"You walked into Damascus alone. Undisguised," she said.

He nodded. "When I set myself to a course of action, it is usually my manner to go straight at the thing. My friends know this, and it is why they were so anxious to make a simple ruse with a detailed plan for me to follow."

"They wanted to keep you from walking into Damascus undisguised again." She felt a twinge in her heart at the deep bonds the four men must have, how committed they were to one another after what they had experienced. "But it seems their plan has been forfeited before it could be put to use."

"Does it not?"

She was taken aback by the smile he sent her as he fetched the bag of food and jug from the cart and returned to the smoking fire on the ground. He removed the cups and poured wine into them but kept the open jug braced on his knee.

"Do we now return to Melk?" she ventured. "Surely it should not take us longer than a pair of days on foot to retrace the way we have come."

Roman had turned one of the cups up against his mouth, and Isra was mesmerized for a long moment while she watched the thick cords in his neck as he swallowed the entire contents. He lowered the cup and sighed even as he was refilling it.

"I think it would not be a good idea to venture through the village in which we were questioned yesterday," he said, and Isra felt foolish at having already forgotten the terror she'd felt at their near discovery.

"And besides," he continued, setting the jug aside and lifting his cup, "I know Constantine Gerard well now. Should we return so soon to Melk, he will likely take it as a sign that this journey is ill-fated, and will do his very best to prevent us from setting out once more." His expression was placid, but Isra understood the underlying message in his benign words. He raised the cup to his mouth and again drank it in its entirety.

"What are we to do?" Isra asked, cringing at her own boldness.

Roman set his cup aside and rose with a satisfied-sounding sigh. "*You're* going to break your fast here by this somewhat comfortable fire. *I'm* going to go retrieve our things."

Her eyes went wide. "From the caravan? Alone?"

"Yes." He walked to the bed of the cart, where the open compartment held the remainder of their belongings, and began rifling through them.

Isra came up behind him. "My lord, forgive me, but you cannot. You do not know the sort of people you will be facing alone. The very size of their party warrants your caution."

"I know they're the sort of people who would steal a man's donkey and the sick flags from around what could reliably be understood to be a corpse," he said, removing a folded piece of leather and setting it on the rough boards. "And besides," he paused while he gathered the long length of his habit and shimmied it up over his wide body. In a moment he had pulled it off, and Isra could not keep her eyes from going to the strip of firm flesh and chiseled ribs that flashed from beneath his white undershirt.

"They came into my camp, very close to where you slept, uninvited," he finished, and shook out the leather to reveal a fine vest with raw lacings up the front. He slipped it over his head and began tightening the ladder of leather ties over his wide chest. "They will answer for that."

Isra didn't know what to say. A part of her was consumed with fear for him, for what could possibly happen to him should he walk into the camp alone and accuse the inhabitants of theft; fear for herself at being left alone for the time he was gone—and perhaps forever should he not return.

The other part of her was thrilled at his daring, his surety. Who could refuse this man? His forearm was greater in size than most men's upper leg. Even his clothing seemed big enough to fit a bear as he removed a wide caped leather cap from his bag and snugged it down over his head before fastening it at his collarbone.

But even though his resolve and confidence were impressive, Isra still feared for his safety. "My lord—Roman," she corrected herself, raising her palm at his frown. "I—"

But her words were cut off by a brown blur that swept through the air of the clearing from behind her, so close to her head that Isra felt the pull on the roots of her hair. An instant later, the brown thing billowed and flapped and shrank and then came to perch on Roman Berg's leather-draped shoulder.

Roman's laugh filled the foggy air as he brought a hand to his shoulder, and Isra gasped.

"Lou!" Roman exclaimed. "I shouldn't be surprised, should I? No, you couldn't miss out on the adventure, could you?"

The falcon had found Roman, the same way it had found him in Damascus.

Lou's painted head seemed to swivel until its brightly rimmed black eye found Isra, and in that instant, she knew what she wanted to do.

"I am coming with you," she announced in a wavering voice, trying to ignore the cringe in her middle. She had just restrained herself from adding "this time" to her statement. "If you please."

Roman turned his still smiling face toward her while he stroked the hunting bird's sleek back. Then he nodded.

"All right."

They walked down the center of the road for what Isra guessed to be at least a mile before they began to see evidence of the party that had passed theirs in the night. Wagons had been pulled off to the side of the road, the animals missing from their harnesses, no signs or sounds of movement from within. She looked up at Roman from beneath the edge of the white linen that covered her head and saw that he was scanning the line of oddly covered conveyances while the falcon on his shoulder scanned the sky—hoodless, tetherless. And even though Roman's steps were calm and measured, Isra could feel his alertness through the thick, scratchy wool of her borrowed gown.

As they walked, they found wagons veered farther off the road and into a spreading field, from which sounds of activity could be heard. Once again, music reached Isra's ears, and laughter. The wagons grew larger, and some had windows, but the oddest thing about them was that they appeared to have been painted and stenciled in bright colors, stylized versions of animals and men and birds decorating their bulky hulks.

Roman, too, veered off the road and Isra followed, walking in the deep, soft ruts left by scores of wide wheels leading into a fallow field where it appeared a common area had been set up. A large fire marked the center, ringed by metal scaffolds of spits and tripods and cauldrons. An old woman with straggly gray hair crouched near the fire, stirring the contents of a pot. Several chickens scratched through the dried and jagged stalks poking up through mud and dead vegetation; a pair of young children emerged, squealing and chasing each other before disappearing between another pair of wagons.

"There she is," Roman said, and after a quick glance at his face, Isra turned to look beyond the fire and past the farthest wagon, where it seemed all the animals had been corralled.

There, indeed, had to be their donkey; it was smaller, fatter, and certainly better groomed than the rest of the animals gathered together beyond the—yes, certainly, that was the long length of sick rope, its red pennants fluttering in the morning air. Perhaps the donkey spotted Roman, for she gave a pathetic and lonely-sounding bray.

The old woman rose from a stool she'd had hidden in her skirts to reach up to one of the tripods and grasp a rope. Isra caught the flash of the curved dome of the bell that had, until recently, been attached to their own cart.

"Cheeky lot," Roman said.

The witchlike figure rang the bell and then cupped her gnarled hands around her mouth, as if readying herself to give a shout.

But Roman stepped toward the fire, giving Isra little choice but to follow, while he called out to the woman. "Hark, mistress," he said in a firm voice. "Who is the master of this party?"

The hag swung around and, although she did not seem surprised at their arrival, she did look appreciatively up and down Roman's large form, her eyes lingering on Lou.

"I'm the master, for all you need to know, Goliath," she snipped. "I've got no scraps to feed the likes of you and neither does he. Be gone." She began to raise her hands again, but Roman interrupted her.

"I've not come looking for a meal," he said, and Isra noted how his voice grew deeper. "I've come for the belongings that were stolen out from under me in the night by someone or some*ones* in this group."

"Bugger off," the old woman muttered over her shoulder.

Roman began to march past the fire toward the corral, Lou maintaining his perch.

"Ay, now! Where do you think you're off to?"

He didn't turn around, and Isra stayed where she was, her hand gripping the knife hidden in her skirt. She was not going to let anyone sneak up behind Roman.

"That's *my* donkey," he called out, pointing with a long forefinger. "*My* sick flags. And I'm taking them back."

Isra felt her backbone tightening. "That is our bell as well," she said to the old woman, who swung her wrinkled face around slowly. "And I believe you are making your porridge in what is meant to be a censer. You shall be ill from that, old woman."

"You don't say?" the hag squealed. And then she reached up once more with her skeletal fingers and began ringing said bell as if trying to shake her own arm loose from her body.

As if by magic, people of all shapes, sizes, and even colors began to emerge from the spaces between the wagons, filling the common area and separating Isra from Roman. Her fledgling bravado disappeared like smoke from the censer, which now contained an unknown portion of contaminated foodstuff.

"He's stealin' the animals!" the hag screamed, pointing her bony finger toward Roman and then swinging around to face Isra. "And *she's* palmin' a blade!"

The crowd began to grumble, roughly one half turning toward Roman and the other half moving in Isra's direction. But Roman's strong voice cut through the rumblings.

"I have come only for what is mine," he called out, and Isra couldn't help but notice the young boy with long, dirty brown hair cut straight across at his collarbone who sank back into the advancing crowd and disappeared. Perhaps he was the thief? But she could not devote further thought to him as Roman continued to advise the group.

"This donkey was stolen from my camp last night, not long after your party passed us on the road. I'm taking her back, along with our bell and censer and the flags indicating an infectious patient in quarantine. I mean no one here harm. Any of you noble enough to claim leadership of this den of thieves and deny me, step forward if you would."

The crowd parted to let a man pass into the center of the clearing, and they backed away from him, leaving Isra a clear line of sight past this new stranger to Roman and the animals beyond.

"Is that so?" the man asked amiably enough, still fastening the thin black belt around his green velvet tunic, looping the long end of it through itself so that it hung down against his leg. His hair was dark, thick, and longer on the top of his head so that it swooped and curved into an attractive wave over his brow. His skin was pale, in sharp contrast to his dark brows and lashes, like charcoaled slashes on his ivory skin.

"If anyone here has deprived you of your property, sir, then I extend to you my deepest apologies," the man said, bringing one of his palms to rest on his chest. "Certainly I bid you retrieve your belongings with my heartfelt thanks for alerting me that there is a *thief* in our midst." At his words, the crowd snorted and twittered.

Roman glanced to Isra and then nodded to the finely dressed and well-spoken man. "Very well. I'll only be a moment."

"Of course," the man continued, causing Roman to pause in turning toward the makeshift corral, "you will be able to prove rightful ownership before you remove them from my family's possession."

"What?" Roman said.

"How do I know these things belong to you?" the man asked, looking around wide-eyed at all gathered there, and then fixing his eyes on Isra. "Perhaps *you* are the robbers, preying upon humble travelers and extorting them of their effects while you distract us with such a beauteous companion."

"That is *my* donkey, *my* sick flags, *my* bell, *my* censer," Roman growled. "And I mean to take them with me. I need not prove anything to you, for you know as well as I that none of these things were in your possession before this morn."

The man shrugged, even as his eyes lingered on Isra. His smile was friendly, curious, and he did not seem at all perturbed at Roman's stern tone. He held up a finger and swung it between Isra and Roman.

"Which one of you is sick?" he asked.

"What?" Roman demanded again.

"You said those were sick flags; I don't believe they are to be flown in an arbitrary manner. The sheriff of the town we passed through yesterday warned of a man transporting a leper on the road ahead of us. But neither of you appear to be rotting where you stand. So I ask you: Which one of you is sick?"

Roman met Isra's eyes again but looked away. "That's none of your concern."

"Well, that is too bad." The man clasped his hands behind his back and looked down at his feet, as if considering. Then he looked up at Roman. "I think you'd better be on your way, then."

"My thoughts exactly," Roman said, and then turned and snapped the line of pennants from the tree, bringing the little donkey trotting to his side.

Isra brought a hand to her throat as a handful of men separated from the crowd after only a single glance from the well-dressed leader. All the men were large, wide, their sleeveless tunics displaying well-muscled arms.

But Roman knew what was about as he quickly turned and faced the five who stopped in a line before him, all crossing their arms over their chests.

"I don't think so, cap'n," one said to Roman.

Roman sighed and tossed the length of pennant in his hand to the ground. He pushed away the head of the donkey, who seemed to want to hide her face beneath Roman's arm. Then he brought his hand to Lou, still perched on his shoulder, and lifted him off into the air. The falcon swooped low over the line of men, causing them to duck and cover their heads for a moment, and then Lou flew a tight circuit around the common, eliciting squeals from the crowd before settling on a branch above Isra.

"I have no wish to injure you," Roman warned them. "Let me pass with my belongings and you'll keep your feet beneath you." The crowd murmured at the implied threat.

"Looks like those things belong to us now," the man responded. "I'd wager the one who'll be showing the soles of his boots to the morn stands before me." Again, the crowd rumbled, but this time there was also laughter and shouts of encouragement.

Roman shrugged. "All right."

The dark-haired leader strolled toward Isra, an easy smile on his face, his arms still clasped behind his back.

"Come no closer," she warned him, trying to keep her voice from ascending.

But he paid her no heed, his smile deepening as his eyes seemed to take in the details of the veil over her head, her face. "I'm not going to harm you," he said with a grin.

"No closer," she reiterated, but he came to a stop only once he had reached her side.

He held up his hands. "Not armed. Let's watch together, shall we? Perhaps you will decide to continue your journey with us should something . . . unfortunate happen to your friend." He turned to face the area where the horses were now wandering away into the camp, but no one gathered seemed to care in the least. Roman faced the five men before him. They squatted down and spread out, likely with the intention of circling him much as the animals had been corralled.

"It's a shame really," he said, leaning to the side to speak to Isra. "He is impressive. Were you slaves together?"

Isra winced at him. But her attention was drawn back to Roman as the first man charged with a yell. In the next instant, that challenger was flat on his back, motionless in the dirt.

To Isra's surprise, the crowd sent up a polite cheer.

"Ah, very good," the man at her side said. "But let us see how he fares against two."

As if on cue, half of the remaining men advanced from opposite sides of Roman, the slighter of the two giving a great leap onto his back and locking his arms around Roman's neck while the man in front took a swing with a meaty fist.

Roman ducked, even while carrying his passenger, and came up with a two-fisted swing under the man's chin, followed by a kick to the groin that caused the crowd to give a collective groan. As the attacker crumpled to the dirt, Roman squatted and reached up over his head, yanking the man riding him in a wide arc, much like he would remove a shirt, and throwing him onto the ground with such force that debris flew up around the fallen man. Roman crouched down to face the remaining two opponents.

The spectators shouted and clapped; some even whistled.

Roman frowned and glanced at Isra, who turned and looked up quizzically at the man still at her side. She was unsettled to find that he was already regarding her.

"I am Asa van Groen," he offered.

Two loud oofs and a strangled yell drew Isra's attention back to Roman, and she saw one of his challengers staggering backward in her direction, his arms windmilling.

Asa van Groen reached out and guided Isra out of the path of the defeated man just as he skidded into the dirt at her feet. He released her promptly, though, holding his palms up again, and Isra was stunned to see that in his right hand he now held the dagger she'd been clutching in her skirts.

Asa grinned at her before flipping the dagger in his palm and offering the weapon back to her, handle first. "I didn't want you to drop it in the commotion; it looks valuable."

The crowd cheered, and Isra looked up to see Roman standing amid a pile of bodies, one of which was attempting to gain his hands and knees and crawl away. Roman bent down and snagged a loop of the pennants and wound them from his palm down to his elbow as he walked toward Isra. The little gray donkey trotted in his wake, as if terrified that she would be left behind, just as some beast gave what could only be described as a barking roar, a sound that was both terrifying and somehow familiar.

"Pardon my boldness," the strange man asked, drawing Isra's attention to him, "but would you happen to be Egyptian?"

Chapter 8

Roman threw the coil of sick flags onto his shoulder as he reached the hag squatted before the fire. She grinned up at him with all six of her pointed teeth while he unhooked the bell. With his other hand he pulled a rag free from a metal frame with a snap of cloth. He wound it around his hand before grabbing the censer, tipping the hinged lid open and tossing the gray, sloppy contents into the dirt. The censer lid clanged as he flipped it closed.

"You may keep the firewood that was stolen," he said to the old woman, who only threw back her head and cackled as Roman turned to walk to Isra.

He didn't like the way the dark-haired man was standing so close to her. But Isra looked to him right away, and although her smile was reserved, he saw a sparkle in her eyes that he'd never seen before. Was that look for him? Or for the peacock who had been speaking into her ear while Roman was fending off five attackers?

She slid her dagger into her skirt as he reached her and then held out her hands, taking the bell and the coil of rope from him.

"Well done, my lord," she said, looking into his eyes, and Roman felt an unusual swelling of pride as he realized the pleasure in her gaze was for him.

"I will echo that praise, if I may," the man at her side said and held out his hand toward Roman as Isra moved behind him to grab hold of the little donkey's bridle. "Asa van Groen."

Roman only looked down at the man's hand and then up into the branches of the tree overhead. He gave a sharp, thin whistle between his teeth and Lou descended at once to land on his caped shoulder.

Van Groen abandoned the gesture with the quirk of a dark eyebrow. "Ingenious disguise you've contrived. Is your master hunting the two of you? Or the three of you, I should say," he added, glancing at Lou.

"I have no master," Roman said. "And I'll warn you now: should our paths cross again on the road, and should any of your people come near, I won't stop at just giving him a thrashing."

"I believe what you say," van Groen allowed with a nod. "But *I* say, why not preclude the chance of an unexpected meeting at some future time? We are headed south, you are headed south; why don't you join us?"

Isra's head swung around to stare at the man, and even though Roman was learning that it was her habit to conceal her emotions, surprise was quite evident on her face.

"You stole from us, set five men upon my protector in hopes of killing him, and now that he has won you think we would travel alongside you?" she demanded, her tone growing haughty, her chin raising.

"Oh, no, my dear; they would not have killed him, never! What on earth would we have done with such a massive corpse, I ask you?" van Groen objected, a look of horror coming over his slender face. "Allow me to point out that there is great strength in numbers. It would be much easier for the two of you to travel to your destination in our midst than on your own. You're both rather . . . conspicuous."

Roman leaned forward and down to gain the man's attention. "Stay away from our camp," he reiterated. Then he straightened and motioned toward Isra to lead the donkey ahead of him. She urged the little gray animal on without so much as a further glance for van Groen. Roman followed.

"Very well, and you have my word!" the man called out behind Roman, but he did not bother to turn to look at him. "From this moment on, none of my troupe's shadows shall fall on your camp. But my offer stands; you are welcome around our fire if ever you change your minds. This day, tonight, a fortnight from now . . ."

"The forty-third of Never?" Roman returned over his shoulder. To his surprise, the crowd gathered in the circle of wagons erupted in good-natured laughter.

He followed Isra and the donkey up the slight rise onto the road and they walked for several minutes before they passed the last of the wagons. Only when they had barren fields interspersed with tiny plots of woodland flanking them did she turn to him.

"You were wonderful, my lord," she said, her voice steady, honest. He looked sideways at her and saw that she wore an expression of openness rather than anxiety or secrecy. "Where did you learn to fight?"

"I had to learn young," Roman said, feeling a heat come up his neck. "My size gave older lads wont to single me out, and there was little supervision of the apprentices. We had to fend for ourselves and for one another."

"Do you often find yourself having cause to battle?"

Roman shook his head. "No. Not for years and years now. When I was—" He broke off for a moment to rearrange his words. "I sometimes had need to break up fights among my workers, usually caused by a woman or too much drink. But I've found that as men grow older, they become more loathe to instigate trouble with someone twice their size."

She was looking down at the road before her feet when Roman glanced at her again, but there was a gentle smile on her lips.

"The intelligent ones," she guessed.

Roman chuckled. He felt very good just then. His arm pained him a bit, but the strain was actually pleasant. He'd done no physical labor since he'd found Isra Tak'Ahn on the hillside, and his body was eager for release. Traveling by cart and then by ship for weeks did not promise to require any effort.

Unless they came across more brigands on their journey, that was. Roman almost hoped they would be a regular occurrence if it meant that same look of admiration from the woman walking at his side.

"What was that man—van Groen, was it?—saying to you?" he asked at last.

"He is strange," Isra said. "He asked me if I was Egyptian."

Roman turned his head toward her. "*Are* you Egyptian?"

"I am indeed," she said. "In part. Perhaps." She shrugged. "I never knew my father or his kin. But my mother's blood is Egyptian, and . . . and English."

Roman's eyes widened and he longed to press her but would not now, noticing how her words were becoming hesitant again, her movements stilted. Perhaps this was a part of her life Isra would rather not expound upon, and although he again felt as if he could demand it of her and she would comply because of whatever debt she felt she owed him, Roman would not take advantage of her in that manner.

"English," he said instead, allowing his voice to convey his interest but looking straight ahead at the road before them.

The birdsong and their own footfalls interspersed with the donkey's clopping gait were the only sounds for several moments.

"My great-grandfather married an English lady," she said in somewhat of a rush, picking up their conversation as if it had never stopped.

Roman looked over at her with a grin. "You mean to say that your great-grandmother was an English lady? Titled?"

Isra nodded and looked over at him. "My mother warned us never to speak it as such. There are many in my country who hate the English. To admit that I am part English—no matter how small the part—could have been very dangerous for us."

"I see. Well, that is yet another reason why you cannot refer to me as lord—you outrank me." He paused a moment and then took a chance. "How did your English great-grandmother fare in Damascus?"

Isra shook her head. "She never saw the city. My great-grandfather died in England. One of his sons—my mother's father—returned to the land of his ancestors, hoping to amass his own fortune." She paused for a moment, letting the birdsong sing them along. "He was unsuccessful. He sold his only daughter into slavery and died penniless."

Roman was shocked at the dramatic story of Isra Tak'Ahn's heritage and wanted to ask after it further but didn't wish to make her uncomfortable by prying.

So it was a surprise when she turned to him and asked suddenly, "Do I appear to be English to you?"

Roman took the opportunity to look directly at her, to study her, with an expression of concentration on his face. In truth, though, he wasn't seeking any specific trait; he was only enjoying her features at his leisure and with her permission.

"Not particularly," he said at last, and then gave a little shrug.

"Not at all?" she pressed.

He looked at her again. "I don't think so. Why?"

Her eyes went to the road again. "My mother said she could see the English in me. In my skin. Huda's as well."

"I do like your skin," he blurted out, regretting it even before all the words had passed from his lips. "The coloring of it, I mean. It's darkrent. *Different.* Dark. Darker. Darker than mine. Which is very pale. You've noticed."

He had to nearly grind his teeth to get his mouth to stay closed.

Isra laughed. "I like your skin, too."

He took the next several moments to grin at the road like a fool. When he was fairly certain he wasn't in danger of complimenting her on the fact that she had hair growing on her head, he tried again.

"Why do you think van Groen asked if you were Egyptian?"

"I do not know," she said, shaking her head. "I am not missing from Egypt; no one knows of me there. If he had asked were I Damascene, I would worry."

Roman agreed. "What of Saladin? Could he have been warned that sensitive information was perhaps lost to a woman from Damascus who is now missing?"

"I suppose it is possible," Isra said, "but not likely. The men I betrayed would rather put an end to me themselves than admit to their ruler that they were bested by a woman. It was a strange question, though. He is a strange man," she repeated.

"Well, you can put him from your mind," Roman said as they came upon the tracks where he had pulled their little cart off the road the night before. He passed Isra and the donkey to walk into the tall grass first. "We shall hitch up our well-mannered girl and be on our way, never to see Asa van Groen again."

He looked up with a smile at their fire, hardly smoldering now, and then stopped, feeling Isra come up behind him. The only other things in the clearing besides grass and tree were the obvious circles of wheel ruts in the mud around the smoking pile of coals.

"That son of a bitch," Roman muttered.

"He knew the cart was being stolen as he gave us his pretty speech," Roman muttered as he walked along with Isra at his side, still leading the reluctant donkey. They were once more going past the long line of wagons pulled off the road and headed into the clearing.

"It could not have been van Groen himself, my lord," Isra said. "There was a boy, though . . ."

Roman raised a hand and Lou gave an uneasy flap of his wings.

"It matters not. Van Groen *knew*." Roman was going to find that ebon-haired peacock and put the man's angular face on the backside of his skull.

The sounds coming from the camp as they entered this time were louder, more raucous than when they'd been there an hour earlier. Every few moments a shout would erupt, or a set of shrill screams. The air was strung with the perpetually panicked, jingly barks of small dogs. As strange as the whole lot of them were, cheering on the man they stole from when he was set upon by five of their own, it wouldn't have surprised Roman should he discover they had taken to poking each other with long sticks to the rhythm of a tune.

As they came into view of the common area, he saw what had to be the entirety of the population of the caravan gathered into a sea of humanity beyond the fire. He slowed, Isra and the donkey keeping close to his side, to observe what the strange group of travelers were about.

He couldn't quite tell, only that the mass seemed to collectively move a score of feet in one direction, heralded by a loud scream or shout. But the next time the flock of people swooped, Roman and Isra's presence was detected by a man standing in the back of the crowd nearest them. He glanced their way and then looked back at them, an alarmed frown coming over his long, sallow countenance.

Just so, Roman thought to himself. *He should be alarmed, the thief.*

The man began flapping his hands in their direction and came at them in a trot. "Go back!" he called. "Run while you still can!"

"Not likely," Roman shouted, standing taller. The man himself was unusually tall and thin, and Roman took rare advantage of his stature. "Find your Asa van Groen and tell him I've come for my cart."

The man seemed to grow thinner as he drew closer, and Roman fancied he could almost see the joints of his skeleton as his clothes flapped on his frame. "Van Groen can't be with you at the moment," he said, glancing over his shoulder as he reached them. "Heed my warning and *run*. Your life is not worth a wooden cart, friend."

Roman shoved the man aside, striding toward the group of folk gathered with their backs to him.

"My lord?" Isra called after him.

"Back in a thrice," he assured her over his shoulder. He was rather looking forward to impressing this Egyptian beauty who had descended, at least in part, from English nobility.

But then a frightful roar came from the crowd knotted together perhaps only twenty paces before him, and the throng seemed to turn at once and stampede toward Roman, swerving around him, knocking him to the ground and sending Lou flapping to safety as they leaped and screamed and dispersed among the wagons.

Roman rolled onto his stomach and looked up in the direction from which the crowd had run.

There stood Asa van Groen in the bed of Roman's own cart, his arms outstretched, a long, curling whip in one hand, turning his body in a slow circle. A boy of perhaps ten with long, stringy hair peeked over the top of van Groen's arm.

"No, Kahn! Naughty! Back!" the man shouted to where the tongue of the cart would be resting. "Go back to your wagon this instant!" He turned slowly, slowly toward Roman, and Roman saw something emerging around the edge of a tall, spindled cart wheel.

Something orange and black and white that walked on silent paws eyed the man in the cart bed with ill-concealed malice and a flick of its whiskered cheek pads.

The moment Roman realized the nature of the beast that threatened van Groen was the moment the tiger noticed Roman, lying on his stomach on the ground. It swung its head from the cart and gave a little start, crouching down and testing the ground with one paw, perhaps waiting to see if he would run.

Which was precisely what Roman intended to do.

He raised up slowly onto his hands and knees. He'd never been a swift runner, but if he, like the crowd that had run, could make it to the labyrinth of wagons, perhaps he would be safe. He glanced over his shoulder and saw Isra, standing as if frozen, the donkey pulling backward away from its bridle, little sounds of distress emanating from her barrel chest.

Isra was staring directly at the tiger. Roman turned his head back.

The tiger was staring directly at *him*.

A loud bray broke the tense silence, and then the thumping of hooves in soft dirt. He wanted to turn around to see if Isra had also fled, for he would not run past her and leave her to the tiger. His question was answered in the next moment when she called out to him.

"Do not move, I pray thee, my lord," she said. Her voice grew louder, as if she was moving toward him. "Remember the words of the wise Wynn."

It could not be possible that she was coming closer. Surely she had seen that there was a tiger preparing to eat him.

"Asa van Groen!" she called out in a sharp voice. "Throw me your whip, and also a staff from the driver's seat."

"There are two—" the man began.

"Either one. Quickly."

Roman wanted to turn his head to see what Isra was about, but he was mesmerized by the big animal staring him down. The tiger flicked its eyes over Roman's back, as if also interested in the activities of the woman behind him.

"Isra," Roman tried in a low voice, "you must find a safe place to hide. You have not come so far to be mauled by a beast."

"It is only a tiger," Isra replied in a strangely calm tone. "A mismanaged tiger, from what I have witnessed. What is it called?"

"Kahn," Van Groen said.

"Where is its home?"

"That wagon behind him."

"Ensure that the door is open and ready to receive him," Isra commanded.

Roman heard the scrabbling of feet against wood, then the thump of boots landing in the dirt.

"Isra," Roman called out warily.

"Shh, my lord," she said, her voice directly above him now.

Roman saw the shift in the tiger's attention as Isra's skirts swished by his arm and then before his face, blocking his view of the animal.

"I'm not certain this is the best time to test Brother Wynn's methods."

"If not now, when?" she replied, and Roman could have sworn he heard a smile in the woman's voice. It was gone when next she spoke.

The whip cracked twice in quick succession. "Hie, Kahn! Hie! Hie now!" And Isra's slippers began to move away from him.

Chapter 9

The tiger was bigger than Princess, even though his matted coat seemed to hang on his large bones like a once magnificent rug neglected for decades, the pattern of stripes muddy, the colors dull. Even the white tufts around the sides of his head were yellowed.

"Hie, Kahn!" she called out again and cracked the whip in her right hand as she continued to move slowly, slowly toward the animal. She held both arms away from her now, the staff—perhaps four feet long end to end—feeling weighty and solid in her grip.

The tiger crouched down and flashed his teeth at her. Isra thought he could be missing several, and she wondered how old he was, what sort of mistreatment he'd suffered at the hands of the people currently hiding from him, or others before them.

She came to a stop, observing that Kahn was refusing to retreat and needing a breath to plan her next move. Isra glanced over the tiger and saw the rear of a wooden wagon with a tall, rectangular box for a bed. An equally tall door stood open and a ramp led from the black interior to the ground. Asa van Groen stood behind the open door, both of his black boots balancing him on the top of one of the wagon's rear wheels.

She needed the tiger to back up or turn around. Advancing on him was clearly not working, and if she should press the issue, Isra was fairly certain the animal was prepared to show her that his remaining teeth still served him in a satisfactory manner. She thought back to when she'd first seen Brother Wynn bringing Princess out into the gallery. He'd never driven or backed her; he'd guided her.

Isra crossed her left foot behind her right and began a slow, sidling semicircle around the tiger, who was now between Isra and the little two-wheeled cart. "Kahn!" she shouted, and then remembered the albino cracking the whip in the opposite direction from where he wished his tiger to go. But she doubted she could make the whip sound should she move it into her left hand.

She raised the staff with her left arm and swung it down as hard as she could against the cart. The tiger sprang to her right, away from the staff, and again showed her his teeth, but he, too, was now doing a cross step with his wide front paws, mirroring Isra's movements.

"Yes," she said in a steady voice. "Nothing for you out here; back to your safe home. *Hie, Kahn!*" she shouted, and whipped the staff down again, only this time it whistled against the air.

The tiger sidled away farther toward the wagon, the ramp of which was perhaps only ten paces from the animal. Kahn was perpendicular to her now and so Isra cracked the whip, causing the tiger to swing fully toward the ramp and continue on in a slow, deliberate pace. He hesitated at the bottom of the ramp, but after a glance over his sliding shoulders at Isra—who cracked the whip again—he leaped up the ramp in two bounds. Asa van Groen slammed the door to the wagon shut.

Even as cheers erupted behind her, the brief glance she'd gotten of the inside of Kahn's wagon was seared into Isra's mind: the filthy floor crusted with excrement, rotting vegetables strewn about in piles, the buzzing of insects that should have died out with the season.

The image was jostled from her immediate attention as she felt herself being hoisted up through the air by many hands until she was riding atop a pair of shoulders, one of them Isra was quite certain belonging to a man Roman had bested only a pair of hours before.

She saw him standing there beyond the crowd with Lou once more perched near his ear, people still running past him toward her, whooping and shouting their delight at her success. But Isra paid none of them any heed; she couldn't look away from the huge blond man and his falcon, his vivid eyes seeming to light up the dreary clearing as he sent her a crooked smile.

Her fingers were clasped and she was lowered to her feet, and Asa van Groen was bowing over her hand. Isra looked past his rounded back in time to catch Roman's frown and see him begin to walk toward her.

"A thousand thank-yous, mistress," van Groen said. "How can we ever repay you for saving us? Name any prize and it shall be yours."

And then Isra remembered what she had seen inside the tiger's wagon.

She snatched her fingers away from the dark-haired man's grasp just as it seemed he'd been about to place his lips on the back of her hand. When he raised his unnaturally pale face to look at her, Isra slapped his cheek.

The crowd gasped and moved a step closer en masse, but van Groen raised the hand not pressed to his face.

"No, let her have her say. She deserves at least that." He dropped both his hands and looked at her. "Although it was indeed one of our own, I didn't steal your things, nor did I order them stolen."

Roman had paused a pair of steps from her when she'd struck the man, but now he came to her side, grasping her right forearm gently, urging her to look up at him.

His gaze was serious. "I'll ready the wagon." But he did not leave her. Isra realized he was asking if she wanted him to stay and intervene for her with van Groen.

He was *asking* her.

"As you wish," she said, giving him a nod. She thought she felt him squeeze her flesh before his hand fell away and he moved to the cart. Isra faced Asa van Groen.

"How long have you had possession of the tiger, and from where did you get him?" she demanded in a clear voice.

His eyes widened and he blinked away the expression. "Kahn's been with us for two months; we bought him from a pelt trader when he realized the old tapestry wouldn't bring as much as we would pay. He's been our greatest attraction." Asa's thin mouth quirked as he added, "When he cooperates."

Isra had felt her eyebrows drawing closer together the longer the man spoke. "Your greatest attraction?" she asked.

"Of course, mistress." The man smiled and then spread his arms, indicating that Isra should look around her. "Think you we travel in such a manner only for pleasure?"

And she did see, finally, now that her attention was not completely taken up with either Roman being attacked or trying to corral a deadly beast into a cage. She noticed that all the wagons pulled in a wide circle in the clearing bore the same kinds of wild, colorful decoration.

And then she noticed the people—or rather the anomalies—in the crowd.

A bearded individual nearly as tall as Roman but twice as wide, and wearing a lovely gown.

A hunter, perhaps, dressed all in green with his quiver at the ready on his back.

A woman holding in her arms four of the smallest dogs Isra had ever seen, while at least four more ran about her ankles.

The old hag who had tended the fire, hunched near the front of the crowd and watching everything with keen amusement.

The variety was too much for Isra to comprehend and so she looked back to Asa van Groen. He lay his hand upon his heart as he had done earlier and stretched out his left arm.

"Welcome, dear friends, to van Groen's Magical Mankind Menagerie!" he announced, and then gave Isra a bow. He grinned at her as he rose. "Of course we now have Kahn, so I am considering removing Mankind from the name."

Isra ignored his display. "What are you feeding him?"

Asa looked at her sideways for a moment. "Whatever we have left over, mistress. You must understand, life in a circus is not the luxury you likely think it to be. Although I'm certain we appear quite—"

"Tigers eat flesh," Isra interrupted. "You are fortunate you have not yet ended up as Kahn's supper. He is starving. The wagon in which you keep him is a disgrace. It is little wonder he wishes to kill you. Or die himself," she emphasized.

"No, no—he can't die," Asa rushed. "We—all of us—used the last coin we had to purchase him."

"Then someone needs to go into the wood and find him something to eat."

"Now?" Asa asked.

"Now."

"But," the man hesitated, "we don't have permission to be here, you see. It's one thing to stop overnight, quite another to poach animals from a lordship's lands. Trust me—they can get very touchy."

Isra only stared at the man.

Asa sighed and then looked over her head and behind him, scanning the crowd. "Dracus!" he called.

The hunter in green stepped forward. "Yes, boss."

"The queen demands her tiger have fresh meat," he said, grinning at Isra as he spoke.

She did not return his smile.

The man nodded and reached his hand behind his neck, pulling an arrow from his quiver. "May I take some for us all?"

"Better not." Asa frowned. "Just Kahn for now."

"Yes, boss." The man called Dracus moved from the crowd.

"There," he said, turning toward her once more. "That should make you more—"

"His wagon must be cleaned," Isra interrupted.

He rolled his lips inward for a moment. "When you say 'must be cleaned,' you mean . . . ?"

"I mean someone needs to shovel out the excrement, scrub the floors and walls and ceiling with soap and water and a stiff brush, and then put some bedding down for him to lie on."

"You're quite concerned about him, aren't you?"

"I would think you be at least as concerned if you hope to use him to earn back the coin you paid for him." Roman joined them then, and he must have seen the distress on Isra's face.

"What is it?" Roman asked, and then he turned his face to Asa van Groen. "What have you done?"

The man clapped his palms to his chest and made his eyes wide. "I've done nothing at all, I assure you, large fellow. But I am dumb-founded at the ideas your woman—"

"She's not my woman," Roman interrupted.

"Your . . . ?" Asa led, but both Roman and Isra let him dangle. "Oh, fine, then." He looked only to Isra now. "If you won't tell me your name, then I will continue to call you queen, which is what I wish to call you any matter. It's as if God himself has sent you to us. It's why I asked you if you were Egyptian earlier. And then you return and direct Kahn as if he has been yours since he was only a kit!"

"What are you talking about?" Isra demanded.

"We need someone capable of showing Kahn. We have had some success leaving him in the wagon behind a curtain and charging a penny just to see him, but not many believe he's real as all he does is lie in a corner. They eventually throw things at him through the bars."

Isra felt her ire rising again.

"If you will stay with us, travel with us however far you are going and train a replacement, I will allow you to keep half of whatever Kahn earns."

"You want me to show Kahn?" she repeated. "To whom?"

"The towns and villages we pass through," Asa exclaimed, and Isra could see the man was becoming excited at the idea. "Perhaps then we might be more frequently granted audience with higher nobles and perform for the courts. I know we could with you—with the Egyptian queen and Kahn!" Asa stood and announced this with such a flourish it was as if he was already before spectators. Isra wondered if the man was ever not performing.

Roman grasped her elbow and leaned his big body between Isra and Asa's. "No. Good-bye."

Roman turned, and although he indicated the direction in which she should go, he didn't pull her or force her. And so Isra went with him, even though she felt a tugging in her heart coming from the direction of the dark, quiet wagon.

"Wait!" Asa called out and ran around to stand in front of Roman. "Wait! Only think of the opportunity I am offering. You can travel in comfort and safety, earning coin along the way rather than spending it."

Roman reached out and swept the smaller man from their path with one swipe of his arm.

But Asa van Groen popped back up in an instant, like a fly that couldn't quite be swatted flat. "At least tell me where you are going," he said. "Perhaps it's fated to be. If we have the same destination, it would be foolish to refuse!"

"Oh, certainly," Roman said with a roll of his eyes. "And there is no chance that no matter where I say we are traveling, that will be your destination as well."

"I'll go first, then," Asa volunteered and then swallowed, took a deep breath, and wiped his palms on his chausses. "Van Groen's Menagerie is traveling south through Venice and then along the coast. We hope to make Constantinople by spring."

Isra looked to Roman's face. She knew her eyes were wide.

But Roman only blinked. "Sorry to disappoint you. We're only traveling as far as Venice." He looked down at Isra. "Are you ready?"

She forced herself to nod, and Roman led her to the cart and helped her onto the driver's seat. The censer was again hung but not yet lit; likely it needed a good scrub. The bell lay on the floor of the driver's perch, and Isra handed the missing staff to Roman, who walked around the wagon and slid it into place. He took the bell and hung it, tying it off carefully.

Isra could not keep her eyes from going to the still, lonely wagon into which the tiger had disappeared. The barred window was dark. She fancied she could smell the animal's wretched quarters from where she sat.

He probably wouldn't live out the fortnight.

The wagon rocked as Roman and Lou gained the seat beside her, and Isra wondered how long she would be allowed to ride with him out in the open for anyone to see.

Likely only as long as it took them to gain the road.

Roman glanced at her as he shook the reins and the donkey began to turn the cart. He looked back to her. "What?"

"Nothing, my lord," she said, looking away into the trees.

The crowd was parting, but slowly, as though reluctant to let them through.

"But perhaps he had a point," she said.

Roman looked at her again. "You want to stay?"

"Have you given it your true consideration, or is your opinion colored by the fact that you have decided you simply do not care for the man? They are traveling to *Constantinople*, my lord," she leaned over to whisper into his biceps.

"I'm not your lord." Roman looked over the head of the donkey. "You think I'm being stubborn."

"I would never think that of you. My lord." Isra rolled her lips inward and bit down on them.

"Hmph," he said. "I don't much care for him; you're right. But we might have better cover, if he can keep the lot of them out of jail."

"And you would not have to play at being a monk," she suggested. "Although it would mean completely abandoning the plan your friends have made for you."

Roman pulled the donkey to a halt and they both looked over their shoulders at the crowd standing in the clearing, staring after them mournfully.

They looked back to each other at the same moment.

Chapter 10

A lthough Roman had convinced himself that he disliked Asa van Groen from the first moment he'd seen the man, he had to admit that the leader of the strange band of travelers had a way of getting things done.

Roman had no sooner stopped the cart—the little gray donkey hanging her head and giving a great mournful sigh—than van Groen had begun shouting out orders to those around him, calling for canvases, staves, paint. Roman turned to Isra and found that she was already climbing down from the seat, van Groen trotting around the wagon to offer his hand to assist her.

"Who has been in charge of Kahn's care?" she demanded as her feet touched the ground, ignoring van Groen's outstretched fingers.

"I have, mistress," the man said, quickly regaining his composure. "There are none other in the band who dare draw near him."

Isra turned her head and looked up at Roman, the question clear in her brown eyes. This woman was not the one he had rescued at Melk. Perhaps he had seen a glimpse of her that night in Damascus, when she had escaped her watchers to come to him and lead him to the prison, but whatever spark of spirit she'd shown that night had been all but extinguished by the losses she'd suffered. Up to this point, she had been afraid, unsure, behaving as if she were no better than a slave.

But when she had faced the tiger alone, knowing it could kill her in an instant, she had become . . . *more*. Perhaps it had been only recklessness; a hope that she would be killed—he remembered with a chill the way she had clutched the little golden dagger in the cell at Melk. But he didn't think so.

He nodded to her. "Call for me if I may be of assistance."

She gave him a slight smile before turning away, and Roman saw hope in her eyes. Asa van Groen kept pace with her, his upper body turned sideways as he chattered and gazed at her.

Roman had little time to stew in his dislike, though, for a group of people approached him now, their arms laden with the supplies van Groen had called for. Roman climbed down from the driver's seat as more arrived with long poles and folded squares of cloth. He turned, his eyes catching sight of a tall, slender woman approaching the group, her white blonde hair twisted tightly back from her face, revealing sharp cheekbones and a pointed chin. She was perhaps a score and ten, her features striking, her eyes pinned on Roman as she walked toward him, carrying a long, shallow box with a dowel handle filled with squat, round crockeries.

She stopped before him and set the box down while two men unfolded one of the large squares of canvas on the ground. She set her hands on her hips and regarded him shrewdly. Her expression was impatient.

"What is your trick?" she asked.

Roman blinked. "I beg your pardon?"

"Your trick. Your show," she said.

"I have no trick," Roman said, glancing sideways as a trio of men climbed into the bed of his cart and began banging straightaway. "I'm only driving the cart."

"You're not the man who bested five of ours only this morning?" she pressed and glanced up at Lou, still perched on Roman's shoulder. "Asa's new darling is your woman?"

"She's not my woman," Roman said for the second time that day.

"The queen's consort," the woman said, ignoring his remark. "I'd warrant you'll have a trick before long, should Asa have a say in it. Hmm. All right." She turned away from him and squatted over her box while one of the men jumped down from the cart and approached the canvas.

He took a piece of charcoal from his pocket and measured with a short stick from each end and corner of the large rectangle, swiftly making black *X*s along the thick material. He was finished in an instant, it seemed, pocketing the charcoal and returning to the cart while the two men on the ground began trimming away the parts outside the charcoaled marks with tapered blades. They gathered up the scraps as efficiently as kittens gathering yarn and were gone, leaving the blonde woman to pull her case closer to the edge of the canvas.

She took a brush from the box, its bristle head round and fat, its handle long and worn smooth. Then she uncorked one of the crocks and dipped the brush inside. A moment later, she was swinging her slender arm in wide, smooth strokes, leaving bold black arches on the cloth. Roman stepped closer to watch from above her.

She glanced over her shoulder. "I'm called Fran," she offered. "I do portraits. And this," she added, now swooping the brush in the opposite direction, until Roman could make out two elliptical shapes, mirroring each other on one half of the canvas.

"You're the one who painted all the wagons?" he asked. The designs he'd seen were quite impressive.

She nodded her head but didn't look at him again, absorbed in the image taking shape before her.

Roman looked around the camp; it seemed everyone was busy with some specific task. He saw no sign of Isra, and that caused him to frown a bit, but he let the annoyance go. The men in the cart bed were now half surrounded by a cage of wooden staves that seemed to grow taller by the moment. Roman spied a discarded hammer on the edge of the cart bed. He looked around again and saw that—besides the old hag who still tended the fire and seemed now to be talking to herself—not one person was idle.

Save him.

Roman walked toward the driver's seat and deposited Lou on the arm of the bell stake; he would have to devise for the falcon a place of his own soon, and fashion another tether and hood as well. But for now, Roman walked to the back of the cart and picked up the hammer, reaching out at once to steady a tall upright for one of the men while he set a tapered iron pin.

The man looked up with an expression of surprise. "Well, all right, big fellow; have at it," he invited in a jolly voice.

Roman slid the hammer up in his palm and banged the pin home in two blows. He looked up and saw that the blonde Fran was watching him once more over her shoulder. Even though she did not smile, Roman noticed again how comely she was.

"Look lively, now," the man holding the stave called, and Roman looked back in time to take hold of the crosspiece while he lashed it to the upright.

And just like that, Roman felt part of the band.

Isra stalked toward the tall wagon that was Kahn's prison, her stomach fluttery and light as Asa van Groen strode along at her side.

What was she doing?

What had she talked Roman Berg into?

Her sudden display of bravado was threatened as old fears rose up within her. She had no idea what she was doing, thinking to join this band of mad and thieving performers, or why. It was just as likely she would fail in her mission to save the exotic beast; he would die from his captivity any matter, or kill her while she was trying to help him.

Or the band could turn on Isra and Roman, robbing them, leaving them destitute on the road. If they found out who they were, that Roman had a large bounty on his head, they would surely betray them for the coin his capture would bring.

But the troubling thoughts wafted away like smoke as she spied the strangely dressed Dracus emerging from the wood beyond the wagon, two long, gray carcasses dangling from his hand. He held them aloft.

"The best I could do, mistress," he called out, his solemn face hopeful.

Isra nodded to him and held out her hand.

Van Groen raised a long arm between Isra and the hunter. "I'll throw them in; you've come close enough to danger this day."

Isra felt her temper flare and she shoved van Groen's arm down so forcefully that it caused the man to step back to keep his balance.

"He shall not eat in such filth," she declared. Dracus came to a halt and looked between the pair with wide eyes in the awkward silence. She ignored the hunter as she continued to address van Groen, who now regarded her with an air of wariness.

"Where is the spade? The water and soap that are needed?"

"I can have them for you in an instant for certain," van Groen allowed. "I am thrilled beyond measure that you have agreed to go on with us, but perhaps we should establish exactly who is in charge of this endeavor," he said with raised eyebrows.

"Indeed," Isra said, and the tremble returned to the pit of her stomach. It brought to mind all the men in her life—and the women, too—who had asserted their authority over her mind, her freedom, her body.

Never again, Isra thought to herself. And *never again* began at that moment.

"So let us establish it," she continued. "I shall have free rein with Kahn. I shall order his care and needs, and my requests are to be heeded. If you think to command me in any way, we will take our leave as my lord wished to do." She stared into Asa van Groen's brown eyes and refused to let her gaze waver; there was too much at stake now, both for herself and Roman and the tiger. "Do you agree or no?"

To her surprise, Asa threw back his elegantly coiffed head and laughed. "So completely perfect!" he shouted. "Yes, my queen! Yes, I will obey." His eyes were still crinkled at the corners when he looked at her. "And now you must understand that I can't risk my life or any of the others' to clean the crate to your precise specifications."

Isra's heart pounded in her chest as she realized the man's shrewdness. She turned toward the wagon. "Is there another entrance?"

"Yes," van Groen said. "It's actually an old prison wagon." He walked to the side of the cart and raised his arm, pointing to a line of round holes down the center of the box. "Iron bars can be inserted here to make two cells."

Her eyebrows rose. "The wooden walls can be removed?"

"They can, but the walls support the bars," van Groen warned.

"I see." She didn't relish the idea of being inside such a close, dark space with the animal, but it appeared she had little choice. "Have the bars fetched and send the supplies I asked for. Quickly, if you please, before the meat cools."

It seemed only moments before a team of men arrived bearing the long black cylinders and shoved them through the wooden panels of the wagon, securing them on the far side with pins. While Isra waited, a pair of children brought a bucket of water and a rough cake of soap, someone else a hoary broom and a long, flat bladed spade.

Isra motioned for the children to come closer and then squatted down so that she was on eye level with them. "Thank you for helping Kahn," she said. "Would you like to help him further?"

Both children nodded, their eyes wide.

"Go into yonder field and gather up as much dried grass and brush as you can. Put it into a pile here by the wagon. Lots and lots, yes? As tall a mountain as you can build."

The children nodded again and turned in a run.

Isra rose from her crouch and picked up the spade. "Open the door."

Van Groen himself once more scaled the ramp and then stepped onto the tall rear wheel with only one boot this time, unlatching the door before swinging it wide.

Isra marched up the narrow plank and passed into the dark rectangle. Her eyes searched the gloom of the far side of the box as she tried to breathe through her mouth. The stench was terrible. She caught sight of the great, defeated beast lying against the opposite door. His eyes were open and he looked at her, but Isra could see the despair in those dull yellow orbs.

Isra began shoveling, always facing the tiger, throwing spadesful of filth behind her through the opening. She was finished in only moments, although when she backed toward the door and held the spade through the opening she could feel the wetness beginning to soak through her gown beneath her arms.

"Broom," she called as the spade was snatched from her hand. "Soap and water."

Isra swept as much as she could through the doorway before tossing the entire cake of soap in the full bucket and then dunking the stiff bristles of the broom in the water. She felt for the firm soap on the bottom and pushed the broom into it.

Isra began to scrub the wagon, the tiger watching her the entire time, never moving, never making a sound, only following her movements with his tired eyes.

When she was finished, she dragged the bucket back toward the doorway and tossed the broom to van Groen. She emptied the bucket out the side of the opening and then threw that out as well. "Ready to remove the bars," she said, and then she held out her hand toward Dracus.

The man came halfway up the ramp, holding forth the rabbits he'd so quickly procured, and Isra took them, turning back inside and facing the tiger.

"Hie, Kahn," she said in a low voice and held up the rabbits by their long feet. She walked toward the bars. "These are for you."

She stopped only an arm's length away from the horizontal iron cylinders, the rabbits nearly touching the questionable divider. The bars were nearly a foot apart; should the tiger desire to suddenly rise and reach through them to claw at her, she would be dead.

Isra swallowed. "Hie, Kahn. Hie," she repeated and shook the rabbits as if the motion would loosen the tremor from her own voice.

The tiger's nostrils flared, his whiskers twitched.

"Hie. Up, Kahn," Isra urged.

The tiger rolled onto its elbows at first, and then with something that sounded like a groan and a sigh, it began to pull itself to its feet.

"Yes," Isra praised as she backed slightly away. "Hie, Kahn. Up." She crouched down and lay the carcasses in the center of the clean space she had created and continued to back away. "Remove the bars," she called over her shoulder as she reached the doorway. "The lowest ones first. *Now*," she commanded when no one moved immediately, fearing Kahn would be frustrated by his inability to reach the meat and associate Isra with torment.

"Aren't you going to come out first, mistress?"

"Do as I ask," Isra said.

Isra watched as Kahn flinched and hesitated when the bar was withdrawn. But then the tiger stuck his head forward, his wide nose waving back and forth in the direction of the rabbits. The second bar slid back, allowing the tiger to push his head through into the half of the wagon where Isra stood near the door.

"Hie, Kahn," she said again.

The third bar withdrew into the wood, and the tiger slowly crept toward the two gray lumps of fur. Isra could see the saliva starting to run from the tiger's mouth. He glanced up at Isra, and she made certain to hold his gaze before she backed out onto the ramp.

"Hie, up. Come and eat."

Kahn slunk fully into the other half of the wagon. Without looking away from the beast, she commanded the bars be returned. The tiger jumped and spun around with a warning scream as the bars slid past with a gritty hiss.

"Easy, Kahn," Isra called, drawing the tiger's attention back to her. He met her eyes and then lay down, curling his front paws around the meat. He looked away at his first crunching, tearing bite, and Isra reached out to close the door gently. She dropped the bar into place and then turned to walk down the ramp.

"He will need more meat," she said to Dracus, who nodded and set off into the wood once more. Isra picked up the bucket and tossed it to van Groen before retrieving the discarded spade and broom. She turned her back on him as she walked toward the other end of the wagon, her work not yet half done.

Chapter 11

Roman and Lou went looking for Isra not long after the sun had reached its zenith, turning the autumn day warm and bright. The camp was alive with clatter and traffic, folk passing to and fro carrying stakes and scaffolds from the fire, clothes hung out to dry from a quick morning's wash; harnesses jangled, wheels creaked. No one stared at Roman or paid him any mind at all really, and he had come to the determination that, to such an unusual band of people, he was nothing unique in any way.

Unlike blending into the brown wool population of Melk, where every man was an identical part of the whole, each individual in van Groen's group was peculiarly distinctive, in some cases in highly bizarre ways. No one was strange because everyone was strange.

Roman approached the tall, rectangular wagon that was decorated like a forest canopy and saw Isra sitting beneath an actual tree not far from the wagon's tongue. Her knees were drawn up beneath skirts that were dirty and dark with damp. She drank from a metal cup while Asa van Groen leaned against the tree next to her, chatting. Isra saw Roman right away, and he was surprised at the pleasure he felt when she smiled at him.

She began to rise, and although both van Groen and Roman reached out to assist her, it was Roman's hand she grasped. Van Groen quickly pulled his velvet-clad arm behind his back.

She looked tired but satisfied as she greeted him. "My lord."

He wanted to correct her again, but it was dangerous to reveal their identities to such a band of semicriminals as this. Especially before their leader, who seemed to be observing Roman and Isra very closely.

"Have you arranged things to your liking?" Roman asked.

Isra's smile returned. "Kahn is much happier. It is my hope that he sees improvement with each new day."

"Well done, then," Roman said, echoing the praise she'd given him earlier.

Van Groen stepped forward. "It will have to do for now," he said, his eyes flicking to the bustling camp beyond them. "We are moving too late as it is. But we are not so far from the Venice road; we will be able to travel much farther into the night than we could on yonder path."

"You plan to perform in Venice, then," Roman repeated.

"If we are lucky. It is in the many small villages before and after that we hope to see the bulk of our coin. The farther south we go, the weather shall warm, and so shall our welcomes." Van Groen signaled with one finger to someone behind Roman before smiling up at him. "I am needed. Will the pair of you walk with me?"

Roman turned, irritated when Van Groen took up Isra's other side.

"I would prefer you travel close to my wagon so that I might look after you until you find your way in our little family," van Groen said. "But I have a feeling you wish to remain as unseen as possible on the road, and as it is I who must contend with constables and the like, it would be best if you found a place farther back in the band." He looked ahead and smiled, his voice gentling to a wistfulness that sounded surprisingly genuine. "Ah. I see Fran has performed her magic once again."

Roman turned his head to regard their now covered cart bed, and saw Isra's eyes widen as she took in the black outline of the bird on the side of the canvas, its wings spread, its hooked beak in profile. The silhouette was filled in with bright gold and surrounded by shooting rays of what Roman supposed was the sun.

"It is beautiful," Isra said.

"Don't stop unless you are stopped," van Groen said, his wistfulness vanishing as he turned to walk backward. Roman suspected he wanted to keep Isra in his sight for as long as possible. "If your conveyance isn't equipped with . . . conveniences, and you must disembark"—he raised his eyebrows and gave a meaningful pause—"you'll have to run to catch up. We mustn't separate for any reason." He raised his hand toward both of them, but his eyes were on Isra. "Until this evening."

She turned to Roman then. "Have we made a mistake?"

Roman looked into her eyes for a long moment, wanting to reassure her but reluctant to lie. There was too much at stake for that.

"I don't yet know," he said at last.

She nodded once and then, to his surprise, she gave him a smile. It was a weary smile, but a smile all the same.

"I suppose we shall soon find out."

He lifted Lou from his shoulder and onto the staff that had only yesterday held the censer, refashioned by Roman's own hand with the scraps left over from the cart's shelter. He hadn't had time to craft a tether or hood, and now he didn't think he would. Lou had proven that he was loathe to be away from Roman, flying all the way from Melk to find him. There was no reason to believe the falcon wouldn't remain close to his side.

Roman held out his hand, helping Isra up onto the driver's seat, inexplicably glad that she would also be sitting beside him on their journey. As she stepped up, Roman caught a flash of white blonde hair, and he turned his head to see Fran, gaining the seat of a wagon close to them. She raised her hand to him before she took up her own reins.

Roman waved and then hoisted himself up beside Isra. Perhaps joining up with van Groen's group would turn out to be a mistake. But in this moment, Roman felt very good about the situation indeed. He smiled and shook the reins to spur their donkey.

He didn't see Fran watching them closely as he turned the wagon in a wide circle to join the line of the caravan.

But Isra did.

It took no more than an hour for Isra to recognize that she was suddenly the happiest she had been since she was a young girl, when she had still been without knowledge of the realities of her life.

She was seated next to Roman Berg in the crisp, sunshiny autumn air, for all the world to see. For the first several moments, the exposure made Isra anxious. She could not recall when she had ever experienced such blatant freedom, and the thought that anyone at all might look upon her—traveling with this man, in a cart as a wealthy woman might, as if it was her rightful place—was so foreign that she trembled.

But then she grasped the edge of the wooden seat and leaned far to the side to look at the line stretching ahead of and also trailing behind them. She saw the top of Kahn's tall wagon and imagined how frightened the tiger must have been and for how long. It was her place now to care for him, and the idea that she was responsible once more for another living thing beside herself calmed her, and also brought to mind the man next to her.

"Have you eaten, my lord?" she asked.

Roman chuckled. "No, *my lady*, I have not. I have regretted my sudden departure from our own camp this morning several times. In preparing our cart for travel, there was little time for a rest, and I'd wager you were too well occupied to notice your own hunger."

Isra nodded while her cheeks heated and then stepped over the seat to escape beneath the arch of the boldly painted canvas now covering the cart bed. She took a moment to slow her breathing, cool her cheeks.

My lady. Our cart.

What a wonderful fantasy that would be to indulge.

But she pushed even the imaginings of it away as she looked around the newly fashioned interior of their conveyance. It was a marvel really how completely it made a shelter. Isra was easily able to access their hidden compartment and, thankfully, the supplies they'd left within had not been discovered when their cart had been stolen that morn.

Likely the capable and determined Roman hadn't given them enough time to explore the cart thoroughly.

Isra wanted to change her gown, dirtied and damp from cleaning Kahn's wagon, but the only other costume she had was barely any cleaner. She did don the other overdress, though; at least it was dry.

After depositing several items in a turned-up portion of her skirt, she emerged back onto the driver's seat. In but a moment, she and Roman were sharing the remainder of the dried fruit and cheese and wine. His grin in her direction meant more to her than the word of thanks he murmured.

She had done well this day. Very well.

It was midafternoon when the caravan began to slow. Isra craned her neck to see what might be causing the delay, but the trees crowding the curving road to either side prevented her from viewing farther than three carts ahead. Slower and slower they went, until at last they were around the bend, and Isra saw they must be joining the wider road to Venice, and there was a village at the crossroads.

Isra leaned this way and that, trying to see ahead without appearing anxious as Roman drove their donkey around the sharp curve in turn. The hopelessly slender man from camp—Barnaby, Asa had called him—commanding the cart before theirs suddenly turned around and pantomimed a sign Isra didn't at first understand. She looked to Roman, who held up both palms toward the man.

What?

Barnaby cupped a hand around his mouth and called back, "Moving through!" Then he pointed past their cart and waved his gangly arm again.

"Ah," Roman murmured and signaled his understanding. Then he adjusted his seat to lean around the side of their shelter and repeated the gesture to the wagon behind theirs. By the time Roman faced forward once more, Barnaby had gained his feet behind his donkey, the reins secured beneath one foot on the driver's seat while he juggled what appeared to Isra to be brightly painted balls.

Their artistic decorations caused Isra's mind to turn to the blond-haired Fran, whose coloring so resembled Roman's. The woman had watched their wagon as they'd left camp, and Isra had somehow recognized the longing in Fran's eyes. She felt a shimmer of jealousy in her chest. How different would her life be now if she had been born of the same culture as the man next to her? Would he then look upon her not as a wretch in need of pity and rescue but as a woman of value? Thankfully, the entertainment ahead distracted her from such useless imaginings.

The villagers standing to either side of the road appeared to be entertained as well. Somewhere fore or aft of their cart—perhaps both, by the sound of the jangled melodies—people began to play instruments. As the caravan crawled through the small cluster of buildings, Isra saw Barnaby reach up and snatch an apple out of the air. Without so much as a wobble, the fruit joined the airborne circle of balls and the people along the road whistled and clapped. A moment later, a roll of bread arced toward the juggler, and it, too, was included in the act, to the sound of roadside applause.

Isra brought her own hands together in delight without thinking, and at her side, Roman chuckled.

She leaned around the canvas to look at the wagon behind theirs and saw what appeared to be a large woman wearing a beard strumming a lute while she drove her wagon, singing along in a warbling, high-pitched voice. A moment later, she, too, lifted a plump hand to snatch some treat out of the air, tossed to her by the stationary audience. She gave a wave and a smile over her lute, singing all the while.

"The villagers are throwing food," Isra said to Roman.

Roman glanced at her with a smile and a shrug.

Isra looked to the faces lining the road: peasant men and women, several children bundled in woolen clothes but with blackened, bare feet. They looked at her with expectant faces and she gave her best smile and a hesitant wave.

The face of a little girl closest to the cart fell into a disapproving frown and then stuck out her tongue at Isra, her attention going to the lute player behind them. Isra felt her face heat and she looked ahead, but at her side, Roman again laughed out loud. She glanced at him, and the sight of his broad grin disarmed the slight sting of embarrassment she had felt. In a moment, she was chuckling along with him.

"I suppose my performance needs some work," she admitted.

"It matters not," Roman said. "We have supplies, and coin to purchase whatever else we need."

"Not enough to last us the journey," Isra pointed out. "We were to sell the wagon and the donkey in Venice."

Roman shrugged. "Van Groen seems to think we will earn our share. I'm not worried."

"Do you ever worry?" Isra asked.

"No," he said. "I act. If I know my actions will have no effect, I do my best to forget about whatever it is."

Isra wondered if that was the reason Roman Berg had been so successful on his own—sold into hard labor when he was a boy, growing up without the love of a family, building a reputation for himself that had brought him much favor and freedom. Isra thought there was great wisdom hiding behind Roman's brawny exterior.

A man along the road caught her eye then. At first Isra thought he was waving to someone else, but as their cart rolled closer to him, it was clear his attention was for Isra alone.

"Hello! Hello there, pretty lady!" he called, waving his arm in a wide arc. In the crook of his other arm was a small pile of what appeared to be bright persimmons, and he plucked one from the bunch and turned it in his fingertips, waggling his eyebrows at Isra.

And so she tried again, smiling and giving the man a wave, and to her surprise, he tossed the fruit to her just as they passed. Isra huffed a breath of a laugh and turned to hold it up in triumph before Roman. Then she looked back over her shoulder at the man to give him a smile of thanks, but when she did, he grabbed his crotch and shoved his hips toward her, running his tongue around his mouth in a vulgar pantomime.

Isra snapped her head back around, her heart in her throat, her stomach somewhere near the soles of her slippers as a sick, dirty feeling washed over her. She looked at the small, soft piece of fruit still in her hand. It was as if it had suddenly become a length of feces.

"Aren't you going to eat it?" Roman asked. "You earned it."

Isra could barely force herself to swallow. "No. I don't want it. You may have it if you wish it, my lord." She lay the fruit down on the seat between them, fighting the urge to wipe her hand on her skirt. "I would prefer to lie down now."

Roman turned to look at her, a frown across his usually open, handsome face. "Are you unwell?"

Isra shook her head but dropped her eyes. "Only quite tired, my lord."

"Of course," he said. "Take your rest."

She needed no more encouragement, and a moment later she was ensconced in the anonymity of the cart bed. She curled onto her side clutching her sack of borrowed possessions, her eyes wide and dry as she stared into the dim shadows of the rocking cart. A cold, heavy stone was in her stomach now, representing the weight of her shame.

Everyone knows what you are. You can never outrun it. You can never change it. It is in your blood, and that man on the side of the road knew it the moment he saw you. You can play at being respectable all you like—in your cart with your handsome blond man—but he would never have you, and you are a fool for thinking any man would.

Whore.

Roman kept the little donkey at an even pace as they moved through the village squatting at the crossroads. He enjoyed watching the faces of the inhabitants as the caravan lumbered along the road, how happy they were to simply watch the wagons and characters roll past, and wondered why van Groen had given the order to move through rather than stop and turn a goodly amount of coin into their pockets. But as it at last became Roman's turn to pass the fringe of buildings marking the proper end to the village, he saw the cluster of men on horseback, several of them with bows resting upon the fronts of their saddles and all of them wearing wary scowls.

The caravan was clearly unwelcome.

Roman turned his face only slightly away from the men as he passed them, attempting to hide his face and at the same time not draw attention to the fact that he was attempting to do so. But the men were more interested in admiring the different decorations on the sides and canvases of the wagons—including his own—and Roman realized in that moment that Fran's duty within the band not only made the conveyances beautiful to look at but also served as a distraction from the individuals within.

It should not surprise him that such a ruse was so well thought out. After all, van Groen and many in his band had likely been living this life for years and knew how to go about it. He was reluctant to give the man any credit at all, remembering the way he looked at Isra, but it did make him feel better about following van Groen across the continent. It was clear the man was very careful about his actions and those of the people who followed him, and the last thing he would want would be to endanger their livelihood.

And, although he truly didn't want to admit it, Roman had to give nod to the idea that he much preferred traveling through this village openly as part of a group. It was unlikely that even one of the villagers would remember his face, but had he driven through alone, many might have recalled the large blond man in the small, plain cart.

In monk's robes.

Ringing a bell as he went through.

Roman chuckled to himself. Really, being part of the caravan or traveling as a monk transporting a diseased body were two sides of a coin. In both instances, Roman and Isra were hiding in plain sight. Neither ruse could be more obvious, and Roman thought Valentine Alesander would very much approve of this turn of events.

Constantine, perhaps not as much.

Roman did wish there was a way to send word to his friends at Melk to let them know of the change in plans, but relaying a written message was too much of a risk. Besides, informing the general that things were no longer following the agreed-upon strategy would only cause him to worry needlessly until Roman returned. There was nothing any of his friends could do to help; it was up to Roman whether he succeeded or failed.

And that suited him very much.

Acceptance of the situation at last settled in his mind for the time being, he allowed his thoughts to turn to the mysterious woman sleeping in the cart just behind him. He didn't know what had upset her so suddenly and thoroughly that she had gone skittering beneath the canvas. Roman sifted through events leading up to her escape but could not identify the cause of her distress.

Perhaps she had wanted the persimmon she'd won but felt she must give it to Roman? He rejected that idea; Isra Tak'Ahn didn't seem the kind to pout or be inclined to stinginess. And besides, the fruit had been on the verge of rot. Roman had spat out the first cloying bite and then tossed the rest of the thing into the weeds.

It was as if she was an animal, once domesticated and content, who had since been abandoned to the wild and forced to survive. She'd forgotten that not every situation was a danger, every person a threat. There would be an hour, perhaps two, when she seemed as though she was at ease, and then with little outward provocation she would retreat in an elaborate defense. As if some invisible demon tormented her without warning.

The sun was sinking low in the sky, turning the gathering clouds heavenly shades of yellow and pink, when the caravan began to slow noticeably again. Soon Roman saw one of the men he had bested that morn making his way along the caravan on horseback, riding alongside each cart in turn.

The man turned his horse from the cart before Roman's and waited for him to draw near before urging his mount to walk alongside the driver's seat.

"Good day, big fellow," the man said affably enough, although even Roman had to wince at his purpling eye and swollen, crusty nose. "How has the road treated you thus far?"

"It is well," Roman returned and glanced at the man. "My regrets for your nose."

But the man waved his apology away. "I've had worse. Listen, pulling off soon. The boss bartered with a farmer for his field and pond. Pull all through and round, right?"

Roman nodded. "Right." He wasn't sure what "pull all through and round" meant, but he was certain he could figure it out.

"And get right to setting up. They'll come about within the hour, I reckon."

"First thing," Roman promised, not having any idea what the man had just said.

"They call me Zeus, the Greek. Good to have you with us." Zeus turned his horse away to wait for the next wagon.

Roman adjusted in his seat and sat up taller, alert for the first signs that the caravan was leaving the road. It was only perhaps a quarter hour before he saw the wagons turning onto a rutted farm path. The rolling of their own cart dipping into the ditch must have woken Isra, for as the wheels rolled up and into the field, she emerged onto the driver's seat at his side.

He didn't think she seemed at all more rested than when she'd disappeared beneath the canvas; in fact, her eyes were swollen. Roman was too unfamiliar with the moods of the gentler sex to know if her appearance was the result of a nap or weeping.

"It is not yet night," she observed, smoothing her hands up over her cheeks and into her hair.

"Van Groen received permission for a field and pond. Perhaps he means to take advantage of a camp where no one need fear being tossed."

Isra shrugged and raised her eyebrows.

They didn't speak for several moments as Roman maneuvered the cart around the long pond, keeping in line. There was another of the brawny men directing the caravan, and Roman realized that the party was forming a single, enormous circle in the field. Even as he was halting the little gray donkey, people were spilling out of carts to the interior and exterior of the circle, bringing cooking apparatus and firewood to the center and setting up poles and awnings on the sides of the carts that fronted the circle.

Everyone seemed to be in a rather large hurry.

Roman looked at Isra, who looked at him.

"What are we to do?" she asked.

But he had no time to come up with a reply before the blond-haired Fran appeared near his thigh, a stack of white cloths in her hands.

"The two of you must have brought us good fortune," she said and then offered up the material to Roman. "For *the queen.* It's not perfect, but it's all I could lay hand to. It will do for tonight."

Roman took the things and turned to give them to Isra. A clatter sounded as something solid fell out of the folds and landed at their feet. When Roman retrieved it and held it aloft, it seemed to be some sort of woven headpiece, coated in plaster and then painted a bright yellow. He turned back to Fran.

"What are they?"

"Her costume," Fran said with a blink. "For the show."

"What show?" Isra interjected, leaning forward to look at the woman.

"Think you anyone at all can just join up with us for nothing, order us about, and disrupt things?" Fran snipped. "We all work. If you don't intend to keep your word, I suppose you might want to take it up with Asa."

She glanced at Roman with something like an apology in her eyes. "The people will be along soon. This will be the first opportunity in days we've had to try to earn back some of what that beast has cost us." Her eyes flicked to Isra for only an instant. "So she might want to hurry along with any further demands she has." Fran turned and stalked away.

Roman felt the amateurish headpiece being pulled from his grasp, and when he looked again at Isra, she was climbing down from the cart, the pieces of her costume wadded into one hand as she lowered herself to the ground.

"Where are you going?" he asked.

She glanced up at him as she shook out her skirts. "I am taking it up with Asa." Then she began walking around the little gray donkey.

Roman stood in the seat, for some reason uneasy about her seeking out the dark-haired leader of the menagerie. "Isra!"

She halted and looked up at him, her tone calm and accommodating but her fine eyebrows knit together. "Yes, my lord?"

He looked at her for a moment, not at all sure what he really wanted to say.

Don't go to him?

Stay with me?

"You don't have to do anything you don't wish to do," he said at last, the words sounding weak even to his own ears.

Her face relaxed a bit and she gave him a smile Roman imagined would be better bestowed upon a child who'd said something clever but naïve.

"Be not troubled by it, my lord." Her smile tightened and she turned away, disappearing around the next wagon, seeming completely prepared to take care of the thing herself.

Roman stared after her, thinking that, unfortunately, she probably was all too well familiar with doing just that.

Chapter 12

Isra found van Groen near the back of his paneled wagon, having a tall, elaborate collar adjusted around his neck by a boy in late adolescence. A squire of sorts he appeared, complete with an open satchel at his feet from which spilled boar's hair brushes, bits of ribbon, a rag stained with blacking.

"Ah, there she is!" van Groen said as the boy bent to the bag once more, and Asa fussed with the stiff embroidered velvet. "Why aren't you dressed? You may avail yourself of the privacy of my own wagon if it pleases you."

"You did not tell me we would show Kahn today," Isra said. "You did not tell me the caravan would stop."

"I didn't tell you because I didn't know, my dear," he said, stepping toward her and reaching out, as if to take her elbow and lead her to the back of his cart. "It's not as if we adhere to a schedule. You must dress. There is no time to—"

"He is not ready." Isra pulled away from him and stepped back. "And neither am I."

Van Groen stopped and seemed to force himself to take a breath, hang a smile on his face.

"I had no idea we would be granted such an opportunity," Asa said as the squire approached from behind and began brushing at his tunic. "It is rare that we come across a land holder willing to host us so close to a village. As I'm sure you noticed, the folk were all too eager for entertainment, even if the governing officials of the town were not so hospitable. I don't know that we will have another such chance to fill our purses before Venice."

Isra only stared at him.

Asa sighed and then looked over his shoulder. "That's fine, Gunar." He turned back to Isra as the boy gathered his things. "If you don't wish to participate this first time, I'm certainly not going to force you." He held up a long, pale finger, its nail white and rounded past the tip. "However, Kahn *will* be displayed tonight. If you wish to have any say about how that unfolds"—he glanced at the costume still hanging down in her right hand—"you will get dressed. Quickly," he added, glancing past her ear for only an instant.

Isra frowned as he closed the gap between them and grasped her—albeit gently—by the very edges of her shoulders. "Don't be afraid," he said quietly, looking into her eyes as he smiled at her. "You are a uniquely beautiful woman who has an amazing way with a magnificent creature. If all you acquiesce to is to stand near his crate and smile, it will benefit us all. And I, for one, would greatly wish to see that."

His smile deepened for a moment and then he released her and moved away, forcing Isra to turn and follow him with her eyes.

"I'll wait for you as long as I am able," he promised over his shoulder, and Isra saw Gunar trot to catch up with van Groen and press the long-handled whip into his hand.

Isra stood there as the sun began to sink even farther beyond the bare trees, draping the field and the circle of wagons in crisp shadows anticipatory of the coming night. She smelled woodsmoke on the air already, heard melodies being strung together as the musicians warmed to their craft. And now, emerging from the gloom in the direction of the road, came the first of the villagers—children running ahead of the adults into the barren field, being transformed into a fair by the burly men setting tall torches in the spaces between the wagons.

Asa van Groen was not going to force her to display herself, regardless of what that icy blonde had said.

You don't have to do anything you don't wish to do.

Roman Berg had advised her the same.

Two men, telling Isra that she had the freedom to choose.

The only problem was, she was so used to being forced either into action by threats of violence or into disobedience by performing the opposite of what was expected of her, she had no earthly idea what to do just then.

She had given her word to van Groen that she would participate in the caravan's entertainment; she hadn't known it would be this soon.

If she did perform, she could earn coin she and Roman Berg might sore be in need of in the coming weeks.

It was all up to her.

Isra looked down at the costume in her hands, the headpiece heavy-looking, possibly resembling a gold crown if viewed from afar and if the audience perhaps squinted a bit. The white cloth material was not silk, but a very fine flax all the same.

How many times had she wished she was someone with power, with wealth enough to command a change in her situation? In her hands, she held the persona of a queen. Or an approximation of one. She could be someone else for a night. All she had to do was change her clothes.

Isra turned and looked at the paneled shelter of Asa van Groen's wagon. The door was closed, but the hasp swung away from the frame, indicating the leader had left his accommodations unlocked.

Her choice.

Isra blew out a stiff breath from between her lips and strode to the wagon.

By the time Roman unhitched the donkey, secured the wagon, and made his way from the interior of the circle to the outer, torchlit ring with Lou on his shoulder, dusk had leaked away into a clear black night. The air was perfumed with sizzling fat and burning pitch, the smell of unwashed men and the faded scent of lavender water mixed with greasy paint.

All around the perimeter of the carts—whose brightly painted canvases and wooden sides had been set alight by the torches—members of the caravan performed their tricks to groups of villagers of varying sizes. There was the juggler, tossing knives and apples over his head, the portions of fruit growing exponentially as he deftly used the blades in rotation to halve the red fruits as they spun in the air.

The woman and her dogs, smallish beasts who yapped and leaped through willow rings whilst wearing tiny vests, sat on their haunches and howled along in time to Helena's direction with her long, painted wand.

Dracus had set up his target some distance away from the caravan, and the archer amazed the crowd with his accuracy as he shot his bow from varying angles.

The fattest man Roman had ever seen in his life sat on a reinforced chair, his arse spilling over the edges of the seat while he strummed a tiny lute. He appeared to be wearing a lady's gown, and his voice was unnaturally high-pitched through his flowing beard. But it was when Roman came around the front of the cart to watch openly that he saw the scandalously deep cleavage and kohled eyes of the performer.

She caught him staring at her, and her fat, bejeweled fingers left the strings to waggle in Roman's direction.

"Hello, dear," she sang out. There were tiny colored ribbons tied into her impressive beard, and at her side looked to be bins of crafted jewelry for sale.

Roman shook himself out of his stupor long enough to nod politely and move away, continuing his search for Isra.

Someone appeared near his elbow, and Roman looked down to find the blonde artist, Fran, walking alongside him.

"Shall I call you Hans, then?" she said by way of greeting, her eyes lingering on Lou.

"Me or the falcon?" he asked.

She smiled up at him before turning her gaze back to the activity around them as they walked along the fringe of spectators gathered before the wagons.

"It seems as though we might hail from the same part of the world, at least originally. You refuse to tell anyone your name, so I thought of one that is common to our heritage. Hans. Have I guessed correctly?"

Roman couldn't help his smile. "I'm afraid not. You are Norse?" he asked.

Fran nodded her head. "And you?"

"How did you come to be entangled with Asa van Groen's band?" he asked, sidestepping her question.

She chuckled, as if indulging his reticence. "I had need to leave my home suddenly, with only the clothes I wore in my possession. Asa's band was camped between the village and my home. I snuck onto the back of one of the wagons. Hid when they stopped." Roman reached out to stay her as a pair of young boys ran whooping in front of them. He released her right away, although she didn't seem to notice as she turned to watch the boys pass for longer than Roman thought was necessary. Lou flapped his wings in a disgruntled fashion at being jostled.

"One of those was Nickle," she said at last, turning back to walk with Roman again but glancing over her shoulder where the boys had run. "Ten years old in the spring. Resourceful lad. It was he who stole your belongings."

Roman paused to look behind him, although the thief was nowhere to be seen.

"He didn't take your cart at first only because he said he doubted he could have made it back to camp without waking you," Fran said with something of a sad smile. "Any matter, Asa didn't discover I was tagging along with the troupe for several days. Almost a week. It's a good thing he did, else I likely would have starved."

Roman watched her from the corner of his eye. "Someone was chasing you."

She nodded and looked up. "You can sympathize?"

Roman only shrugged.

"Yes, someone was chasing me. I killed my husband on our wedding night, apparently, although I hadn't set out to. I was only ten and six and my husband a very old man. I'm quite certain his heart merely gave out. His just reward, if you ask me."

"Why are you telling me this?" Roman asked.

Fran drew a deep, easy breath in through her nose, her eyes still taking in the crowd milling around the perimeter of the circle. "All here know my story, where I'm from. I'm not so enamored of this life as I once was, but perhaps I can somehow be of help to you in finding your way here." She looked up at him, her face still solemn, sad. She looked as though she wanted to say something further but only shrugged and turned her gaze to the gathering.

Roman nodded, his hands behind his back as he strolled. "Thank you."

"The woman you are with," Fran hedged. "She is wanted, too? Is it because of you that she is, or the other way 'round?"

"Have you seen . . . her?" Roman asked, catching himself just before he let Isra's name slip.

Fran rolled her pale lips inward with a little smile, as if surrendering to the idea that Roman was not going to talk about the dark beauty traveling with him.

"No," she said. "Not since she came from Asa's wagon." Fran looked up at him, daring him to think what she was alluding to. "I thought that was where you were going just now—that you knew."

"I knew she was going to find van Groen," Roman said, trying to mask his unease. "But I've been settling our wagon and don't yet know where van Groen is camped."

Fran raised her pale eyebrows and scanned the ground as her slippers at the end of her long legs kicked out before her. "Ah. *Our wagon*. But she is not your woman." She looked up at him.

"We are traveling companions," Roman said feeling the back of his neck heat. "What of you?" he asked, turning the tables on Fran's inquisition of his personal life. "Have you no mate in this band of merry performers?"

"No," she said. "Not for a while anyway." She gestured with her head, and Roman looked to where she'd indicated, not realizing he'd been studying her fine profile. "We've arrived just in time."

Roman stopped a fair distance behind the sizable crowd gathered in front of a draped rectangle of curtain. More torches had been placed around this area of the camp, and the many flames lit up the ocher-colored fabric better than any gilded candelabra at a noble feast. Although he and Fran were at least ten paces behind the crowd, Roman's height gave him the advantage of seeing everything as clearly as if he was in the front row.

Suddenly, a slinky, rippling shadow flowed from the seam of the curtains, revealing a coif of dark hair that was somehow swept even higher than Roman remembered. Asa van Groen held his long arms out from his sides, the pale skin of his hands seeming to glow. All his wide white teeth showed in his broad smile, and even from such a distance, Roman fancied he could see the sparkle in the man's eyes.

"Gentle folk!" he called out in a rich, robust voice. "Yours have been favored to be the very *first* western eyes to behold the miraculous and *dan*-gerous spectacle that waits behind this curtain. *If . . .* you dare look upon it." Van Groen's mesmerizing voice inflected the words in such a way that even Roman found himself leaning forward, as if he'd no idea what was behind the curtain.

He felt Fran's shoulder press into his arm. "He's very good, isn't he?" Roman nodded.

"For it is *not* a sight for the faint of heart—or for those *easily* swept up in the tide of *romantic longing!*" Van Groen paced the width of the curtain now, his gaze flowing over the audience, his white hands waving hypnotically in time with his words. "*Thousands* of miles! From the *strangest* land ever inhabited by man! Where the people are ruled by golden *statues* and *beastly sorcerers*, and where the sand stretches away farther than the horizon at sea and a simple traveler might wander and wander . . ." Here, van Groen held his arm before him and stared past his fingertips before whispering, "*Forever.*"

He whipped around to the crowd again. "*But tonight!*" he cried, causing a good portion of the audience to startle and then laugh nervously at themselves. "Through a *highly* secret agreement with *none other* than the *king* of that very land himself, I bring to you *two* of Egypt's most prized and coveted jewels. *Kahn the Terrible* and his mistress, the *queen of the River Nile!*" Van Groen held up his arms again and stepped to the side as the curtains split in the center and spread open.

The crowd gasped and clapped.

And there was Isra, standing before the wagon with van Groen's whip in one hand, looking rather startled herself at her abrupt revelation. Her dark eyes were wide beneath the awkward crown upon her head, but Roman had to admit that, from a distance, the complete costume was quite impressive. The white cloth he'd only seen folded in her hands was a long, flowing sheath. It shimmered in the torchlight against her raven hair and dusky skin, and when she raised her hands to indicate the cage behind her, Roman saw a cape attached at her shoulders, knotted tassels along the undersides of her arms.

The painted wooden sides of Kahn's conveyance had been dropped down to reveal ceiling-to-floor bars, and in the far left corner of the crate the tiger lay, his glittering eyes taking in the crowd apathetically. He licked each of his cheek pads in turn and then looked away.

The applause died away after several moments, and soon the only sounds in the chilly night air were the shuffling of feet, the hissing of the flames, the sounds of the night insects. On Roman's shoulder, Lou gave a pair of short cheeps.

"Does it do a trick?" someone from the crowd shouted.

" 'E's only lying there."

"I want to touch it."

"I want my penny back."

The grumblings grew louder and more discontented with each passing moment, and Roman felt a knot of unease in his stomach as he saw the panic creeping across Isra's face.

"Uh-oh," Fran murmured at his side. "She's losing them."

"How can she lose them?" Roman demanded. "She hasn't done anything."

"Exactly," Fran said, and her eyebrows flinched up a bit. "Don't worry. Asa won't let it carry on much longer. He'll save her, mark my words."

Roman's frown grew deeper, as if his growing concern was burrowing trenches in his face while the crowd's calls became more sinister.

"I don't think it's real. It ain't movin'."

"Strike it with the whip!"

"I've paid me coin. I'll see it move," said a skinny, balding man, and he strode toward the wagon with his stick held like a battle sword, as if he had not the least intention of paying Isra even the courtesy of a nod.

Isra's eyes went wide as she watched the man approach the bars. Then her fine brows knit together, and in the next instant the whistle and crack of the whip rang out and the crowd once more gasped itself into polite attention.

The walking stick now lay in the dirt at her feet. The man's face was slack for a moment, and he rubbed the hand that had so recently gripped the stick.

"Ay, now!" he cried out in a warbly, wounded tone.

"Do not approach Kahn," Isra said, the accent of her words sounding so exotic and smooth and beautiful, Roman felt a tingle in his ears and gooseflesh on his arms.

He leaned toward Fran. "I don't think she'll be requiring van Groen's assistance."

"I should say not," Fran whispered in return, and Roman could see the perhaps grudging admiration on the blonde's face.

"All of you," Isra continued, turning toward the crowd. "For your own safety, I must ask you to stay back from the cage. This . . . this tiger"—she paused, licked her lips—"has a reach twice the height of a grown man. His claws are . . . over a foot in length." The crowd murmured worryingly. "Should you come too near, he will reach through the bars and pull you in." She paused again. "The parts of you that fit between them."

"Thank you, Queen," the man who'd thought to breach the cage said, dropping to one knee before Isra and bowing his head. "Thank you for saving my life."

Isra looked down at him with such a perfect expression of royal haughtiness, Roman wanted to cheer. "Take your cane and go."

Once the man had melted back into the crowd, Isra turned her attention to them again.

"The tiger is hypnotic, magical. There are many legends from my land about his strength and power. From his teeth and claws drip venom. In a blink"—she snapped her fingers and the crowd seemed to flinch—"he will have appeared and pounced on you. You have no chance," she said, shaking her head as if in regret.

Roman happened to catch a glimpse of Asa van Groen, leaning against one of the curtain poles beyond the edge of the crowd. His arms were crossed over his velvet-clad chest, and he was smiling at Isra. This caused Roman to frown, but only for a moment, as the woman in white demanded his attention as well.

"Only I, mistress of the wild Kahn, have any hope of survival," she said. "And so now, I will risk my life for your pleasure."

"What is she doing?" Fran murmured.

"I don't know," Roman said with growing unease as he watched Isra walk to the back of the wagon. A young man stood on a rear wheel with one hand on the door latch and what appeared to be a brace of rabbits in his other fist.

Isra placed one slippered foot on the ramp and then held out the hand not gripping the whip to take the rabbits. She nodded to him, but then seemed to remember the crowd, leaning forward in anticipation.

She turned her face slightly toward them and commanded, "Open the cage!" The lad swung the door wide and Isra started up the ramp.

"She's goin' *in there*!"

"No, my lady—don't!"

"Oh, mercy, I can't look."

Roman, too, felt more than a little trepidation at Isra entering the wagon before all these people. Even though she had done as much earlier this very day, she had been separated from the beast then and Kahn had since eaten. Perhaps he would be feeling stronger, more resentful of his space being invaded by this human. Roman wanted to call out to Isra as the crowd was doing, but he would not distract her. Isra was doing as she wished and, in truth, she had everyone in the field enthralled, villager and performer alike—especially Roman.

So he tightened his jaw and watched, controlling his breathing as if he could send a sense of calm to the woman no one could take their eyes from.

As soon as Isra crossed the threshold, the lad on the wheel shut the door behind her and dropped the bar in place. Isra was trapped now. If the tiger chose to attack, there would be little chance of getting her out of the cage before she was mauled. The torchlight rippled over her white gown and the crowd was so silent Roman could almost hear individual breaths from the audience over his own.

"Hie, Kahn!" Isra called out. "Hie! Up!"

The tiger stared at Isra for what seemed to Roman to be an eternity but was likely only a heartbeat. And then he began to pull his great, lithe mass from the corner with a low growl, growing longer between the bars, like a striped tide rising.

The crowd gave a muffled gasp at seeing the beast uncoiled and at attention, and they gasped once more as Isra took a deliberate step toward the tiger. Roman forced himself to swallow, to remain still.

"Hie, Kahn!" she commanded again, and the tiger took another rolling, hesitant step toward her. She held up the brace of rabbits.

Roman thought he would shout out despite himself when Kahn suddenly reared up on his hind legs with a scream, pawing at the air with one great forearm. In the next instant, Isra flung the pair of rabbits and sent them spinning across the floor of the cage. The tiger pounced on the carcasses as they shot past him, turning himself away from Isra and causing the cage to rock wildly.

Isra backed to the door and rapped twice, and the lad released her onto the ramp, which she strode down while swinging her doubled whip. She seemed to glide over the ground as she came around the side of the wagon again to face the crowd

Then the scared, hunted woman Roman had found near death on

Melk's hillside held out her arms with a beaming smile, her gown shimmering, her crown shining as brightly as the purest polished gold.

"Kahn the Terrible!" she said.

And the night air above the torchlight in the field vibrated with the sound of the cheers for Isra.

Chapter 13

Isra felt as if she was living in a different world. Bundled in a blanket next to Roman on the driver's seat as they made their way south of Venice, she was tempted to believe it was true.

The air had turned icy the night before, leaving the spiny branches overhead black with damp as the early morning sun burned off the frost. Her breath billowed out in front of her, mingling with Roman's as the little gray donkey plodded along the quiet road.

"Not quite as lively as it was yestermorn, is it?" Roman asked, as if he'd read her mind.

"No." She smiled and turned her head to look at him. In the dawn's light, his curling blond hair and the falcon on its perch over his shoulder gave him the look of a character in some of the little painted Christian icons she'd seen. He was such a beautiful man; she wondered if anyone had ever told him so. "It is peaceful, though. I like it."

"As do I," he replied, and his crooked grin encouraged her to lay her temple against her forearms and continue to watch him as he spoke. "I would have wagered the coin you earned last night that we would not have broken camp before the noon hour."

"I am glad you did not," she said. "I have never seen a people imbibe as much drink as these have in the last week."

"I have," Roman admitted. "But not often, and when I did, the group was comprised wholly of laboring men. Even the . . . I don't know what to call him. Her."

"Delilah," Isra offered with a chuckle.

"Yes, Delilah. I reckon she could fell Samson herself with forearms that size, not to mention outdrink him."

"I think she likes you," Isra teased. "Her beard would be tickly."

Roman cast her a sideways glance that conveyed the fact he knew she was tormenting him.

"Do you think women should not drink?" she asked.

He glanced at her again. "Is this a trick question?"

"It is not." Isra turned her face to rest her chin on her wrists now, closing her eyes and feeling the wind of their passing crisp on her face, numbing her cheeks. "In my country, the women are not to drink. They are to cook and tend the home, the servants. Bear children."

"I've not seen you drink much," Roman said. "Does that mean you are an accomplished cook?"

"No." Isra opened her eyes now, lest the words she spoke caused unwanted images to bloom in her mind. "I would often play in the kitchens when I was small. I had no playmates and so the cook would take pity on me and send me to fetch wood or water, though she never thought to teach me to prepare food. The little chores became Huda's when . . ." She looked away to the side of the road, wrinkled her nose, pressed her lips together before turning forward again. "After my mother was killed."

He was quiet at her side for several moments, and Isra was angry at herself for ruining the peace of the morning. He was clearly uncomfortable with the subject of her past. Why had she brought it up? It wasn't as if her life was filled with pleasant memories to recount.

"I can cook," he said at last, his voice steady and even, as if there had been no lull in the conversation at all.

"Can you?" She turned her head on her arms again to look at him, thankful for his rescue. Did he even know he was saving her yet again?

He nodded and still looked at the road ahead, his expression mild, content. Just looking at him made Isra relax.

"The brethren at Melk rotate the differing duties, and that includes time in the kitchens and serving. My stews have become quite good, although my puddings are only passable."

"I am surprised a man of your size and strength is a capable cook." And it was the truth. Of all the things she would have guessed Roman to be talented at, culinary proficiency wasn't one of them.

"You must make me one of your stews," she said with a smile. "And a pudding, too, so that I might judge it."

"I will," he promised. Then he did glance over at her. "You're enjoying yourself with Kahn, aren't you?"

"Yes." She had answered him before she'd consciously formed her reply, but now she realized it was true. "I am still very afraid, though."

Roman chuckled. "No one can fathom it. Certainly not I. Why do you go in the cage and not simply stand outside, as van Groen suggested?"

Isra turned her face forward once more to gaze over the donkey's head, this time forcing herself to collect her thoughts while the low, brushy trees inland of the coast waited politely for them to pass. She pressed her mouth against the backside of her forearm for a moment, and then reminded herself that she had vowed to always tell this man the truth.

She pulled her head back only far enough that her lips could form the words. "I want them to like me."

Roman glanced at her twice. "The villagers?"

Isra nodded and rested her chin on her arms now, leaving her mouth free to converse. "The villagers. Asa and the troupe."

You.

"Why would you care what the villagers thought of you? They're all strangers. You'll never see any of them again."

"But I have seen their kind a thousand times in my life. Only the city they live in and the color of their skin is different. Simple villagers, no one of import, true. But poor people are often the most vicious, my lord. I could not leave my home in Damascus without being spat upon or called vile names in the street. And that was only by the women. Even the beggars knew I was beneath them. They all felt it necessary to remind me and one another at every opportunity." She paused to swallow and take a deep breath. "I want to at last show someone that I have something to offer, too. I did not know what that thing was—or if I had the ability to do it—until I saw Kahn. Perhaps even when I first saw Princess."

Perhaps when I first saw you.

He was quiet for a very long time, and for most of that time, Isra was afraid to look at him. She was afraid she would see disgust on his face at being reminded of what she was, where she'd come from, what she'd done. And so she continued to stare at the wagon ahead of theirs, watching the little plumes of dust and gravel shoot toward the sides of the road while her shoulders wanted to creep closer to her ears.

"I think they believed you," he said at last, and again his voice was completely placid. "Perhaps if you do it enough times, you will eventually believe it, too."

She looked to him quickly but didn't challenge his comment. Her shoulders began to fall back to their normal position when she realized he wasn't going to pursue the conversation. "Will you work for Asa?"

He shrugged. "A duty would pass the time. I am not suited to idleness." He looked over at her with an easy grin. "I certainly don't have half the talent or beauty you have, so I suppose I must content myself with the occasional menial labor."

Isra felt her heart expanding inside her chest so rapidly that, for a moment, it interfered with her ability to breathe. In that moment, she wanted to blurt out that when she was with him, she felt capable of attempting things she never would have dreamed. She could do anything if he was waiting for her on the other side of whatever trial was placed before her.

The general in Damascus.

The long, long journey to Melk.

Defying Constantine Gerard.

Facing Kahn for the first time.

Performing with the tiger to ensure her and Roman's survival in Asa's band.

But she managed to find her breath at last and pasted a weak smile on her mouth before looking away from him and saying, "My lord, you are already the queen's most trusted adviser. What more important duty is there?" It was as close as she could come to speaking the truth without making a total fool of herself.

"An adviser, eh?" Roman mused, nodding his head. "That doesn't sound like a strenuous position, but very well. I accept. And so my first duty as your adviser would be to advise you to fetch us a drink. The dust has me parched already, and you must preserve the royal voice."

"As you wish, my lord," Isra said, ducking her head and turning on the seat to disappear into the wagon. She collapsed onto the pile of folded blankets and drew deep breaths as she stared at the staves crisscrossing above her, her heart pounding merrily in her chest.

"And stop calling me my lord!" he cried through the opening.

Isra brought her fingertips to her mouth to cover her smile in the dim interior. Then she whispered behind her hand, "Yes, Roman."

They had no luck that day or the next, passing over the rocky road through clusters of ramshackle dwellings of poverty-stricken villages littered with ruined fishing nets and heaps of discarded shells. No happy peasants stood along the road waving and throwing fruit as they had before the caravan passed Venice, although they did receive several sideways glares and longing looks as they drove through as quickly as they dared. Asa's men had given the word to roll swiftly; they had been mobbed by destitute bands on more than one occasion apparently. Don't make eye contact, women in the back.

Which caused Roman to wonder about the tall blonde, Fran, who drove her own wagon. She kept to herself, never joining in the nightly gathering around the communal fire, although everyone who spoke her name did so with a hushed deference—save for van Groen, who seemed never to mention her at all. Was there no one to look out for her?

It was an odd thought for him, used as he was to caring for only himself and Lou until Isra Tak'Ahn had come to Melk. He considered for long hours as he drove their wagon in the midst of the caravan whether he might convince himself to fancy the private, artistic woman who claimed coloring so like his own, and he likened the awkwardness of his thoughts to someone imagining what it would be like to suddenly be a fish or a tree; how abruptly different the world would become.

Having a woman of his own would be much the same for Roman as transforming into a different species. He'd never entertained the idea of it before, even as a youth. His adolescence had been spent in backbreaking labor, early adulthood in striving to make a name for himself. Yes, there had been women in his life, in his bed, but it had never progressed further than the physical, and never for longer than the time Roman was in whatever city required his talent. Usually much shorter. A wife would only be left behind in a faraway village or city to tend their children while he was gone for months, years at a time. His babes would have grown up without knowing their father, his wife overburdened and resentful.

He wouldn't put someone he loved through such agony.

But if he survived his mission to warn King Baldwin, if he and his friends were never exonerated, if Victor one day grew weary of the Brotherhood's presence at the abbey, could he be someone's man? Someone's provider?

He imagined it for a long time, letting the well-behaved donkey drive the cart herself. From his cloudy childhood memories he constructed a scene of a northern meadow at the base of a snow-capped mountain, the fjord just visible through a break in the hills. He would build a cottage in that meadow with a barn attached to it for the few animals they would keep. He would break ground for a small food plot, perhaps some fruit trees as well. There would be plenty of fish in the nearby waterway, plenty of elk and bear in the mountains. In the winter, his wife would spin the wool from their sheep for his garments, and Roman would spend many hours before the fire with their children, teaching them to read Latin and to order numerals, and he would never send any of them away.

The warm season would mean work in the nearby villages, earning coin or goods to support his family. Two babes, three, six? Boys for certain, and girls, too, likely. In his mind, Roman was seated at a finely hewn table he'd built himself, the firelight flickering over the little faces leaning over the slate next to his. He somehow knew the snow outside this dream place was deep. He heard the crackle of the logs, the gentle hum of his wife as she worked her handicraft, and in his mind he raised his face to look at her.

It was not tightly coiffed white blond hair he saw, but a long, silky-looking fall of ebony beneath a sheer lavender shawl; long, tan arms holding forth the spindle as hammered gold bracelets danced and tinkled up to her elbows. The shawl moved as the dark-haired woman began to turn toward him, and her profile emerged.

"What are you looking at, my lord?" Isra asked.

The shuddering light was no longer cast by some dreamy fire but by the red evening sun stuttering through the trees on the right side of the road. When had Isra emerged from the cart bed, and how long had she been watching him? Roman's neck felt hot, as if she could somehow see his domestic imaginings.

He became intensely aware of his surroundings at once and nodded at the sight of the wall still some distance down the road. "We've reached Dubrovnik."

"You must have fond memories of this place, you were smiling so when it came into view."

"I've not been here before," he admitted, the tingling of his neck intensifying. He couldn't very well explain to her that he'd been smiling at a daydream of being a simple cotter, with a wife who looked suspiciously like Isra. "Van Groen says it's half way to Constantinople, though."

She gave him a confused look but did not press the subject as the caravan drew nearer to the city gates.

The sea stretched out beyond the rooflines, painted with the fiery sunset. No tall buildings interfered with the dreamy view save for the pair of citadels minding the port on the seaside corners of the wall and a single delicate church spire. While the road leading through the surrounding cluster of dwellings had been rough and pocked with holes, Roman now drove the donkey onto a finely paved stone thoroughfare, and the many hoof falls echoed in the valley created by the steep terrain behind and the mortared wall ahead.

Roman saw Zeus approaching on his horse.

"Going into the city," he advised. "There's an alley leading to a lot against the northern wall we'll camp at. This is a port town; there'll be a tax to enter. Only a couple pence. Asa wants the pair of you with him, once through."

Roman nodded his understanding and Zeus moved on to the conveyance behind them. Isra was climbing once more over the driver's seat to disappear beneath the canvas before Roman could ask her why. He thought she'd want to see the entrance to the city, having been subjected to such depressing villages for the past days, but it was as if the directive from Zeus had prompted her escape into the cart bed.

He didn't care for being ordered about by van Groen himself, but for no obvious reason. Roman had never been one to chafe at legitimate authority. Every tier of society, indeed every undertaking by man, must possess some sort of hierarchy of leadership, and Roman certainly had no interest in governing this menagerie of traveling misfits. Van Groen was not only knowledgeable about the trade in which he and his people engaged, he had treated both Roman and Isra—especially Isra—with naught but kindness. Vain, ebon-haired, silk-tongued, blinding-toothed devil he might be, van Groen had ensured that they were well included and provided for.

Especially Isra.

Roman shoved away the thought that he could be jealous of the leader of the caravan as Isra rejoined him on the driver's seat with a huff of breath.

"It is accounted for, my lord," she said, and when he looked to her with what must have been a bit of a frown, she averted her eyes. "Roman." Then she held out a clenched fist, not raising her face toward him.

"What's this?" he asked, even as he opened his palm beneath her fist. In the next moment, a trio of coins fell into it, warm with the heat of her skin.

"Our tax," she said, facing forward on the seat, her hands clasped in her lap, her gaze straight ahead.

"Isra," he began, glancing down at the coins again, "I have my own purse. I will pay the tax."

"I have no wish to disobey you," she replied. "Of course you will pay the tax from your purse if you feel that is what should be done. I only request that you add the coins I gave you to your bag so that I may be held accountable to you for my portion."

"Accountable for your portion?" Roman said. "Isra, there is no need for you to—"

"Never in my life," she interrupted as she swung her head to face him, the color high in her rich cheeks, "have I had the chance to pay my own passage with coin I earned in the light of day." She looked at him boldly, but Roman could see the anxiety in her eyes, the wildness to be understood, even if what she must explain further wounded her already battered soul. "Never have I purchased a bolt of cloth, a piece of fruit, a skewer of meat. *Never*. No one would accept my coin, even had I been allowed to keep what I earned. Everything I have ever had, I have been given or forced to steal." She paused, and now Roman could see her chest rising and falling quickly, shallowly.

"I would pay my portion. Roman," she added, looking into his eyes.

Roman looked at her for a moment as he tossed the coins in his hands. Then he nodded and looked away, slipping a finger into the drawstring of his purse to widen the neck just enough to slip the coins inside.

He wondered if she knew how brave she was.

They inched forward on the road toward the entry in the wall and Roman took advantage of the stilted silence between them to appreciate the fine feel of the sea air on his skin, the scent of lemon trees flavoring the breeze and making his mouth water. The temperature was dropping along with the sun, but it was still so much warmer than the weather they had left behind at Melk. Seabirds circled and called to one another overhead, and as if the gulls' cries were challenges he could not ignore, Lou flapped from his perch and headed into the painted sky.

At last the gray donkey came to the gates, and Roman urged her to a halt as the sentry lifted his arm and stepped to the side of the wagon. Another man carrying a shallow basket trailed behind him, looking from all accounts to be a beggar rounded up for the task. Roman guessed the guard would not even come to his sternum were they both standing on level ground, and so, seated in the tall driver's perch, it was as if he was looking down upon a child.

"Donkey; cart; driver. Three pence!" the guard trilled and held out his hand, his tiny, squinting eyes glancing once, twice at Isra.

Roman fished three coins from his purse, feeling a deep satisfaction at the idea that there was no way to ever know if the little discs of metal that found their way into his fingers were Isra's or the ones he could claim ownership of.

"Wait!" the little man barked and held his palm up. He frowned at Isra and then swung his glare to regard Roman. "You have slave." He placed his thumb against his palm. "Four pence."

"No," Roman replied, and continued to hold forth his pinched fingers. "No slave. Three pence."

"Dress of a slave," the man insisted. "Look of a slave. Your wife?" he challenged.

Roman shook his head and pressed his lips together. "No. She is my—"

"Ah!" the man said in a nasty little sigh of comprehension. "Four pence, all the same. A different kind of slave."

Roman heard Isra's gasp even as he gained his feet in the wagon, now towering over the guard in truth.

But the man did not seem intimidated in the least. "You not pay tax, you not enter Dubrovnik. All slaves taxed here."

Roman tossed the reins to the seat behind him and hopped down to the ground before the guard, his boots raising twin clouds of dust.

"You shall apologize to the lady," he said, still being forced to bend his neck at a ridiculous angle to glare into the man's upturned face.

"I apologize," the man replied earnestly, and then his eyes narrowed. "*After* you pay four pence."

"Ho, there!" a genial voice called, and both Roman and the guard turned their heads to see Asa van Groen cantering up on his black horse from the city side of the wall. "Can I be of assistance to you, good fellows?"

The guard stabbed a miniature appendage in Isra's direction. "Slave is one pence more. Four pence."

"She's not a slave," Roman growled, his fists clenching at his sides.

"No, no, my good man," the leader said with a concerned frown and swung down from his horse. He joined Roman and the guard, placing a hand on the guard's forearm. "That's exactly right; this lady is no slave."

The guard flung off van Groen's touch. "Slave or not, the tax is four pence for you now, ugly bear," he sneered at Roman. "Pay or go."

"I'll pay the extra pence," van Groen said, his hands already at the purse hanging from his black belt.

"No," Roman said, and added to the three pence already in his hand. He held the four coins to the little dictator. "Four pence." He smiled as broadly as he could as the man snatched them away and flung them into the basket still held by the beggar behind him. "I'll be looking for you."

"You don't frighten me, you big, stupid yellow *ox.*" He swept his fingers toward the cart. "Go on. Go away now, lest I tax you again for your noisy mouth." He turned to van Groen. "I watch you myself. At any trouble, the jailer will—"

"No trouble," van Groen promised, backing away with his hands up and then swinging up onto his horse. He looked at Roman pointedly. "Are you coming?"

Roman turned and regained the driver's seat, adjusting himself and twitching the reins.

Isra did not seem to have even blinked while the exchange had taken place. He glanced at her again as he drove the cart into Dubrovnik beneath the violet hues of a passionate sunset, the wheels clattering on the ancient cobbles.

"Are you all right?" he asked, trying to keep his voice even.

She nodded, her eyes looking straight ahead. "I am very well, my lord," she whispered.

Roman sighed.

Chapter 14

Isra was racked with nerves so that she trembled as she donned the white flax gown in the back of her and Roman's cart, him keeping watch beyond the bed. The interior of the cart beneath the canvas was shadowy dark, only filtered light from the torches outside allowing her to tell up from down as she struggled to dress.

She thought for a moment how nice it would be to have a wooden shelter like the one Asa van Groen boasted of in his own wagon, and the distraction helped calm her. Asa's conveyance was much like a tiny cottage on wheels, with a copper brazier and rimmed shelves and baskets attached to the wooden walls. He had a shaded lantern hanging from a pulley in the ceiling, and a tabletop that could be folded away into the wall. A plush bunk piled with coverlets nestled against the front wall, and Isra couldn't help but think how comfortable it would be to sleep there rather than on the hard cart bed that was currently her pallet.

Likely, though, her bed was much more comfortable than the ground Roman slept upon nightly.

Her fingers fumbled in the darkness, attaching the cape to the gown by feel alone. They would require a larger cart bed—one with two axles. And a wooden shelter would add so much weight that they would need another donkey, or a pair of horses like Asa's, to pull it. It would all cost a goodly amount of coin, but perhaps she could eventually afford it with her proceeds from working with Kahn. A place in a corner for a perch for Lou; trunks for the clothing and belongings they would acquire. Two bunks of course, one of them unusually long to accommodate Roman's height.

Or perhaps one very large bed . . . ?

Isra slipped the curved headband of her pretend crown behind her ears and pulled the two thin plaits she'd fashioned on either side of her face in front of her ears. Once her costume was complete, she paused with a frown.

You are dreaming as if you will spend the rest of your life as part of this caravan, with Roman at your side. You foolishly plan a future? Wake up, girl! You are en route to the land of your enslavement to achieve your revenge and assist Roman and his friends in freeing themselves to return to their old lives. Lives that do not include a Damascene whore.

What if she returned to Asa after her and Roman's mission was complete? Would the caravan have her? She tried to imagine herself living in Asa's wagon, but the image was blurry, watery, and popped like a soap bubble.

Must she become Asa's woman to stay on? Must she become anyone's woman? Why could she not keep her own cart—this cart— and drive it herself? The blonde artist, Fran, did as much. Isra could purchase the conveyance from Roman with her own money—the donkey, too.

Her own home . . .

"Are you all right?" Roman's voice cut through the reverie of possibility.

"Yes."

Isra inched toward the back of the cart on her knees, handfuls of her long gown clenched in her fists to keep from trapping the beautiful fabric between her skin and the rough boards and ripping it. She was careful to drop her skirt before edging her head beyond the canvas. Roman offered his hand and helped her disembark from the wagon, and she didn't realize how chilled she had become until her fingers were wrapped in Roman's warm grasp. He let her go too soon.

They were standing between the cart and the smooth stone wall of the city, and Isra could see that Lou had finally returned from his hunt, the falcon's noble outline clear atop Asa's nearby wagon. A handful of the tall torches had been placed along the wall to navigate the maze of the caravan, but Isra couldn't help feeling more than a bit trapped by the darkness and the task that awaited her. She could not see the area that had been set up for the performance, but she could hear the swell of the crowd beyond, smell the alternately pleasant and noxious odors that were common to cities. It was so much more than a simple crowd gathered in a field now.

"You plaited your hair," Roman said, his blue eyes taking on an even lighter cast in the torch glow as his gaze went to the sides of her face.

"Oh." Isra felt heat come into her cheeks. "Ah . . . I . . . do you—"

But her stuttering inquiry was interrupted by the larger-than-life leader of the caravan, as Asa came striding through the wagons, his costume and collar, his tall, sleek hair seeming to take up more physical space than Roman's mighty frame.

"There she is!" Asa beamed, holding his arms out wide and then folding one hand across his middle as he gave a grandiose bow, and Isra could see he carried a bundle of items in his left hand. He rose and took one of her hands, lifting it to his mouth and placing a kiss on the back of her palm before giving her fingers a little shake and then releasing them. "You are breathtaking, my dear. Not nervous, are you?"

"I am, yes," Isra admitted, glancing at Roman's slight frown. "Has Nickle . . . ?"

"Everything is in place," Asa assured her with a confident smile, and then he turned to Roman, seemingly oblivious to the crossness on his face. "What of you, big fellow? Are you averse to lending your talent to our endeavor this evening?"

Roman's eyebrows rose, as if Asa's request had caught him off guard and taken the sting out of whatever slight Roman had perceived.

"Have you a thing in mind?" he asked.

"*Magnificent crowd*," Asa crowed, raising clenched fists as he addressed the sky. "The take is already substantial, and has likely grown since last count, with word spreading through the city about the presence of the Egyptian queen." He looked back to Roman now, and his expression of rapture had sobered. "But I am concerned about the number in the audience. I've my strong men on the perimeter around Kahn's cage, but . . ." He raised his eyebrows and looked at them both. "There are a lot of folk."

"You want me to assist with keeping the crowd away," Roman said, and Isra liked the way his face relaxed, his shoulders squared even farther.

"Yes," Asa replied, but it was with a wince. "That. But in a less—how should I say it?—obvious capacity."

Isra and Roman exchanged glances and then Roman looked back to van Groen.

"Perhaps you should explain."

"Certainly." Asa smiled. "As you know, we are forming our lovely queen's character after that of the mighty and mysterious Cleopatra, whose paramour, as you likely also know, was a soldier by the name of Marcus Antonius. While your coloring is perhaps not quite what one might imagine when thinking of a centurion, your impressive stature is just the thing for discouraging enthusiastic admirers from approaching our Nile royalty and possibly endangering the tiger or the queen herself."

"You want me in the act?"

"No, no, good man—not necessarily in it," Asa assured. "But visible. Between the crowd and Kahn's cage. To lessen the distraction, though, it would be best if you dressed the part." He presented the items in his hand to Roman with a flourish.

Roman took them and separated the individual pieces: a short brown tunic with what appeared to be wide leather flaps hastily sewn about the hem, and what looked suspiciously like a large wooden bowl, its outside covered over in cloth with two long, rough-cut pieces dangling from either side.

"What the hell are these?" Roman demanded.

"Your centurion tunic and helm, noble soldier." Asa grinned. "Fran is putting the finishing touches on your shield just now. A useful prop, I'd wager, if control becomes necessary. Here, try it on." Asa reached out and snatched the bowl from Roman's grasp, and then had to stand on tiptoe with his arms completely outstretched to perch the vessel on the tall blond man's head.

Roman was scowling, and when he turned to look at Isra the limp cloth flaps that were likely meant to portray protective side pieces waved like little pennants against his cheeks.

Isra was shocked at the abrupt snort of laughter that escaped her and she brought both hands to her mouth. It was too late, though; Roman was already turning back to van Groen and shaking his head, his helm shields flapping, forcing Isra to turn her back on the pair.

"I'm not wearing this. I look ridiculous, obviously."

"No, no!" Asa said. "It will look perfect to the crowd! You'll see!"

"No."

Isra was trying to compose herself enough to turn back around, but the conversation between the two men made it difficult.

"What if we find you a spear to hold as well? A dull spear. Perhaps a spoon on the end of a han—"

"I'll run you through with it," Roman promised. "If it's dull, it shall take quite a long time."

"Listen, big fellow: You wish to keep our queen safe, as do I. You will be a magnificent addition to the performance. And I can't keep referring to you as 'big fellow' for the entirety of our acquaintance. With this costume, you'll have a place in the troupe, a true identity!"

"You want me to answer to Marcus?" Roman asked. "No, thank you. He had an agonizing death, did he not? Let's not give anyone any ideas."

"No, no," Asa agreed. "We couldn't go that far. You'd be . . . you'd be . . ." Isra could almost hear the wheels in Asa's mind turning. Then she heard a crack, like a finger snap. "The queen's Roman consort!"

Isra's eyes widened and she turned back around to find Asa clutching the bowl to his chest. Her eyes went to Roman's slack face.

Van Groen held out the pretend helm. "Won't you at least try it? Just this night. Unless there is trouble, you'll need do nothing more than stand there and look menacing, which doesn't seem to be a problem most of the time, any matter."

Isra thought she saw the shadow of a grin play about Roman's lips when next he spoke to her. "Do you think you could call me Roman?"

Isra tried to suppress her own smile. "If it means I might keep you nearby, I will do my best, my lord."

He turned back to Asa and snatched the bowl from him. "I accept."

"Good man!" Asa clapped Roman on the back and then held his crooked arm toward Isra, which she took, although she wished it was Roman escorting her. "Fran will be along with your shield." Then he pulled Isra into the labyrinth of wagons, patting her arm as they went.

They arrived at the rear of Kahn's wagon, and Nickle was waiting for them with a large cloth-wrapped bundle, the widely woven fabric soaked through in macabre red patches. The sight of the package made her stomach clench, although she didn't understand why. The lad held out his fist toward Isra, and she gave him her open palm with a quizzical look.

He deposited several coins into her hand. "I told him he could attend the exhibition for free so he only charged half, milady."

Isra smiled in surprise at the boy's honesty and resourcefulness. She and Roman had thought Nickle nothing more than a very talented thief, and although she still thought him gifted, she realized that Nickle's thievery might have at times meant the difference between eating or not for the troupe. Isra recalled all too well those long weeks when she had been forced to take what was not hers to survive.

She divided the coins evenly, handing half of them back to Nickle. "Well done," she said.

The lad gave her a short bow. "My pleasure, milady."

"The same sequence as before," Asa said, forcing Isra to focus on the task at hand. "The speech you give is brilliant—"

"Most of what I say of Kahn is untrue," Isra warned.

"Of course," Asa said, waving his hand. "The folk don't care about the truth; they only want to be mesmerized, frightened, entertained. Say whatever you like—the more fantastic, the better really. As I said, the crowd is large; try to drag the first part out a bit; build the suspense. Once you're inside, it's over rather quickly. By necessity, I understand," he rushed to add, then opened his mouth as if to speak, then closed it again on a smile as he looked over Isra's shoulder.

"I must say," he mused, "when I am right, I am right."

Isra turned and saw what appeared to be a centurion soldier from the ancient world walking toward them, a large, polished bronze shield on one arm.

And a tall, smiling blond woman on the other.

Asa van Groen had been correct: From a distance, the helm appeared authentic; the tunic, rugged and battle worn. The shield looked as though it must weigh a hundred pounds, but the way Roman was swinging it, Isra suspected it was yet another piece of artistic magic rendered by the beautiful Fran.

Isra's stomach knotted and the knot tightened as Fran gave a chirp of laughter at something Roman had said.

"Don't be discouraged," Asa said near her ear, surprising her. His words contained a hint of something beyond a leader managing the outcome of his venture, and Isra felt his concern. "The crowd will adore you."

"Thank you," she managed to strangle out and drop her eyes just as Roman and Fran reached them. She didn't want to look up at the two blond people, so well matched; didn't want Roman to see how disconcerted she was by Asa's comfort. But she wanted to see Roman more.

"Our Roman!" Asa boomed, releasing Isra and throwing his arms wide. It startled her so when the leader called him by name that she flinched. "Incredible! The crowd will swoon with excitement! Fran, the shield is a masterpiece as usual."

Fran only stared at him, a decidedly bitter look about her mouth. Isra thought for a moment that the blonde would outright snarl in reply. But to Isra's surprise, Fran looked instead to her, a bright smile suddenly curving her thin, pale lips.

"Just look at them both together, I say. Very good." The blonde's eyes narrowed a bit, and Isra couldn't help but think that there was anger behind the woman's friendly smile, although why it should be directed at her, Isra didn't know. "All *she* needs is an asp hanging from her tit, yes?"

There was a heartbeat of thick, awkward silence, and then Asa and Fran burst out in jovial laughter.

"Sometimes my humor is vulgar, I confess." The blonde chuckled. "Perhaps I have traveled too long with such a virile and fecund group."

Isra tried to smile, but she suspected the attempt was rather pathetic, and she didn't dare glance at Roman.

"Van Groen," Roman said, interrupting the lurching silence, "I'd have a word with you first."

"Certainly, certainly," Asa acquiesced, and then his gaze went to each of the two woman. "Gunar's in place. Fran, you'll stay with her until her prompt."

"Oh, why not?" she answered and looked away into the darkness with a quirk of her mouth.

Isra felt the flesh of her arm being pressed and looked down to see Roman's large hand.

"I'll be right there this time," he said with an encouraging grin. "Naught to fear."

She returned his smile, feeling a little of her uncertainty melt away. "How could I be afraid of anything at all with such a capable Roman soldier to protect me?"

His touch lingered.

Her smile deepened.

"Roman?" Asa called out. "Shall we . . . ?"

His hand fell away, but he held up his palm in a wave and Isra half turned to watch him following van Groen until they had disappeared around the side of Kahn's wagon.

"Is that what you do?" Fran's low voice drew Isra's attention. "Play the stricken, frightened innocent so that whatever unfortunate man you happen to be with at the moment will be sure to take care of you?"

Isra's heart wanted to rise into her throat at Fran's bitter scowl. "I—I do not know what you mean."

"The big, brawny man has kept you safe thus far, yes? Spirited you away from whatever trouble it is you caused for yourself? Now that you've found our band and have charmed Asa with your skill with that dumb beast, you think to better your match, *don't you*? Ready to cut the Norseman loose and latch on to Asa, *aren't you*? Let him be your champion while you steal the coin that rightfully belongs to everyone in this group right out from under our noses."

"N-no," Isra protested, her mind in such shock at the dreadful accusations that she couldn't form a coherent argument. "I—I lay no claim to—"

"*That's right*," Fran snapped, stepping closer to Isra. "You have no claim to anything or anyone here. You're a stupid nobody. You might have fooled some by your helpless disguise but *I'm* not stupid; no one could put on the *show* you have without years of practice. And I'm *not* referring to Kahn."

Isra couldn't swallow, her throat was so tight. But Fran did not relent.

"How many men has it taken you to get this far, hmm? A score? No, more than that, I daresay," she said with a wicked smile and stepped even closer, until Isra was forced to pull her head back lest she breathe in the hot air the blonde was expelling from her slender, flaring nostrils. Breath scented with strong drink. "I can see it on your face—you who think yourself so clever and secretive. That's what I do in the band; I notice details. So, how many? A hundred? Two?"

Isra stepped back a pace. "You know me not. I have done nothing to offend you."

"What if I take your protector away from you?" Fran said, ignoring Isra's protest. She closed the distance again. "I think I could lure him away. And away is exactly where I wish to go. So you are welcome to Asa and this hellish life. You deserve each other."

Isra felt as if she might vomit. She tried to swallow again but failed.

Suddenly, Asa van Groen's voice cut through the hush of crowd chatter somewhere on the other side of Kahn's wagon. It was time for her to perform.

"Go on," Fran urged with a smile. "Go to him, then. He's calling you."

"*Kahn the Terrible and his mistress*, the *queen of the River Nile, along with her Roman soldier!*"

The crowd sent up a loud cheer and Isra began backing away toward the curtain, looking at the woman who'd just verbally attacked her in complete confusion. Why would Fran say such wicked, hurtful things to her?

And how could she be so close to the truth about her past?

Isra turned and ducked behind the edge of the drawn-back curtain, her knees feeling as though they would give out on her at any moment.

She held out her tingling arms before the crowd, sending the fringe swaying, as Roman in his centurion attire and with Lou once more on his shoulder, paced in a defensive manner before the applauding, whistling mass.

No one could put on the show you have without years of practice.

She turned from side to side, her eyes roving the crowd that was packed in like roof thatching and stretched away into the city night. The applause faded.

Roman halted several paces away but facing her now. He raised his shield in what Isra supposed was a salute, and then he bowed his head and sank to one knee for a moment.

What if I take your protector away from you?

Isra cleared her throat, tried to find the words she was supposed to speak as her arms fell back down to her sides. The crowd stared at her, ogled her; a man in the front nudged his friend and whispered something to him, looking at Isra all the while.

Stupid nobody.

Isra was horrified to feel the hot trail of wetness streak down her cheek.

If she ruined the performance, it would be the end of her and Roman traveling with the caravan. They were farther south now and would either have to carry on to Constantinople on their own or inquire as to ship travel from Dubrovnik—risky after being seen by so many of the residents of the city. They would be remembered for certain.

No. No, she would not allow that to happen. Roman had already risked too much.

She inclined her head toward Roman, who was frowning at her in a concerned manner. She drew a deep breath.

Isra raised her arms again and looked to the crowd once more. "Good people of Dubrovnik!" she enunciated, letting her accent curl the words, then clip them tight.

"The tiger is a hypnotic, magical creature. Many are the legends of his strength and power and the deadly spell he casts over mortals to lure them to their doom. . . ."

Chapter 15

It was nearly midnight before the last of the city revelers left the encampment near the north wall, and the members of Van Groen's menagerie were alone to recount tales of the evening and gloat over their take. The dog show had been a huge success, and the yappy little creatures now lay scattered about Helena's feet as if they'd been shot dead, full up with the endless scraps and treats fed to them by the charmed crowd.

Delilah had been propositioned twice—by both a man and a woman.

Barnaby had greatly increased his personal possessions by encouraging merchants in the crowd to bring him items to hurl into the air while he invented witty rhyming stories on the spot about the owners. The people were so entertained and eager for the next round that hardly anyone had asked for their merchandise to be returned, and the juggler was currently going about the encampment with his pack, selling off the excess. Roman had purchased a rather nice little pot for two pence, thinking of the stew he'd promised to make for Isra.

Mother had foretold of approximately sixteen marriages, a score of impeding pregnancies, and one imminent, bloody, torturous death—although that unfortunate fortune had been assigned to a miserly individual who had ruthlessly haggled with the old woman over the price of having his future predicted.

"You pay half price, you get a short future!" the hag cackled.

Roman shook his head, but he had to smile as he and Lou walked about the small circle behind the wagons near the wall. All the members were packed in like herring around the communal fire, but no one seemed to mind. There was even more of a festival air to the place than when Dubrovnik's citizenry had been about, and it was obvious everyone was quite pleased with the coin they'd made that evening.

So although he was hailed and cajoled by several small groups of people, urging Roman to come and sit and drink, he did not pause for long with any of them; he was looking for Isra and, unfortunately, van Groen.

The smooth-talking leader had vanished with her almost immediately after Isra had shown Kahn to thunderous applause that seemed to go on for a quarter hour. It had taken all of Roman's self-control not to use his faux shield to shove his way through the crowd when van Groen had held up one finger toward Roman, perhaps intending to reassure him that they would soon return.

That had been more than an hour earlier. And while he wasn't yet concerned enough to be worried for Isra's safety, he was sufficiently preoccupied with the idea of her and the handsome van Groen secreted away somewhere together to be growing quite cross.

"Lose something?"

He knew who had spoken before he looked to his right and saw Fran's half smile looking up at him, her hands behind her back as she strolled in his direction. He turned toward her.

"Have you seen"—he broke off as Lou suddenly took flight from his shoulder—"van Groen?"

"Asa you're looking for, then, is it?" Fran smirked as she glanced up at the departing falcon and then came to a stop before him. "He and his new darling seem to be working on a vanishing act together."

Roman didn't want to agree—especially with the part about Isra being van Groen's darling—but he did nod. "They've been gone a while. I just—" He broke off again, sighed, looked over the sea of heads toward the fire. He turned back to the attractive blonde. "Nothing. Not important."

"Good," she replied with a smile, and he noticed that her eyes were unusually bright, glittering. "Because I have something for you."

Roman felt his eyebrows raise. "Something for me?"

Fran nodded and then took one fist from behind her back and held it toward Roman. He opened his palm beneath her hand and she uncurled her fingers and pressed a small, warm length of metal into his skin. She withdrew her arm to behind her back once more and looked up at him. Roman looked down.

It was a key.

"It unlocks my wagon," she said. Roman looked up to find her watching him brazenly, and he had to admit he was flattered by this beautiful woman's boldness in pursuing him. "Everyone knows you have been sleeping beneath your cart. Perhaps you've tired of being cold and wet. There is room in my bed for two."

Roman looked back down at the key in his hand, his neck feeling hot. "I would not be at ease leaving my traveling companion unprotected," he said, and then added, "And I would never wish to compromise your reputation by accepting your most generous offer."

To his surprise, Fran laughed and stepped closer to him, reaching out her hands to grasp his tunic on either side of his hips.

"I'm not worried about my reputation," she said through an indulgent smile. "The little queen isn't keeping you warm, is she?"

"No," Roman allowed, his neck heating even further.

"Do you not find me pretty?" She pressed herself closer to him, and Roman smelled strong drink on her breath as she wobbled on her feet.

"You are a very handsome woman," he assured her and reached out to grasp her elbows to steady her.

"But not as pretty as *herrrr*," Fran mused. Her tone was still mild, her eyes smiling.

"Your beauty is unique to you," Roman defended, and indeed, he did feel it important to let the woman know he did find her attractive. "In another circumstance . . ."

He stopped himself. What other circumstance could there be? He was free from Melk, free from any authority save his own for the first time in years. Yea, he could sore use the comfort of a woman. So why did the image of dark hair and eyes, of a whispered, twirling accent prevent him from taking what was being willingly offered?

Did Roman want Isra Tak'Ahn?

"I wish to return north," Fran said. "I tire of the feast or famine of this life." She shook her fists, still clutching his tunic. "Come with me."

"But," Roman hedged, taken aback by her offer, "what about the people looking for you? Your husband's benefactors?"

"That was so many years ago," she said. "They were all old men even then. No one is looking for me now. And besides," she added,

"I have more than gotten used to a common life. I only want a home of my own. Somewhere clean, and quiet, and still."

Roman heard the longing in her voice, softened by drink, and he recognized the reflection of his own wants. He remembered the fantasy he'd had in the wagon, of the little cottage he would build. Hadn't thoughts of Fran spurred that dream?

But Isra's absence was making it impossible for Roman to think of anything or anyone except her.

"While I admit that my desires are very much the same," Roman said gently, "I am not free at the moment to pursue them. I have . . . obligations to fulfill."

"To her?" Fran pressed.

Roman nodded. "And others. I don't know how much longer we shall be traveling together. We have a specific destination in mind."

"Venice?" Fran gave a knowing smirk, reminding him of what he'd initially told Asa van Groen.

"No. Not Venice," Roman admitted.

"I don't care," Fran said. "If not now, then later, in the spring. And I want you to use the key, regardless of whether you decide to come home with me or not. Come home," she urged. "Don't you want that?"

He found himself looking at her mouth, wondering what it would be like if he kissed her now, followed her back to her brightly painted wagon. But the arousal he expected to feel never manifested.

A sudden cheer went up around the fire, and Roman and Fran turned their heads in the same instant to see a beaming van Groen leading Isra toward the fire by her hand. They were both beaming.

Isra's eyes scanned the crowd, and Roman knew she was looking for him—*he knew*, and it made his heart beat faster. Her gaze lighted on him before he could raise his hand, and she stared, her smile becoming stiff.

He'd forgotten the lovely Fran was still in his grasp.

And so he set her from him, took her hand, and pressed her key into her palm. "Thank you," he said. He closed her fingers around the metal and left her, moving through the crowd to reach the woman who was no longer looking for him but had turned away and was now being sheltered under Asa's green velvet-clad arm as he addressed the band.

* * *

"God save the queen!" someone from the troupe shouted, and Isra couldn't help the bit of a smile that returned to her mouth as the crowd applauded and whistled.

"Indeed!" Asa praised with a laugh. "The good mayor was so taken with her, he has requested we stay on to entertain some visiting dignitaries arriving on the morrow! So it is another night in Dubrovnik for us, good folk. And I'd wager the take this time tomorrow evening will be twice today's!"

The crowd cheered again, and Isra felt a tug on her arm. Both hoping and dreading it was him, she looked up and saw Roman's concerned face looking down at her.

"Where have you been?" he asked, glancing at Asa's arm about her shoulder.

Isra opened her mouth to answer, but her words were precluded by the dark-haired man's at her side.

"And let us not overlook the contributions of our noble Roman!" Asa cried. "Surely his commanding presence lent an air of such authenticity that the pharaoh himself will soon be demanding a return of his kin!"

The crowd laughed good-naturedly, but Roman paid them little heed as he looked down at Isra, still waiting for an answer.

"The mayor called us to audience," she replied, hearing the coolness in her own voice. After the dreadful things the blond woman had said to her before the performance, the sight of Fran making good on her threat to lure Roman had been more than terrifying.

Lure him away from what, though? Isra demanded of herself. *You do not own him. He does not want you. Has he no right to a woman if he chooses?*

"Well done," he said with a smile, no trace of concern left, no raised eyebrow at her tone. "You were in fine form tonight."

"And now," Asa called out, squeezing Isra's shoulder ever so slightly, "we celebrate!" He looked to her and then to Roman. "We will all drink together, yes?"

Isra looked to Roman, hoping he would acquiesce to join the party so that she might also, but then a blonde head appeared once more at Roman's right arm, and Fran leaned up to whisper something behind his shoulder. He turned his head toward her but said nothing as she slid away into the crowd with only a glance at Isra and the dark-haired leader of the band.

"I find I am quite tired," Isra heard herself saying, although she hadn't planned on begging off at all. She was finally being included, celebrated for an accomplishment, and she had looked forward to partaking of the company of people who accepted her for who she was.

Or who they thought she was.

But Isra was no fool, and she was experienced enough to know that a woman only whispers such things in the presence of others when it is obvious to everyone what she is offering.

What she had already offered Roman, if the scene Isra had witnessed upon her and Asa's return was any clue.

She ducked out from beneath Asa's arm. "I wish you both a festive evening in whatever amusements you find worthy."

"Wait," Roman called and reached out to take her elbow lightly.

Without thinking, she jerked her arm from his grasp. "Is there something you require of me, my lord?" she asked, but her eyes were trained on the flickering shadows on the ground.

"No," Roman said after a heartbeat of time. "I was only going to escort you to the cart."

"I know the way." Isra left him then, without so much as a glance, walking into the dark maze of wagons alone.

The flickering fire did not penetrate past the first semicircle of conveyances, and by the time she reached her and Roman's royally decorated cart, she had tripped twice, stubbed her toe on a wheel, and rammed her hip into a corner of a lowered wagon bed. Even the donkey was away in the communal corral, and that suited her greatly. She needed to be alone now. To relive this night in all its glory and agony; to cry in private.

She had just set one knee upon the board when she was seized by her hips and pulled backward through the air, landing against something hard and warm and definitely human. A moist, stinking hand clamped over her mouth before she could scream.

"Good evening, slave," a nasal voice hissed into her ear.

Isra did not struggle against the guard from the gate; she knew from past experience that if one resisted immediately, it only brought about the violence sooner, precluded any hope of escape. So, although she didn't relax, she willed herself not to strain away, to stand perfectly still against him.

"Your woman friend says you will welcome my company if I find you away from your great idiot guard. If you are nice, I return your pence."

She nodded her head as best she was able with the hold she had been placed in, but waves of panic crashed in Isra's head all the same, threatening to turn the blackness behind the cart into a wash of red. This could not be happening to her again.

The woman friend could be none other than Fran. No one else in the band had had so much turned a frown in Isra's direction. The woman's vitriol before the exhibition had only been a precursor to her true rage.

Why did the blonde hate her so much?

"Very good," he cooed in her ear. "But if you are ill-tempered, I shall strangle your throat and do what I will any matter. You understand?"

Isra nodded again but had to squeeze her eyes shut. The red haze was growing. Although she wished to appear complacent about the man's detestable plan for her, she had no intention of letting him have his way. She had vowed to herself in Damascus that she would never again be taken against her will; this man truly would have to kill her first.

But better he not know that just yet. She waited to see what his next move would be, and she didn't have long to wonder.

"Anyone waiting for you in the cart?"

Isra shook her head.

"Good slave tells the truth. I watch it for hours and know the answer." He urged her forward by pressing his groin into her bottom until she was trapped between him and the cart bed. "I take my hand from your mouth. If you scream, I knife your kidney; it shall not damage the parts I'm interested in. Now, go."

Isra gasped a breath in through her mouth, relieved that the sewage stench of the man's flesh was gone. She grasped the edge of the bed and hoisted herself up very carefully, slowly, thinking through each inch of movement. She forced herself to be still, not to scream or kick out, when the man grasped her buttocks with both hands.

He was bluffing; he wasn't holding a blade.

For some reason, the idea that he intended to rape her without thinking he needed a weapon to restrain her increased Isra's rage tenfold. Her jaw trembled in her fury—she couldn't still it; her eyes felt wide in their sockets, as if her eyelids had disappeared. She was a wild animal, moving, acting solely on instinct.

She clambered over the end of the bed and onto her pallet with exaggerated care, stretching out her arms beneath the satchels and parcels tossed against the board behind the driver's seat as the man behind launched himself up against the wood and hooked a boot over the end.

Isra's fingers scrambled under the pillow of her satchel and then she turned to rest on her heels and brace herself with her hidden hands as she watched the man pull himself the rest of the way inside.

He crawled clumsily, quickly, over the blankets toward her, pushing his stench ahead of him, his shadow rising above her against the canvas ceiling. She pulled Maisie Lindsey's long dagger from beneath her satchel and held it forth in the darkness.

"Do not come any nearer," she warned, but it came out as a strangled whisper.

He descended. "Shut up, sla—"

Isra felt the pop of the blade tip piercing the man's clothing—or his flesh—reverberate up her arm as he fell onto her, and his answering scream nearly pierced her eardrums. She launched herself backward on her heels through the front flap of canvas, leaving the blade stuck somewhere inside her attacker. She fell over the driver's seat, hitting her head on the footboard as she landed in the narrow well beneath the bench, while inside the cart the man continued to scream. She didn't know where the blade had touched him, had been unable to see more than shadow on shadow in the pitch black of the shelter. He could be seriously wounded, or he could only be scratched and able to come after her.

She scrambled to her feet, trying to find her bearings to get down from the cart, but the world was spinning, tumbling her around and around.

"Roman!" she cried out, her voice still strangled in her panic-clenched throat as she clawed her way up from the foot well. "Roman!"

She fell out of the cart onto her shoulder and face in the dirt. Her cheek felt seared and she heard the crack of her pretend crown as it slid sideways and was crushed beneath her head. Above her the cart rocked as the man shouted and thrashed as if he could not find his way out of the blackness. She staggered to her feet, her screams becoming clearer, louder, as she backed away from the wagon.

"Roman! *Roman!*"

She heard the sound of footfalls pounding in the dark, the cry of a hunting bird pierce the alley. "Isra? Isra! Where are you?"

"Roman!" She seemed to be unable to say anything but his name.

In the next heartbeat, he grabbed her arm, turned her around. "What is it? Are you hurt?"

"A man," she stammered as the roar of many running feet grew and the glow of carried torches bobbed and flashed between the carts. "A man in the cart. He—he attacked me."

More of the band reached them then, and the torchlight cast Roman in black silhouette even as she was revealed by it.

Asa van Groen was the next to reach them. "Good God, what's happened? Is that blood?"

Roman released her and leaped onto the driver's seat in two great bounds.

Isra looked down to see her pristine flaxen gown splashed with bright red and thought of the leg of lamb Nickle had earlier procured for Kahn.

That was what Fran had intended: that Isra be offered up as a sacrifice. To be devoured by the fiend in the cart.

But she had no time to think on it, for in the next moment there was a gurgled scream and the cart lurched a final time. Something thudded onto the dirt beyond the cart and half the band left Isra and van Groen in a run to investigate.

Isra turned and saw Roman approaching her again, but this time his face was nearly unrecognizable. It was as if he wore a mask resembling the man she had come to know, but this man's features distorted the pleasant expression into something undeniably dangerous and fearsome.

"Is he dead?" Isra asked, her voice breathy with anxiety and dread when faced with this different Roman. "Did I kill him?"

"What in hell is going on?" Asa demanded. "Is who dead? Why are you covered in blood?"

Roman ignored the man. "Yes, he's dead." Even his voice sounded different; flat, emotionless. "But you didn't kill him. I did."

Zeus came around Roman from behind. He glanced at Isra apologetically and then looked to van Groen.

"We have a problem, boss."

Chapter 16

A sa van Groen swept past Isra, touching her arm in what might have been meant as a comforting gesture, to follow his man around the side of the cart. The rest of the band, who had been standing there staring at Isra, followed, leaving her alone with this huge blond man who looked so much like Roman but at this moment was not.

"Are you hurt?" he asked again in a gruff voice, his eyes sweeping over her ruined gown. She could only barely see the dark washes over the wide skin of his forearms in the gloom.

Isra shook her head and then wondered if he could see the motion. "No." She didn't know if she had cut her head when she'd fallen, but she couldn't feel anything now, so she chose to believe it was only bruised.

"I'm sorry, Isra," he said, and she could hear the loosening of his voice, as if the Roman she knew was trying to return. "I should never have allowed you to return to the cart alone. I failed to protect you. Please forgive me."

Even though an instant ago terror had still gripped her, turning her skin to ice, her heart galloping in her chest, his words melted her fear like a scrap of old candle wax dropped into a fire. Her chest seemed to expand, her nostrils flared.

Here before her stood the most noble, capable, honest man she'd ever known. So completely had he assumed the responsibility of her that he was prepared to bear the burden of wrong perpetrated by a lecherous, soulless criminal. He'd killed a man for the sake of protecting her, and Isra knew full well the weight that action carried on a person's heart, no matter how much the one killed might have deserved his fate. What that man had tried to do could in no way be Roman Berg's fault.

But Isra knew whose fault it was.

"I owe you my life, again," she said, struggling to make her voice steady.

It was Roman's turn to shake his head. "You did well enough on your own. I'm only sorry you were forced to defend yourself." He paused, his head turning toward the cart slightly for a moment. "Everything in the cart is ruined. The bedding, the clothes."

Isra rolled her lips inward. The blade must have struck the man in a vital location. Now Roman had lost many of his possessions and Isra had nothing once again. Her anger grew.

She knew whose fault it was.

"I wish to return to the fire now, my lord."

"I'll come with you," he said, stepping to her side.

"No," she said, holding up her palm. "I will be safe there."

"Roman." Asa van Groen stepped from behind the cart. "A moment?"

Roman looked back to Isra, his uncertainty obvious.

"Only nearer the fire," she promised. "In the light."

"Van Groen can wait."

She laid her hand on his chest when he approached her, and she could feel the steady thump of his heart through his thick musculature. What a precious organ it was beneath her palm, what a pure and spotless soul it powered. Her eyes shimmered with tears and she was glad for the darkness.

"I will be fine," she said.

He reached up and grasped her wrist with his palm but did not remove her hand from his chest. "I feel as if I can never let you from my sight again," he said.

"I am too much trouble," she acknowledged in a whisper.

His thumb stroked the inside of her wrist. "No."

"Roman?" van Groen called again.

She pulled away from him through sheer will—a will to exact an answer for what he had been forced to do for her sake. "Asa needs you."

"Wait for me at the fire," he said, and she knew it was no command but rather his way of giving his blessing for leaving, his way of telling her he trusted her judgment in whatever it was she meant to do, even after she had so recently failed him.

"As you wish."

And then she turned and left him, heading toward the communal area that had been all but abandoned now by the members of the band, called away from their revelry by the disastrous goings-on at Roman and Isra's cart.

She stepped into the close, quiet ring of conveyances, her eyes scanning the wooden and canvas walls until she spied the small, expertly painted wagon directly across the fire. The woman had to be inside it; she was nowhere else to be seen and she certainly hadn't come at Isra's panicked screams.

Isra walked steadily toward Fran's wagon, her eyebrows lowered, the ghostly echo of Roman's heartbeat still thumping against her palm.

"This is not good, Roman," van Groen said as Roman came to his side. The strongmen joined them in standing over the crumpled body of Isra's attacker, while the rest of the band clustered some distance away, whispering among themselves and casting furtive glances in their direction.

"You had no choice, I understand," van Groen assured him, "and I am in your debt for not allowing harm to come to Is—" He broke off. "Our queen."

Roman grimaced in the dark. He hadn't realized until now that he had shouted Isra's name in his panic to locate her. He didn't know who else had heard him besides van Groen at his very heels, but Roman's respect for the man grew more than a bit at the idea of him catching himself and not repeating her name before those gathered.

"Who knows what other mischief he might have caused," van Groen added. "But now . . ."

"Now we have a body to contend with," Roman finished for him.

"You want we should take it to the shore?" one of the men asked.

Van Groen shook his head. "No, the gates are already closed. Besides, that won't work this time with the tide."

"This time?" Roman asked, raising his eyebrows and looking to the leader of the group. "Do you oft find yourselves with unwanted corpses?"

"We've yet to possess a wanted one," van Groen quipped and then squatted down. "It's the guard from the gate." He flicked the fringed purse on the man's belt, slid some sort of folded wooden measuring device partially from its leather holster and then returned it. "He'll be recognized when he's found. And we have all of the morrow to wait until our performance."

"Surely the city wouldn't immediately blame anyone here," Roman suggested. "He could have been killed by any number of people. You witnessed his behavior at the gate, van Groen. He likely had enemies, considering what he attempted this night."

"Oh, certainly," van Groen agreed, rising to his feet and brushing his hands together. "But that's an inherent danger of our trade, I'm afraid. And it's why, for the most part, we avoid staying long in the cities; we are easy targets upon which to blame the more distasteful transgressions. It is infinitely more palatable for the officials to seize our things, hang one of us, and send the rest of us packing than to contend with the political strife of trying one of their own."

"Especially if one of their own happens to be a noble or official," Zeus offered bitterly, and Roman wondered about the man's experience in that situation.

"Indeed," Asa agreed. He looked to Roman. "And it's why we are oft not permitted entrance to the cities. Things seem to . . . happen when we're about." He looked down at the body again. "Things such as this."

"What do you . . . typically do?" Roman asked. "In a situation such as this?"

"Well," Asa sighed, "as I see it, we have two options. One, we hide the body in our midst until after our performance. Then we leave it somewhere it will not likely be discovered until we are well out of sight and out of reach."

"What's the other option?" Roman asked.

"We leave Dubrovnik at first light, as soon as the gates open, eschewing the morrow's performance and dumping the body into the sea. The first option allows us to at the very least double our profits, although we run the risk of him being discovered. After all, your cart might resemble a slaughterhouse in the light of day. The second option gives us a better opportunity of distancing ourselves from the area before the body begins to decompose and stink in this mild weather, but our abrupt departure after such a gracious invitation to stay on by the mayor himself will inevitably seem suspect."

Roman nodded. Van Groen was incredibly composed about such

things, and it gave him confidence in the man. "We'll not be sleeping in the cart now. We could hide him within."

"Aye, stay," Zeus said. "We need the coin."

"Stay," another strongman added.

"My advisers have spoken," van Groen said, "and I must admit I agree. Of course we must speak with the queen to be certain she will be able to perform again so soon after enduring such an ordeal. All right, lads, let's get him up and into the cart." He turned to Roman when he bent to take hold of an arm. "No, man, not you. You've eliminated the threat; we shall dispose of it. Your job continues to be looking after our lady." He leaned to look around the side of the cart. "Where is . . . ?"

"She went to the fire," was all Roman said, because in truth it was all he knew. "I'll see if there is aught she requires from the cart, though I doubt it."

"As do I," van Groen acknowledged. "Quite the spot of luck she had, hitting that vein in the dark. It certainly made a hellish mess, though." He held out the long dagger, hilt first, to Roman. "I don't know if she'll wish this returned or not."

Roman took the blade. "It was a gift from a friend," he murmured, looking down at the fantastically forged handle. He wondered that Maisie Lindsey hadn't set out to save Isra's life that morning they'd left Melk. "She'll want it. Eventually."

"Very good," van Groen said, unfastening the green velvet of his frock and shrugging out of it. He hung it on the edge of the cart bed and squatted with the men to take hold of the corpse. "I'll join you both in a trice," he wheezed as they lifted the body in one motion.

Roman began backing away. "My thanks, van Groen," he said, and found that he truly meant it. He turned toward the fire and was halfway through the maze when he heard a woman scream in fear for the second time that night.

Isra had not bothered to knock on the low door at the back of Fran's wagon. She'd seized the latch and pulled, and the door had swung wide.

"Thought I'd leave it unlocked because you had so foolishly returned my key," the woman slurred from somewhere within the blackness of the shelter. "Come in, my Roman."

Isra's heart pounded like a hammer in her chest. The woman had thought to have Roman well busied while Isra was being raped. Instead, Fran had forced that good and noble man to commit murder. The only time in the whole of her life Isra could recall being in more of a rage was the black day when she'd found Huda.

She climbed into the darkness of the wagon readily, flung herself into the unknown environment with her hands outstretched, her fingers hooked, clawing through the blackness. She felt her nails skitter across flesh for the briefest moment, and the woman gave a shriek.

"Roman? Ow! What—?"

Isra lashed out again just above where the sound of the woman's voice emanated, and her fingers tangled in silky hair. She tightened her hand into a fist and gave a scream of rage, yanking the woman after her as she backed out of the wagon.

Isra hopped down through the door, dragging the screaming Fran. She gave a mighty heave and the woman fell away into the dirt, the firelight playing over her rumpled skirts and undone hair. From somewhere over her head, Isra thought she heard Lou screech.

Fran looked up, her face a pale mask of fright with reddened eyes. When she saw Isra, though, those eyes narrowed with ill-concealed malice.

"Who do you think you are, coming into my wagon and putting hands on me?" she demanded.

"Get up!" Isra shouted.

Fran suddenly looked about her and saw that the fire ring was deserted. Her face shot back around. "Where is everyone?"

"Get up!" Isra screamed.

Fran's porcelain features hardened so that they resembled polished ivory and she drew her knees beneath her, her hands steadying her as she staggered to her feet, her eyes never leaving Isra.

"I would have thought you busy with your little admirer," she slurred, swaying on her feet. It was obvious Fran was more than a bit affected by drink, but Isra didn't care.

She drew her arm back and struck Fran in the face, spinning the blond woman around and knocking her to the dirt with a cry.

"Get up," Isra insisted again.

Fran looked up sideways at Isra, and it appeared a touch of reality had come back into the blonde's eyes as she took in Isra's bloodied appearance.

"What's wrong with you, you savage?"

"*I* am the savage?" Isra asked, taking slow, measured steps closer to the blonde, who began to pull herself along the ground, trying to increase the distance between them. "Did you hope he would kill me? Or just humiliate me?"

"I—I—" Fran stammered. She gave up and looked around the fire again. "Mother!" she cried out, seeing the old hag who had shuffled over to tend one of the numerous pots over the fire. "Mother, help me!"

The old woman looked up and frowned in their direction. "What's this about now, Franny?"

"She's going to kill me!" Fran shrieked.

Mother looked to Isra. "Well," the hag drawled, "we should likely confer with Asa before all that. I'll fetch him." She began to shuffle away into the darkness.

"Mother, no!" Fran cried. "Don't leave me here with her." Fran's head swiveled back around. "You stay away from me, you . . . you rubbish! Leech! Asa will throw you out of the band now, attracting the like of such predators!" she taunted.

Her words brought back the image of Roman's hardened, unrecognizable face, the scream of the man, and the lurch of the wagon when Roman was inside.

Isra fell onto the dirt atop the woman, her arms flailing. In her mind she heard every feminine voice that had ever insulted her, degraded her, humiliated her.

"You evil, wretched woman!" Isra screamed. "What you made him do!"

"I didn't make him do anything!" Fran shouted, fending off the blows as best she could. "You invited it!"

Isra shrieked, and her next slap caught Fran across the mouth. She took great handfuls of the woman's blond hair in her fists and raised her head so that her face was close to Isra's.

"*I am speaking of what you made* Roman *do!*"

Fran gave Isra a belligerent, drunken smile. "Oh, I see. Jealous, were you? How d'you like it?"

Isra raised her arm again, but she was snatched into the air in the next instant, her feet sailing out in front of her, long silken strands of blond hair floating down lazily like fairy streamers.

She knew it was Roman's arm around her middle, Roman who

held her suspended against him, her feet still far from the ground, and so she struggled, pried her fingers around his arm.

"Let me go, my lord!"

"No," Roman said. "Isra, what is this?"

She saw Asa van Groen and the rest of the band streaming into the fire circle around Mother, who only looked on with her arms crossed over her flat chest, shaking her head.

When Asa caught sight of the blond woman on the ground, he broke into a run toward her, skidded to a stop in the dirt on his knees by her side. He lifted her by the shoulders.

"Fran! Franny! What is it? What's happened?"

"She's mad!" Fran cried, seizing the front of Asa'a white undershirt. "She came into my wagon! She tried to kill me!"

Roman let Isra slide to her feet but retained a hold on her arm. "Isra?" he asked. "Why would you attack Fran?"

She looked around and saw that every pair of eyes around the fire was trained on her, the performers sharing similar looks of astonishment. But Isra looked only at Fran when she spoke.

"She sent the guard to our cart," she said. "She told him I would be alone."

Fran snorted. "He was harmless! Such attention hasn't seemed to bother her before."

"He would have raped me!" Isra screamed and lunged forward, but Roman held her firm. "Are you blind to my costume?"

"Did you, Franny?" Asa asked.

The blond woman frowned, looked from Isra to van Groen and back again. "He said he wanted to meet her, give her a token of his admi—" She broke off and looked back to van Groen. "Asa? What happened?"

"He's dead, Franny," van Groen said.

Fran looked back at Isra, who was shocked at the genuine horror that seemed to come over the woman's face as she appeared to look at Isra's gown for the first time. Or perhaps it was only now that the sight of it could penetrate the fog of drink enveloping Fran.

"Are you—are you hurt?" Fran asked, and her chin flinched.

Isra could only stare at the woman.

"Did he . . ." Fran pulled away from Asa and struggled to her feet. She put out a hand and began walking toward Isra. "Are you hurt?" she insisted again, and her eyes filled with tears.

"Stay away from me," Isra warned.

Fran halted, although she let her hand remain outstretched. "I didn't think he—I . . ." She couldn't seem to form a coherent sentence. She looked around at all gathered, first in one direction, then the other, before turning back to Isra. "I'm sorry," she choked. "I'm—I only . . ." She looked to Asa. "There's a body now?"

He nodded, his expression grim, sorrowful, but Isra couldn't fathom the complexity of it. There was much going on beneath the surface of this scene that she did not understand.

"I'm sorry," she said again, but this time she turned to address the group as a whole. "I'm sorry, everyone. I did go a bit mad, I suppose. It's only that . . . it's been a year now. I know it's warm here, but . . ."

Many of those gathered glanced away, as if it pained them to look at Fran.

"I'm sorry!" she cried out. "*I'm so sorry!*" Her words deteriorated into a sob and she brought her hands up to cover her face.

Asa went to her, his own face creasing into a mask of—pain? Regret? Isra couldn't tell. But he wrapped his arms about her, murmuring into her ear while he steered her back toward her wagon. He looked over Fran's head to where Isra and Roman still stood.

"Take my cart," he said. "I'll need to stay with Fran. I should have been staying with her for a while now," he said, his voice heavy with regret. He helped the blonde into the wagon and pulled the door shut after them.

Isra looked around at the others, who were dispersing to sit around the fire, the mood considerably subdued. Some of the women were even weeping quietly.

Only Mother was walking toward her and Roman now, a tall mug in each gnarled fist, and when she reached them, she offered the drinks.

"Here you are, children," she said with a touch of breathlessness in her voice, as if carrying the mugs had been a physical trial. "I suppose someone ought tell you what all this is about." She turned around and began shuffling back toward her perch on the far side of the fire.

Isra looked up from the steaming mug to see that everyone gathered around the flickering flames was now looking at her and Roman expectantly. Zeus stood up from a three-legged stool and looked to Isra as he swept his hand toward it, a clear invitation to sit.

"You might as well," he said, moving away to lower himself down onto the dirt beneath the sturdy chair in which Delilah sat. "It'll take a fair bit."

"Not really so long," Mother said as she resumed her perch on her tall stool. She sent a bowl and a bundle of rags around the circle of people to place near the stool Zeus had offered. "I suppose we shouldn't be surprised at Franny's behavior of late. And I further suppose we all share some of the responsibility for it."

She looked across the fire at Isra specifically, her old, colorless eyes seeming to bore into Isra's skull. "It's a year since we lost Max."

Somehow, Isra knew in that instant; she could see the signs, the clues, and it caused a cold, bitter dread to creep into her heart.

Roman voiced the question Isra thought she had already answered. "Who is Max?"

Now Mother's eyes left Isra and looked at Roman. "Franny and Asa's son. He would have been six years this winter, we reckon. Although that's only a guess. We didn't know how old he was when we found him."

Isra did sit down then, feeling as though all the strength had gone out of her legs. She pulled a rag from the pile and dipped it in the bowl of water. "You found him?"

Mother nodded her old head as she stared into the fire. "On the side of the road outside of Budapest, four years ago. It was winter, the snow unusually deep that year. The baby was crouched in a ditch, only a long shirt on him that barely covered his little legs." The old woman paused, her mouth pursed with the memories Isra was glad she couldn't see. "Dirty, cold. Hungry. Franny and Asa'd been together for nigh on ten years at that point, and no babes had come."

Standing just behind her stool, Roman took the wrung-out cloth Isra had handed him and then offered, "I didn't know van Groen and Fran were married."

Mother looked up from the fire and sent him a kind smile while he wiped at his arms. "Things like that aren't of much import to people like us, big fellow. Any matter, 'twas Franny who found him. We stayed about Budapest for weeks, mostly because of the snow, but also to see if the babe's parents were searching for him. By the time the snow melted, it was clear the child had been abandoned. Max was Franny and Asa's, as certainly as if she'd borne him herself.

Maximilian George van Groen," Mother finished in a gentle voice, as if in prayer.

"He worshiped Nickle when he joined the troupe two summers ago," Zeus added, and Isra looked up, her eyes instinctively seeking out the boy. She saw him sitting with his slumped back to the fire just behind Mother, his long, straight hair hiding his face. "Treated him like an older brother. Followed him everywhere."

Nickle stood from the stool and walked into the maze of wagons, and Isra's heart flinched.

"Max was ill when we found him in Budapest, and although Franny and Asa did their best to care for him, he was never a healthy lad. At the slightest chill in the air, he'd come down with the ague; keep it for weeks, it seemed. Last winter he was especially touched. He never recovered."

Helena was stroking her favorite pet, asleep in her arms. "Neither did Fran."

"Things became uneasy between her and Asa," Zeus said. "We . . . we were all mourning. In different ways. It seemed they were better apart than together for a time. But we could see Fran slipping away from us all. We could see."

"We should have seen," Mother corrected with a frown. She looked up at Isra and Roman again. "We're a superstitious lot, we are. You don't talk about a thing lest you want it, you see? We'd hoped they'd find their way back to each other."

"Then we came," Isra said to no one in particular. She felt the warmth of Roman's hand on her shoulder, and without thinking, she reached up and grasped his fingers.

"This is not your fault, child," Mother said. "But now you know." Her dark eyes bored into Isra's. "Now you know."

Chapter 17

Roman helped Isra into the back of van Groen's wagon as most of the rest of the band dispersed from around the fire. He got the feeling no one really wanted to sleep then, but even though they would not begin performing until the noon hour, there was a watch to keep now over Roman and Isra's cart until the moment they left Dubrovnik, lest the body hidden inside it be discovered.

She ducked through the doorway and then turned to look over her shoulder, her eyes fixed somewhere on the ground. The gown Helena had lent her was clutched in her fist.

"Are you coming?"

He paused in closing the door, his own rough tunic borrowed from Zeus rustling against the painted wood. "Ah . . . I'm just going to . . ." He pointed in the direction of a wheel.

Isra did raise her eyes to his then, and he realized at once how frightened she had been this night—not only by the man who had attacked her but by her own reaction to Fran, the news of van Groen and Fran's relationship, their dead child. Roman himself could pretend Isra was as calm as she sounded until he looked into her eyes. Like a window into her very soul, the emotions she'd likely long ago learned to hide thrashed and wailed and relived their damnable memories. When faced with the truth in Isra's eyes, Roman faltered.

She blinked. "You have no blanket, my lord. Everything in the cart—"

"It's mild here," he said, looking away from her as if he would observe the weather. He didn't think he could be so close to her tonight.

"Then I shall sleep on the ground with you," she announced, grasping the door ledge with both hands and beginning to reach her foot toward the dirt.

"No," he said, reaching up to stay her. She looked at his fingers on her knee and then back into his face. He dropped his hand, his neck warming. "You've had a harrowing evening and—"

"As have you," she interrupted.

"Isra, I can't," he said, looking up at her again. "It wouldn't be wise."

"Is it not time that you slept inside," she asked levelly, but the wild emotion in her eyes were legion when she added, "with me?" She reached out with trembling fingers and touched his jaw.

His heart slowed nearly to a stop at her words, and he tried to construct an alternate meaning behind her query; some way she could have meant something besides what he wanted her to mean.

"I'm not certain you know what you're asking me to do this night," he pressed.

He saw the line of her throat move as she swallowed and then nodded. She backed inside once more, and Roman grasped the door frame and pulled himself inside Asa van Groen's wagon after Isra and shut the door behind them.

He sat on his heels in the blackness until the scrape and spark of flint flashed in the dark and then the interior of the wagon was filled with a soft yellow glow and Isra was pulling a lantern up closer to the ceiling. Roman felt like a giant within the confines of the cart, as if he was looming over the small woman who mirrored his pose, her hands on her thighs.

"My costume is ruined," she said matter-of-factly and then rose up on her knees. "I apologize for my appearance." Her fingers began curling and uncurling against the flaxen material along her thighs until she grasped the hem of her gown in each fist. Then she pulled it up to her waist, and Roman realized the stains had penetrated all the way through her underdress, and that it was both thicknesses of material that were being peeled from the smooth, tan skin that was glowing in the lantern light. In an instant, Isra was completely nude, kneeling before him.

The crushed tunic fell from his grip as he struggled to breathe. Her body was so perfect, so marvelous in its natural state, she could have been the inspiration for sculpture.

"Is that more pleasing to you?" she asked with a bow of her head.

He forced himself to take a deep, hitching breath. "I've never seen anything more beautiful in all my life."

She came toward him on her knees, her shadow self already reclining on the cot fitted into the front wall of van Groen's cart. She reached out and placed her palms on his abdomen before leaning up and pressing her lips to his chest through the material of his shirt, hesitantly at first, but then she rolled her cheek into him and drew a deep breath through her nose.

Roman brought his hands up behind her and he looked at his palms as if seeing them in a dream. Isra was pressed to him, his hands just inches from her bare skin—*and now touching her.* The peaks and valleys of her shoulder blades, the pearl-strand fineness of her spine. Her skin was silk lain too long near the fire, smooth and searing and shining in the light. The smell of her like incense and bright blossoms, an offering for a flaming altar so hot that it surely must be an atonement for sin.

Was this sin?

Roman reached down and cupped the side of her jaw, turning her face toward him and then lowering his lips to hers. She answered his kiss readily, and the eagerness of her mouth made him groan in surprise. He pulled away from her.

"Isra," he whispered. "I—"

"Shh, my lord," she whispered against his skin, bringing one hand around the back of his neck and pulling his head toward hers once more. He could feel the trembling of her body against his. "Only tell me how you would have me first. I shall give you whatever pleasure you desire."

He pulled her even closer before the ugly subtlety of her words penetrated his passion-absorbed mind. He tried to ignore it, wave it away as if it was no more than a passing odor on the breeze. He might have been able to disregard the elusive bit of trouble her words alluded to had she spoken no more.

"It is the least I can do for you, after all you have done for me."

If he had jumped into the cold sea beyond the wall so close to van Groen's wagon, his desire could not have cooled more quickly. Roman grasped Isra's shoulders and moved her away from him, pulling her lips from his chest once more so that he could look into her wide, dark eyes, glistening with—passion? Fear? Resentment?

"Do you mean to sleep with me as . . . as payment for coming to your aid tonight?"

Her smooth forehead wrinkled with what perhaps might have been confusion. "Not only tonight, my lord. I owe you my life, many times over. I have nothing else to give you."

Roman felt the first stirrings of anger in his gut, a new experience for him when holding a nude, willing woman.

"You've made a fair amount of coin with Kahn by now, have you not?" he challenged.

Now it was true confusion he saw on her face. "Yes. I . . . would you rather I give you silver? I apologize." She crossed one arm over her bosom and sat back down on her heels, dropping her eyes as her cheeks bloomed and reaching her other arm around for Helena's gown. "I thought it was me you wanted."

He seized her again by her shoulders, and this time it did not matter to him whether she was clothed or not. The import of his words trumped any desire of the flesh he felt for her.

"I do want you," he insisted, "but I don't want to be . . . *paid* with your body. How could you think that of me? Of yourself?"

She turned from him as she pulled the gown up to her chest and then flipped it around her hip. "I misunderstood."

"You misunderstood?" he pressed.

"Yes," she said, rising up to her feet and turning toward the cot. She exchanged the gown for the coverlet, wrapping it about her in a one-shouldered manner, causing her to look even more like the work of some ancient artist come to warm life.

"I don't believe that," he said. "If I deserve anything this night, it's the truth, Isra. What have I done to make you think so little of me?"

"I do not think so little of you!" she insisted and turned to face him. "It is simply what I *do*, Roman! You do not understand! It is what I *am*!"

"What?" he demanded, also gaining his feet but finding he had to bend his neck in the shallow conveyance. And so he pressed between her and the cot and sat down. "What exactly are you?"

"You know," she said. "Everyone knows."

"I know the living you were forced into in order to give your sister some sort of life," he challenged. "That was what you *did*, not who you are."

"There is little difference," she said bitterly.

"I think there is a bloody lot of difference," he said, his voice growing louder. "And it's insulting that you liken me to a man no better than any of those you knew before."

"No!" she said, her eyes wide as she turned to him. "You are nothing like them."

"There was little difference between us a moment ago, was there not?" he challenged.

She stared at him for several heartbeats. "I do not know how to be with you in any other way."

"We seemed to be doing just fine before tonight," he said, and when she had no reply for him, he rose from the cot and shuffled to the door.

"Where are you going?" she asked, her voice tight, and Roman didn't want to think it was with panic. Even as angry as he was, he could not cause her any further anxiety.

"Beneath the cart, as was my original intention," he said and opened the door. But then he paused and looked back at her. "And if you still don't mind," he said, and reached out to seize a fold of the coverlet she had wrapped about her body and yanked. She was nude again in the next instant, but Roman averted his eyes before the magnificent sight of her flesh could warp his mind.

He hopped to the ground and slammed the wagon door behind him.

It was only after he'd situated himself with the thin blanket and settled down on his side to face the fire that he noticed old Mother still about, tending the flames. She was looking toward him and shaking her head, something of an exasperated expression on her face.

Roman shut her out by closing his eyes, but the sight that awaited him there was no better, as Isra Tak'Ahn's bare skin glowed as brightly in his mind as the sun.

Either way, he thought it would be a very long, uncomfortable night.

Isra lay in the plush cot belonging to Asa van Groen for what seemed like hours, staring at the golden arc of light cast from the lantern she hadn't bothered to put out. Or, rather, she hadn't wished to be locked alone in the dark with the memories that were sure to plague her after she'd humiliated herself before Roman. The same old horrors, fertilized by fresh pain, were only just bearable in the light; she knew all too well that they were strangling in the lonely dark, where memories of colors and sounds and smells could explode in bright relief against the blackness of her mind.

At least with the lantern lit, she could keep her eyes open.

She had wanted so much for Roman to see her when he looked at her—to somehow be able to forget about her past and perhaps believe that she might be of value to him as a woman. Perhaps as his woman. But her actions had only reinforced her insignificance. Reminded him of the other men she had been forced to know.

He was right; she had treated him no differently.

Roman hadn't understood that he was intrinsically different, though; she'd never wished to give herself to any man before him. She'd *wanted* to share her body with him, to give him ease, to be close to him, to show him how much he meant to her. Wasn't that what a woman did for her man? But now she understood that even though her instinct to love him had been correct, the way she'd offered herself to him had been all wrong.

Should she have played coy? Or lain back and pretended disinterest? Those were the tales she'd heard of some wives' behaviors. But neither one of those would have been the truth; Isra wanted to know what being had by a man you loved was like. Now she might have only the memory of the way Roman's lips had felt on hers to try to fill the aching chasm in her heart.

Isra turned over on her side to face the door, pulling the borrowed gown down over her legs as she drew her knees up on the pallet. She had disappointed him, and he would never look at her differently now. Isra found that she wasn't so very surprised; she didn't think she'd ever look at herself differently.

She must have dozed, for the image she held in her mind was not a memory—small Huda, only the top of her dark head visible as she crouched in the dirt of the alley behind their apartment, playing with stones in a circle she'd drawn with her finger. Yes, that image Isra had seen many happy times, but it was the tiger pacing in circles around the little girl that made the memory a nightmare. Kahn, perhaps, saliva running from his yellowed beard, his glowing eyes watching the oblivious child hungrily.

Isra wanted to call out to the Huda in the dream, to warn her to be still, be very quiet, and perhaps the tiger wouldn't see her. And then she remembered that that advice had failed so miserably in the waking world, and little Huda was dead. Brutally, and forever.

The child in the dream suddenly lifted her face and Isra saw the swollen eye, the bruised and bloodied mouth, the torn ear missing its jewel, as if Huda was immediately before her.

"Isra!" she cried in alarm.

Isra's eyes snapped open as the door to the wagon was pulled wide with a whoosh of cold air.

Roman stood in the square of night, the lantern light causing him to squint.

"Hurry," was all he said.

She didn't question him, only pushed her legs from inside the gown and stumbled toward the door, half in, half out of her nightmare, the reality returning to her like the blast of chilly December air outside the wagon: Huda only came to her in her dreams when there was impending disaster.

Isra all but fell into his arms and he set her on her bare feet in the dirt, the tiny pieces of crushed shell and sand that comprised the soil biting into her softened instep. Roman pulled her into a run as they crossed the fire circle and dashed toward the tall wagon that was lit up by torches now.

Kahn's cage, Zeus and the other strongmen struggling to pull the wooden walls away from the bars, quickly, frantically; Asa van Groen pacing near the rear door.

"What is it?" Isra called out to Roman in the cold, humid air. "Is he ill?"

"No," Roman said.

And then they were before Asa and he turned to them and reached out to grasp Isra's other hand, clearly intending to pull her away from Roman.

"Come, hurry, hurry," the dark-haired man urged, and there was something of a sob in his normally suave voice.

"Wait," Roman said, and pulled Isra back to him. "What do you expect her to do, van Groen? Go in there now? That's madness! Shall we lose them both?"

"He'll kill her!" van Groen gritted between his teeth. "She *wants* him to kill her!"

"What is going on?" Isra demanded.

Then the final wooden wall was lowered from the cage, and as the torchlight fell upon the occupants within the tiger's wagon, Isra understood the urgency.

Fran was standing in the cage staring at Kahn, who lay in his corner with only his head raised, as if he'd been woken from his slumber, which surely he had. His tufted mane, now fuller and whiter as his health improved, swung toward Isra as the edge of the wooden wall bit into the dirt, and she would have sworn before God that the animal was blaming her for this bizarre turn of events in his already confusing existence.

Wasn't it her fault, though? Wasn't everything?

Asa dropped Isra's hand and stepped toward the cage. "Fran? Franny?" he cajoled. "It's all right; we're all here now. Only back toward the door and Gunar will—"

"We're all here?" Fran interrupted in a disinterested tone, her gaze never leaving the tiger still lying across the wooden floor from her. Too close to her. "Are we now, Asa? I would disagree with you. Max isn't here, is he?"

"Franny, please," Asa pleaded in a cracking voice. "This is . . . this is *madness!*"

"Oh, and well I know it," she mused on a breath of laughter. "How I do! It was I who released Kahn the day we were joined by my fellow Norseman and your special new pet. Had you guessed it was I?"

Asa stared at the blond woman through the bars, his face slack.

"Had you?" Fran demanded in a sudden shout.

"No," Asa replied. "Fran, why . . . ?"

"Because." She paused to swallow, and one might be tempted to think she was working up courage for what she was about to say—or do. "Because even though your plan was to move south, I never know when you will suddenly change your mind, Asa. The next big surprise. And I could not risk you deciding to lead the troupe farther east. Not with . . . with winter. The cold. I thought if the tiger escaped and had to be killed . . . that with no grand show, we would find somewhere to winter. We could stay in one place for a bit so that I could . . ." She broke off again and drew a deep, jagged breath. "So that I could *mourn.*"

Isra looked to van Groen's face and was surprised at the silvery threads of wetness glowing against the man's pale cheeks.

"The troupe moved on after Max died, as did you," Fran said more calmly now. "But I can't move on, Asa. I can't move another step, now that I am without you both."

"Franny, *I love you*," van Groen insisted. "I've never stopped loving you. But you pushed me aw—"

"So since *we are all here!*" the blonde cried out and then raised her arms from her sides, and Isra saw Asa's whip in Fran's right hand. "Let's have a show, shall we? Rouse the city! Why do you lie about in slothful slumber when there is still a shilling to be had? *Hie, Kahn! Hie!*" The whip cracked, and the tiger flinched and showed his long fangs to the blonde.

Isra yanked herself free from Roman. She marched toward the cage, clapping her hands over her head. "Kahn! Kahn!" Her heart snapped against her breastbone like the whip in Fran's hand when the tiger swung his head toward her voice.

"And still you challenge me?" Fran asked in a bemused if weary voice. "Is it not enough that you have my man? My people? Go away, troublesome woman, and let me have my bloody end."

"I do not want Asa, Fran," Isra said in a stern voice, all the while holding her hands in the air and keeping her eyes fixed on Kahn's as she walked backward toward the rear of the wagon. "And he does not want me. Whatever end you think to be had is a fanciful wish. Kahn is full. He will only maul you should you continue to intrude upon his den."

"Go away."

"I cannot let you do this to the people you love," Isra said, glancing at Gunar, who stood with his hand on the door latch. "Come out now or I am coming in to get you."

"No!" Fran shouted, and Kahn flinched again, this time with a quiet hiss. "I've already told the rest and I will tell you: If the door behind me opens, I will throw myself upon him, I swear it."

Isra froze. Had they left even one of the walls up, perhaps they would have had time to insert the separating bars. She believed the blonde was speaking the truth; Isra could see the desperation and pain on her face, hear it in her words. There was a time, not so very long ago, when that kind of pain had been Isra's constant companion as well, only she'd had no beast to sacrifice herself to.

"I know what you are feeling," Isra said.

"You don't know anything," the woman spat.

"I lost a child, too: Huda. She was my sister, but I raised her as my own. She is dead, too, Fran. Dead at ten years. And not from illness, a weakness of the lungs as with Max; Huda was killed by very bad men. In the worst way a woman could be killed, and that which is unfathomable for a little girl."

Isra saw Fran pause and swallow again. "What did you do?"

"I killed the man who was their leader," Isra said, ignoring the tense thickness of the air, keeping her eyes on the tiger and the woman as she walked toward the center of the cage on cold feet. "That is why I am hiding with the troupe. Why I am running. I stabbed a man through the heart with a dagger while he lay in my bed."

"We are not so very different then, you and I, are we?" Fran mused in a choked whisper. "Did killing him make the pain go away?"

"No," Isra answered, surprised at the tears that came from her own eyes now, although her voice was steady. "I believe the pain will never go away. It will never get less. But perhaps we will one day become strong enough to bear it."

"I don't want to bear it any longer," she gasped. "I can't."

Isra turned her head only slightly to catch Roman's eye. Then she glanced at the door behind Fran, even as she continued to walk toward the opposite end of the wagon.

"You must," she insisted to the blonde as Roman sidled around the petrified van Groen toward the door she'd indicated. "You gave your son more years than he would have likely seen had you not pulled him from that gutter in Budapest. You had the honor of being his mother for four years. Will you now discredit the man he called father, the people he knew as his family, by placing them all in jeopardy and forcing an innocent creature to take your life?"

"Please, be still," Fran mewed on a sob. "I never meant you true harm, I swear it; but please, please, don't speak anymore."

Roman was in place now. Isra looked at him and he shook his head, as if he had only now realized what she was going to do.

She looked back to Fran as she stepped up on the wheel near Kahn's head. "I am coming in, Fran," she warned. "If you move any closer to Kahn, it is likely one or both of us will be badly injured. I shall not let you torment him. Or yourself," she finished. She reached for the latch.

Fran began shaking her head, her eyes once more on the tiger, as if hypnotized. "You'll be killed," she whispered.

"Kahn," Isra said in a low voice as she turned the latch. She had to take his attention from Fran, from the door behind which Roman stood at the ready. "Kahn, hie."

The tiger pulled fully onto his elbows and turned his head to look over his shoulder, the long muscles along his spine bunching. He could reach through the bars and maul her from here if he chose, but her proximity beyond the cage wasn't enough of a distraction from Fran.

"Now!" she cried, throwing open the door while the tiger shot to his feet with a half scream, backing his haunches against the bars, confused about which direction to lash out.

Fran let out a shriek and stumbled forward toward Kahn. She seemed to stop in midair and begin a retreat, but it was not fast enough. The tiger rose up with a scream and swiped his huge paws at the woman, batting her blond head as if it was nothing more than a white bit of seed fluff from one of the dried autumn pods along the early road they'd traveled from Melk. Fran went limp and Isra saw Roman's wide form behind her, dragging the blonde back toward the door.

"Kahn!" Isra screamed and stepped into the cage with her hands over her head. "Kahn, to me!"

The tiger spun around and backed into a crouch as the far door closed, his ears laid back against his skull.

"Easy, Kahn," she said in a firm, steady voice. "Easy. It is only you and I now; all is well. It is over. Easy."

The tiger hissed at her, his ears still flat, but he seemed to recognize her even if he didn't completely trust her after the debacle that had taken place in his cage.

"I am sorry to have disturbed you," she said and began to step back toward the door. "Easy. Rest now. Easy, Kahn."

His ears came erect again in hitches and starts, swiveling around to catch the commotion of sounds coming from outside his cage, but he kept his eyes trained on Isra and took a step toward her.

Isra froze once more, the words of the pale Brother Wynn so loud he could have been standing at her side, speaking into her ear.

Don't think to run. Only be still, and don't turn your back . . .

Another step and the tiger was before her, his head chest high to Isra, although, unlike the first tiger she had come into contact with, Kahn did not require the benefit of standing on the wide, raised edge of a fountain. Kahn sniffed her midsection, her arm, up her shoulder to her face.

Isra closed her eyes and closed her mind to everything except how beautiful Kahn was, and how very much she cared for him and wanted to protect him.

Then the tiger's hot breath was gone, and she felt the cage rock and a warmth close to her bare feet. When she opened her eyes, she saw that Kahn had circled around to once more lie in his corner, apparently pleased that his unwanted visitor was gone.

"Good boy," Isra whispered and stepped backward from the cage onto the tongue of the wagon. She reached for the door, but it was snatched from her hand by Zeus, and Isra herself was pulled from her perch by arms she now recognized.

Roman turned her to him, held her close.

Isra wrapped her arms as far around his wide shoulders as she could reach. She neither shook nor sobbed, but her skin was numb in the face of the stiff night wind and the horrific ordeal she'd just taken part in.

"Is she dead?" she whispered.

"I don't know," he said into her hair. "But we're leaving Dubrovnik tonight."

Isra pulled back. "You and I?"

Roman shook his head, and then Isra heard the clattering and crashing of animals being pulled from their slumber against their will; supplies tossed haphazardly inside wagons; Kahn's wooden walls being raised up tight; Lou's panicked cries from some perch he had found nearby. Isra looked over Roman's shoulder as the licking glow of flames rose above the circle of carts and wagons belonging to the troupe, and he answered her. "All of us."

Chapter 18

The city gates nearest their camp had been thrown open readily at the troupe's shouts of fire, and Roman led the caravan out of Dubrovnik in the small, black hours before dawn, driving van Groen's wagon as fast as he dared. Behind them, the flames from their abandoned cart had spread to a solitary shed and bells began to ring throughout the cold stillness of the city, alerting others to the danger that crept and crackled and sent up shimmering waves of heat in the frosty air.

The troupe was in chaos. Animals had been seized from their pens, hitched to whatever conveyance was closest or led away by men running on foot. There was no time for sorting, for order in their departure; they took advantage of the pandemonium they'd created in order to escape the city before any officials thought to stop them, question them about the fire that was meant to dispose of the body left behind in the tidy little cart with the clever hidden compartment.

The cart, their clothes, their supplies—all gone. Their plan had been in disarray nearly since they'd left the abbey weeks ago, and now it had been completely destroyed. They had no belongings, no transportation outside the sumptuous and ungainly wagon Roman now drove save the one small gray donkey, whose whereabouts were unknown at that moment. The only things Roman could claim were Isra and Lou and Constantine's letter for Baldwin, tucked—as it had been since their departure—close to his skin. He and Isra should have already sailed the Mediterranean, disembarking at Alexandria in Egypt, should now be refining their plan to attempt to warn the king of Jerusalem about the threat to his life. Instead, they were fleeing a hostile city as members of a traveling faire heading east toward the Balkan Mountains, and Fran might be dead.

Roman was pushing the team as fast as he dared on the rough, dark road; one missed curve and he would not only overturn the wagon but the conveyances behind him would quickly pile atop them, led by the lantern swinging wildly at their rear. He tried not to think of poor Lou, locked away behind the door of van Groen's wagon, but it was the safest place for the falcon until they stopped in the daylight. He guessed the caravan was at least a quarter mile long. They would have to travel for some distance to be far enough away to be out of reach and to find a place large enough to accommodate their camp. And so, while the darkness hid their flight, it also threatened their destruction, and Roman rushed to meet the dawn at the horizon.

Isra was at his side, her thin gown and bare feet hidden by the coverlet she clutched around her with one hand, while her other gripped the edge of the seat. She'd not said anything since they'd fled the city, and Roman wondered if the combined events of the last evening had finally broken her. He could not devote a moment to recalling what had taken place; it had shaken him so to see Isra endanger her life for the troubled Fran, and now that she was safe beside him, it was all he could do to simply drive the wagon, telling himself that he was carrying her farther away from the danger that lay behind them when in truth he knew they were likely only hastening toward danger of a different sort.

He began to slow their pace incrementally after what he guessed to be two hours, but he did not stop. Even when the sky grew gray and even colder than the black of midnight, Roman drove on. They passed through a small village, mostly abandoned by its appearance, and just outside the last ruined shelter he spied a ramshackle barn, half burned some time ago by its dark and crumbled appearance. The building leaned into the dawn, showing the sun's bright rays through its pitched doorway as if it was a mouth singing glorious praises to the morn.

Roman felt like doing the same after such a hellish night. He called back to Zeus, riding on horseback just beyond the rear of van Groen's wagon. As soon as Roman had given the command, the bald man turned his horse to relay the word, and Roman drove the tired team around the bright side of the ruined barn and stopped.

Isra was clambering down from the wagon before it had even rocked to a halt, and although Roman looked after her as she fled, leaving her coverlet to dangle from the floorboard, he did not call out. He knew where she was going.

He stood in the driver's seat and stretched his back for a moment before climbing down stiffly and unhitching the horses, holding them by their bridles while the last of the carts passed before him. Then he joined the group of men setting up a corral on the sound side of the barn. Within moments he was engaged in the work, trying not to think about where Isra was and what she was seeing.

Asa van Groen was sitting on the side of Fran's cot when Isra pulled herself into the back of the gaily painted wagon. Old Mother shut the door behind her, darkening the interior once more. The single lantern light gave the quarters a moribund, heavy air, combined with the thick stench of life leaking out of a person. Asa's marvelous dark hair stood up in great, thick tufts through his fingers, which gripped his skull. He looked up at her entrance, his face gray, drawn, deep lines having suddenly appeared at the sides of his mouth in the hours since Isra had last seen him. His white shirt was no longer white but instead resembled the blood-soaked queen's costume Isra had discarded. Van Groen was not painted with a criminal's blood, though; it was Fran's blood. The blood of the woman he loved.

Behind him, the coverlets piled high and tucked in taut around her thin body, lay Fran. Isra could not see her face, for Mother had returned straightaway to the stricken woman's side, and was bent over her, seeming to mop at her face with a rag that she dipped periodically into a shallow earthen bowl.

"Where are we?" Asa asked in a gravelly, tired voice.

Isra shook her head. "Outside a village. Almost deserted."

Van Groen nodded slightly. "Everyone escape from Dubrovnik?"

"I think so," Isra said, but in truth she didn't know. She steeled her nerves and glanced toward the still figure on the cot. "How is she?"

"Bad." The word was reedy and crackled. "Mother has stitched her as well as any could. But—" He stopped, pushed the tips of his long fingers deep into the corners of his eyes. "Part of her scalp is . . . I could see her *skull*."

The hag turned then, dropping the stained rag in the bowl with a little splash and holding it tight to her middle. "I've need of some things from my own cart. I'll carry you back a bite, Asa."

He waved a hand. "Not hungry."

Mother waved back with a nod. "All the same . . ." Then she opened the door and ducked out, shutting Isra inside with van Groen and Fran.

He didn't look up again, and Isra hesitantly moved closer to the cot, both dreading and needing to see the condition of the woman lying on it. She caught her gasp before it could escape, but now it sat lodged painfully in her throat.

Fran's beautiful, smooth, Nordic complexion was gone; the left side of her face was no longer symmetrical with the right, hitched up higher on her skull, stretched tight by the ugly black strands of gut running in a jagged, mismatched track from in front of her left ear to the crown of her head. The blond hair—so like silk, Isra had thought at one time—had been hacked away close to the mottled scalp. The wound was puckered, weeping; her thin, pale lips flattened and pulled to the side. Her eyelids were purple, swollen, even as her sockets appeared to have doubled in size. There must have been another wound on the back of her skull, for the embroidered pillow beneath her head showed concentric rings of dried and fresh blood, like a macabre halo in a painting.

Fran now looked like the monster Isra had called her, and in that moment, she was shamed to the core of her soul. Regret seized her heart and squeezed with a mighty fist so that she whimpered.

She went to her knees at the side of the cot and reached out a trembling hand to place it over Fran's chest, heaving unsteadily with each breath.

Forgive me, Fran. Forgive me for judging you as I felt judged. Forgive me for not seeing how similar we are; for not asking. Forgive me my cowardice and my fear that shrouded my heart in anger toward you. Forgive me, forgive me.

"She might not awaken," van Groen said, but his inflection made his words seem a query rather than a statement, and Isra knew he was seeking any shred of reassurance.

"No one can know except God," Isra managed, and nearly choked on the words. Had God saved Huda or Max? Did God even care to save the dying from this life? She saw the motion of Asa nodding from the corner of her eye and thought she heard a muffled sob.

Was it up to the dying to live?

Please, Fran, I beg you, live for Asa.

But Fran didn't so much as twitch.

Isra rose slowly to her feet, letting her palm linger on the still woman. "How can I help you, Asa?"

Asa scrubbed his face with his palms and sighed. "Send Roman to me. I won't leave her, not even for a moment."

"Of course." Isra hesitated and then reached out to place her hand on van Groen's stooped shoulder. "I am sorry, Asa. Sorry for Fran and for . . . for Max."

Van Groen gave a sniffling inhalation and then reached up and grasped Isra's fingers. He turned her hand and pressed his lips to her palm, and she was reminded of the first morning they'd met, when he'd sought to kiss her hand. It had been a flamboyantly courteous gesture, and one Isra had taken as playacting, but now she understood that everything about Asa van Groen was larger than life—his occupation, his hair, his teeth, his personality, his enthusiasm and flair for the dramatic.

His loves. His losses. His grief.

She squeezed his fingers in return. "I shall fetch Roman."

He nodded and let her go, turning his eyes toward the mangled visage of the woman lying on the cot. And Isra saw love sweep over his face.

She escaped Fran's wagon with a gasp, pressing her back against the closed door. The folk who were busy near the cart stopped what they were doing and looked to her.

"She yet lives," Isra called out.

The camp gave a collective sigh and then turned back to their work without comment.

We're a superstitious lot, we are. You don't talk about a thing lest you want it, you see?

Isra did see now. She stood aright from the wagon and looked around for Roman. She didn't spy his tall frame over those gathered, but when she heard the echoing pings of a hammer coming from inside the ruined shelter, she knew where she would find him.

He and several of the other men appeared to be attempting to brace the interior of the falling-down barn with some timbers they'd salvaged. He looked up when she entered the crooked doorway as if he'd been waiting for her, and she thought he looked very strong and capable then, his tool in his hand, his shirt already wet through from his efforts. He walked toward her.

"Asa wants you," she said in greeting.

Roman nodded and looked out the doorway over the rolling land-scape—stark and winter empty, though not frigid in the bright morn-ing sun. "Is she dead?"

"No." Isra began to turn away. "I must look in on Kahn."

"Isra, wait," he said and reached out to take her hand.

She looked down at his fingers gripping hers and then back into his face.

"If he asks us to stay . . . ?"

Isra blinked. "Here?"

"With the band. If he asks *you* to stay," he clarified. "You needn't go on with me. It would only put you in greater danger. Once I have done what I set out to do, I will return to Melk."

His meaning hung in the air between them: He would return to his friends at the abbey and Isra would be left alone. In an instant, im-ages flashed through her mind of the moment when she would bid this man farewell. The weeks without him, when she would be won-dering where he was on his journey, if he had arrived, succeeded, survived. She might never know if he lived to return to his friends at Melk. If she let him go now, it would surely be forever.

How would she even breathe without him?

"I go where you go," she said calmly, although the emotions trapped in her chest were anything but calm. "Until the end of it."

"You're certain?" he pressed, and she couldn't help but recall with a stab of regret that those same words had crossed his lips only last night, when she had thought they would make love.

"I came a very long way to find you," she replied carefully. "It was I who insisted you return. Even for this moment, I was destined; this barn. The guard who attacked me; Fran and Kahn. It was always intended for me to flee Dubrovnik in the middle of the night."

"Why?" he asked intently, as if very certain he must know her an-swer.

"I do not know. But if all of this is not part of something bigger, something better, then my suffering—yours, and that of your friends—was for nothing. Huda's death only a random evil."

"I would like to know for certain that we are doing the right thing," he confessed. "If it is for naught . . ."

She squeezed his hand and then slipped away from him.

She could not tell him that she had dreamed of Huda.

* * *

"I should have known better than to grant them entrance, let alone invite them to stay another night," the mayor said, falling into his chair with a sigh. "Monsters and criminals, the lot of them! It's a miracle they didn't burn down all of Dubrovnik. The woman, though—ah, she was a pleasure. Would that you had had the chance to see her with her beast, my lord. An amazing sight, I must confess."

"Your courtesy is much appreciated, Lord Mayor," the guest said, settling into his own chair and taking the chalice from the tray held forth by the servant boy. "Though I am too much enamored with my new bride to have any interest in a random encounter, no matter how exotic the creature. I have seen my fill of strange beasts in the past several months. They hold little appeal for me now."

"The Holy Land, eh?" the mayor guessed with a scoffing laugh. "I have heard tales of the savage ways there."

Glayer Felsteppe shrugged one shoulder. "There, and lands across the sea. Regardless, I wish I could tell you that our party passed them on the road so at least you could give chase and bring such criminals to justice."

"Bah. Good riddance to them," the mayor said with an annoyed grimace and a wave of his thick hand. "Although I am surprised you have come overland and not by ship, if you are in such a hurry to return to your home with your wife."

Glayer let a boyish grin creep over his face. "Indeed, it was my original intention to return by sea. In fact, although permission had already been granted us by the king, we were not to be married until after my return to England."

"Oh?" the mayor's eyebrows rose.

"Without causing my lady undue embarrassment . . ." He looked over at the woman sitting apart from them in a chair by the window, her beautiful face devoid of any expression as she stared through the glass, her rich brown hair twisted into a thick, spiraling rope over her shoulder beneath her veil. Her hands in her lap, the refreshments offered to her sat untouched at her side. "She gave me quite the surprise by arriving in Jerusalem unannounced. We soon discovered we had need of an early ceremony, lest the legitimacy of my heir be held in question. Travel by sea was no longer in my wife or child's best interest."

The mayor threw back his head and let out a roar of laughter, which, at last, caused the woman to flinch. "Ah! Well, my best to you both, and let us raise our cups in hopes of a boy, shall we? To the future of your great endowment—may it prosper and forever find favor."

Glayer Felsteppe, Earl of Rosemont, lifted his chalice with a grin. "Indeed."

Chapter 19

They left van Groen and Fran behind before the sun reached its zenith in the sky the next day. Although everyone in the band was still exhausted and frazzled from the sudden flight out of Dubrovnik, they would not jeopardize the couple by drawing attention to the dilapidated barn. Roman and Zeus and the other men had shored it as much as they could, and then led the horse pulling Fran's wagon inside, guaranteeing cover from the road by any who might pass by, as well as making the animal easy for van Groen to care for on his own.

Old Mother had wanted to stay and help nurse the menagerie's artist; perhaps she had even intimated to Asa that Fran might live. But van Groen had sent the hag—like the rest of the band—away with his kind apologies, expressing the sentiment that he wanted Fran's last hours, last days of life to be spent in solitude with no travel, no guests. At last having the full attention and care of the man who still loved her so deeply.

Everyone had left an offering of some kind. Mostly foodstuffs and drink to sustain him during his wake, although some had left talismans, charms of sorts, along with mementos they possessed of the woman who lay dying. Bits of costume she'd created, drawings she'd made of the troupe members. Perhaps they thought to leave a part of themselves behind as witness. But no one had argued with van Groen's wishes, and so now Roman led the caravan southeast over the dusty road toward Constantinople, Isra on his right upon the driver's seat, Gunar on horseback beyond her; Zeus riding to Roman's left on his own mount.

Roman didn't know how he had come to be the leader of this strange band of folk, who, upon their first meeting, had stolen from him and attempted to have him beaten to a pulp. But he would do his best not to disappoint them. Or van Groen.

Or the once more quiet woman at his side.

"Will you show Kahn again?" he asked. "Van Groen told me he gave you leave to do with him what you would."

Isra looked over the tan stretches of fallow field, so like the sand they would soon be surrounded by, but with the thick smell of plant matter lingering like ghosts of crops past.

"I do not wish to," she said at last, her voice faint, distant. "What happened with Fran was no fault of Kahn's. But . . ." Her words faded away and she was quiet for a time. "I see little reason why the act should be revived."

Roman agreed, and in truth, he was relieved by her answer. It would be enough of a task to keep the band together and out of the jails of the various municipalities as they traveled farther south; enough to keep everyone safe and fed and distracted from the heartbreak they carried away from van Groen and the ruined barn. To think of Isra continuing to climb in the cage with the tiger night after night gave him a searing pain in his stomach.

"We have plenty of coin to last us the remainder of our journey," he said in an effort to cheer her. "A surplus, in fact. Considerably more than we left Melk with."

Isra gave a disinterested hum and was quiet for so long that Roman thought she was simply not able to speak to him at the moment, and he had resolved to let her be.

"Now we must only survive the journey," she said at last and then looked to him. "And the destination. We have no plan for once we reach Syria. How we are to locate Baldwin, gain access to him."

Roman pinched his lips together. He was surprised that she had been thinking about the task that lay yet before them. If he was to be honest with himself, there had been entire days when Roman had forgotten the real reason he and Isra were on this mad journey together.

"I work best without a plan," he reminded her. When she didn't answer him, he looked to his right and saw Isra was regarding him with a weary smile, her cheekbone propped on a fist, one eyebrow quirked.

"You're very pretty when you're exasperated with me," he said.

Her smile widened. "I could never be exasperated with you. My lord."

"Is that so? Well, I see *you* have no compunction in exasperating *me*."
And, having been well caught out, Isra at last laughed.

They passed through only two villages in the next five days, and
the first burg was still too close to van Groen and Fran for reaping
from it what coin they could. The second village ordered them
through in no uncertain terms. By the time they reached the first
signs of the metropolis of Constantinople on the afternoon of the fifth
day, Isra could plainly see the crease of worry that had taken up residence between Roman's light eyebrows.

Some in the band were running out of food, and grazing had been
scarce for the animals. They needed to find hospitable hosts willing
to sell to them that night—on the morrow at the latest—if everyone
shared what they had left and they could find a meager patch of land
to overnight on.

Zeus returned to their cart from his patrol with his horse at a gal-
lop and a gap-toothed smile on his face, and within an hour, the
troupe was pulling all through and round a fringe of dwellings lying
just two miles outside the city walls. Isra was glad to once more see
Roman's ready smile as the folk procured their supplies from the village merchants. They set up the round as dusk fell and the musical
cacophony of readying for an audience Isra had become so fond of
filled the air.

But she watched Roman's frown gradually return as she leaned
next to him against Kahn's paneled wagon, and the dusk turned to
night and the moon rose high into the air over the sounds of the lute
and drum and the yapping of Helena's dogs . . . and the audience
didn't come.

Save for a few bored adolescents who appeared to scoff at the performers, none of the villagers bothered to attend van Groen's Magical
Menagerie. Not one shilling was made. The troupe was subdued as
they tore down the awnings and bundled and strapped the extinguished
torches and retreated to their wagons for the night.

Tomorrow, they called to each other.

Tomorrow, they repeated like an incantation.

Roman was one of the last to quit when he crawled into Asa van
Groen's wagon; Isra guessed it must have been past midnight. Lou
flapped for balance on his thick shoulder.

"You are taking your duties very seriously," she observed from the cot, the silken embroidered coverlet fisted under her chin. "There was little reason for you to stay so late."

He dropped to one knee and pulled the door behind him, then deposited his falcon on its perch before settling onto his hip against a side wall with a sigh rather than stoop beneath the ceiling. "I promised van Groen I would look out for the troupe as far as Jerusalem," he said. "Or wherever we end up." He scrubbed both large hands over his face and then dropped them to his lap while he leaned his head back to gaze up past the lantern. "I don't think I'm doing a very good job of it."

"It is through no fault of yours that no one came," Isra argued softly. "The troupe ate tonight. The horses are grazing. I count that as a success."

"I badly underestimated van Groen for a very long time after we joined the caravan," Roman mused, ignoring her arguments. "I thought him little more than a peacock. A petty thief with no usefulness at all."

"A peacock?" Isra asked, intrigued, liking when he spoke at such length.

Roman continued looking at the seam of wall and ceiling. "A man who has better costumes than I." He rolled his head along the wall to give her a slight smile.

She returned his smile and allowed, "Asa is a good man." She swallowed, giving herself a moment to rethink what she was about to say. "Roman?"

He looked at her, his eyebrows raised. The fatigue, the worry was clear on his face.

"Will you sleep with me tonight?" His eyebrows shot up even farther, and she rushed to add, "Not . . . no! I mean, will you take your rest here, in the cot? I cannot bear to think of you sleeping on such an unforgiving surface when you have toiled so diligently."

"I would crowd you," he said, looking away from her and reaching up and pulling his folded stack of blankets from the narrow shelf along the wall. "There is barely enough room in that bed for a slight thing like yourself; I don't know how van Groen and Fran managed all those years." He made a show of arranging his makeshift pallet on the floor. "I'll be fine here."

Isra knew she had a choice to make in that moment. She could demurely agree and thank Roman for his consideration, roll over, and go to sleep in the bed alone.

Or she could own the knowledge that the days they had left together might likely be counted on both her hands. She could own it, and she could look for a bit of bravery somewhere deep inside her, where the horrors of her past had somehow failed to reach. She could be brave enough to try again.

Did she have any bravery left?

She felt tears welling in her eyes as the fear of what might happen in the next several moments became a near tangible thing sitting heavy upon her shoulders. She didn't know if she could survive another rejection by him, but she wanted him close so badly, needed him, and she knew he needed someone, too. Perhaps it wasn't her, but she was there, and perhaps she would be enough for a time, any matter. She could try her very hardest to be.

She reached behind her for the long, thin pillow she'd been using, and her other hand balled the coverlet onto her lap. She dragged the bedclothes from the cot as she slid over the side to her knees and then crossed the short expanse of rough wood in that manner to settle onto her hip at Roman's side against the wall. She didn't look up at him as she dragged the covers along the floor after her, bunching them up onto her legs and then slowly, incrementally, pushing them over onto Roman's lap.

He didn't stop her hand, didn't protest, so Isra then spread them out deliberately, reaching across to tuck the hem of the coverlet beyond the long length of his leg. When they were both covered over with the blanket, she tucked her arms inside, pulling the top up over her shoulder. Then, without daring to peek up at him, she hesitantly lay the side of her face against the thick hardness of his arm.

Her eyes were wide in the dim light of the wagon, the painful, obvious quiet. She tried not to breathe, as if she could somehow suffocate her nervous trembling.

It seemed an hour later before his deep voice rumbled, and the sound of it caused her stomach to leap.

"Isra, you cannot stay like this."

There it was, then. She began to rise to a seated position once more, feeling the absence of his warmth already from her face, the despair sinking into her stomach and eating through the bottom. What a pathetic fool she was.

"If you are going to insist that both of us sleep on the floor, you might at least turn over so that we may lie flat," he said, and it took every shred of physical self-control she had not to gasp in giddy relief.

But she said nothing, only moved her bottom along the rough boards so that she could recline. She turned onto her left side, facing the empty cot, Roman's large body between her and the door.

The lantern light swung wildly for a moment and he gave a huff behind her before the interior of the wagon went pitch. In the next moment, his long warmth seemed to envelop her as he lay down behind her. She squeezed her eyes shut and brought a hand to her mouth; she could not weep now, even in happiness.

She had been right; he did *need her.*

But then his arm came around her just below her shoulder, and it was so the embodiment of everything Roman Berg had done for her already, stood for, meant to her, that Isra could no longer hold back her quiet sob.

He didn't question her weeping, though, only drew her more closely to him. Isra took her hand from her mouth and lay it along Roman's forearm, a smile coming over her entire face in the dark even as her tears ran free and soaked the thin pillow beneath her head.

"Shh," he said against the crown of her head, and then he pressed his lips there for a long moment. Even when he turned his mouth away from her scalp she could feel the heat of his breath cutting through her hair.

And then Isra slept.

Chapter 20

Roman led the caravan into the city proper the next day, not bothering to send Zeus ahead. Constantinople was an enormous, messy mix of humanity, filled with holy houses and brothels, princes and criminals. The troupe were paid little heed as they passed through the gates, and Roman felt his heart lighten further at the idea that the band following him would change their lack of coin into a surplus that night. The streets were teeming with people: merchants, children, pilgrims, soldiers. It took the caravan the better part of two hours to make it through the crowded thoroughfares while exotic and lively music seemed to manifest from the very air of the city itself.

They settled most of the wagons in a long line along the city wall, paying a shopkeeper two nights' rent in advance to pull the main performing wagons into the alley along his place of business. There they would entertain the city dwellers as night fell, although some of the performers—Barnaby, old Mother, Delilah—set up works right away. Even Lou took the opportunity to be off on the hunt. It wasn't the best location in the city to be certain, but their prospects were better here than anywhere they had been in the past week. Roman helped shoo the last of the animals into a temporary corral in a corner created where the alley met the city wall and then turned to Zeus.

"Have you need to be away from the troupe?" he asked plainly.

"Not at once, big fellow," he answered with a grin. "What would you have me do?"

A moment later, Roman strode through the narrow alley, his eyes scanning the heads of the band in search of long black hair and—

"Isra," he said near her ear as he gently took hold of her elbow, pulling her away from the stack of beaded necklaces she was helping Delilah untangle.

She spun around, a smile already on her face. "My lord, how may I serve you?"

"I fancy a walk about the bazaar. Would you care to join me?" He knew his grin was foolish, but he didn't care.

Isra's eyes widened. "I do not—I have never . . ."

"Come," he said, tucking her hand beneath his arm and leading her from beneath Delilah's awning. He paused and turned back toward the wooden bin of crafts the bearded woman had produced, and reached inside to pluck a small circlet of dull beads strung on a thin leather strip from among the trinkets.

He held it up to the hirsute Delilah. "May I?"

"Certainly, dearie!" she called out in her childishly high voice. "With my love!"

Roman smiled at her and then took Isra's left hand and slipped the beaded ring onto her middle finger.

"There," he said and returned her hand back beneath his arm. "Now no one will question your right to purchase whatever your heart desires."

She said nothing, and when Roman looked down at her, she was staring in the direction of her hand.

"Only don't pay them what they first ask," he cautioned.

She looked up at him. "What?"

"The merchants—they are terrible cheats. They always begin with a price that is at least twice the item's value. You must refuse their first offer."

Isra blinked. "What?"

Roman felt his smile soften and he stopped in the street, turning his body toward hers. He brought his left hand up to touch her cheek.

"Are you happy, Isra?" he asked.

"I—yes," she said, her eyes still wide with confusion, doubt.

He leaned down until his nose touched hers. "Good. So am I. Let's don't spend all the money." He pulled her along once more into the milling crush.

It took her almost an hour to warm to the experience, but once Isra had lost her anxiety, she picked and haggled, chose and refused from the vast and seemingly endless variety of items for sale at the market. Two long silken scarves in aqua and green; a pot of balm for her skin. A leg of lamb for Kahn. His back had been turned to her when she made her final purchase, and Roman was speechless when he saw the long white tunic, open on the sides and slit high in the front and back for ease of walking and riding. A long, narrow belt completed the costume. The garment reminded him of the Templars', and although he didn't know if Isra had intended the costume to allude to the fighting men he had lived in such close proximity with for so long, he was touched by the gifts.

"Now you can be a peacock, too," she said, and it caused him to laugh up into the smoky, sunny sky and squeeze her hand.

He saw the thin copper circlet, wrapped around smooth, polished tigers' eye gems, and broke his own rule by purchasing it outright at the merchant's first offer. It was the only one of its kind among the cheaper, duller hair decorations, and he knew it was meant for the beautiful woman at his side—the woman who could command such a beast as the gem was named for. He slipped it over the plain scarf she wore on her head, and at her smile, Roman knew he would have paid any amount to see such happiness on her face.

They acquired meat on long sticks and sisal-wrapped jugs of wine and then took their meal on the edge of a common. Isra was fascinated by the tremendous diversity of the crowd, and Roman was fascinated by Isra.

How could such a gentle soul still be contained inside a woman who was so strong? How could she continue to reach out over and over to others—to him—when Roman doubted she had been shown care by anyone at all for years? When necessary, Isra would defend herself and those she wished to protect. But her physical beauty was so blinding, no one who met her could at once have any idea that even greater treasures lay beneath her exquisite exterior.

He wanted to kiss her then, but it was not yet time.

She caught him staring at her and he held her gaze for a long moment before rising and leading her back through the maze of streets to the alley they had rented. Performers all across the city came alive around them as they walked, the sky grew darker, the music grew louder, and endless torches and lanterns lit up Constantinople.

The nightly party began.

Roman waved a farewell to Zeus and the other men as they headed into the city's interior, looking for fights and female companionship. He didn't for one moment consider trying to mask the men's intended destinations from Isra; she wasn't stupid, and he would not disrespect her by treating her as such.

"Does it bother you?" he asked, suddenly looking down at her, surprised to see her face rather than the crown of her head, as was her usual posture when they were in public. At her frown, he clarified, "Being in the city?"

She gave a shrug of her slight shoulders and turned her eyes away, but only forward, not down. "It is a city," she said easily. "Not my city."

She was quiet for a moment as they neared the rear of van Groen's wagon. Lou was already waiting for them, perched on top and obviously fatter for his recent excursion.

"I should have left when our mother was killed," she said as they came to a stop, and Lou hopped down onto Roman's shoulder. "Huda was beginning to question our life and not understanding what it meant, she had talked about the day when she would enter into the common room to be called on. Perhaps in the way that other girls with other lives dream of the day they shall marry. She thought it all jewels and perfume and being told that you are pretty." Isra took her eyes from the falcon to look directly at Roman. "She was wearing one of my scarves, one of my robes, the day it happened. Playing pretend that went too far. I thought that by staying I would protect her, provide her with a place to live while I tried to find a better way. But instead it is my fault that she is dead."

Roman looked down into her deep brown eyes, tearless now, but filled with a painful sincerity that seemed to pierce his own heart. He had not been expecting this admission, or this insight into the damage her heart had sustained. But he had always welcomed heavy weight.

"It is not your fault, Isra," he said. "Nothing you did, nothing Huda could have done, warranted the actions of the animals who killed her."

"I should have left with her after—"

"And gone where?" Roman interrupted. He took her parcels from her and set them inside the door of the wagon so that he could take both her hands in his own. "Where could you have gone alone, with a young girl? Tell me true and I will accuse you as you seem to want me to do."

Her eyebrows rose into a sad frown. "Anywhere."

"You say that now," he said. "But you know the truth as well as I.

Anywhere would have been as bad but likely worse. You both might have ended up dead."

"Or just me," Isra insisted. "Huda might have lived."

"You're right," he said with a nod. "You could have died and Huda could have lived. She could have married a wealthy foreign mercenary and moved away to Spain and borne many children and lived a long and happy life." Her chin flinched then, and that was all right; it was warranted, expected.

"I know what you are feeling, Isra Tak'Ahn," he continued in a firm voice. "Why was I spared that day at Chastellet? Why was I forced to watch hundreds of men I'd lived with, worked alongside, die bloody, horrible deaths? My own apprentice—a good man, already with a wife and child at home—struck down while urging me to safety. Had he not done that, his child might still have a father.

"Why did Constantine survive the battle, survive the torment of Saladin's prison, only to learn that Glayer Felsteppe had murdered his wife and only child? What of Asa; should he lose Fran after also losing their son to this life on the road?"

Her eyes were big and round now, perhaps with fright at the things he was saying, the wide open, bottomless, cold truth that Roman knew now stretched out before Isra like a black chasm. So he released her hands and grasped her shoulders, showing her that she was not alone in this discovery.

"I don't know why I lived. I don't know why Huda died. But I do know that neither of us can claim responsibility for any of it."

"Perhaps," she said quietly. "Perhaps you are right, Roman Berg. It does not make my regret any less, though."

"You wouldn't be the woman you are if it did," he said and then released her. "Now come, enough of this sadness and remorse. Let us revive our happiness of the day by letting our friends amuse us."

Old Mother had done a fair business for the day, being situated nearer the end of the alley closest to the thoroughfare, but to earn her coins had meant calling out to the passersby all the long day and the elderly woman was clearly exhausted. She was packing up her small table when Isra and Roman reached her, the drawstring pucker of her mouth even more pronounced.

She was shaking her frizzled gray head. "Too far away," she

complained, her tone more concerned than plaintive. She flicked her hooded eyes to the street behind Isra and Roman. "Too many players."

Mother's words were echoed by the rest of the troupe—collectively, they'd not even earned enough coin to replenish what they'd spent on the rent of the alley.

Isra looked up at Roman's face, and the worry was back in full force, carving great lines on either side of his usually smiling mouth.

"I'll set out at first light," he said. "Try to find a better location."

Dracus shook his head, twirling his bow around on the toe of his boot. None of the pedestrians had been interested in his displays of marksmanship. "We can't afford a better location now, boss," he said. "We've got one night of rent left, food yet to buy on the morrow."

Isra looked around while the two men discussed the surprisingly dire turn of events the troupe found themselves facing. This was Constantinople—one of the most decadent cities in all the world, filled with travelers, nobility, soldiers. Gaining this town should have earned the band coin aplenty to continue on toward Syria, but as Isra took in the other offerings now lighting up the night streets, she thought she realized why.

There, across the way, a man juggled long sticks of fire, alternately lighting and extinguishing each of his feet as the batons twirled.

She walked to the end of their all but deserted alley and looked in both directions: a man in the center of the avenue with a long sword poised half in and half out of his throat; a woman dancing in front of a tavern, her body covered in nothing more than a multitude of sheer scarves; farther down the thoroughfare, the familiar tall humps of camels dressed in red and gold costumes, ferrying drunken patrons in circuits.

Van Groen's menagerie had dogs. A bearded woman. A juggler. Perhaps enough amusement for the northern continent, but here, in this city of excess, dogs were no better than lice.

"We stay much longer, we won't have coin enough to leave," Dracus was explaining to Roman behind her in an apologetic tone.

Isra turned around and looked past where Nickle had joined Roman and Dracus to the tall, shadow-draped wagon standing silently near van Groen's.

It was one thing to go walking in the bazaar with Roman Berg in the daylight, quite another to draw attention to herself at night, when the exact manner of men she was seeking to hide herself from would be about the city streets. They were so much closer to Damascus now . . .

But Kahn needed to eat tonight, any matter.

And so did the troupe.

Isra could not simply stand by while Roman thought himself a failure when she might be the only one who could turn the troupe's fortune. She knew he would never consider abandoning the caravan here, although they had plenty of coin to purchase horses of their own and continue on to Jerusalem without the troupe. Roman had given his word to van Groen, and Isra herself would not leave Kahn; after Fran, no one else was brave enough even to feed the tiger. They might have more than another week of travel out of Constantinople ahead of them, and—as a group, as a family—they needed coin and supplies.

She turned back to the street, and to the flame thrower whose circle of spectators was large and well-lit by the score of torches standing at the ready to aid his performance. Bright light danced over the crowd and across the street to barely tease at the entrance of the alley.

All that bright, rippling light would turn Kahn's striped coat into exotic treasure.

Isra took a deep breath before spinning on her heel and marching toward the small cluster of folk now gathered around Roman.

"Ready Kahn's wagon to be moved," she called out in a clear voice as she approached. "Pull it into the street at the end of the alley, but do not let down the walls."

They stared at her as if she had just commanded them all to fly, but she only continued in her instruction.

"We have no time for a curtain, but we will draw a bigger crowd if they can gather around."

"Mistress," Dracus cautioned, "we've paid no tax to perform in the street. If we are cited—"

Isra didn't understand the intricacies of which Dracus spoke, and in the heat of the moment she didn't care. She only knew she must act immediately if she was to retain her nerve.

"We will pay whatever fine we incur," she said, and then gestured to the man at the end of the alley, who appeared to have accidentally or otherwise set his hair on fire and was dunking his head in a nearby barrel to the delight of the crowd. "Think you Kahn and I are no better than that buffoon?"

"Isra," Roman said quietly, "the last time you were in Kahn's cage, he attacked Fran. How will he react now, in this strange setting, with an unpredictable crowd? We are without even Zeus and the other men to ensure their distance."

"Fran attacked *Kahn*. And I have no need of strong men," she said. "I have a Roman soldier." She held his gaze, forcing herself to be brave. "And I have faith in Kahn. Would that you have some in me."

"I do have faith in you," Roman insisted. "It's only—"

"We are part of this troupe," she interrupted. And then, more quietly, "*I* am part of this troupe. Everyone works," she added with a smile, echoing some of the first words Fran had spoken to her. "If you do not like it, take it up with Asa when next you see him."

Dracus was looking back and forth between Isra's face and Roman's, and Isra could feel his anticipation. Finally, he blurted, "Well, boss?"

"Do whatever she asks," he said at last.

Isra hesitated for only a heartbeat of time, afraid that if she spoke so much as a word of thanks her bravado would leave her. And so she strode toward the wagon, her heart pounding in her chest, her skin tingling.

She enlisted Delilah's help with her hair, and the woman made quick work of Isra's long tresses, producing a mass of thin plaits twisted with flowing, silken ribbons. In the bottom of a flat, shallow trunk beneath Asa's cot she found one of his short, fitted green tunics and slipped it on over her gown. The last two pieces of her costume were the black leather whip and the tiger's eye circlet given to her by Roman only hours before. She placed the bejeweled copper low on her head, bisecting her forehead, then turned and held out her arms for Delilah's inspection.

The woman's beard twitched as she considered Isra's costume. "It's a strange combination," she admitted and then nodded her head. "I think it will be a great success."

They left the wagon, and Isra saw right away the crowd that was already gathering on the thoroughfare at the end of the alley, curious about the contents of the painted wagon and about the large man dressed in the long tunic and belt, his leather hood lying over his shoulders where Lou perched regally. Together, man and bird paced in a circle around Kahn's wagon. Gunar was atop the fantastically painted cage, Asa's long staff in one hand and the stiff collar around his own neck, striding along the edges, his words rolling over the crowd.

"From the darkest corners of the jungles lining that great river, where even the bravest men dare not tread, comes the most exquisite pairing of beauty and terror ever seen by northern eyes." Gunar glanced down the alley and saw Isra approaching, and then turned his attention back to the crowd while sweeping his arm behind him. "Brace yourselves for the most thrilling sight ever witnessed by man: Kahn the Terrible and his queen!"

Isra swept into the circle of light on the thoroughfare and felt the eyes upon her, but she gave herself no time to succumb to fear. She advanced, circling the wagon herself as she spoke, throwing her arms wide and gesturing with the leather whip.

"Many years ago, in a city so rich its streets were lined with gold and silver," she called out in a robust voice, "there lived a great prince. He claimed great wealth and commanded powerful armies, but his most longed-for treasure was the heart of a poor young woman from a village under his rule."

She stopped in her march and reversed direction as she noticed more and more people drawing near the wagon. Even the flame thrower himself had paused in his performance and now looked toward Isra with interest. Dracus and Helena and Nickle were circling the crowd with the baskets and Isra was encouraged by the tiny clinks she heard in the still night air.

"His station would not allow him to make the poor village girl his wife. Eventually she was married to a man of her class and soon had a family of her own. The great prince was heartbroken and swore he would have no other. Instead, he took to leaving his palace in the dark of night to stalk the jungle around his love's village, watching her as she tended her house and raised her children. The pain of departing from her grew greater with each rising of the sun, until he could no longer bear leaving the jungle even for a short time lest he miss catching a glimpse of the woman he loved.

"The prince soon became wild; his hair grew long and striped with the shadows of the thick forest, his teeth became great fangs with which he caught his own game to eat, and he soon developed a taste for raw flesh." The crowd gasped and Isra reversed directions again. "The people of the city mourned the loss of their ruler. Many,

many years later, the village woman's husband died, and as the prince was by all accounts no longer a prince but a feral creature, there was no law that said he could not now claim his love. So, one evening as dusk was settling over the village, he left the shadows of the jungle to approach his heart's desire as she drew water from the well.

"When the old woman looked up, she saw not the handsome young man she might have loved in her youth but a huge, vicious beast, creeping toward her in the low brush with growls and tossing of his great maned head." Isra stopped and threw out her hands. "She screamed in terror, '*No!*' and backed away from the beast, who followed the woman, trying to speak words of comfort: 'It is I, my love; I've come for you at last.'"

Isra spun around and stalked in the other direction. "But the woman only heard terrible roars and, thinking she would soon be eaten, she dropped her water bucket and ran for her life toward the village, shouting for help.

"The prince, seeking to calm her fears, gave chase. He caught her quickly, reaching out his arms to embrace her, lowering his head for that first sweet kiss. But when she did not respond, the prince looked and saw that his love was dead, mauled by his long claws and sharp teeth."

The crowd was tomb silent, and so Isra lowered her voice and stepped around Roman's solid form, nearly whispering to the crowd now pressed together in hushed expectation.

"And so the prince retreated back into the jungle, damned for eternity to live out his days as a tormented beast, never to be seen again." She turned and walked toward the wagon, pulled herself up on the rear wheel. "*Until tonight.*" She looked up and saw that Gunar was already unfastening the latches at the top of the wooden walls, and then Isra looked over the crowd, where streams of people still trickled in from alleys and other parts of the city.

Word was spreading. The baskets were filling.

"Ladies and gentleman, Prince Kahn!" Isra pushed the edge of the front wall away as Gunar trotted along the roof, freeing the other three walls that crashed to the dirt, and the crowd gasped in delight.

Isra looked to her right and saw, as if she had trained him to do so, Kahn rising up on his haunches in the center of the cage, pawing the air with his fangs bared.

A shiver ran up her spine at his magnificence, at his power. A shiver of pride, and yes, a little fear.

Nickle appeared near her feet, bearing the wrapped portion of butchered meat she had procured for the tiger, and in the next moment, Gunar hopped down on the opposite rear wheel.

"Ready, mistress?" he asked in a low voice.

Isra nodded, and van Groen's squire opened the door enough for Isra to slip inside the cage. Again the crowd gasped, and Isra unfurled her whip.

"Hie, Kahn!" she called, and the crack split the air.

The tiger snarled and tossed his head, spittle flying from his whiskers.

She flicked the whip again. "Hie, Kahn! Come!" Her heart felt as though it would burst in her chest.

Then the tiger reared to his full height again, his scream pressing against Isra's eardrums. The wagon shook as he fell back to his front paws, and Isra knew it was enough. She flung the meat to the far end of the wagon, where Kahn chased it down and pounced on it. Isra backed quickly to the door, and in the next moment she was free, swinging herself around the end of the wagon on top of the wheel, one arm extended over the crowd.

"Prince Kahn!" she announced in a triumphant voice.

And Constantinople welcomed the menagerie at last.

Chapter 21

Roman sat on the floor of van Groen's wagon, watching Isra in the lantern light as she removed her tiger's eye crown and released her hair from the numerous plaits—twice as many as she had worn on her first performance in Constantinople three nights before. Her eyes were kohled and her cheeks rouged so artfully that he thought Fran herself would approve. The shape of Isra's face was sharper now, her eyes at a dramatic, dark slant.

Roman found her nearly irresistible.

They were in the very center of the city now and had held private performances for the mayor and his court and, tonight, a visiting emir and his entourage. Isra was the darling of the city, and the troupe now had enough coin to journey the entire way back to Austria without performing if they so desired. But because she was the darling, Roman feared Isra's continued presence in Constantinople, her spreading fame, was becoming more and more dangerous.

And so the time had come to discuss the future.

"I've spoken with Zeus," he began. "We'll leave for Jerusalem on the morrow."

Isra's hands slowed on the last of the ribbons and she looked to him. "As you wish."

"It is unsafe for you here now; word is spreading," he explained, although she had not asked for any explanation.

"I understand." She carefully folded van Groen's familiar green tunic.

Roman ran his tongue along his teeth, buying himself a moment of time. "I don't want you to show Kahn again."

Now her eyes flashed, her mouth thinned. But she only replied, "As you wish."

Roman was frustrated. He had expected some sort of argument, at least a press for an explanation, and instead Isra was giving him curt obedience, almost as if she was angry with him.

"Do you not have anything to say?" he asked at last. "No disagreement with my decisions, no questions?"

"Yes, I have questions," she said, placing the tunic in the trunk carefully before pushing it beneath the cot. "But they are nothing to do with leaving Constantinople."

Now he was more confused. "Then what are you angry with me for?" he asked.

She looked up to him. "I do not wish to discuss it."

"You have questions, but you won't ask them? That makes no sense, Isra."

She turned around quickly. "It makes no sense? It makes no sense? I offered myself to you weeks ago and you refused me. I think you do not want me, and I accept your decision. But then you treat me like your woman, you protect me and care for me and buy me gifts; you lie with me at night and hold me in your arms. You kiss my face, my hands, you have my very future in your hands, and yet you let me linger, not making me yours in truth. Is that because you only plan to leave me behind? Or because you would regret taking me?"

The wagon was silent except for the quiet squeak-squeak of the lantern set swinging by her speech. Roman looked up at her and his frustration melted away.

"You're angry with me because we haven't made love?"

"No! I am angry with you because I do not know what I am to you!"

He held his hand up to her. "Come here," he said.

She lifted her chin. "No. You answer me first."

"All right," he said and dropped his hand, unable to hide his smile. She was nearly unrecognizable from the woman he had found on the hillside at Melk.

"I will ask you to be mine," he said, looking into her eyes.

"When?" she pressed. "The forty-third of Never?" Her accent trilled the words, making them so much more amusing coming from her mouth in anger.

He chuckled. "Sooner than that, I hope. But I can tell you one thing . . ." He held up his hand again and lifted his eyebrows to her in unspoken question. After a moment's hesitation she came to him and placed her fingers in his palm. He pulled her down onto his lap and cradled her against his chest.

"When we decide our future, it will not be in Asa van Groen's wagon. And it will not be until you feel you are truly free."

She turned her head against his tunic to look up at him. "What do you mean?"

"You still feel beholden to me," Roman explained. "And your past is yet between us. Not on my part but on yours. I am not your master or your keeper or your lord, and I don't ever wish to be."

"But I I—"

He placed his finger over her lips and shook his head. "There are things in my heart that I would have you know. But I will not be free to speak them until we are finished with this business hanging over us."

"After we find King Baldwin?"

"*If* we find King Baldwin," he corrected. "We shall see how you feel about me then."

"You are a terrible master," she said and lay her head back down. "To deny me so. You say yourself that we don't even know if we will locate the king. He could be dead already, and then we would be more likely to find the forty-third of Never."

Roman smiled at the frown in her voice and opened his mouth to speak, but he was cut off by a polite knock on the door of the wagon. He eased Isra aside, mindful to disguise the discomfort in his chausses, and leaned over to open the door.

"Boss?" Zeus asked, half his face flickering by the torch he held. "Some men requesting to speak with you."

Roman glanced over Zeus's shoulder but could only make out the shadowy outline of a trio standing in the common, backlit by the few torches still alight by those members of the troupe loathe to retire from the festive atmosphere of Constantinople at night.

He looked back at Isra, who still wore a frown, though now it was tinged with worry.

"Lock the door behind me," he said in a low voice. At her nod of understanding, he slid the dagger Valentine had given him back into its place beneath his belt and pulled himself from the wagon.

"Is there a problem?" he asked, looking to the silhouette of strangers.

"No problem," the man in front replied, stepping toward Roman in a completely nonthreatening manner. As he continued speaking,

Roman noted his heavy Frankish accent. "We only wish to commend you on your successful performance and extend to you an invitation on behalf of our lord to perform for his household and esteemed guests. We hope you will accept."

Roman frowned. They could stay no longer in Constantinople; it had already been decided. "It is not the menagerie's habit to disappoint an eager patron, but we are moving on with the dawn."

"Then let us attempt to persuade your direction," the man said with a smile. "We have come to invite you to the Castle Kerak at the request of Raynald of Chatillon. Certainly you have heard of him."

Roman's blood seemed to freeze in his veins. This was the lord who'd been accused of breaking Baldwin's truce with Saladin. Was it possible they would be led directly into the assassin's den?

"Not being of the soldiering ilk, I'm sorry to say I have not," Roman lied. "It is possible Kerak is much farther south than we planned on traveling."

"Perhaps it will sway you to know that my lord wishes your entertainment for none other than the king of Jerusalem himself," the man rejoined. "Soldier or nay, everyone in this part of the world is familiar with Baldwin. The Leper is in poor health, and my lord wishes to bring joy and comfort to his dear ally. You will be paid handsomely for your performance, and given leave to advance through to Jerusalem if you so desire. The winter weather there is much more tolerable, I should advise you."

"I'll need to speak with my men," was all Roman would say, and he felt an odd trembling in his hands, usually steady and untouched by anxiety.

Roman marveled at the idea that a laugh could be accented. "That is noble of you," the stranger allowed. "But our request is only a courtesy. My lord insists you accept. If you have any intentions whatsoever of traveling south of Constantinople and prefer to do so safely, perhaps you will quickly consider our *request*."

"I see," Roman said and thought of how van Groen would handle the situation. He gave a bow. "Certainly, we would be honored to entertain the king at Kerak."

"*Bien.* We will send an escort to your party at dawn to lead you from the city. There will be no performances along the route for commoners; we must travel quickly. You will be compensated for any loss of income. *Adieu.*"

Roman watched the three men turn and depart the alley while Zeus stood at his side.

"I've got a bad feeling about this," the strongman said.

"So do I, Zeus," Roman said, clapping the man on the back and then turning toward the wagon once more, where Isra waited. "So do I."

Despite the man's initial reluctance, traveling from Constantinople through the county of Antioch was an uneventful pleasure. Surrounded front and back by Raynald's soldiers ensured that the caravan was completely safe from thieves, and the camps at night were festive things, the fighting men intermingling with the troupe beneath warm, starry skies filled with music and laughter and plenty of drinking.

Isra felt layers of anxiety peeling off her like the woolen skirts she had discarded as the familiar scents of her homeland surrounded her and the horizon beckoned to her like a beloved acquaintance. They were going to a Christian stronghold, far from Damascus and from anyone who might know her. Although it caused a prickle at her spine to even think it, she had reason to believe now that Roman would soon accomplish his mission and he and his friends would be free.

As would she.

Would she then be his?

She watched him as he sat around the campfire, discussing things she had little interest in with a small group of soldiers, his expression intense in the midst of the conversation, but his posture relaxed, easy. Any concern that his true identity and connection to Chastellet would be discovered was soon relieved as the men in Raynald's company had not been in the Holy Land at the time and knew little about the trouble at the Templar fortress, which seemed to have happened ages ago to them in this place of constant strife. All the troupe referred to Roman as boss, and it had been assumed that Roman was nothing more than the leader of a band of performing misfits who traveled the map for coin.

Isra had handily excluded herself from scrutiny when her nationality was questioned by implying that Roman had purchased her from her master years ago. This had made the blond man frown fiercely at her as the soldiers congratulated him on his good sense, but to Isra's mind, the idea of Roman acquiring her wasn't entirely untrue. The night she had met him on the Damascus street had been the moment when her life had changed. When the first thoughts of rebellion had been tiny seeds planted in her mind, the first time she had deliberately disobeyed the rules of her life up to that point.

Her master's name had been fear, and now that master was gasping its last breaths.

She sat next to Roman as he drove the horses over the hard, bumpy road, and it was she who pointed out the long, rectangular shape of Kerak as it came into view. Sitting atop a great hill over the city, it seemed a forbidding place—stark and silent and enormous against the white sky at noon. But while Isra was disconcerted at the sight of the fortress, Roman was fascinated, pointing out to her details of its construction, naming the parts of the stronghold and their purposes. His knowledge of and obvious passion for building was evident, and she found herself proud of his intelligence and skill.

He craned his neck in all directions as they pulled through the first gatehouse into an enclosed bailey, the citadel itself still some distance away and behind another walled barrier. The caravan progressed slowly through the compound until they were in the inner bailey, and at last the long train of vehicles came to a stop.

The troupe set up the round in the bailey, directed by the stewards of the house, and Isra and Roman fell into their established routines of helping erect awnings, stake festive pennants, and adjust the spacing of the carts. The inhabitants of the compound paused to smile and point and whisper to their companions as they crossed the dirt en route on their various errands, or took a moment to lean over the long, smooth half walls of the verandas suspended on the side of the keep overhead and peer at the activity below.

The stable master had refused in no uncertain terms to house the troupe's ragged animals alongside the fine beasts of the lord or the garrison, so Roman and Zeus made do with a splintered trough in a corner of the bailey and piles of fodder brought by two young boys. Isra had to smile at the sight of the now tattered red sick flags ringing the makeshift corral, remembering that first camp she and Roman had made together.

"He's quite the handsome fellow, is he not?" Delilah said in a whispered giggle and nudged Isra's ribs with her wide, round elbow so that she staggered on her feet. "I fancied him a bit myself at first. Even if his face is oversmooth."

Her cheeks warmed over her smile and she dropped her eyes, but she said nothing as she continued sorting Delilah's little beaded jewelry into the wooden display bins. There wasn't time for her to sit and stare after Roman; the steward had commanded that she would perform within the hour. It was much sooner than Isra had expected; she'd thought perhaps on the morrow, after everyone had had time to rest and Roman would have time to surreptitiously seek out the Christian king.

Isra dropped the last bag of carved bead rings into a little niche, continuing to smile to herself as she caught sight of the identical one she still wore, and then left the bearded woman with a wave, walking around the side of van Groen's wagon. There was just enough time for her to change into her costume and prepare for the performance. But when she raised her eyes across the compound she stopped short at the rear corner and pressed herself back against the wood.

There, walking across a far corner of the bailey toward the wide opening that led into the main building was a pair of Damascene soldiers, the telltale colors of their sashes like a slap to Isra's face. She looked as closely as she could at their dark faces, so out of place here in this compound of reddened, pale complexions—and so much like Isra's own—but she could not say they were familiar at such a distance.

Neither could she say they were not.

A hand grasped her arm from behind and Isra barely stifled her scream as she jumped and spun around, pulling free of the grasp.

But it was Roman who had touched her—of course.

"What is it?" he asked, at once alert to the fear on her face.

"Those men," she began and turned around to indicate the pair of soldiers, but they had vanished. "They must have gone inside." She looked up at him again. "Two men. Perhaps from Damascus."

Roman's brow fell into a frown. "It's possible they are only mercenaries, but there is no way of inquiring unless we wish to incur suspicion. I've just been told the king is feeling exceptionally poorly this evening and will not be present for your performance."

Now it was Isra's turn to frown. "I thought it strange they wished the troupe to perform so soon after our arrival. Think you they would make their attempt this night?"

"It's brilliant really," he said, although his tone bore no real admiration. "The Saracen mercenaries, the troupe—all of it is the perfect cover. It would be impossible to mark the king's murder as treachery with so many strange visitors about to blame it on."

"You think it is the machination of Raynald," Isra said.

But Roman surprised her by shaking his head as his gaze skittered over the features of the exterior walls of the keep. "No, I'm not entirely convinced he's involved at all. But it must be someone under his command." He looked back to her. "If whoever it is thinks to take advantage of the performance tonight to do this evil, it means I must reach the king beforehand."

He took her arm again and turned her to face the keep, nodding toward one of the long balconies partly hidden by an olive tree. "Baldwin is there, in those apartments."

Isra glanced up and then looked back to Roman. "How will you reach him?"

"He must be housed in the royal wing. Which means there is likely only one direct access from the common area. It will be separate from the other living quarters, with chambers for his personal security." His gaze was intense. "Once we are inside, I must try to gain the upper level while you have the fortress distracted, and hopefully before anyone else with ill intent can reach him. Which means you must show Kahn without me."

A chill of fear swept up Isra's spine as she looked into his eyes, but she could not refuse. Hadn't they come all this way to do this very thing? Hadn't they been given almost the perfect opportunity to do so?

"Zeus and the others will be present. If I have not returned by the time you are finished, you must rejoin the troupe and all of you must leave Kerak as quickly as you can."

"As you wish," she said as calmly as she could, although her heart pounded so that she could feel its reverberations along her throat.

He pressed her arm and held it securely for a moment, looking as though there was something else he wished to say. Then his touch was gone and he walked around the end of the wagon and opened the door for her. "I'll wait here while you dress."

Isra obediently climbed into the shadowed interior and Roman closed the door behind her. She left the lantern unlit and sat for several moments in the darkness, absorbing the feeling of being safe, of having the man she loved within her reach, guarding her, protecting her.

But then Huda's bruised countenance burst into torturous relief against the blackness of her vision, and Isra fumbled in the dark with shaking hands to light the lantern, frantic to fill the wagon with wildly swinging light and to convince herself that it meant nothing.

It meant nothing.

Chapter 22

Barnaby led the procession into the keep, his fingers plucking a lute and his strong, clear voice ringing off the stone walls. Nickle followed with a jangly tambourine, and when his little capped head disappeared beyond the doorway, applause echoed politely and Isra's insides clenched and twisted into a ball.

Helena went next, leading her line of little darlings dressed in their finest, and the shouts of delighted laughter tumbled along the stones of the wide corridor where Isra walked as if in a funeral procession.

Kahn's wagon eased to a halt, pulled by the strongmen Zeus and Arpetto, and Isra stopped too, turning to place her hands on Zeus's stooped shoulders, her slippers in the stirrups of his hands. Gunar scrambled up the wheel and onto the roof of the cage behind her.

She looked over her shoulder at Roman, who waited in the entryway to the bailey, leaning against the thick wall with his arms crossed over his chest, watching her.

"*Ena, dio, tria,*" Zeus said, and on three he hoisted Isra into the air.

She reached up and took hold of Gunar's hands, pulling herself atop the wagon.

"If you would, mistress," the young man commanded, indicating an area where he had spread a square scarf. Isra eased down onto one hip, her legs crooked to the side, one arm out to brace herself. Asa's whip and staff lay waiting, the latter of which Gunar bent down and retrieved, tossing it into the air before snatching it in his fist. Isra thought he would make a very capable leader of his own troupe one day.

He swung down from the top of the wagon and straightened his stiff collar before striding boldly ahead through the doorway, where

Barnaby's gay melodies still filled the air and the yaps of Helena's dogs elicited bursts of laughter.

"Fine people of Kerak!" Gunar cried out while raising his arms, and the wagon began rolling forward slowly.

Isra looked over her shoulder once more and saw that Roman was still watching her. He winked and his mouth crooked in a grin. She tried to return it, tried to memorize how he looked just then, in the long white tunic she had purchased for him with her own money. The late afternoon sun filled the bailey behind him, lighting up his blond hair like a halo.

"Kahn the Terrible and his queen!"

Isra looked forward, relaxed her face into what she hoped was an expression of haughty disinterest as she and the tiger beneath her rolled into the huge stone hall.

Isra's heart pounded as her eyes flicked over the crowd crammed into the cavernous room. It seemed as if every person living or working at Kerak must be gathered there, which caused her dread to increase. Roman's suspicions of using the performance as cover while the ultimate evil was committed above everyone's head seemed more than possible; it appeared to be guaranteed. Surely no one was missing from the audience.

No one but the king and whoever had been charged with seeing him dead.

The wagon rolled to a stop and the performers circled around it twice, encouraging the audience in their welcoming applause while the wagon swayed almost imperceptibly beneath her seat; Kahn was awake and pacing.

Her eyes scanned the crowd closely now, and she took stock of the spectators: the seated nobility and their companions, the fighting men gathered around next, with their array of weaponry on shining, deadly display at their sides; the servants and lesser residents of the castle pressed against the walls, leaning up on tiptoe to peer over the sea of people crushed together.

And there, standing just behind the lords in their ornate chairs, were the two Damascene soldiers, their turbans causing them to stand out as if alone in the room. Isra's blood ran cold as their dark eyes watched her closely, their heads leaned together.

Gunar introduced her again and Isra rose to her feet, her knees weak, the muscles of her thighs quivering with dread. She picked up her whip and held her arms from her sides.

"Many years ago, over a city boasting streets of gold," she began, projecting her voice from deep beneath her diaphragm to steady its tremble, "ruled the wealthiest prince in all the land. And although his riches guaranteed him anything his heart could desire, his most longed for possession was the love of a poor young woman from his own village."

She caught a ruffle of movement out of the corner of her right eye and turned that way to continue her story.

"All his gold would not allow him to make the poor village girl his wife," she said as her head turned, and she caught sight of another turbaned head, moving from a doorway along the front wall through the crowd toward his similarly dressed comrades. The man glanced up at her and Isra's heart clenched, stopped.

Even from across the room, separated by hundreds of faces and months of time, Isra knew that black, evil gaze. She would know it after a hundred years, a thousand.

Hamid.

He slowed and turned his head toward her once more, his body following his gaze as he came to a complete stop.

Isra swallowed, very aware of all the eyes upon her, and broke gaze with the man. "Eventually, she was married to a man of her own status and soon had a happy family. The great prince was heartbroken and would have no other for his bride."

Another flash of movement at that same doorway caught her attention and Isra looked quickly. It was Roman, and he paused now, watching her, one foot already on a stairway that disappeared around a turn. The question on his face was clear.

Are you all right?

Isra glanced back to Hamid, and his face was a stone mask as he brazenly stared at her, his long arms hanging at his side.

What would happen if she alerted Roman that the man who had set murderers after her, who had commanded the monsters who viciously killed her sister, who had allowed it to happen in his very presence, was in this room? Was in this room and *recognized her?*

Would Roman stop in his mission to save the king in order to save Isra?

Did he care for her enough to do that?

The better question might be: did Isra love him enough to allow him to do what he had come all this long way, all these many years to do? To at last redeem his friends, his brothers, even if it meant placing herself within reach of the man who would kill her?

Perhaps then she would feel worthy of him, of surviving Damascus when Huda had not.

So she shone her brightest smile in the direction of the doorway before swinging her gaze back over the crowd, sweeping over Hamid's head without pause. She kicked the first latch free.

"Instead, the prince began leaving his great palace in the dark of night to pace the edge of the jungle around his love's village, stalking her." Now she let her gaze come back to Hamid, whose eyes were black as any devil's. She looked at him directly, daring him to act. "Waiting. Waiting years for even a glimpse of the woman he knew he *could never have*."

The general began to push through the crowd toward the wagon as if mesmerized, and so Isra walked to the edge of the roof nearest him. With a flick of her slipper, the second latch came undone with barely a click of sound.

"Soon he could no longer bear leaving the jungle even for a short time lest she slip past him unnoticed. The prince became wild, unpredictable, his skin discolored by the shadows of the forest, his teeth great fangs. He soon indulged"—she felt her eyes narrow—"unnatural appetites for flesh."

The hall was silent like the air before a great storm. Isra turned from Hamid and paced to the rear of the wagon as she continued her tale. She released the third latch without breaking stride.

"His subjects mourned the loss of their once-noble ruler, but he was eventually forgotten, as all men are wont to be. And then, many years later," Isra said and paused, unlatching the final clasp and sitting down at the edge of the roof, her slippers dangling. Zeus and Arpetto, waiting on the wheels, grasped her by her wrists and upper arms.

They lowered her to the ground, and the movement of air caused her scarves and her plaits to flutter and stream behind her, eliciting delighted sighs from the crowd. She landed on her feet and sauntered around the front of the wagon, playing to the enraptured crowd and ignoring the man she stepped ever closer to.

"The village woman's husband died. Now, the prince was no longer a prince but a desperate, feral creature, and thusly felt ruled by no law. So, one evening, as dusk settled over the village, the beast left the shadows of the jungle to approach his heart's desire as she drew water from the well."

Isra stepped her feet one over the other in a sideways manner, feeling the cold hatred emanating from Hamid as she came closer and closer to him, and yet she refused to give him her attention yet. She circled her arms, gestured with her whip, and Asa van Groen would have crowed with delight at the way she had mesmerized the crowd.

"When the woman looked up at the sound of footfalls in the grass, she saw not the handsome benefactor who once might have protected her innocence but a vicious monster." Isra stopped and threw out her hands. "Oh, how she must have screamed in fear when faced with such a fiend!" Isra lifted her face, her ear-piercing shrieks ricocheting off the high ceiling and walls.

"Help! Help me! No! Stop! Please! Someone please help me!" Isra lowered her face and took a step away from the crowd before continuing her sidestepping movement around the perimeter. Her throat was raw, but the pain felt wickedly good.

"But the beast came on, trying to speak to her words of what he felt was his triumph at last: 'I've come for you. You are mine. You belong to me now.'"

Just as she would have come even with Hamid, she defied him further by turning on her heel and stalking slowly back in the direction from which she'd just come.

"The woman only heard terrible growls, and thinking she was soon to be devoured, she dropped her bucket and ran for her life, still shouting for help."

She turned suddenly to walk toward Hamid yet again, the heads of those gathered in front turning the slightest bit with each of Isra's slow steps.

"The beast, seeking to ease her fears, gave chase. He caught her quickly, reaching out his arms to embrace her tender flesh, lowering his head for a sweet kiss." Now Isra stopped, feeling not cold hatred but a burning rage, so that she knew she would be face-to-face with Hamid if she but turned her face forward.

And so she did.

As she spoke her next low words directly into that soulless gaze, her fear vanished. "But when she did not respond, the beast looked and saw that the girl was dead, mauled by his long claws and sharp teeth."

The crowd gave a shocked gasp, and there were several cries of distress. Isra spoke quietly but clearly, her face only inches from Hamid's.

"And so the beast fled back into the jungle, damned for eternity to live out his days as a tormented monster, never to be seen again." She paused, and even she was surprised at the twitch of her mouth as it longed to smile.

"I will kill you myself," Hamid said in a whisper of their shared tongue. "You . . . *whore*."

Isra leaned forward until it must have appeared to the crowd that she was going to kiss the turbaned man who so resembled her. Her smile widened and she even chuckled.

"Come then," she whispered, her nose circling his in the air.

She backed away quickly with her arms, her whip raised high, and a gust of air rushed in to fill the space between her and the demon of a man, although her eyes never left him.

"Never to be seen again . . . *until tonight!*"

She heard the footfalls of Gunar, of Zeus and Arpetto, take their places behind her, and she turned toward the crowd, spinning around once completely so that her scarves and her plaits flew.

"Ladies and gentleman, Prince Kahn!" Isra pushed the edge of the front wall away and then the other three fell to the stone floor with earsplitting cracks. Even those nobles who considered themselves too precious to stand in the presence of such base performers rose to their feet then, and the hall roared with approval as the magnificent tiger was revealed.

Hamid left the fringe of the audience, his eyes bulging, his mouth a sneer. Several of the people around him pointed and whispered as he advanced, and it was clear they thought him part of the performance.

Isra backed up until her feet were on the wagon tongue. She turned and leaped sprightly up the narrow beam while Hamid continued his measured stalk toward the wagon. She held out her whip.

"And now," she called out to the crowd, sweeping her whip across her chest and then before the crowd, "you will all be witness to a display of courage unlike anything you could imagine!"

Her head whipped back around and she saw Hamid was standing at the end of the wagon tongue. Isra flicked the long leather whip in her right hand and it licked Hamid's forehead, leaving a thin line of red that immediately began to drip into his eyebrows. The crowd gasped and his brown hand came up to touch where she had struck him. He looked back at her, his face darkening even further. He stepped onto the beam.

"Hamid!" one of his comrades called out. "What are you doing? It is a tiger!"

Isra turned and opened the door of Kahn's cage and stepped inside with the pacing animal. His cheek pads flinched at her entrance, but he seemed more agitated by the crowd as his big head swung toward the sea of faces through the bars.

"It is only a trick animal!" Hamid shouted over his shoulder, and the pleased murmurings of the crowd died suddenly as they realized what the turban man intended to do. "He can be nothing but tame. This woman, however, is a runaway slave. She belongs to me and I would retrieve her."

Isra stopped, knowing her back was to Kahn but more willing to offer her vulnerability to the tiger rather to the evil man who now stood in the doorway.

"I wouldn't do that if I were you, fellow," Zeus warned in a not-so-friendly voice. He and Arpetto stood on either side of the tongue, Nickle having retreated to the safe embrace of Helena. Isra saw from the corner of her eye that Barnaby was sidling toward the doorway with them both, the dogs trotting after them, for once, silently.

Hamid stepped one boot inside the wagon and Kahn turned his head, knowing the instant his sanctuary had been breached.

"I shall wring the life out of you before all gathered here, and I have no care for it at all," he said. "You have caused me great grief from my master and you will pay for it. Come with me quietly and perhaps you will live."

"I am not afraid of you," Isra answered, lifting her chin.

"No?" he challenged with a despicable smile and a glance toward the whip in her hand.

Isra tossed the long leather weapon to the floor with a clatter. She raised her eyebrows at Hamid.

He stepped closer. "I mean what I say: I will wrap my hands around your throat and . . ."

"Stop talking about it and do it, then," Isra snapped. "I do not think you will. *Coward.* Coward who rapes little girls."

His smile actually deepened and he held his hands out like claws. "No, I shall not kill you at all, I think," he said in a conspiratorial tone. "I shall keep you. You shall be my toy."

Isra shook her head. "Never."

Hamid nodded. "Watch me."

"I will," Isra whispered. And then she commanded, "Hie, Kahn!"

She felt the heat of the large tiger through the layers of tunic and gown on her left. His wide head swayed in the air, taking in the scent of the turbaned man.

And then Kahn did a very strange thing; he took two steps forward, coming to stand at a perpendicular between Hamid and Isra, and his flank pressed back into her skirts. She wanted to reach out and touch him, but the fur over his shoulders was rigid, prickling.

"I have no fear of your cat," he said with a condescending tilt of his head. And then Hamid reached over Kahn's back.

The tiger twisted and raised up so quickly that Isra saw little else beyond an orange-and-black-striped blur and then a spray of red. Hamid screamed and was clutching at his middle on the floor of the wagon as Kahn landed on his paws on either side of him.

The crowd didn't know whether the display was part of the performance or not; they seemed to be frozen in macabre concentration.

"Help me!" Hamid shouted in his native tongue, his hands struggling to keep the top and bottom halves of his torso together as a flood of blood pooled around him. His voice grew louder, shriller. "Help me! Help me! *Help m—*"

Kahn swiped at the man's head with a roar, sending a spray of blood out onto the audience. Hamid screamed no more.

The crowd erupted in panic and began to scatter, stampeding in all directions, while Hamid's comrades approached the wagon at a run.

Zeus and Arpetto convinced them to change their minds about approaching, and in an instant both Damascene men lay in a heap on the floor. Kerak soldiers appeared to be regaining their bravado, several now headed toward the wagon.

"Come, Isra," Zeus warned.

Isra froze; Zeus had used her true name.

He looked at her with exasperation. "We've known who you both were since the second week you were with us. Asa makes it his business to know the sort of people living with him. Now I need to shut the door and pull out of the keep before they close the gates!"

Kahn chose that moment to leap from the wagon.

Zeus and Arpetto ran.

Isra had no choice but to step around the gory mess that had been Hamid to follow the tiger, who sent the soldiers scattering until the hall was empty save for the backsides of the poor folk desperately trying to push through the doorways.

There was no time to try to lure Kahn back into the wagon and she couldn't leave him to wander the halls of Kerak; eventually some brave soul would come bearing a bow. And so Isra picked up the whip and skipped quickly down the wagon tongue. The crack of leather cut through the air.

"Kahn! Hie, Kahn!" She walked backward toward the steps up which Roman had disappeared. "Come, boy. Come, Kahn." And then, with the albino monk's warnings loud in her ears, Isra turned her back on the tiger and ran.

Chapter 23

"Who dares invade my chamber?" the hoarse voice called as Roman eased into the room. He had to hurry lest the soldiers lounging in the antechamber be alerted to an unannounced visitor. "I have no desire to be placated like a child by Raynald's banal entertainments. I said to leave me!"

"I cannot, my liege."

"Who goes there?"

Roman closed the door quietly and entered the luxurious chamber that was thick with the smell of sickness and decay. Three sets of double doors stood open to a walled balcony, long white curtains twitching in the meager breeze that did little to lessen the odor. The king was reclining on a couch, his back toward the door, and when he pushed himself up and looked over his shoulder, Roman could see the long, discolored dressings that bandaged the king. He was unrecognizable as the man Roman had last seen three years before at Chastellet.

"Who goes there, I say!"

"A friend," Roman said, stepping toward the couch as if in a dream, a nightmare.

"Your name," Baldwin barked in a hoarse voice.

"I regret that I cannot give you that, my liege." He knew a moment of fear when Baldwin reached for a bell on a nearby table, but the king's arm swung like a pendulum as he struggled to sit up and his bandaged hand only knocked the alarm to the carpeted floor, where it gave a dull clank and was still.

That was when Roman saw that the gauzy strips continued over Baldwin's eyes, and he realized the king had not deigned to be present at the performance in his honor because such amusements were beneath him but because he could not see them.

The leprosy had taken Baldwin's sight.

"Get out," the king cried hoarsely. "Whoever you are, get out!"

Roman's throat constricted at the sight of the brilliant young man so decrepit and weak.

"I've not come to harm you," he said, his voice strained. He was grateful Constantine was not present to see his friend—the man who at one time had meant so much to Stan—in such poor health. "I've come to save your life."

The king stilled in his agitated floundering. "Who are you and what do you want? Your voice sounds familiar to me and yet I cannot call your face to mind."

Roman stepped closer to the couch, the odor of the king's disease causing his stomach to clench. "You are not safe here, my liege," Roman began. "Raynald has broken your truce with Saladin. There is word that a traitor among your vassals has conspired to make an attempt on your life."

"Raynald has only defended himself from like attacks," Baldwin muttered, waving his bandaged hand. "There are many tales of treachery about each of my vassals, likely perpetrated by one another in an effort to steal any power they can before my corpse is even cold. If I believed every rumor on the breeze, I'd have no lords left."

"It is no rumor, my liege," Roman insisted. "The very plan was relayed by a Saracen general to a woman from Damascus some months ago."

"Yes?" Baldwin challenged and reclined once more against his bolsters with a groan. "And who, pray tell, is this vassal who seeks to see the end of me? Or can you not reveal that either?"

Roman swallowed. The king's reaction to the answer Roman was about to relay would reveal whether Roman was likely to leave Kerak alive.

"Lord Glayer Felsteppe."

Baldwin stilled, and the tremble of roared applause suddenly wound its way up the staircase. "I would know your name."

"I have brought a written message to you," was Roman's reply, and he took Constantine's letter out of his tunic and held it toward the king until it touched Baldwin's bandaged hand. The sealed page was wrinkled and soft, scuffed and dirtied from the many miles it had traveled from Melk.

"I can read it not," Baldwin said bitterly. Then, after a moment's pause, "You claim to be here on a mission of assistance; perhaps you would indulge me?"

No one's eyes save Baldwin's. If you cannot place it in his hands, burn it.

"Of course, my liege," Roman said quietly.

"Come closer," the king demanded. "When the light is right . . ." He let the statement trail away. Roman didn't know if the king would recognize him or if it was a bluff on Baldwin's part, but either way, he felt that after he'd read Stan's letter, it wouldn't matter.

Roman knelt by the king's side and slid his finger under the seal of the message. He unfolded the page and cleared his throat, surprised at the prickle in his eyes at Stan's flourishing handwriting. His friends seemed so far away at that moment . . .

"Beloved Baldwin, It is my hope that this missive finds its way into your hands, and that your health is tolerable.

Although it has been many years since last we met, and you have meanwhile set your sword against me, I urge you to consider the warning that has been placed in your ear. Perhaps it is because of me that your life is now endangered; had I succumbed to my imprisonment and torture in Damascus or simply failed to rail at the injustice perpetrated by one of Chastellet's own against you and our brethren, there would not now be one so intent on seeing you dead. You cannot know how it pains my heart that you would think me capable of betraying you. But even so, I cannot allow you to be in such danger, and so I reveal to you the truth of it, in my own hand.

I vow to you on my honor that Glayer Felsteppe is the man who perpetrated the siege on our great fortress of Chastellet. It is he who is to blame for the slaughter of our friends, the destruction of your hold at Jacob's Ford. Baldwin, he has murdered Patrice and little Christian in hopes of drawing me out so that he might at last destroy me. I have only persevered thus far for my friends, good men exiled along with me, their lives also stolen.

Dear Baldwin, though you may consider me beloved no more, I beg of you, heed the warning brought to you at great risk by our friend. Hie yourself and your trusted men as far from Raynald of Chatillon as you can be, and charge not into

*hasty retaliation at his word while his integrity remains in
question. Remember your loyal vassals and keep them close.*

*It is my fervent prayer that by the time this missive reaches
you, God will have shown me mercy and I will at last be dead.*

Non nobis Domine, non nobis, sed nomini tuo da gloriam . . . "

"Constantine," Baldwin croaked.

Roman looked up, his own cheeks wet, to see the king had thrown
one of his forearms over his eyes. The king turned his head into his
elbow and gave what sounded like a gasping sob. Roman rubbed
firmly at his face and then, in the next moment, was caught off guard
by the hand wrapped around the back of his neck. Baldwin's face
was before his, cloudy eyes rolling in their sockets between the slits
of gauze, a dagger point dimpling the underside of Roman's chin.

"Who . . . are . . . you?" the king demanded in a raspy whisper.

Roman had to smile at the king's feign and quick reflexes. Constantine did not admire many men, but Roman now better understood
why he had respected and loved this young, sick king.

"My name is Roman Berg, my liege," he at last admitted quietly.

Baldwin's hand on the back of Roman's neck relaxed, even as
screams echoed through the corridor—screams that sounded suspiciously fearful rather than amazed and entertained. The king's dagger,
too, retreated, and Baldwin ran his bandaged fingers over Roman's
head and shoulders.

"Roman?" Baldwin repeated incredulously. "My good stone
master?"

"It is I," he allowed.

Baldwin threw one arm awkwardly about Roman's shoulders.
"Thanks be to God that you are alive." The king withdrew. "Where is
Constantine? Hailsworth? There was a Spaniard who cast his lot with
you as well, was there not?"

Roman hesitated. Baldwin had already shown that he was sly. "I
fear I cannot say, my liege."

But the king only nodded. "I understand. It is not—"

His words were interrupted as the chamber door whooshed open.
Roman turned to see Isra rush inside the king's royal apartment and
slip quickly behind the door—

And Kahn bound into the chamber behind her.

"Who is it?" Baldwin demanded, sitting upright on the couch.

Roman's blood froze in his veins as the tiger started and then crouched, hissing in his direction, his wide nostrils flaring, picking up the scent of the room.

Kahn's front paws were red with blood.

"Be still, my liege," he warned as calmly as he could.

"Who is it?" the king insisted. "Mine enemies?"

"No," Roman said as Isra eased the door closed on the sounds of approaching footfalls pounding on the stairs, the shouts of soldiers. She slid the bolt into its home. "It is a woman and—" he swallowed "—her tiger. The entertainment provided for you."

"A tiger?" Baldwin repeated. "You cannot mean the beast?"

"I do," Roman confirmed. "Only be very still," he urged as Kahn began to take hesitant steps toward Roman, still kneeling at the side of the couch, at a clear disadvantage to the giant animal now rolling toward him, lapping at the air with his great, sniffing inhalations and trailing bloody prints behind him.

"Roman," Isra said, her back pressed against the door. "Hamid was here, at Kerak. He was at the performance."

He didn't know what to fear more, the tiger swaggering toward the king of Jerusalem or the words coming from Isra's mouth. He swallowed. "Did he see you?"

"Yes."

"Did he recognize you?"

She nodded and took a gasping inhalation. "Yes."

"My liege," Roman said quietly, "Hamid is the Saracen said to be in league with Felsteppe. *Isra?*" His voice rose on her name as Kahn was now close enough to reach Roman with one long swipe of a striped foreleg.

"Hie, Kahn!" she called, her voice strong even with its warble.

The tiger paused, dropped his head.

"Kahn, come!" she continued. "Hie!"

Baldwin's voice was low, contemplative, behind Roman's head. "I can smell him."

"He wants a bath, my liege," Roman admitted. "Isra, are they looking for you?"

As if in answer, a polite yet insistent rapping fell on the king's door, and although it caused Roman to flinch, it had the effect of turning Kahn's attention to the would-be intruders.

"My liege," an alarmed voice called from beyond the door. "There are criminals about this wing of the castle, and a wild beast. Are you undisturbed?"

Baldwin hesitated for only a moment before calling out, "Damn it all, I am resting! Inform me when they are captured."

"The lord has bade me search your chamber, my liege," the voice explained, and the door rattled against the bolt. "There is a tiger that's been loosed on Kerak. He's already killed a man."

"Baldwin!" another voice called through the door. "Are you well?"

"That's my man," the king said calmly and then called out, "Send those idiots from the corridor, Judd. And ready the men; we depart Kerak within the hour."

There was no argument, no questioning, and Roman would have had cause to breathe a sigh of relief...

Until Kahn let out an agitated roar.

"Break down the door!" the voice belonging to the man Baldwin had called Judd cried.

The king turned to Roman and said in a raspy rush, "Go, go—there is little I can do for you here. I must return to Jerusalem if I am to have my full resources. Do what you must to flee."

"My liege, if they break down the door, the tiger might attack your men. He's...he's killed before."

"Then go off the balcony, man!" Baldwin shouted. "Am I not the only one in this chamber without sight?"

"Isra?" Roman prompted. "Can you climb down?"

"We are two stories up," Isra insisted. "I do not know if Zeus and Arp—"

The first blow fell on the door.

"Hie, Kahn!" Isra shouted and marched toward the tiger, cracking the whip and turning the beast toward the closest double door. Once Kahn caught sight of the sky, he quickly padded onto the stone balcony, and Isra disappeared after the tiger.

Roman rose to his feet but paused to grip Baldwin's shoulder. "God's blessing upon you, my liege."

"Tell Stan," Baldwin said, grabbing Roman's forearm and keeping him, "forgi—"

The door burst open and the first of the soldiers flooded the room with great battle cries, their swords drawn.

Roman pulled free of the king and ran toward the open doors of the veranda. In two great strides he was on the balcony, his hands raised over his head, and he launched himself over the low wall, reaching, reaching for the thin branches of the olive tree beyond.

Prickly twigs, wads of leaves, sliced across his palms as his body fell and he tumbled down through the branches. He landed with a shout on his left shoulder in the dirt, feeling the joint slip. For an instant he was in Chastellet's bailey again: the sand in his mouth, the sun in his eyes, the pain in his arm as the arrows fell around him.

Then Zeus was leaning over him, and suddenly others, pulling him to his feet, ducking as they ran together to the shelter of van Groen's wagon.

"Isra!" Roman shouted, looking around.

"With Delilah!" Zeus replied, pushing him up onto the driver's seat. Roman saw the violet-painted wagon already pulling ahead toward the gate, but his attention was disrupted by Zeus's mighty shove, which nearly sent Roman off the other side of the wagon. "Go, go!"

"How? Where is Kahn?"

Zeus threw himself up next to Roman and slashed at the horses with the reins. The wagon jerked forward, and Roman cried out and clutched at his arm as the myriad of conveyances that comprised van Groen's Magical Menagerie sent great clouds of dust into the air of Kerak's bailey.

One of the last sights Roman noticed was the string of red sick flags, torn down and trampled and left in the dirt.

They roared toward the first gate, their pair straining past Delilah's cart and taking the lead, and Roman saw with dread the score of white tunicked soldiers forming a line across the opening, the red crosses on their fronts like warning signals.

Templars.

Defenders of the king.

Zeus began to rein in the horses. "We're dashed!"

"No! Go, Zeus! Faster!" Roman gritted his teeth as his unseated bone sent stabbing pain into his chest. He struggled to stand in the footwell, bracing one knee on the driver's seat.

Roman locked eyes with the captain standing in the center of the line, a tall man with a twisted red scar across a diagonal on his face. And then Roman gathered all his strength, all his breath.

"*Non nobis Domine, non nobis, sed nomini tuo da gloriam!*" he shouted. "For Chastellet!"

The captain seemed to become a statue for a frightening heartbeat as he stared into Roman's eyes, a light of recognition dawning across his face, and then he sprang into action, shoving the men nearest him away.

"Let them pass! Let them pass! Clear the way!"

The wagon flew through the gateway, sending one soldier spinning to the dirt, the rest diving for cover, and already the captain was running alongside the caravan, shouting ahead.

"Clear the way for the king's envoy! Let them pass! Open the gate!"

Roman held on to the edge of the wagon's roof and looked behind as the caravan raced after them, Delilah's face closed down in concentration until her head seemed nothing but hair, her beard split and blowing to either side of her wide shoulders. And beyond their troupe, scores of white tunicked soldiers closed in behind them, blocking the way of chase for Kerak's dark-clothed army.

Roman looked down at Zeus, whose face was a mask of panic, although they were through the last gate now and ploughing up the road at top speed.

"I don't see Isra!" Roman shouted over the sound of the cartwheels on the road.

"She's with Delilah!"

"I don't see her!"

Zeus's mouth thinned. "She's in the back!" He hesitated. "With Kahn!"

Chapter 24

Isra's hand was on the latch of the wagon door, the cloying smell of Delilah's perfume mingling with Kahn's musky scent and the odor of drying blood. With each rustling scuff of fur against wood she thought of flinging open the door and hurling herself from the cart, but by the wild rocking of the conveyance, she knew it was likely she would only be broken to pieces by whatever animals and wagons were racing after them: death either way.

Were they escaping Kerak?

Were they being chased?

Had Roman managed to flee Baldwin's chamber?

She was almost completely blind in the back of the wagon, the cracks in the chinking of the boards only revealing themselves as faint, glowing threads. The rumbling of the wheels were like thunder, stirred and thickened by Kahn's occasional short growls of unease.

But then the wagon seemed to be slowing, and it rocked to a halt at once, throwing Isra forward. She caught herself with her hands, and Kahn gave a snarl at the abrupt movement. The wagon was flooded with warm light and she was dragged through the doorway at such speed that she left some of the skin of her forearms on the floor of the wagon.

But then the door slammed shut and she was crushed in a one-armed embrace against Roman's chest.

"Are you hurt?" he rushed and then dropped her to her trembling legs, where she nearly collapsed to the dirt. He yanked her aright with one hand rather roughly and held her from him, his eyes roving her, his expression strained, wild as he demanded, "Isra! Are you hurt?"

"N-no," she managed to say at last and noticed his left arm hanging useless at his side. "Your arm?"

"You're not injured? Kahn didn't—"

"I am fine, Roman," she insisted and then looked around. It seemed half of the troupe had gathered round them, and still the rest of the conveyances were pulling up short, drivers disembarking and sprinting toward them. She looked back at Roman. "Where are we?"

"Just beyond Kerak," he said and then leaned back against the rear of Delilah's wagon with a ragged sigh, his eyes closing. He reached out and pulled her to him once more, dropping his lips to the crown of her head as he had been wont to do the past several weeks.

It was the sweetest feeling Isra had ever known. And yet she could not pause to revel in it.

She pulled away.

"Hamid's men will follow us," she warned. "They saw me."

"The king's men will put them off, if not stop them altogether," Roman said. "But you are right; we must be away. Even if Hamid's men are prevented from giving chase, I doubt Raynald will be pleased with us once the king departs. He's not a stupid man and will likely link our sudden departure with the king's withdrawal of favor." He stood aright from the wagon and looked to Zeus. "Head out. Make haste."

"Aye, boss," the strongman replied. "Which direction?"

Roman stepped away from the cart and looked around. He pointed with his right arm. "Up the first of those hills. The climb shouldn't be bad, and we will have a view of the road from there. Zeus, you drive for Delilah; she's had a fright." He reached out to take Isra's hand and pull her toward van Groen's wagon.

"Boss?" Zeus called out. "Your arm?"

"I've had to do more than drive a cart in this condition, friend," he said over his shoulder. "It's not the first time it's happened. There's not a Spaniard in the troupe I don't know about, is there?"

Isra didn't understand what he meant, but she followed him anyway. "Are you certain you can drive?" she said. "Perhaps Zeus could—"

"I'd have you with me," Roman said, and he sounded angry.

Isra didn't question him, only preceded him onto the driver's seat and gathered the reins. She handed them to Roman after he hauled himself up with some effort and sat down with a grimace.

She looked forward at the rolling sand as they lurched ahead, the future rushing toward her, yet it was hidden all the same.

They gained the top of the rise in less than an hour, the sun blazing magenta beyond the stark outline of Kerak as it snuck below the horizon. It seemed the whole of the troupe held their breath as they formed a line along the ridge, watching the road.

"It's late," Dracus offered. "Perhaps they'll overnight and leave at dawn."

Roman shook his head. "If I've learned anything about Baldwin, it's that he doesn't take betrayal lightly. If we don't see him and his entourage on the road before the sun sets, he's either dead or he's decided he doesn't believe me after all, meaning he'll send men after us at first light."

"Not good either way," Dracus mused.

"I'm afraid not."

The moments dragged by. Isra's legs felt as if they could no longer support her, so she sank to her bottom in the silt before the cave, crossing her legs and dropping the crown of her head into her palms.

Huda's face bloomed in her mind, but it wasn't the last images of her, which had haunted Isra's dreams. It was the Huda of happy times: the giggles and dimples colored by the sheer silk as they had hid in their little makeshift tent over their bed, telling stories and secrets, drinking tea.

The sun on her face when they'd run through the fields of short-lived flowers outside Damascus. Huda had run and run, her arms outstretched, her smile turned up to the sun, her head barely visible above the tall grass.

Her eyes looking up at Isra with an innocent grin. *I am fine, Sister. Do not worry so. I am very well and happy.*

Isra started and raised her head, opened her eyes.

When had she said that? Isra could not place the memory. She had appeared to be small still—six years, perhaps—but the voice had been recent, untouched by Huda's childish lisp.

Isra jumped again as the troupe suddenly sent out a cheer. She looked ahead, down the valley, and saw a thick cluster of horses emerging onto the road leading from Kerak's sandstone motte, a red and white banner flickering like a tiny scrap in the sunset.

She looked up at Roman, but his face was turned to the sky now, as if he was contemplating something only he could see.

Then he turned his head toward her, held out his hand.

Isra placed her fingers into his palm and let him pull her to her feet. Once she was standing he drew her against his chest slowly, deliberately, wrapping his uninjured arm around her shoulders, and Isra held her breath as she looked up and he lowered his head.

"I can wait no more," he whispered against her mouth, and then he kissed her.

Isra had never been kissed in that way before, even by Roman on that disastrous night in Asa's wagon when he'd wanted her. Now, his lips pressing against hers felt as if she was at last taking a deep breath of fresh air after being underwater for what seemed like years.

"Er, boss?" Zeus's voice interrupted the perfect moment, and Roman pulled away from her slowly, his easy, boyish grin shining even in his eyes.

She tried not to feel bitterness toward the caravan's lead man; after all, the troupe had been convinced she and Roman had been lovers since they'd begun sharing Asa's wagon. They couldn't know the significance of a single kiss—what it stood for, the weight it carried. And so Isra forgave the man, even though she guessed what he was going to say and had hoped to postpone it for at least a few more precious moments.

"We'd best take to the road before the day leaves us," Zeus continued.

Roman's smile faltered and he let Isra go from his embrace, although he did keep hold of her hand. He looked around at the troupe. "Where will you go?"

The question hung in the air, and Isra noticed several people glance questioningly at one another. Zeus himself pursed his lips a moment before answering.

"North, of course," the man said quietly. "We must retrieve Asa. And I hope Fran as well." He paused. "You're leaving us, then?"

"The events that occurred here tonight are of great import to some friends of mine. I must return to them as quickly as possible."

"South?" Isra offered, so glad when his face turned toward her again, like the sun on her skin. "Perhaps follow in Baldwin's wake?"

"It is likely many of the king's vassals remain convinced of my guilt; if I were discovered, our long journey to save the king's life might end with the loss of my own."

Isra knew too well that Roman could not circle to the east, for behind them lay Damascus.

As if he could hear her thoughts, Roman spoke again. "The only way for us to go is west. To the sea."

"Through Kerak?" Zeus exclaimed. "That's madness, boss! Raynald will have watchers posted."

But Roman ignored his friend's warning as he turned once more to Isra. She braced herself.

"We must leave Kahn behind," he said, and his sympathy was clear on his face. "Even in his wagon, a ship might not agree to take him on."

"No one else save me will go near him," she argued. "He is as wanted a criminal as we. Has he not been through enough? Has he not saved us both enough that he deserves his reward?"

"I understand. But Isra, what shall happen to him if we must leave him at the coast?" Roman asked in gentle exasperation.

"I will not leave him at the coast." She thought perhaps the realization of what she intended to do was beginning to dawn on him, and yet she could not let him continue to wonder.

"I will not leave him at all."

Roman stared at her until Zeus broke the heavy silence as he stalked into the spreading gloom. "I'll ready his wagon with fresh bedding; it's yet a mess with—" He broke off and moved away with his head down, the rest of the troupe following him quietly, as if sensing the impending tragedy.

Roman's handsome face wore a confused frown. "You . . . you're staying with the caravan? But I want you to come with me." He took her hand. "Isra, surely you know I love you. I think I've loved you since Damascus. I know I've loved you since we joined the caravan."

She wanted to speak, but her teeth were clenched so tightly, her throat so rigid, she felt that if she tried in that moment, she would shatter into a thousand pieces.

Roman blew a short breath out of his nose. "Do you love me?" he demanded, his voice rough.

"Yes," she whispered. "Yes, I love you."

"Then come with me to the coast," he urged, drawing her hand to his heart.

She shook her head as the first tears fell from her eyes. She forced herself to be braver than she ever had.

"Why?" he pleaded and tried to urge her into a one-armed embrace.

But she pulled away from him, stepped back, swiping at her eyes. "My whole life I have been owned. Commanded. Afraid. I have had to depend on someone else for my very existence." She looked up at him, feeling enough of the confidence in herself Roman had always believed in to speak the words without faltering.

"I do love you. But for me to come to you, I must first live in freedom without you." She paused. "I do not know who I am now, who I can be. Who I want to be. I must discover that on my own. I must be whole on my own. If, after I do that, you still want me, I will be yours."

"I want you now," he insisted. "Have we come all this way together only to part?"

She placed her hands on either side of his face and raised up on her toes. He lowered his head to meet her lips, and Isra kissed him hesitantly, sweetly, for a long moment.

"I must learn to live with myself before I can give my life to you," she said against his mouth. "Please. Do not despise me for it."

"Never could I—" He broke off and then looked down at her, and his throat moved as he swallowed. "Isra Tak'Ahn, you are the strongest woman I have ever known—perhaps the strongest person. You have given me so much and asked for nearly nothing in return. Can I now refuse you this one thing?"

He raised his right hand to stroke her face and then leaned forward to press his mouth to the crown of her head one final time, and when he breathed in deeply, his inhalation was jagged. Isra squeezed her eyes shut against the heat of his breath.

"I vow," he murmured into her hair, "I will never again return to this country. It has broken my heart for the last time."

Isra's sob caught painfully in her throat and she clutched at his tunic.

"Take care," he whispered.

Then he pulled away abruptly and turned toward the horse Zeus was walking toward them. He paused and looked up at the roof of Asa's wagon, where Lou perched. Roman whistled and held up his forearm.

But Lou turned his head, adjusted his wings.

Roman dropped his arm back to his side and looked at the bird for a moment as the rest of the troupe stood watching. There were no good-byes, no stiff-lipped farewells; the crowd was uncharacteristically silent. Roman turned from Lou and gained the saddle awkwardly, immediately kicking the horse's sides and riding toward the Mediterranean in the warmth of December, toward Melk. Leaving van Groen's Magical Menagerie, his falcon, and Isra behind.

Everyone else was abed—indeed, the hour was late. Certainly the two other members of the Brotherhood who could boast of warm companionship had sought it after such a wretched night. Taking their comfort. Constantine would not begrudge them that. He hoped that if Roman still lived, he was safe. Warm. Perhaps the Damascene woman had shown him care.

Constantine turned on his heel and began to circle the secret library in the opposite direction now, his hand reaching out occasionally to run his fingertips along the edge of a shelf, or the smooth turn of the tabletop, the back of a chair. He looked at the manuscripts lining the walls, the creamy wax as it beaded on the side of the candles in their holders. He tried to look anywhere but at the center of the table, where the message still lay.

Victor had left it. Constantine supposed there was no need to keep it anywhere else but here since they all now knew. Save Roman. Roman, who was at this moment likely somewhere deep inside the Holy Land, risking his life on a mission that no longer mattered.

Finally, Constantine sat down in his chair. He stared at the tabletop directly beneath his gaze for a very long time before reaching out with one hand and sightlessly placing his fingertips on the edge of the parchment. He drew it to him, sliding it beneath his gaze. He placed his hand beneath the tabletop on his lap, clenched into a fist like the first.

He let his gaze skitter up the page until it reached the top and, at last, he read the words himself.

To celebrate the installation of Lord Glayer Felsteppe as Earl of Rosemont, as well as his marriage to our beloved Lady Theodora while on their travels to that Holy City of Jerusalem, 21 November, in the year of our Lord 1181 ...

Constantine reached up and pushed the paper away slightly, unable to bear reading any further. The parchment seemed to itch under his fingertips, and so he slid the message back and forth quickly.

Now it burned. It vibrated. It shook the very table . . .

Constantine rose up with a roar, flipping the huge oaken slab into the air. He kept screaming, his fists clenched and shaking, his vision blurring, his temples pounding.

His last shred of caution, of sanity itself perhaps, slipping from his grasp as the damned missive floated and twisted through the air to land on the rug.

His arms fell back to his sides at last and he stood there, his chest heaving, for several moments. When he was once more calm, he untied his cincture and lay it along the chair near the window. He removed his monk's robe, not minding the bite of cold winter air in the stone room. He stood in his shirt and chausses, his boots. Then he turned to the long, thin cabinet wedged between the final shelf and the gatehouse wall.

Opening it, he withdrew his long sword and sheath, his battered cloak, his ragged purse containing only a handful of the damned Chastellet coins.

All of these he put on.

Then Constantine quit the secret library, walking through the corridors dressed in a manner that no man there save Victor and his brothers had ever seen. He strode through the gatehouse, Michael's stony eyes watching him, but the archangel made no argument as Stan pushed open the squeaking gate and left it wide.

He disappeared into the quiet stable for the better part of an hour before emerging once more with a sleepy black mount. Together they crossed the frosty bailey to the main gate. Constantine struggled with the brace for a moment and then opened it just enough to lead the horse through.

And then General Constantine Gerard was gone into the night, the whole of sleeping Melk unaware that they had lost him.

Chapter 25

Roman walked up the muddy path leading around the village of Melk, a rough satchel slung over his back. The air was crisp, still cold, but it contained a whiff of the freshness that sets men's minds to the coming spring. The ground was soft, thawing now, and the sun blazed down with enough cheer to make up for its lack of warmth.

He paused to look toward the center of the town and saw the bustling market, villagers meandering among the stalls he had once known so well. Everything seemed rather foreign to him now. Then a flash of red caught his eye, a lock of curling hair escaped from beneath a hood, and he knew of only one woman with tresses of such a bright hue.

His heart ached as he drew near them, Adrian—oddly enough in the dress of a layman—escorting Maisie down the street, unaware that they were being followed. Roman was nearly upon them when someone threw themselves upon his person, causing him to stagger in the street.

"Roman!" Mary Beckham cried, her slender arms not even reaching halfway around his body as she embraced him.

Roman laughed and lifted Valentine's wife in a swinging circle, kissing her cheek before setting her back on her feet. He looked up quickly and saw the handsome Spaniard only ten paces from him, the quirk of his mouth so painfully welcome as he bounced a much grown Valentina on his arm.

"We were beginning to think you preferred the warmer climates, my friend," he said. "What took you so long?"

"I had to travel half the way here with my arm dislocated because there was no sneaking Spaniard to reset it for me."

Then Valentine handed his daughter to Mary, and he and Roman came together in the center of the street, embracing with laughter.

"What?" Valentine insisted, drawing away but still clapping Roman's back. "Your shoulder again? Who did you enlist?"

"Another Spaniard, I'm afraid," Roman began but was interrupted as Adrian and Maisie joined them, and the greeting was just as warm, just as heartbreakingly sweet.

He touched Maisie's cheek allowing himself to think only for a moment of the woman's blade, which had saved Isra's life. He turned back to Valentine.

"I ran into a spot of trouble while trying to enlist a ship on Crete," he said. And when Valentine raised his eyebrows, Roman expounded. "Pirates."

His eyes widened. "Francisco?"

Roman winked. "He and Teresa left me in Venice. I am to give you both their love." He looked at the cherished faces before him and knew a twitch of unease that one was missing from the group. "Come, let us hie to the abbey and call for Stan. I have news for you all."

No one moved, although their smiles faltered.

"Where is Isra?" Adrian asked instead.

Roman cleared his throat. "I don't know, Aid."

Maisie frowned. "You doona know? She didna return with you?"

"Ah, no." Roman looked away for a moment and then back to his friends with a smile and a shrug. "Any matter, Valentina has grown!" He reached out and rubbed the hem of the baby's long gown, but she buried her face in her mother's neck so Roman dropped his hand. "Is Stan in the rotation this week?"

"Let us go back to the abbey, yes?" Valentine said suddenly and with great enthusiasm. "We will have a drink, hear about your great adventure. Come!"

They began to turn away, but Roman stopped them, placing a hand on Valentine's arm. "Wait." None wanted to meet his eyes. "Where is Constantine?"

Adrian at last looked up. "He's gone, Roman."

"Gone?" Roman repeated. "Gone where?"

"We doona know," Maisie offered. "He left nae word."

"I would guess England," Valentine said.

"But why now?" Roman demanded. "I risked my life to return to Syria. I found Baldwin. Isra and I saved his life and the king believes—"

"It does no matter now, my friend," Valentine interrupted gently.

"Felsteppe is a peer," Mary Beckham said in a tight voice. "A powerful peer—an earl. He married in the fall. At the same time you left Melk."

"Even if Baldwin pardons us," Adrian said with a trace of his old bitterness, "we can't touch Felsteppe now. He's above the law."

"He is the law." Mary grimaced.

"Why didn't you follow Stan?" Roman demanded. "Has he gone after Felsteppe? What if he needs help? What if he—"

"We were waiting for you," Valentine interrupted. And then with a smile, "We were waiting for you, Roman."

Roman's head was spinning. "I need to see Victor, hear his thoughts."

"Of course, my friend, of course. But there is something else you must know," Valentine said. "Lou is gone, too. I was giving him his exercise the day you departed and he simply did no return to the mews. I thought perhaps he followed you, but . . ." The Spaniard looked pointedly at Roman's empty shoulder.

"He did follow me," Roman said. "He chose not to return with me, though." He felt the stoop in his posture as he turned from his friends and began climbing the path toward the huge abbey over the Danube. When he'd left Melk all those months ago, he'd envisioned his homecoming as a triumph, a victory. Even at Kerak, he'd held in his heart the idea of returning to his friends against the pain of his departure from the woman he loved.

Now, Isra had refused him, Lou had abandoned him. Even Constantine, the one to whom Roman had hoped above all the others to carry the news of Baldwin's favor, had gone.

And Glayer Felsteppe was now an earl.

Roman's world had fallen apart both slowly and all at once.

He walked toward the abbey ahead of the others and they followed him, bearing witness as he carried his grief and his anger home.

Chapter 26

Isra left the village behind her, her long, silky train draped over the arm holding the lead, the bracelets on her other arm tinkling as the circled whip swung in her hand. The troupe was setting up in the round in the very center of town of course; what village could refuse such entertainment as offered by van Groen's famous menagerie?

She drew many looks and several frightened shrieks from the folk she passed. Isra didn't mind, though. She knew it wasn't often they saw such a dark-skinned woman walking through their village dressed in shimmering green silk and adorned with gold jewelry, a glittering crown atop her head.

Especially such a woman walking with a tiger at her side and a falcon on her shoulder.

Kahn stopped to sniff at a butcher's stall, causing the fat man to fall backward into his pile of sausages with a scream.

"Hie, Kahn." Isra chuckled. "Come. My apologies, sir," she called to the butcher. "He is not hungry, only curious."

The tiger reluctantly dropped back to the road and continued up the hill next to Isra toward the great abbey, shimmering in the warm air much as the jewels on Kahn's great collar sparkled.

She walked through the gates, marveling as much at the relaxed posture of her shoulders, the proud tilt of her chin as at the statuary that decorated the manicured gardens. Lou danced on her shoulder, his talons pressing the thick leather patch sewn onto her costume—her costume, which she'd commissioned from her own design and paid for with her own coin. The falcon did not fly from her, although his head swiveled and he seemed to be looking, searching.

Several brethren were hard at work in the bailey, but when they saw Isra and Kahn, they dropped their rakes and crossed themselves.

Isra stopped and looked about the bailey, the scores of darkened archways that led to different parts of the compound.

Which way was she to go?

As if in answer to her unspoken prayer, a skinny, bald monk walked toward her with a smile. Victor, who had blessed her before she felt worthy of such a thing. He gestured toward a corridor, where their conversation wouldn't disturb the holy silence.

"God's blessing upon your return, my child. Welcome," he said with a nervous smile, glancing at the tiger. "Seek you Brother Wynn or Roman first?"

"For the sake of your charges, I should probably see Wynn," Isra returned.

"It really doesn't matter," Victor said, skittering back a pair of steps as Kahn reached out his neck to sniff the air in front of the monk. "Where one is, we're certain to find the other. Good day, Lou. I know someone who shall be quite pleased to see you. Follow me, please."

Through a pair of corridors and then down the wide stairs Isra trailed Victor, Lou clutching and releasing his talons on her shoulder, the tiger staying close to her side while his ears pricked, his coat bunched, his whiskers twitched.

If Isra had possessed whiskers or wings, hers would have twitched, too. She could sense Roman nearby. Her stomach clenched.

Brother Wynn was the first to see them coming, standing just beyond the bottom of the wide apron of stairs, moving large piles of straw. The albino monk dropped his pitchfork with a great clang, his white hands going to his head.

"Thanks be to God," he cried out and then raised his hands and dropped to his knees, his eyes on the stone ceiling. "Thank you, Lord. I knew you would answer my prayers, merciful provider!" He got to his feet quickly, his eyes only for Kahn, but his words for Isra. "His name?"

"Kahn," she said with a smile and then amended, "*Prince* Kahn. He has performed, but now it is time for him to be at peace." *For both of us to be at peace.* She slid her wrist from the braided lead and let it drop.

The tiger sauntered across the stone floor as if he already ruled the subterranean domain, his wide head swinging. He went immediately to the first cell on the right, sniffed loudly, and then rose up to his full height to look through the small barred window.

"He is magnificent," Wynn breathed.

As if to prove the monk's statement, Kahn let out a roar that shook the stones and was immediately answered by a shriller scream. Then Princess's door did in fact shake as the tigress launched herself at the window.

"Wynn?" a familiar voice called out. "Is everything—"

Isra turned and her breath froze in her chest as she caught sight of the large blond man coming from the shadowed end of the gallery. Isra was not surprised to see a mallet in his hand, his bare arms hanging down by his sides. He tossed the tool to the floor with a clang.

She thought she heard him whisper Lou's name; then, an instant later, his sharp whistle pierced the air.

Lou crouched and took flight from her shoulder, his light underbelly flashing in the gloom of the gallery as he glided silently over the fountain to land on Roman's shoulder.

With Lou and Kahn gone from her side, Isra suddenly felt very alone. And as she stood, watching him, the old doubts tried to creep up from her past, gasping their last breaths in hope of resurrection, hope of once more having Isra's tender consciousness to feed from.

He does not want you now. He has come to his senses. Go back to your circus now, before he has chance to denounce and humiliate your foolish, tender feelings. Whore.

No; she reminded herself of the realization she'd had during these months on the road with the troupe without Roman. *I am not a whore and I never was. Roman Berg does not give his heart lightly, and he gave it to me. It is mine, and I have come to claim it.*

Isra flung the doubts from her mind once and for all as she tossed the whip to the floor behind her and ran toward Roman, holding up her skirts as she crossed the stones. Her crown slipped off and clattered across the floor, her silken head scarf fluttering away to land in the water of the fountain. Lou swooped from Roman's shoulder to disappear into an open cell as Roman began to stride toward Isra. She did not slow but held out her arms and leaped.

He caught her, pulled her so tightly against him that she couldn't breathe, but Isra didn't care. She wrapped her arms around his neck and kissed him as she'd wanted to for so long, with the passion she was no longer afraid to feel or show, with the love in her heart that she knew was nothing but pure.

She pulled away. "I love you, Roman. Do you still want me?"

"Forever and ever," he said and kissed her again. And then he turned with her in his arms back toward the doorway of the cell that had once been her prison, her sanctuary, at Fallen Angels Abbey. And he kicked the door closed behind them.

"See here, now," Wynn shouted down the gallery. "You'll have to stay in there. I don't know how Princess will accept—"

"Wynn," Victor interrupted, "I don't think you need to worry about them interrupting anything, hmm?"

"Ah!" the albino said with a light in his eyes. "I see now. Yes, well, all right." He took the short whip from his cincture and let it crack in the air.

The tiger dropped from the door and spun around.

"Hie, Kahn," the monk said firmly but kindly. "Come now, boy, let us have a marriage today, shall we? Victor, will you preside?"

"Lord have mercy."

He lay her on his cot, which he had moved to Wynn's domain along with his other meager possessions once it was clear it was no longer necessary for the Brotherhood to remain in hiding as monks. Even Lou's old perch stood in a corner, and his beloved falcon sat content-edly upon it once more. Roman had filled his days since his return to Melk as a lay helper of Wynn, and he had been as happy as he could have been with it. It had been a companion, and a tiger.

Isra stroked his face as he kissed her jaw, her neck. There were so many questions he wanted to ask her, but not yet. Not until he had loved her and made her his and she could not take it back.

He raised up and looked into her eyes. "It's all right now, isn't it?" he asked.

"Yes," she whispered with a smile.

And so he took his time unwrapping her, like a precious gift sent from far away—which he thought was not an inaccurate description. Each inch of her tanned skin he revealed he covered with his mouth, replacing the sheer silk with his breath.

She had scars; old, pale lines and patches. Someday he might ask her about them, but right now he loved them all; they were a part of her, comprised her beautiful form that Roman hoped with all his heart now belonged to him.

In moments she was nude below him, save for her hammered

gold bracelets and the chains around her neck, the jewels dangling from her ears and lying against her skin.

"Now remove your clothes," she said quietly.

And he did, feeling his passion rise even higher as she watched him brazenly, that little smile never leaving her lips, her dark hair fanning over his pillow.

He didn't want to go too fast, nor did he want to hesitate with her, giving her cause to think he wasn't certain. But when he lay down beside her, thinking her too small, too fragile for his hulking, clumsy self, she reached for him eagerly, kissing him again and causing all thoughts, all second guesses, to fly from his mind, leaving only the immense depth of feeling in his heart, in his body.

Their joining was so sweet, so perfect, Roman felt emotion welling in his eyes, but he was not shamed, kissing her face tenderly as her breaths, too, became labored. He forced himself to slow, slow, and Isra gave him the gift of her surrender when she cried out beneath him. Roman lost his caution and joined her, feeling as though he had at last found his rightful place in the world.

They lay together in the bed as the candle burned low, talking of all that had happened to each of them since their parting at Kerak.

Her temple was against his chest, his forearm across her slender back when she said, "Fran is dead."

Roman felt his mouth turn down, a vision of the blond, troubled woman blooming in his mind. "Before you returned for Asa?"

She nodded, her hair like brushes of silk against his skin. "Two days after we left them. Asa buried her himself and then waited alone for us."

"She was very sad," Roman allowed. "But Asa?"

"Asa is at peace. He told me once that he didn't think Fran would ever have recovered from Max's death, that she would have eventually come to the same end in one way or another. I do not know if I agree with him." Isra was quiet for a moment. "She should not have left Asa."

Roman tucked his chin to look down into her beautiful face as she tilted her head up to do the same.

"She should have fought for herself. Fought for him."

Roman stroked her cheek, downy and smooth. "Not everyone is as strong as you are, Isra."

She nuzzled into his chest once more. "The troupe is waiting for us in Melk. Asa is very much looking forward to meeting you again. We have a home with the caravan if we wish it."

"Without Kahn?"

"Only without Kahn," Isra answered, more than a touch of sadness in her voice.

"Is that what you want?" he asked, his heart skipping a beat.

"I have had the time I needed," she answered. "I am grateful for the home Asa and the others have offered me. But now I shall go where it is best for both of us."

Roman drew a deep breath. "I'm not certain where would be best for us to go, but I'm fairly certain where we're going. Isra, Constantine left Melk on his own some months ago, while we were still in Syria. Glayer Felsteppe has married into an earldom. There's little we can do against him now, regardless of Baldwin's clemency."

Isra stilled and then lifted her head from Roman's chest to look into his eyes with a worried frown.

"He has gone back to his home," she said. "To avenge the deaths of his family."

Roman nodded. "Perhaps," he said. "We were hoping for a message from him, or news. Hoping . . ."

"Hoping he would still be the general?" Isra guessed.

Roman felt his mouth thin. "I suppose so."

She lay her head back down on his shoulder. "I do not think Constantine is capable of that anymore. He needs his brothers with him."

"As do I." Roman stroked the delicate hills of her shoulder blades, like silk beneath his hand. "We've already made plans to leave Melk. A fortnight from now, you would have been too late."

"I would have found you," Isra said, and there was no anxiety in her voice. "Lou and I, we always find you. Where are we to go?"

Roman kissed the crown of her head, relishing the smell of her hair he remembered so well. "Perhaps to Adrian's father's until we can make a better plan. Constantine was always the one who made the battle plans, and he hasn't been himself for some time. We cannot fathom his mind. None of us are sure exactly where to start."

This time Isra sat up. "You do know where to start."

"You are so beautiful. Will you marry me, Isra?"

"You *do* know where to start," she repeated and placed her palm along his cheek. "It is the same as when you saved him from the prison."

Roman frowned. "Damascus?"

She shook her head. "No. You did not know where to look, but you went any matter. You went and your heart led you to your friends."

"You led me to my friends," he corrected.

"And I will go with you now," she said. "To England, to Norway, to Cairo—to the ends of the earth." She lay her forearm along his chest and then rested her chin. "You are my family, Roman. My soul. These men are your brothers; now they are my brothers, too. Even though that particular brother has not cared for me in the past."

"I know he will change his mind," Roman said.

Isra nodded. "Then let us go. Tomorrow. *Tonight*," she insisted. "Let us band together, the family that we are, and go after our own. Nothing can stop us."

Roman felt chills sweep over his skin. How could he ever be worthy of a woman so brave and true?

He leaned his head up and kissed her mouth. "Isra, for the second time: Will you marry me?"

She smiled against his lips. "As you wish, my lord."

Epilogue

March 1182
Thurston Hold

Dori walked down the corridor, the fingers of one hand trailing the stones, the other placed atop her round belly. She had to stop twice; the twinges were shockingly strong and they made her head swim. Only for a moment, though, and then she was once more heading toward her sitting room.

She walked through the door and started as her husband turned from the window and gave her a head to toe look of disgust.

"What are you doing in here?" she demanded.

"It's my house; I'll go wherever I like," he sneered.

"It's my house," Dori insisted. "You just live here."

She shouldn't have said it; she should have learned by now, but years of being headstrong were hard to overcome.

Glayer Felsteppe stomped toward her and twisted her arm painfully behind her back until her shoulders and ribs screamed. Soon, Dori was screaming, too.

"Stop!" she pleaded. "The baby, please!"

Only then did he release her and shove her away. "Watch your snappy mouth around me, woman," he warned. "You won't always be carrying my child, and when you're not I'll have little use for you. Mind your tongue."

When Dori failed to acknowledge his threat, he strode toward her quickly, grabbed a great handful of her hair, and jerked her head back. "Did you hear what I said?"

"Yes!" she screamed. "I'm sorry!"

He pushed her away once more and then regarded her with a look of contempt. "For the love of God, if you're going to go about the keep in the daylight, at least drape yourself with a cloak or *something*. Your shape is revolting."

And then he quit the room, slamming the door behind him.

Theodora Rosemont choked on her sob as she stood aright, dizziness overtaking her once more, the twinges starting again. She gasped and lowered her head, praying for the pain to pass. When it finally abated, her chest and face were covered in a thin layer of icy perspiration. She walked toward the window Glayer Felsteppe had been looking out of when she entered. It was his favorite spot in all the house, to her great dismay.

The door opened again, and the pinch-faced nurse her husband had hired came in, carrying the afternoon repast.

"Your tonic, milady," she said, and set the tray on the table Dori had only recently left.

"I don't wish it today, Nurse. I think it makes me . . . ill."

"You must drink it," the sour woman demanded. She couldn't have been more than a year or two older than Theodora herself, although the woman's bitter countenance belied her youth with every deep line on her face. "For your strength in childbirth."

"It gives me pains," she admitted. "Makes me dizzy. I don't want it. Take it away."

"Very well. I shall inform milord of your wishes."

The two women stared at each other for several moments. The last thing Dori wanted now was for Glayer Felsteppe to return.

"Fine," she said, stalking to the tray and picking up the cup. She drank the foul liquid, like raspberries, only green and bitter, then slammed the cup back on the tray. "Now take it and yourself from my sight."

"Yes, milady," the woman sneered and quit the room.

Dori brought a hand to her throat and went back to the window. She might throw the whole mess up after all.

But the view commanded her as well—the rolling hills only just beginning to show signs of the soft green of spring as the first tender stalks of grass and early crops pushed through the chilly soil. And in the far distance, a tiny, jagged black speck. Anyone else unfamiliar with the horizon might have mistook it for nothing more than another tree.

The ruins of Benningsgate Castle. What a haunted place it must be now, its lord in exile as a traitor and presumed dead; its lady and heir burned to death in a fire that had destroyed most of the keep. The grounds were held by the crown now, while the king determined the rightful successor.

Glayer Felsteppe was campaigning in earnest to the king for a chance to purchase the tragic remains.

Dori felt her head swimming again, so much so that she fell into the window seat with a gasp. Her vision began to throb and pulse and turn reddish at the edges.

She cried out at the pain in her abdomen, in her bottom, and then felt a trickle of wetness on her knees where she crouched. She tried to raise up to inspect herself, but her head seemed to explode with the sea, her throat swelling, her nose closing.

She heard herself gasping and choking as she tumbled off the window seat and onto the floor, feeling a thickness like seafoam bubbling at her mouth, pooling in her throat. The room grew dark, and now footsteps thumped across the floor . . .

And in the window above Theodora Rosemont's body, the skeleton of Benningsgate Castle bore witness to yet another tragedy against mother and child.

ABOUT THE AUTHOR

Before writing historical romances, **Heather Grothaus** worked as a successful freelance journalist, short story writer, and magazine writer. She lives with her family on a small farm in Kentucky.

Readers can visit her online at www.heathergrothaus.com or connect with her on twitter and Goodreads.

Please turn the page for an exciting sneak peek of
CONSTANTINE
Heather Grothaus's next installment in the
Brotherhood of Fallen Angels series
coming in December 2016!

Prologue

July 1179
Chastellet

Glayer Felsteppe swaggered into the king's antechamber, his heeled boots—so vain and out of place here in this land of sand—clicking conspicuously on the red floor tiles striped black with cool shadows. None of the Templar soldiers in retreat from the heat of the day paid the thin man's entrance any heed, and Constantine kept to his own vantage point in the shadows behind where the king sat. He had waited a long time for this moment.

Felsteppe came to a stop before Baldwin and sank to one knee, spreading his arms and dropping his head of flaming hair in a grandiose display. "You called for me, my liege?"

The king flicked his bandaged hand, releasing the man from his show of homage, but Felsteppe was too entrenched in his performance to notice. "Lord Felsteppe, it has been alleged that you have once again taken to fraternizing with Saladin's envoys," Baldwin said, his tone more tired than irritated. "More than fraternizing."

Felsteppe's head snapped up and he rose, his gaze going to the darker area behind Baldwin's chair as if by instinct.

Like a cockroach that senses the raised boot above it and skitters away before it can be stomped, Constantine thought as he emerged from the gloom. He left the evidence of the charges he had levelled still hidden on the table behind him. There would be no skittering this time.

When Felsteppe saw Constantine, his already beady eyes narrowed farther before he looked back to the king of Jerusalem. "My liege, General Gerard constantly seeks to besmirch my good name with his outrageous claims. The man is clearly obsessed with me."

Constantine said nothing, refusing to be baited.

The king's sparse eyebrows rose. "Do you then deny that you were fraternizing with the Saracen legates?"

"I spoke with them, certainly," Felsteppe scoffed, drawing back his coiffed head as if shocked at the absurdity of the question. "It was my duty to chaperone the men of lesser ranks while you met with Saladin's general. Unlike some"—here Felsteppe levelled a haughty look at Constantine—"I felt it would not further our cause to be overly combative. After all, Saladin sent his men seeking peace."

"He's seeking an end to Chastellet!" Baldwin barked and slapped his hand on the arm of his chair, causing many of the soldiers lounging about the quiet, shadowed room to glance toward the king. Adrian Hailsworth, architect of Chastellet and the only man Constantine could reliably call his friend, did not look up, absorbed as he typically was in the sheets of plans spread out before him at his table in a far corner of the room.

Baldwin ignored the looks of the soldiers. "Saladin knows that while our mighty fortress stands, there is no chance of him seizing control over the crossing at Jacob's Ford. It's imperative we remain, no matter the cost to us, and no matter how many dinars he offers in bribes."

"Your communications with the Saracens were far from mere courtesy," Constantine added, unwilling to let Felsteppe attempt to turn the charges against him into a pointless political debate. "You're a liar. And a traitor."

"General," Baldwin warned in a low voice, turning his head only slightly toward Constantine. "The man shall have his say."

"A traitor as well now, am I?" Felsteppe sneered. "And what fantasy, pray tell, have you concocted in your mind this time that I am to held liable for?"

"Selling Templar weaponry to the Saracens. In the very bailey belonging to the men it was crafted to defend."

At these allegations, the soldiers who before had only glanced in the direction of the king now fully turned toward the trio of men, prompting many more to do the same. The quiet murmurs of conversation ceased, and an air of expectation swelled against the stone walls.

Felsteppe's laughter cut through the silence and seemed to echo. His smile was wide as he threw up his hands. "That's preposterous." Baldwin spoke. "You deny General Gerard's accusation?" "Of *course* I deny it!" Felsteppe scoffed. Constantine turned back to the table behind him while Felsteppe continued. "Surely you must see that the general's claims become more and more outrageous? I would never—"

His words were cut off as Constantine turned, his arms laden, and tossed the evidence to the floor between Baldwin and Felsteppe. If any in the room hadn't been paying attention before, the echoing crash and clatter of weaponry ensured that all eyes were on the three men at the head of the tense room.

Even Adrian looked up from his plans.

Felsteppe stared at Constantine for a moment, but then he blinked and shrugged. "Am I supposed to be moved by this rather noisy display?"

"The weapons you sold to the Saracens," Constantine clarified through gritted teeth.

Again, Felsteppe laughed. "Oh, really? Then why are they in *your* possession rather than the Saracens I supposedly sold them to?" He rolled his eyes.

"I bought it all back from them," Constantine said. "From General Abdal himself."

Felsteppe looked to the king with an air of exasperation. "Ridiculous, my liege. It is Gerard's word against mine. Perhaps a Saracen's, as well, if even his scheme went so far."

Baldwin was staring at Felsteppe, but when he spoke, his words were directed at Constantine.

"How much did Abdal claim he paid?"

"Three hundred dinars, my liege," Constantine said.

"That is a paltry amount for such steel." Baldwin looked away for a moment, as if collecting his thoughts. "Judd," he called out, and his summons was answered at once by a lanky soldier who levered himself aright from a woven mat beneath a far window, shuttered against the baking heat.

Judd bowed before the king. "My liege."

"Take possession of Lord Felsteppe's purse, there on his belt," Baldwin commanded. "Empty it before us all, and let it be counted and the nature of the contents noted."

Constantine's jaw clenched as he saw the panic enter Felsteppe's eyes and the man's hand twitch toward the bulging leather packet hanging upon his side.

Judd turned to Felsteppe, his palm out. "If you please."

Now Felsteppe's hand did cover the purse, as if trying to protect it. He looked up at Baldwin. "My liege, I am greatly disappointed that you would think I—"

Baldwin interrupted. "Take it off, Lord Felsteppe. Or I shall have Judd do it for you."

Felsteppe's bony throat convulsed. He hesitated only a moment more before loosening the purse strap from his belt, his voice noticeably trembling when next he spoke.

"I cannot see how the contents of my purse could possibly incriminate me. It is common knowledge that all men in this country must trade in many currencies. I—I—" he struggled with the knot for a moment, and Constantine thought his fingers must be shaking. He at last worked the strap free and handed the weighty purse to Judd before looking once more to Baldwin, his pointed chin lifted. "I have done nothing wrong."

Judd turned slightly and dropped to one knee, so that his actions could be seen by both Felsteppe and the king. As he opened the purse, a handful of Templar soldiers rose and drew nearer, not daring to encroach on the scene outright, but clearly interested in the outcome of Judd's accounting.

The tinkling wash of coins on the tile floor was like sudden rain on a roof, and even before Judd began to sort the coins near the pile of weaponry, Constantine knew. He knew from the raises and shadows of the coin faces; the color of the metal; the number of stacks equal in height.

"Three hundred dinars, my liege," Judd said without emotion. "Two pieces of Chastellet gold; one penny."

The men gathered outside the circle raised their voices in sudden outrage, and Felsteppe seemed to shrink away from the crowd, turning to face them, backing closer to the wall.

"It's not as you think!" he cried. He looked to Baldwin, his eyes wild. "My liege, I—"

Baldwin stood. "Clear the chamber!" he shouted, and then looked around at the angry group of soldiers. "*Clear the chamber!*" The king waited, his chest visibly rising and falling as the Templars streamed through the far door, leaving Felsteppe and Constantine—and the once more oblivious Adrian Hailsworth—alone with Baldwin.

"It's not as you think," Felsteppe repeated, then licked his lips, advancing a step toward Baldwin. "These pieces are clearly broken, useless; surely Gerard retrieved them from a refuse heap. I-I—"

"The pieces *were* discarded. For *repair*," Constantine growled. "Regardless of any excuse you might concoct for your thievery, you cannot deny the coin in your purse."

"Constantine," the king warned. He looked back to the accused man. "You understand that every allegation General Gerard has levied against you now has many times more weight."

"He is a danger to Chastellet, my liege," Constantine insisted, the words out of his mouth before he could stop himself.

Baldwin looked between the two men with a sigh. "I was to leave for Tiberius on the morrow, and I'll be damned if the pair of you will cause me to shirk my duties." His eyes pinned Felsteppe. "*You* were to be left in charge of the hold during my absence, but it could mean danger to the fortress or yourself should I leave you unattended—with or without my authority. You shall accompany me to Tiberius."

Felsteppe's jaw flexed and his sneer was just below the surface of his skin. "As you wish, of course. My liege."

Then Baldwin turned to Constantine. "Which means that *you*, General Gerard, must continue to attend to your duties at Chastellet until my return."

No, no, no, no.

"Bal—*my liege*, surely you have forgotten that I was to depart for my home within the fortnight. Am I to be punished for bringing the actions of a thief and a traitor to light?"

"I have not forgotten. Nor do I mean to punish you, Constantine," Baldwin said, and although he had twice used Constantine's given name, the king's tone was still stern. "But what did you think would happen if your accusations were found true? Would you now leave Chastellet in his care?"

Felsteppe's face reddened further, but he was wise enough to not comment. It was Constantine who felt the fool now.

"What of Hailsworth?" Constantine said, pointing toward the man still hunched over his plans in the corner. "He's been in residence as long as I. And he's titled. Surely he could—"

"No." Adrian Hailsworth did not so much as look up as he called out. "Not a soldier. Don't care about the lot of you."

When Constantine looked back at Baldwin, the king had one eyebrow raised. "It's a short journey. You will be free of my tyranny forever upon my return."

It was not in Constantine's nature to beg, but he could not help expressing the yearning pain in his heart. "I want to go home, Baldwin. My son Christian was only four when I last saw him—little more than a baby; he's nearly seven now. He needs me. Have I not served you faithfully for two years?"

"You have, and I am grateful. But you'll stay until my return or risk besmirching an otherwise exceptional career." Baldwin paused and then pressed, "Your answer, General?"

Constantine's anger simmered. "As you wish, my liege."

Baldwin turned to Felsteppe. "I've not passed judgement on you before the men as of yet, and so you will probably be safe. All the same, it is best if you do not encroach on the soldiers' common areas this eventide." He glanced at the pile of coin and weaponry still on the floor. "You may, however, see the return of your purse and your *penny*."

The king turned and, as he limped toward the doors that led to his private chambers, called out, "And do pick up the mess on the floor before you're off." He slung the door closed with a crash behind him.

Constantine looked back at Glayer Felsteppe, whose reddened, watery eyes and curled lip gave evidence to his rage. Constantine didn't care. He had done his duty, and would now continue to do his duty until Baldwin's return, no matter how much he resented it.

"You son of a bitch," Felsteppe snarled. "You just couldn't stomach the idea of me being in charge of Chastellet, could you?"

"I couldn't care less who Baldwin retains to fill my appointment after I am gone," Constantine replied, turning his back on the loathsome man to walk to the large cask mounted on its side against the wall. He watched the liquid flow into his cup and he wished it was wine. "But while I am responsible for the welfare of this hold, I will report anything I feel the king needs be aware of. Especially if it is of a traitorous nature."

"You're only trying to further your rank." Felsteppe continued behind him, as Constantine raised his cup to his lips and let the cool water flood his mouth. "Lazy, entitled bastard! You deserve not even the tiniest fraction of the power you claim at Chastellet."

Constantine swallowed and then sighed, his eyes trained on the smooth stone above the cask. He called to mind the verdant landscape stretching out around Benningsgate, the wet greenness of the very air in her forests. He imagined sitting in his own hall of an even, drinking from his own casks and speaking of things such as crops and flocks and servants. Hearing the gossip about the town. He thought of the moment—delayed now, true, but only by weeks—he would approach Benningsgate and see the blond little boy running for him, leaping into Constantine's arms . . .

He felt slightly calmer. "Any power I have here has come hand in hand with my duties, and both were given to me after I proved myself worthy."

Felsteppe sputtered. "Did you earn your title? Benningsgate Castle? Did you work your way into your earldom? Your wife's bed? I've heard the latter at least can be done with little effort."

Constantine ran his tongue along his teeth and closed his eyes for a moment before turning to face the man, who seemed so distraught that Constantine wouldn't have been surprised to see him collapse to the floor to pound his fists and boots against the tile.

"You can't keep blaming others for your failures, Felsteppe. Eventually, you will have to claim responsibility for your life and the choices you make."

"Choices?" Felsteppe said on a false laugh. "You mean like the choice Baldwin has made? You know it's only a matter of time before Saladin orders the attack on Chastellet now that our *king* has turned him away yet again. The fortress isn't even properly completed!"

"It's almost done," Adrian Hailsworth muttered from his corner, his head still down. "Only the glacis to complete. Strong enough now."

"The foundation is exposed!" Felsteppe cried out to the architect. When Adrian failed to respond, Felsteppe faced Constantine once more. "You're all fools! Baldwin has guaranteed your deaths."

Constantine's eyes narrowed. "It is our duty to defend this stronghold and the river crossing below. That's what you swore to do when you accepted your charge."

"I came here to make my fortune, same as all the others."

"Perhaps you should have sought assignment in one of the ports then. Promise of riches is not why men come to Chastellet."

Felsteppe stared at Constantine and then sniffed a half laugh, his thin lips quirking in some semblance of a grin. "Oh, of course. That's not why *you're* here, is it, Gerard?"

Constantine's back stiffened, but he kept his expression neutral as he gestured to the pile of armaments still littering the floor. "Do as the king commands and retreat to your cell before the sun sets. Some may lie in wait for you." He turned and started to cross the floor, heading toward the double doors and his own chamber in order to grieve the delay of his departure.

Perhaps many men's futures—indeed, the future of the world— would have been quite different had Glayer Felsteppe held his tongue and allowed Constantine to leave without further comment.

But, alas.

"*You're here* because your wife is a very rich whore with a constant itch, and everyone doubts the son she bore is yours!"

Constantine halted, still facing the door.

Baiting you again. That's all.

He started forward once more, and this time he saw that Adrian had raised his head and was now watching Constantine with a wary expression.

"That's right—I know. *Everyone* knows," Felsteppe taunted. "Who can predict how many children you'll have to your name upon your return? Perhaps even now, little *Christian* is on some other man's lap, sitting in your chair at supper, calling him Papa."

Constantine stopped again, his feet sticking so firmly that he swayed in his stance.

"You'll never outstay *that* rumor, Gerard," Felsteppe chuckled. "It will live with you—and the boy—for the rest of your lives. Christian will never *really* know if you're his father or not. Rather sad, isn't it? I feel sorry for the lad, truly. Whore for a mother, and a coward—"

Felsteppe continued to talk as Constantine turned and stalked back toward him, but he had no idea what the man said, as the blood was roaring in his ears so loudly that it drowned out all other sound. Felsteppe, however, must have realized that he had finally hit his mark for now he drew his sword and sank into a defensive posture with a satisfied smirk.

Constantine, too, swept his weapon from its sheath as he continued to rush forward. When he was nearly close enough to strike, Felsteppe changed tactics and charged. But Constantine was ready and in two swings, Felsteppe's weapon went sliding and clanging across the floor. Constantine was upon him then, and rammed the butt of his hilt into Felsteppe's nose once, twice, sending blood spraying from the man's face like a fountain.

Felsteppe staggered back with a cry, his hands covering his dripping face while Constantine sheathed his weapon—if he didn't, he was certain he would kill the man outright. But even though he was no longer readily armed, he wasn't yet finished with Glayer Felsteppe.

And neither was Felsteppe finished. Once he saw the weapon was sent home, he charged at Constantine with his bloody fists clenched, a scream of rage coming from his sticky mouth. Constantine met his fury with his own, ducking Felsteppe's swing and coming up with a fist under his chin and then two swift blows to the man's abdomen. When the redhead doubled over, Constantine grabbed him by the back of his leather hauberk and slung him around in an arc.

Felsteppe flew through the air toward Adrian Hailsworth's corner table and landed across the end of it, sliding through the piles of parchment as his hands scrabbled for purchase. Adrian pushed his chair back with a screech and stood.

Constantine stomped after Felsteppe, seizing him and flipping him over on his back, a shower of crumpled ivory pages raining down around them. Felsteppe swung with a weak yell, his fist clenched around a wad of parchment, and Constantine took the blow on his chin. He hardly felt it though as he drew back and hit Felsteppe in his already battered face, his knuckles making sick, splashing sounds by the third blow.

Before the sixth could land, Adrian hooked his arm around Constantine's and pulled him backward with a mighty heave, allowing Glayer Felsteppe to slide to the floor in a crumpled, gasping heap.

"Killing him won't make Baldwin change his mind," Adrian said near his ear as he pushed between Constantine and the bleeding, wheezing man on the floor. "You've made your point."

As much as Constantine appreciated the friend he had found in the brusque, scholarly Hailsworth, he was not quite satisfied that he had indeed made his point. He swept Adrian aside and after two strides sank to one knee over Felsteppe, seizing the front of his sodden tunic and pulling the limp rag of the man close to his face.

"Dare not speak my son's name again. Verily, never be in my

sight after this day, Glayer Felsteppe," Constantine said as calmly as his still seething rage would allow. "Whether Baldwin allows your return from Tiberius or nay. Perhaps I could not prove them before today, but I have not forgotten—nor will I—your many, many misdeeds at Chastellet. The rapes of the merchants' slaves, the thefts, the traitorous discords with which you sought to infect the men. You are *scum*, and you deserved to be wiped from the land. The next time I see you, I *will* kill you."

"You think everyone is afraid of you, Gerard," Felsteppe rasped, bloody spittle flying from his split lips. "I'm not. You're not *holy*; you're not *superior*. You're a pampered house cat whose been made to believe he's above covering over his own shit."

"I do believe this particular housecat has shown you his claws," Hailsworth muttered as he returned to his chair, his eyes for naught but his precious scrolls as he straightened his exploded stacks.

"Fuck you, scribe," Felsteppe snapped, and then he glared back into Constantine's face. "You'll pay for what you've done today. Today and every day since you've come here and tried to ruin me." Felsteppe pushed at Constantine, and he stepped back and allowed the beaten man to stagger to his feet at last.

Felsteppe pointed a bony, stained, trembling finger toward Constantine, his other hand still curled around the ruined parchment he'd dragged from the table top. "I will see everything you love burn. Everything."

"You couldn't come within a score of miles of anything I love, Felsteppe. You're lucky the king didn't dismiss you outright. I believe he still might. Then where will you go? Back to Land's End to herd sheep?" It was a low blow, but his fury seemed to let the words flow like the water from yonder cask.

Felsteppe's face matched his bright hair, between the blood in and on his cheeks. "Everything you love," he repeated. "No matter what I must do."

"Get from my sight," Constantine demanded and then turned away from the man before he was tempted to fall upon him again.

He heard the door open, and Adrian Hailsworth called out in a sardonic tone, "Oh, no, please—do keep those parchments. They weren't quite right and rather covered in your blood, any matter."

The door slammed shut.

"Maggot," Adrian muttered.

The air in the room seemed to tingle with the altercation that hadn't fully resolved Constantine of his anger. And when his gaze fell upon the pile of contraband Felsteppe had failed to collect and return as commanded by the king, Constantine sighed. Even though his muscles still burned and his breath left a metallic scent in his nostrils, he crossed the floor and began gathering the broken swords, the cracked shields, and the worn pads himself, his hands still wet with Glayer Felsteppe's blood.

It was his duty, after all.

Glayer Felsteppe staggered through the narrow, dark interior corridors of Chastellet, his humiliation unrelieved by the fact that he passed no one. It mattered not—by now, Glayer knew every warrior monk, every base laborer, even the meanest slave had been apprised of the going's-on in Baldwin's antechamber. No one at Chastellet would ever let him forget what had happened. Perhaps it was best that he left.

He swiped at his dripping face with the wad of soft paper in his hand, then paused near a tall, wide tapestry to press a finger to one nostril and blow the contents of the other into the seam of floor and wall. His breath hitched in his chest as he coughed and spat—he thought perhaps at least one of his ribs was cracked. He stood there a moment, looking at the tapestry while he tried to regulate his searing breaths. The symbols of the Templars seemed to mock him as they hid among the trees and rivers woven into a rich, fantastical battle landscape: a dragon flying from a castle perched on a craggy peak; giants treading through a surf littered with wreckage; a figure with flowing red hair hovering above it all, seeming to stare down the corridor in the direction from which Glayer had just come.

Baldwin would never elevate Glayer to senior officer of anything now. Bastard leper, prancing about as if he were fit to command battalions when he was barely out of nappies.

Glayer reached up suddenly, flinching at the stabbing pain in his side as he grasped the heavy tapestry and wrenched it from the wall. He spat again upon it, then strode across it down the corridor, his pace quickening as his mind urged him on.

Bastard Gerard, behaving as though he owned the world, with his title and his estate and his heir. His pious standards and pharisaical morals.

Glayer had been sincere in his threat to destroy Constantine Gerard, but in truth, there was nothing for Glayer to go back to if he was turned away from the Holy Land. He'd come here to make a name for himself—to earn lands, riches, perhaps even a fief of his own. He would not become Baldwin's servant in Tiberius, traded to some Frankish baron as if he were little more than a page. To be laughed at here, then forced back to his mother's poor cottage on the westernmost point of England with nothing to show for his years away than a nose more crooked than when he left.

His vision blurred as he came into the blinding light of the bailey and the shimmers of heat floated up from the baked earth. Glayer threw up a forearm and ducked his head as he struck out into the center of the space, to shield his eyes from the sun and from the sight of whomever might be watching him, laughing at him. He walked quickly.

He hated Gerard. And Baldwin. And his mother. Hated this damned oven of a fortress; hated the men it sheltered. He glanced up and saw the light colored robes of Saracens still gathered near the wide gates, obviously readying to depart. In their midst was General Abdal himself, the soldiers around him protecting both the messenger and the coin Felsteppe knew he still carried. An ambitious man, Abdal, who knew how to wield the power he had been given in this land of enemies and thieves.

Unlike weak, sick, stupid Baldwin. Glayer wondered if anyone else but he knew how many thousands of dinars Saladin had offered in exchange for the razing of this godforsaken place. For Christ's sake, the foundation wasn't even . . .

Felsteppe stopped suddenly in the blinding hot bailey, his heart pounding, and looked down at the crumpled rendering of Chastellet's most secret parts that he still held in his hand. His skin went icy, clammy as he raised his head, and the tall General Abdal turned toward him as if Felsteppe had called his name. The two men stared at each other for a long moment.

And Glayer Felsteppe realized that his time had at last come.